Ryan Stark is the pseudonym of Austen Gower.

Alongside a successful career in IT, he has been writing fiction in various forms for around twenty years. Since 2015, he has published three novels in the Daley and Whetstone Series: *Killing by the Book, The Farm, and Unnatural Selection*.

Proof of Life is the first in a series of international crime stories in the *Amber Rock* series.

Married, with a wife, two grown-up children, and a new granddaughter, Austen lives in Worcestershire, England.

Twitter: @RyanStarkAuthor
Facebook: RyanStarkAuthor
Web: www.ryanstarkauthor.co.uk

Also by Ryan Stark

The Daley and Whetstone Crime Stories

Killing by the Book
The Farm
Unnatural Selection

For Amelia, who came into our lives at a dark time and shone a bright light on us all.

The Beckett Chronicles

PROOF OF LIFE

Amber Rock Book 1

RYAN STARK

Fuldean Press

Proof of Life

Copyright © 2021, Ryan Stark.
All rights reserved.

The right of Ryan Stark to be identified as the author of this work has been asserted in accordance with sections 77 and 78 of the Copyright Designs and Patents Act 1998.

This is a work of fiction. Names, characters, corporations, institutions, organizations, events or locales in this novel are either the product of the author's imagination or, if real, used fictitiously. Any resemblance to actual persons (living or dead) is entirely coincidental.

No part of this book may be reproduced or transmitted in any form or by any means, electronic or mechanical, including photocopying, recording, or by any information storage and retrieval system without the written permission of the author, except where permitted by law.

ISBN 9798540163958

Ryan Stark

ACKNOWLEDGMENTS

Proof of Life is the first in the Amber Rock series of novels. I have carried out extensive research and, hopefully, most of the facts are correct. However, I am just a wordsmith, so I would like to thanks few people for their help and guidance outside my area of expertise.

I am indebted to Tom Sperrey for his advice on sailing, part of which helped with the initial plot.

Also, Giovanni Discenza, an old school friend, helped ensure my Italian/ English translation was up to par.

A quick thanks to the folks at Orbit Homes, the Royal Institute of Chartered Surveyors, and Enterprise Inns, for a loan of their meeting rooms before and after work, so I could keep writing.

Finally, I'd like to thank my wife and family for their forbearance. The creative process can become a little obsessive.

Ryan Stark

PROLOGUE

London, May 4, 1990

Were they still out there?

Joanne McKenna straddled the toilet bowl. Her knees were shaking. Outside, the footsteps were deliberate, pacing past the stalls, pausing, then moving on. Her heart was booming so loud in her ears. Could the woman hear it?

There were always three of them. The woman she called *Helga the Hell Bitch*—a name she could spit with venom. The short man looked like a pig and the tall, surly man with the crooked nose always looked grumpy. *Pinky and the Brain*—somehow, she could cope if she gave them each a silly name.

Three constant faces in a sea of humanity.

She held her breath, releasing it, slowly, open-mouthed, as quietly as possible, but it roared in the silence. The lock on the cubicle door rattled, and Joanne stifled a yelp. The woman let out a frustrated sigh, then started pacing again.

Why had they started following her again? Why now when Max was away?

She leaped as a timer valve clicked, water running into the cistern behind the wall panel. She needed to pee as much through fear as anything else. How long could she hold it? Still, the footsteps paced the tiled floor.

Helga had been outside Ashad's shop when Joanne bought her lunch. As she turned to leave. One fleeting moment, their eyes met before the woman looked away and her stomach knotted. Tall, ungainly, like an *Anglepoise* lamp, left slightly folded. Her dowdy gray twin set and white blouse made her look old, though she was probably only around thirty. The same woman she'd seen before. The eyes were unmistakable. No doubt about it. The woman had turned. Her thin lips curled into a smile as she fished out a cigarette, click-clicking a lighter.

Maybe she should have spoken to the cow? Marked her card once and for all? But she hadn't.

Damn her tight-arsed British reserve.

Yesterday, someone had stolen her bike, compelling her to take the Tube. It must have been them. Who else? Still, the Tube. An easy place to shake off a tail. Yet it was the Tube. Tight, airless passages, the spooky echo of buskers bouncing off the tiles. Crowds weren't her thing. Body odor, grime, and dust on her skin, the unsavory crush on the platforms. The unworldly moan of the trains as the bow wave howled through the tunnels. The rats scurrying between the rails. Especially the rats. Then there was the crash. Okay, it was fifteen years ago, but forty-three people died at Moorgate. What if it happened again?

Raising her pace, Joanne had headed for Liverpool Street Underground, seeking cover behind the forest of pillars in the ticketing hall. Instantly, she felt the familiar panic. Nausea, the difficulty breathing, the cold sweats. Steeling herself, resisting the temptation to glance behind her, she zigzagged through the hordes of milling passengers toward the escalators and down to the Central Line. She knew there were lavatories there. There would also be people, smells, filth, but she could hide. Sit it out, literally.

Like that worked!

Finally, with a huff, *Helga* gave up. Her heels clicked loudly across the lavatory floor. The door squealed open, then slowly wheezed shut. After about a minute, in the echoing silence of her own terror, Joanne climbed down and unlocked the cubicle door. The lavatory was empty. At last, she allowed herself a breath.

Come on, Joanne. Man up. You're being silly.

Three years ago, they'd all been afraid. Carl Hayes, a colleague in the US, was convinced someone was watching him. But that was America. Over there, everyone watches everyone else. Then when he committed suicide, the silliness turned to paranoia. Max Anderson, her boss, suggested they should be vigilant, change their routines, even their routes to and from work. Or buddy up with a colleague. It all became very silly. Joanne even convinced *herself* she was being followed for a while.

Then Harvey Brooks and Max had reluctantly told her about the others. Not just Hayes but Pete Fernandez and Todd Gruber, maybe more. A string of suspicious deaths. Rumors of a cover-up. Amber Rock. Sometimes Max Anderson really got on her nerves. She wished to God she'd never listened to his spy stories. He'd put the willies up everybody he knew, and now they were all looking over their shoulders, seeing spooks around every corner.

But it was possible? Amber Rock had a long memory.

The inquest found Carl Hayes suffered depression. Maybe suicide was inevitable? Eventually, like these things do, it all sort of petered out. Until recently. Max had arranged a meeting with Professor Rossi in Geneva. She hoped he wasn't stirring up that whole mess again. And if he was, maybe, they *were* all being watched, and she was the only one who had realized?

Joanne! For God's sake, listen to yourself!

Edging open the door, gingerly peering out, she jumped back as two girls came blustering in, chatting, tinny music escaping the inevitable earphones. After an awkward smile, she took a deep breath and left, immediately shunted along by the train of people heading down the corridor.

Proof of Life

Helga was leaning on the grubby white tiles beside the sign for the Central Line. Her face was thunder, studying the passers-by, brightening up when she caught sight of Joanne.

Toilets? One way in, one way out. Really?

Raising her head, staring forward, Joanne walked briskly past, stemming the panic, frustrated that now she was going away from her train. Still, she could head toward the Metropolitan Line, or Hammersmith and City, even across to the Central Line. Onto the platforms, then double back. How well did the woman know Liverpool Street, anyway?

Then she saw the two men. *Pinky* was standing by the entrance to the Metropolitan Line tunnels. *The Brain* was behind her, leaping from the escalator, making up ground.

The three constant faces in a sea of humanity.

Still, she pressed on. *The Brain* took a nod from *Helga* and turned to follow. Joanne picked up her pace, pushing through the crowds, hoping for a place to hide. A nook, an electrical cupboard, anything. The Tube was always warm, always crowded. Today more so than ever. The warmth robbed her of her breath. She wanted to scream but the sounds stuck in her throat. The people, the stench of bad breath, sweat, and sickly sweet perfume, tainting each lungful. She took a tunnel to her left, another to her right, then a platform yawned wide. A series of sonorous staccato beeps, and the doors slid shut behind her. Ducking down, tying shoelaces she didn't have, she saw *The Brain* pull up as the train left, smacking his hands on his thighs in frustration.

As the train motors whirred up and the platform slid away, Joanne squeezed her eyes tight. This couldn't be happening, could it? Not in London? Not in real life? Her heart was beating so hard she thought it would burst through her ribs, but she had escaped. She had beaten them—at least for today. And tomorrow, she would be wiser.

Which train was she on? She checked the route map over

the door and breathed a sigh of relief. Metropolitan westbound. That gave her options. Off at Moorgate and South to Bank or continue on to Baker Street. Either way, she could reach the office. Reach the sanctuary of a building full of people she knew.

But isn't that what they would expect, Joanne?

It was the obvious move. So instead, when the train pulled into Moorgate, she would cross platforms and head east, away from her office. She could travel to the terminus at Aldgate and take the Circle Line train from there.

As she left the train, Joanne ducked back into a small crowd of commuters. Amazed at her calmness under pressure. Moving along, she almost forgot her anxiety, buoyed by her success.

Take that Helga!

She remembered the words of Franklin D. Roosevelt from her time at Oxford. *The only thing we have to fear is… fear itself—nameless, unreasoning, unjustified terror which paralyzes needed efforts to convert retreat into advance.* Anxiety, fear, and paranoia had dogged her all her life, increasing tenfold since Carl Hayes' death. Maybe now was the time to see sense?

She would call Max Anderson when she reached the office. Insist he spoke to the Police.

Over her platform, the scrolling ticker showed two minutes for her train. Thirty more and she would be back out on the surface. *Helga, Pinky, the Brain* were nowhere to be seen. Today she had outwitted them. Joanne took a deep breath, tasted the grime and the ozone, and smiled. Maybe she should take the Tube more often. Acclimatize herself to it. Confront her fears.

Ahead, the wind moaned down the tunnel, ghostly echoes through the hubbub of people. A yellow glow bounced along the electric conduits, sparking in the dark. She stepped back, letting others find their lucky spot, where the train would stop, and its doors open miraculously before them. A small man, Iranian, Egyptian, mumbled past, apologizing in broken English. She started, reprimanding herself immediately. Thousands traveled every day, safely, efficiently. One day she would look back on this and laugh.

"Sorry, Miss McKenna, but you have become a problem to Amber Rock. Goodbye."

Something thumped into her back and she was falling into the abyss, the black, the squirming rats. There was a metallic squeal of brakes, a flash of light, and the open mouth of the startled driver.

Then the headlights burned her eyes.

Ryan Stark

PART ONE - ROME, ITALY

Proof of Life

Chapter 1

Wednesday, September 4

Luciano Moretti had to die.

He was fifty-eight years old, divorced, with two daughters, a son, and three grandchildren he rarely saw. A native of Lombardy, Italy, he enjoyed horseback riding and collecting Renaissance art, which filled the sprawling villa in the hills north of Monza. However, since the divorce, he preferred to stay in Rome, the epicenter of business in Italy. Moretti also traveled widely, brokering deals across the world, oiling the wheels of commerce, enabling the movement of products and services across borders.

Except every deal was illegal, immoral, or both.

Arms, drugs, endangered species, information, even people. He matched the buyers to the sellers for an obscene fee and without dirtying his own hands. The information he dealt in could topple governments, oust dictators and send the financial markets into free-fall. It could get people killed or, if acquired, prevent it.

Moretti had to die so countless others could live.

Of course, I felt bad for his family. I am sure he loved his children and doted on his grandchildren. They would be generously provided for, though they may have to look over their shoulders for a while. No one else would mourn his loss. Especially not those he stole from, or hurt, or whose loved ones never came home. Especially not me. For me, it was just a job. Luciano Moretti needed to be removed from the ecosystem and the world would be a better place.

Proof of Life

A week ago, I received the call from Pliskin, my boss. Moretti had set up a private auction on the dark net, restricted to a select few with deep pockets and loose morals. The lot? Information. Pliskin informed me it could not go ahead, instructing me to stop it. My brief was simple. Visit Moretti, recover the information, and eliminate him. Of course, I'd never met the Italian; he could have been one of many unprincipled bottom-feeders living in the shadows. I had to take Pliskin's word that the information he was selling could be dynamite in the wrong hands.

So, posing as Franklin Farrell, internet entrepreneur, I endured the red-eye from a gray, wet Dulles Airport and landed in Italy before the sun made an appearance. Flying was not my thing. Too much nothing between the fuselage and the ground. They say every landing is a controlled crash and a competent pilot is one with the same number of take-offs as landings. Fortunately, my pilot was competent enough. Even so, when I descended the steps, my head throbbed like a steam hammer and my legs ached. Leonardo da Vinci International, Rome, passed by in a blur of corridors and conveyors before I rapped on a cab window, threw some euros at a dozing tassista. Then I napped the forty minutes to the city center.

Rome was one of my favorite cities. I'd visited with my folks as a kid and fallen for its hectic vibrance, the chaos and noise. In the Fall, the weather is less predictable, the leaves brown and the tourist thin. There is also half a chance of a seat in one of the over-priced coffee bars. Now, it was closed, waiting for the sun to rise and coffee to percolate.

I awoke with a jolt as the driver pulled up outside the Castel Sant'Angelo, squat and solid, lit orange against the dawn. I needed a walk. Loosen up my limbs and wake up. The worn paving across the Ponte Sant'Angelo was slick with rain, greasy underfoot, and there was a faintly fetid odor rising from the Tiber. If the stench didn't kill me, the walk would do me good. I kept to the side-streets. Chasms of stillness between the baroque and the gothic, away from the tourist traps. And away from the city's CCTV cameras.

Pliskin was as good as his word. The anonymous white Ford Focus sat amongst a row of identical ones. I found the keys under the wheel arch, popped the trunk, and swapped my bulky overnight bag for a much slimmer one. Then I locked it up and negotiated the empty streets to the Via della Posta Vecchia, a dog-leg alley connecting somewhere to nowhere. However, this somewhere was one of the most breathtaking sights in the city.

The vast expanse of the Piazza Navona.

Once, long ago, while my mom pointed her Olympus Trip at the architecture, my dad regaled me with stories of the Stadium of Domitian. A roaring cauldron of cheering spectators applauding their heroes, jeering the villains, and holding their collective breath as chariots overturned, spilling their victims beneath the pounding hooves and scything wheels. Now, two millennia later, the fountains were off and the gray dawn was the domain of street cleaners vacuuming up yesterday's detritus. A few of the cafés and restaurants were yawning into a new day and the smell of freshly baked dough reminded me how hungry I was—*Eat when you can, sleep when you can, soldier*—so I stopped off to grab a monumental Americano and a slice of warm focaccia from a bleary-eyed barista. I knew how she felt.

Searching the facades, I found the small discreet wooden door leading up to an apartment, rented by the day. Redbrick and pantiled, perched on the rooftops over the square, it resembled a bungalow lowered by crane onto the roof four floors up, only daring a peek over the edge down onto the cobbles. Inside, it was spartan, painted walls, tiled floors, artwork that tried too hard. Über modern, über chic, soulless. Still, it had a bed, a couch, and a balcony with a view of a similar apartment across the piazza.

Proof of Life

Moretti also rented his apartment by the day. A temporary office in town to conduct his auction. My appointment with him was at 1:00 pm, but by 10:00 am, I was getting antsy. The Americano had been a mistake. So, I freshened up, shaved the overnight growth down to a fashionable Mediterranean stubble, and put on a fresh shirt. Then I checked the small holdall. American Airways gun policy being what it was, I had relied on Pliskin to supply the hardware. A Glock 19M semi-automatic, a model I was familiar with. This one came with an aftermarket threaded barrel and suppressor to keep things quiet. I would have half a chance of making the shot without deafening myself, or startling the pigeons.

Down below, the piazza had woken up. Chattering tourists milled aimlessly, maps and coats flapped. A guy in yellow coveralls had emptied the Fontana del Moro and was jet-washing the algae and chewing gum, revealing a tired turquoise beneath the dirty green. He was singing to himself, loving life as he picked up loose change, throwing it into a yellow bucket. Another guy, as brown as mahogany, animated and wide-eyed, spindly in a heavy woolen overcoat, was trying to entice the gullible into buying his handbags. His low, creaking sales pitch almost lost below the harsh sound of the jet-wash. Across the way, in the other apartment, net curtains played in the open French doors. A young woman was leaning on the balcony railings opposite. She was slender, with blonde hair tied into a ponytail, a formal black two-piece, and just a flash of knee as she crossed her slim ankles. Around twenty-one, around my height. The sort of generic receptionist-cum-assistant look of a million hotels and offices. Her face was round and pale and she looked as bored as I did. I caught her eye and she flashed an uninterested smile. I smiled back. She turned away and continued staring indifferently into middle-distance. Then, at exactly 11:45 am, she looked down, sighed, and hurried inside.

A small, rotund, middle-aged man appeared from the shadows beside the Museo de Roma. He wore a pale blue shirt and beige chinos, with a cream cashmere cardigan covering his shoulders like a cape; no knot, just the sleeves overlapping in the European metrosexual way. A pretentious goatee and spectacles beneath waves of gray hair hid a purposeful face. In one hand, he swung a stylish leather briefcase whilst he pressed his cellphone to his ear with the other. He was moving expediently. Not rushing, but with an air of self-importance some people have. Places to go, people to see. In contrast, the tall, stocky man accompanying him wore a regulation black overcoat and mean expression. His cautious eyes scanned every face in the square.

Luciano Moretti was here. The carnival had to begin.

The woman reappeared on the balcony, dressing a white cast-iron table ready for lunch, clipping down the edges of the flapping tablecloth. Moretti emerged into the doorway, in animated conversation, the phone still at his ear. Pliskin told me Moretti always lunched at noon, come rain or shine. It was a ritual. By 2:00 pm, he would be ready for a siesta; the best time to strike a deal. The best time for *me* to strike.

The woman finished dressing the table, picked up her wooden box, and eased past Moretti back into the void of the apartment. I had bargained for a minder; one shot for him and one for Moretti, but the girl was a problem. She was someone's daughter, partner, even mother. Back in Iraq, we called it collateral damage. Heartbreaking, but it was something to which I'd become annealed. Make it quick, don't think too much about it. Even the sweetest girl could smile as she detonated a suicide vest.

Then I jumped at the sound of a tiny crack, more a *phut*, like someone spitting an olive pit. Then another, and a halo of red peppered the flapping table cloth. Moretti's eyes bulged large and rolled as he dropped the phone and tipped backward into the room.

Proof of Life

Chapter 2

At first, I was annoyed. I'd traveled halfway across the globe, psyched myself up for the kill, and someone else stole my thunder. Was it the woman? Was the whole PA thing a ruse? After all, there had only been two shots. One for the minder, one for Moretti. Or perhaps a third I hadn't heard, and she too was staining the carpet crimson? More concerning was also the question of my fee. If Pliskin learned I hadn't pulled the trigger... Then there was the information Moretti was auctioning. If the killer found it first, where did that leave me? With the Glock stashed beneath my jacket, I set about finding out. Below, the Piazza had woken up. Tourists meandered everywhere, prey for the pickpockets. A thousand cameras, a thousand eyes, hopefully, all trained on the architecture. Keeping my head low, I made for the blue doors of Moretti's block, a small sliver of black between the flaking panels, just as his minder had left them.

Inside, the hall was a musty mausoleum of peeling paint and shadows. Shabby chic; the odor of mildew and polish to disguise the smell of money. The hubbub outside the doors had died away, leaving a clinging silence beyond the pulse in my ears. I followed the checkerboard tiles past a side-table, a statuette of some roman god, a pot plant begging for light and water, then onto a stairway, stone steps hollowed by thousands of footfalls. I eased out the Glock, chambered a round, and climbed the marble stairs. The higher I climbed, the smarter it became, tiled floors gave way to carpets, laminated doors to solid oak, plastic numbers to polished brass lettering, landings with ranks of brown varnished doors and nameplates that didn't interest me, then a single stairway to an attic studio where Moretti lay cooling. One way in and one way out. What could go wrong? In the Marines, I was never alone. More than one pair of eyes. Now I was on my own.

More haste, less speed, Beckett.

I took a deep breath, waited a beat, and listened. Behind Moretti's door, a floorboard creaked, feet scuffed at the furniture, curses whispered in Italian. Aiming a foot just beneath the handle, I sent the door splintering open. Rolling forward, I stretched out the gun. A tall, shaven-headed man swiveled around and, for a split second, the muzzles of our guns eyed each other. Instinctively, I fell sideways as, with a *phut,* a bullet buzzed past my head. As I regained my balance, I sent a couple back in response. My aim was as bad as his, He grunted. Plaster dust peppered his leather jacket as he turned for another volley. I let loose a third round, clipping his arm. In a howl of pain, his gun tumbled to the floor. My next shot slammed into the wall, missing the assassin as he leaped for the shattered door. Still on my knees, I spun the nose of the Glock out of the doorway into the stairwell. But he was gone. Somewhere below, a door slammed.

My heart was hammering but I didn't have the luxury of time. The room held a couple of brown leather tub chairs and a dressing table-cum-desk against the wall. A door led off into a small kitchen area, another into a bedroom. Stretched across the carpet, face planted in his own gore, lay Moretti's minder. Small caliber weapon at close range. Around the window, the expensive wallpaper was spattered maroon, like some kids had thrown jello at it. Moretti lay on his side, across the threshold of the window, with half his head missing. Once inside Moretti's skull, the bullet would have pin-balled around, turning his brain to whipped blancmange. Merciful and quick. If I'd used the Glock, most of his head would have gone.

The minder's pockets were clean; he was working. Moretti had a cellphone, wallet and keys. Most of the drawers were out, cheap pens and tourist leaflets over the carpet, hairdryer hanging from its coiled flex. I searched the rest, opened the minibar, but there was nothing resembling information worth €500,000. Slamming the desk with frustration, I cursed the gunman who had beaten me to it. Resigned to failure, I took a picture of the bodies. Even though I hadn't made the shot, my employers would want an assurance he was dead before they fired me.

A movement made me catch my breath. A reflection in the mirror above the desk, then an immense impact on my neck made my eyes spark.

In the split-second before unconsciousness, I felt an wave of disappointment. After a decade in the Marines, a year in specialist training, I'd been suckered. My legs turned to latex, and I collapsed like a badly built wardrobe. Growing up, I had been all too ready to solve an argument with my fists. And look where that had gotten me now.

Proof of Life

Chapter 3

"Don't move." British accent, female, frantic, panicking. Above me, the suppressed muzzle of the assassin's Smith & Wesson swayed. Beyond it, the young woman from the balcony, shaking, almost hysterical, eyes screwed tight and tears tracking mascara down her cheeks. Her blonde hair was loose, quivering around her face, like cobwebs in an earth tremor. There was a smell of vomit and, as I couldn't taste it, I assumed it was hers.

My head hurt like hell and a cut above my eye stung. I was confused. Why hadn't the assassin finished me like he had Moretti and his minder? Neat, tidy.

I screwed up my eyes, tried to shake away the stars. It didn't work. Outside, sirens were sounding.

"Listen, lady, the Polizia are on their way. We need to leave now."

"What are you doing here?" The girl waved the S&W closer as if that would loosen my tongue. Her panic was palpable. It made her unpredictable.

"Do we really have time for twenty questions?" I spotted my Glock out under the sideboard.

Her brow furrowed. "You were across the square. In the other apartment?"

"Uh-huh." Slowly, I heaved myself upright, keeping my hands raised, my eyes on the gun. "I had a meeting with Moretti? Franklin Farrell, 2:00 pm? Someone jumped me when I arrived."

"You're American?" Her eyes darted about the room,

Proof of Life

over to Moretti's corpse, then back to me. She found no answers. She pointed under the sideboard. "You were carrying a gun."

"Everyone who deals with Moretti has a gun. It's healthier that way. Not for him, though." The assassin left the S&W when he fled. A blessing in disguise for him. He vamoosed, leaving me in a room with two corpses and the gun that killed them.

"I don't have a gun." The irony was obvious even to her as her eyes flicked down to the S&W. "Not usually, anyhow."

"Seriously," I pleaded. "We have to go—now." In the Piazza, the sirens were echoing from the stonework. An anxious murmur had sprung up amongst the small crowd in the square. Things had turned to shit.

"We're staying right here until the police arrive." Her pupils were flicking left and right, her breathing labored. Her mind was in overdrive. I needed her to see sense, if only for my sake.

"Look, lady. My gun is over there. Ballistics will show it didn't kill Moretti. Now, the other guy..." The angry sirens were growing louder. Time was almost up.

"What other guy? I didn't see..." The S&W had ceased to point anywhere dangerous, and she was gnawing at a hangnail.

"He was searching the place, and I disturbed him. They were dead before I arrived." I cast a hand at the maroon wall, the bodies. She winced. "He left the gun so I would carry the can. Smart move. But, lady, he was wearing gloves and so am I." I flashed my Napa leather jazz hands.

"And?"

"You're not, and you're holding the weapon that killed them both. Fingerprints?"

She shrieked and the S&W tumbled to the floor.

"You're English, right? Foreign country, dabs all over an unregistered firearm? Two violent murders? I am sure they will understand—eventually. Or you can come with me and get the hell out of Dodge so we can find out what really happened here."

The girl's eyes flicked about, her breath puffed in short pants, but she didn't budge.

"Okay. Your choice. Shoot me or come with me." Hauling myself upright, I left the S&W on the floor, performed a quick reconnoiter and, confident there was nothing to find, I resolved to quit while I was ahead. Keeping one eye on the girl, I gingerly lifted the Glock. For a moment, I cupped the trigger, gripped the stock, and aimed at the girl's forehead. She gasped, transfixed. No loose ends.

But I couldn't shoot.

The deal was to recover Moretti's information, ice Moretti—and by association, his minder. An honest transaction in my business. The other way round, neither of them would have hesitated to return the favor. The assassin did not hesitate before trying to plug me.

But the girl was different. Wrong place, wrong time. Even though she'd aimed the killer's gun at my face back, she had no intention of using it. She was terrified, on autopilot. Having failed to kill Moretti, how could I kill an innocent bystander?

I slid the gun into my belt, knowing I would regret it eventually. I stepped towards the door and turned.

"What are you? One-hundred-and-forty-pounds? I could have taken the gun off of you easily. But I didn't. Make the smart move, lady. Let's go."

But she was rooted to the spot, open-mouthed, quivering like a moth in a hurricane. The A-line skirt was creased and her hair was a mess. She had the pathetic, tearful, needy expression women know men cannot resist. It brings out the chivalry in them. They feel obliged to be big and strong. I didn't need the headache; she'd already given me one of those, but equally, I couldn't leave her. Eventually, she would open up about the moody American with the Glock automatic. Besides, Moretti's briefcase was resting against her ankle. Quickly, I grabbed the S&W and flicked on the safety.

"*We have to go.*" I grabbed her hand, feeling a tug of reticence. Confused, her eyes flashed between Moretti's corpse and me, then across at the open window. Finally, she grabbed the briefcase and her handbag, and moved.

Outside the apartment, the front doors rattled, echoing up the stairwell. Someone barked orders in Italian. Footsteps clattered on the hall tiles. That way was out. Across the landing, there was a door marked *Uscita di Emergenza*. I dragged the girl across and leaned on the bar, briefly blinded by the sun bouncing off the pantiles. Three yards in front, it was straight down onto the canopies of the restaurants. Police cars were drumming over the cobbles, scattering the tourists, making the hawkers anxious. The laborer had turned off his jet washer. Instead, he smoked a cigarette and watched the cabaret. Ten yards to our right, a sheer drop led to the unforgiving pavement outside the Museo di Roma.

"Wait." The girl stopped jerking me back. She removed her heels and pointed left across the rooftops. "The church—there's a terrace café up by the dome. If you can get out, then you can also get in."

"Good work. Let's go before they figure that out too."

Together, teetering like a high-wire act, we picked our way across a landscape of viciously raked rooftops, cracking tiles and startling pigeons, climbing down onto a flat-roofed attic which ran across towards the dome. I jumped down and held out my hand for the girl. Then we hunkered down behind the low parapet wall and took a breath. We were on a colonnaded terrace. Empty, except for a few fake bay trees in pots and pigeon guano in gallons. The immense dome towered above, casting its shadow reprovingly over us.

"That way, right?" I pointed across the terrace to a small balustraded wall. Beyond, white tables flapped and blustered in the breeze. She nodded, panting, red-cheeked her eyes round and tearful.

"Yes, we can go through the cafeteria. Hang on!" She threw off my hand "What am I doing helping you?"

"Saving your own neck, lady, just like me. Now, act normal, calm. We're just tourists. Okay?"

"Don't tell me to act calm. I was perfectly calm until you two started shooting."

"Hey! I haven't fired a goddamn shot." A white lie.

"You expect me to believe that?"

"Whatever. Just listen. We're going to head down through the café to the street. We hold hands and pretend to be tourists. Give me the briefcase."

"Not bloody likely!" She pulled it to her bosom as if she were protecting a favorite kitten from a rabid Alsatian. "I'm not stupid. I know this is what you were after back there. How do I know you won't shoot me once you have it?"

"For God's sake. What is it with Brits and guns? No one is going to get shot. Now give me the goddamn case." The sun was scorching the felted rooftop. I was hot, fractious, and losing my patience.

"Why should I?"

I raised my eyebrows and puffed. "Because—because Italy is a patriarchal society, and it is more believable, out of a guy and a girl, the guy would carry the case. Okay?"

"Murderer, stalker, and a bloody chauvinist. Take the bloody thing." My ribs flexed as she thrust the case at me.

"You have a cell, er—?"

"—Stephanie, Stephanie Jordan," she replied reticently as if she had given away a state secret. "I was working. It's in my handbag switched off." She climbed to her feet, brushing an errant wisp of hair back behind her ear.

"Good. No one can trace you. How long have you worked for Moretti?"

"Just today. They hired me for a specific contract."

"You, me both."

Somehow, I think the irony was lost on her.

***

The steps down avoided the church, so there were no awkward *Forgive me father for I have sinned* moments as we descended to a swish restaurant. Just distracted waiters frenetically breezing about with trays. Through the kitchens, a fire door was wedged open for the cigarette breaks, and beyond it, a small airless yard led to a deserted backstreet.

"Where are you taking me?" Again she stood, her heels unsteady on the cobbles.

"Away. I have a car."

"If you think I am going anywhere with *you*…"

"Can we please just stop arguing? For one moment?"

She puffed and spoke in her politest plummy Brit voice. "So, *Mr. Franklin Farrell*. Pray tell me, where are we going?"

"Okay—okay." I held out my hands, defeated. "Right now, I just need to get out of this city before rush hour starts. I fly out of this goddamn country tonight."

"Fly out? What happens to me then?"

"Can we just get away from here? *Please?*" At the end of the street, blue flashes were bouncing off the brickwork. Soon they would fan out and we needed to be gone. With a shrug and a huge, anxious sigh, she finally relented. As calmly as she could, she took my hand, and we strolled down another anonymous side street, leaving the wailing sirens behind.

Maybe she had figured I was her best chance of avoiding a night in the cells and a tough phone call to the British Embassy? Maybe it was her turn to run out of options?

Proof of Life

Chapter 4

Tears had spoiled the girl's makeup, I pulled a clean handkerchief from my pocket, offered it to her. Chivalry wasn't dead. Then, I held her wrist and, moving with an ungainly shuffle, dragged her the five blocks to the rental Ford. I clicked the key fob, looked along the line for the flash, and opened the passenger door.

"Get in."

"If you think I am getting in there with *you*..." She pulled her wrist away defiantly. Her eyes were moist and red. The mascara blurring again.

"Listen, lady."

"Stop calling me *lady!*"

I took a breath and steadied my voice. "Stephanie. The Polizia are all over the Piazza. Anytime now, reinforcements will arrive and start combing the streets. We need to get out of here—now, *so get in the frickin' car.*"

Reluctantly, she yielded the battle of wills and dropped into the front passenger seat, scowling as her skirt rose over her knees. I looked away as she yanked it back down.

"Now stay put. Believe me, you are better off in this car with me than waiting here for the cops to arrive."

On any normal day, driving through Rome is tough. Hordes of irate drivers clogging the streets, leaning on their horns, believing their journey was the most important. Today, it seemed every police vehicle in the city had responded to the call, and traffic jammed up in their wake. After around thirty minutes, I caught the odor of burning metal, which I hoped wasn't our motor. The temperature needle was uncomfortably jammed in red and the afternoon sun was sticking my shirt to my back.

"Okay. So I got in the car. Now tell me where we're going." She was clinging to the belt, trying to sidle to the furthest part of the seat away from me. Her eyes flicked about nervously, peering out, trying to find a landmark, something—anything—familiar.

"An alley, a side street. I need to check out Moretti's briefcase. He had something my employers need."

"My God! And you killed him to get it?" She shrunk away still further.

"No, I didn't. The other guy. *He* killed Moretti."

"But you were going to."

"I'm sure it wouldn't have come to that," I lied.

Finally, the traffic eased as we hit the suburbs. I veered onto a side street, sending the satnav lady into a fit of unnecessary instructions. Pulling in a hundred yards along, I killed the motor and hauled Moretti's briefcase from behind the seats. It was one of those aged leather floppy man-bags, like an overgrown school satchel.

"So, you fly back to the States, or wherever, and forget all about this? What am I supposed to do? Walk into the police station and give myself up?"

I glanced over. She had pulled down the sun visor, and was using the mirror to repair her makeup, her jaw hoiked to one side in concentration.

"Of course not. I'll think of something. I promise."

"Like I am going to take a promise from *you*? More chance of Elvis riding down the street on Shergar carrying the holy grail."

"Okay, okay. Let's just settle this once and for all, shall

we?" The annoyance and frustration bled through in my tone as I pulled the assassin's gun from the side pocket of the door. She shied away, mouth flapping.

"What is it with Brits and guns?" I flipped the gun and proffered it butt first. "Here are the facts. A day-rate assistant turns up for work. Her client and his minder are both killed. The police arrive and both the assistant and the gun are missing. The Polizia may or may not have information about me, or about the other guy, but they sure as hell know about you. Like it or not, you're in the frame for a double homicide."

She stared at the stock of the gun, eyes round and scared, the bravado sliding off her face like hot greasepaint. "I wish I'd stayed in the bedroom, in the back of the wardrobe."

"But you didn't. I wish I'd asked Mary-Jane out in eighth grade, but I didn't. Right here right now is all that matters."

"This is not my problem. I never asked for any of this. Just take me back into town and drop me off with the Polizia. You can take your plane back and I will take my chances. They will know I couldn't have done—*that*." Her chin quivered, flicking off the teardrops that made it past the mascara. She rubbed her eyes, smearing black onto her hand.

I needed to turn the screw, drive the message home.

"So you walk into the precinct house and this all goes away? What about the guy that *did* shoot Moretti? You think he'll just drive into the sunset? Job done? You're a loose end, Stephanie. Right now he's using every resource he has to find us and tie up those loose ends. And not even the police will be able to stop him. So, we can keep on bickering like this until the Polizia or the killer find us, or we can start being smart. Until we can prove neither of us killed Moretti, we need to work together. Okay? Take it from me, you're better off with me than with them. And certainly better than looking down an assassin's gun barrel. Understand?"

Proof of Life

She nodded; the faintest of nods, non-committal, just enough to satisfy. Then she grabbed for the gun, taking me by surprise, wresting it from my grip. She turned it and squeezed the trigger. All her anger, frustration and fear concentrated on a small piece of cast aluminum that did not budge. Annoyed, she growled and squeezed again. Then, defeated, she let the pistol swing free and slumped back against the door. Her shoulders shuddered as the tears flowed and every hint of resistance slid into the footwell.

I spent ten years in the Marines. I wouldn't have lasted ten days without the ordeal of boot camp. Every recruit is treated with brutal harshness, every recruit has the civilian pummeled out of him and the Marine forced in. You have to break a man down to build him back up. Now I would need to build this girl back up.

"Look, Stephanie. What's happened has happened. The police want us. Moretti's assassin wants us. We have to keep one step ahead so we need to pull together until I can figure some way out. Okay?"

She had turned to the window, looking through a smear of condensation at a blank wall. Anywhere but at me.

"You're not my prisoner, and you need to decide. Right here, right now. You can take the gun, take a hike, take your chances but you'll be on your own. No one will look out for you. Or you can stay with me and we'll work this thing out."

I took back the gun. "Look, Stephanie. I don't want to debate this anymore. And, if you're going to shoot me then do it but you need to take the safety catch off first."

Chapter 5

My objective had been simple. Meet with Moretti, remove him and recover what he was auctioning. I had to hope the briefcase contained something I could take back. I was rewarded. Moretti traveled light. Lip salve, tissues and antacids, his passport, a Mont Blanc pen and some loose coins; teeny-tiny European play-money that won't buy jack. All useless, except for a transparent slip folder and one sheet of A4 paper, the thicker kind for writing special letters.

***

Amber Rock

The following items are provided as a single lot:

Maxwell Anderson

Information on recent investigations into the disappearance of Maxwell and Katherine Anderson in 1992, suggesting they may still be alive. Max Anderson is of interest to Amber Rock and therefore his whereabouts carry a high premium.

Amber Rock

Extensive documentation covering the work of Max Anderson, the Sentinel Group, and the scientific community, into Amber Rock and its activities. This information is known to a closed community and not in the public domain. It has recently surfaced in its entirety, having been presumed lost with Max Anderson. This dossier also contains information regarding Trueman, Velasquez and Gilbués. Information on Amber Rock is rare and therefore extremely valuable.

Sentinel Group

A dossier of information regarding the Sentinel Working Group, detailing times and dates of its findings. Scans of original documents including signatures and images. The information

Proof of Life

suggests collusion between Amber Rock and the Sentinel Group to suppress the information. Along with the other parts of this dossier, it has a high value.

Bidding

Only sealed bids in excess of €500,000. These must arrive no later than 23:59:59 on December 31, 2019.

Only valid bids received into the following TOR encrypted mailbox will be considered:

x865C4676zB896.4353345u35Mmss@nzh3fv6jc6jskki3.onion.

Messages will be opened in the presence of a certified notary.

The winning bidder will be informed by 15th January 2020.

The lot will be delivered on encrypted removable media to an approved ESCROW location following clearance of 20% of the winning bid.

The Encryption key will be delivered to the same location following clearance of remaining funds.

No correspondence will be entered into at any time.

***

"This letter? What do you know about it?" I held up the transparent binder, but she kept her face towards the window and gave a petulant shrug.

"Please. Look at it." I shook it testily.

"How should I bloody know?" she mumbled. "Sr. Moretti turned up, ordered me to prepare his lunch, and carried on gabbling down his phone. I took the briefcase through to the other room. I didn't bloody open it."

I skim read the page again: *The lot will be delivered on encrypted removable media...* I hunted around the bag again, checked the front pocket, reached into the corners, feeling the seams, looking for anything hidden.

"And he didn't give you anything else—an envelope, a small package, a computer drive?"

She paused again and huffed. "No. Just the briefcase. I

was a pretty face for the day. To distract his clients."

"It's not here. Shit!" I slammed the steering wheel with my palms, feeling the ricochet in my injured shoulder. The girl jumped.

"What isn't there?"

"What he was auctioning. A thumb drive, a data card, even a damn CD."

Moretti was no fool. He believed the information to be valuable. Upwards of €500,000. Why would he risk bringing along anything more than a taste of the goods to whet the appetite? The rest he'd keep somewhere safe. That left me with a problem.

Moretti had a villa north of the city. I needed to look around it before my flight home. So did his killer. Except I had the girl to worry about, too.

***

I was booked on the 03:35 back to Washington, DC. The afternoon was drawing on and I needed to make progress, so I turned West, then North at a cloverleaf onto the autostrada, blending into the traffic for a couple of junctions until I saw a motel badge on the satnav.

"Right, we're going to book a room. Like civilized people. You think you can do that?"

"Fuck off." She was hunched down in the passenger seat. She'd been quiet for a while, perhaps considering her options, deciding she had none.

"Is that a yes?"

She gave a tiny, resigned nod.

I threw in the guns into the briefcase, then hauled the girl out of the car. There was money in Moretti's wallet, more than enough for one night in a motel. The girl moped around a display of tourist leaflets with her back to the reception until I grabbed her arm and we both strode quickly off down the corridor. At least it would give her time to get her shit together while I decided what to do next.

"You take the bed. I'll take the couch." There was no couch. The joke fell flatter than New Jersey roadkill. She sat in a chair in the farthest corner under the window, yanked the curtains closed, and drew her legs up to her chest. I poured water, handed a glass over.

"Why were you really there?" She shuffled her butt on the uncomfortable seat. Assessed whether she should drink the water or throw it at me. Whether she would reach the bed alive. Decided not to risk either.

"I was there for what Moretti was selling. I didn't kill Moretti. I've never killed anyone." Another white lie.

"Excuse me if I don't believe you." She turned to the window, peered through the drawn curtain. Then she looked me right in the eye. "I have done everything you asked, so now you need to level with me. Secret meetings, automatic pistols. Just who the hell are you, really?"

I threw the briefcase on the bed and huffed. "I will level with you if you promise me you won't freak."

"You have two bloody guns. I am already freaking!"

Carefully, I removed the Smith & Wesson, checked the safety, and set it down on the bedside table in front of her. I removed the Glock and tossed it onto the bed, far away.

"Happy?"

"Happier. So who are you really?"

"My name's Beckett. I work for the government—indirectly. Franklin Farrell is my cover name."

"Beckett what?"

"Beckett. Just Beckett."

"Your mom and dad called you *Just?*"

"Don't be a smart-ass, Stephanie."

"Steve. Everyone calls me Steve."

"Your mom and dad called you *Steve*," I parodied, raising my eyebrows. "Each to his own."

She scowled, pulled her legs tighter "Twat! What were you really doing there?"

"Just what I said. I was there to meet with Moretti, is all." The white lies were flowing thick and fast.

"Sure," she scoffed. "And I'm the Pope's podiatrist!"

"Steady job. People always going to have bad feet."

"And Moretti? Were you there to kill him, too? Like the other man?" Considering the small arms I was toting, I figured the question was rhetorical, so I let it hang like wet mud on a windowpane.

"What else do you know about Moretti?"

The girl shrugged. "He pays €100 a day for six hours work. Agency recommended him. That's all."

"Moretti is an information broker—amongst other things. He sells it to the highest bidder, regardless of how many people suffer. My boss found out he had information we needed, so he sent here me to get it before anyone else could. Only someone beat me to it."

Steve shuffled uncomfortably, her eyes drifting to the gun on the bedside table, measuring the distance. "Alright, Mr. *Farrell*, I'll buy it. And did you? Stop the auction?"

"I stopped a table lamp with the back of my head, is all. Moretti is dead, so maybe I delayed it a while."

"And the other one? The one who…?"

"He was probably there for the same reason."

"On the same date? At the same time? Bit of a

coincidence." Her tone had changed. Less panicky, more confused. She sipped her water.

"Moretti upset many people. I am surprised there wasn't more of a queue." But she was right, and I didn't believe in coincidences. The gunman had taken a colossal risk walking through the door. There was only one conclusion. He knew I was coming and needed to get to Moretti first.

I'd expected her to dive for the gun. Her eyes were flicking between it and me. When she did, I let her. I'd emptied out the slugs, anyhow. She squeezed the trigger, squeezed it again, then sighed, deep and purging.

"Look, Beckett. I am scared out of my mind. I saw two people murdered, the police are chasing me and I have run away with a thief and a killer. I—I need to just—just understand what's going on." Her wide eyes were fiery reflections of the dim bedside lamp. I wanted to throw an arm around her, tell her everything was okay, but I knew it wasn't. Not yet. Not while Moretti's killer was out there looking for us. Not while she was wanted by the Polizia.

"And you want to compound that by shooting me? No one knows you're here. No one is coming after you. You're safe for now. You even have the gun, for Chrissakes. What more do I have to do?"

"I was terrified back there. Then I find you lying on the carpet. And if you are who you say you are, I'm frightened of you. I'm trapped here with a maniac who kills people."

"Maniac is a little strong, Steve."

She shuffled in the chair and smiled, an awkward, nervous flick of the mouth, quickly redressed. There were furrows across her brow you could plant crops in.

"So what happens now?"

"As I said, you take the bed, I take the couch. Things will look different in the morning."

Chapter 6

The sheet of paper in Moretti's briefcase was an invitation to bid. An appetizer. What I needed was the main course—the *removable media* he'd referred to. A single thumb drive in a city the size of Rome. Fortunately, I had an idea where to look. Moretti owned a villa a few miles from the motel, up in the leafy suburbs surrounding the old French Cemetery. Hopefully, he'd kept the thumb drive there, unless he'd lodged it in ESCROW or his killer already had it. Still, I had to risk a look before I flew out.

The problem was the girl. She'd taken a good hard look at my face, knew I'd entered Italy as Franklin Farrell. She even knew my code name—Beckett. As soon as I left the motel, she would phone the Polizia and the airport would be awash with armed security waiting for me to turn up.

I couldn't take her with me and I couldn't leave her in the motel. That left only one other option.

No loose ends.

I picked up the Glock, checked the magazine. The girl was curled up against the headboard of the bed, pulling the blankets about her like chain-mail armor. Eyes darting between me and the gun, tiny pinpoint fireflies in the weak light from the lamp. Her mind was several steps ahead. Her mouth flapped, unable to keep up. But even as I leveled the gun, I felt my resolve waiver again.

"By rights, I should've killed you back at the apartment, you know that, right?"

She didn't move.

Proof of Life

Pulling back the slide, I chambered a round. More for effect. "Right now, there is a mean-looking assassin out there, who wants you dead because you saw what he did. You saw his face. Then there's me. I was there too, and you saw my face. You're a loose end, Stephanie, and loose ends have a habit of tripping people up. Tripping *me* up."

Still, she sat, curled up, fetal, gripping the edge of the sheet, her eyes screwed up tight. Did she know I couldn't shoot her? Not in cold blood? What would it make me?

My resolve finally crumbled.

"I still have work to do. You need to stay here. Don't answer the door. Don't use the phone. I'll leave the other gun. Don't touch it unless you have to." I reached down and pointed to the safety catch. "You need to flick this off, remember? Otherwise, it won't work. I'll be gone in a couple of hours. I'll bring back some food."

Gathering all my things, I wondered if she knew I wasn't coming back. Whether I knew the moment I left, she would pick up the phone.

***

I parked up on a derelict lot a few streets from Moretti's villa, near the the French Military Cemetery. Far enough away not to arouse suspicion. The house on the lot was forlorn and neglected. Even prime real estate suffers in an economic downturn. Yet, the street was anonymous—high walls and spiked automatic gates. Rows of ordinary parked cars and no one about. Moretti's street was much the same; terracotta-colored stucco walls towering higher than necessary, pock-marked and dirty, with broken glass cemented into the top. Wooden gates dressed with more spikes, a small brass plate with a number above a slim mailbox and numbered access pad. Overhead, the trees joined to cast a pall of cool darkness over the road as evening drew on. Behind the gate, it demanded privacy. Perfect for a successful international arms broker with plenty of free time.

Entering via the front gates was out. Whilst one of Moretti's minders was in a fridge at the morgue by now, he would have others. Staff at home looking after the silver. So I chose a more discreet approach. The neighboring gates were a shade of bright blue, faded and peeling, carrying a sign which read *vendesi*. Another victim of the downturn. Inside, the garden was unkempt and overgrown, with a crisp carpet of leaves, tall grass, and unruly shrubs. There was a smell of damp, as if not even the sun paid a visit. No vehicles, shutters closed, mail and free papers tumbling from the mailbox behind the gate.

I shinned over, heaved myself onto the flat roof of the garage. Moretti's property was a modern, glass-fronted villa, an island in a sea of gravel and lawn, bathed in the ethereal orange glow of a setting sun. A double garage ran along the far edge of the property and, out back, an aquamarine pool shimmered under its own lights as the fine breeze crazed its surface. The blinds were drawn, a kaleidoscope of colors flashed across the inside. Someone was home, eating his cookies and drinking his milk. The perimeter bristled with lights and CCTV, but the adjoining wall seemed to be a blind spot. Maybe Moretti got on with his neighbors and didn't see them as a threat? Maybe he did, and he buried somewhere them in the overgrown yard?

Dropping over, I hugged the hedging before darting across towards the double garage. Immediately, the place lit up like Macy's in the holidays, so I rolled onto the path and hunkered down in the shadows beside the garage. Over at the house, the front door latch popped and the nose of a gun poked out. A voice shouted in Italian. Did Moretti's house-sitter know his boss was not coming home? I held my breath, hearing more gabbled Italian and footsteps on the gravel, following the figure along the barrel of the Glock. He was tall and broad, bald as a newborn, almost a clone of the dead minder. Eventually, he stopped, puffed heavily, and scratched his scalp. Then he mumbled something under his breath and began half-heartedly sweeping the drive again. Reaching up, I hoisted myself onto the garage roof. Lying flat, smelling the warm bitumen, expecting another blinding light that never came.

"Gattino. Vieni da papà." Something about a cat?

For a moment, the man stood, the top of his head reflecting the white glare of the lights. He huffed and began shuffling down the path.

"Dannato gatto." *Damn cat?* I had been called worse.

As he passed into the rear gardens and the lights extinguishing I took a breath.

The garage roof led to a first-floor balcony and a French door ajar in the humid evening. Inside, the room was über modern, minimalist and empty—a utilitarian dresser, a plateau of a bed, and a monumental TV. My nose prickled to an expensive cologne and stale cigarettes. Somewhere an electric clock ticked. At one end, a massive en suite occupied more footage than my house in the States. Out through another, an oak-balustraded mezzanine spanned three sides of the landing, culminating in a fiddly Italianate staircase sweeping down onto the marble of the ground floor. Again über modern and open plan, soulless. Below, an enormous arc of couches corralled the stone fireplace and massive plasma TV above it. There was a match on, soccer, maybe. Across the room, the front door latched with a clunk, and the goon mumbled to himself as he slumped onto the sofa and started throwing Latin expletives at the players.

Six painted doors lined the landing. Empty, dark bedrooms, a palatial bathroom and, in the corner, the den—a small but well-equipped office. I knew Moretti had a safe. The key was on his keyring, tubular with a transponder head.

Ultra-secure, difficult to duplicate. Easing the door closed behind me, I shone my flashlight over the bookcases, the Roman sculptures and Renaissance art, wondering how much was authentic and how much for show. One wall teemed with photos and certificates and, in front of it, an ostentatious desk claimed the deep-pile cream carpet. On the desktop, an antique silver desk set. The blotter was fresh and a photo frame beamed with several young, sunny smiles.

I caught myself thinking about the girl, Stephanie. Wondering if the Polizia were on their way. If Moretti's assassin had traced us to the motel. If she was dead already.

Focus, Beckett.

The safe wasn't hidden, just securely bolted down behind the desk. Inside, there were several high-end watches, jewelry, and some wads of cash in various currencies. There was a Heckler & Koch VP9 handgun and a box of 9mm rounds. On the more capacious lower shelf, there were stacks of paper, manilla folios and envelopes. And a small silver thumb drive attached to a luggage tag bearing a single word: C1r1v1gg34. With Moretti's love of Renaissance art, not the most secure password but memorable. Closing the safe, I started pulling drawers, rifled through papers and keepsakes. *Information* covered a broad church, so, finding a *Moleskine* notebook, I thrust it into my pocket.

Outside, a floorboard creaked. I noticed the silence, an eerie blanket of stillness, and I stopped breathing, my heart pumping in my ears. The TV was switched off. Had the game finished? Readying the Glock, checking the chamber, I stepped behind the door as a shadow crossed the light, sneaking under it. Then the door slowly opened, and the shadow stretched across the wall.

Proof of Life

Chapter 7

Pietro Castellano eased open the door, fed the nose of his Sig Sauer through. His heart was pounding, spooked by the cat, then hearing the noise on the landing. Why did Moretti keep the street-vermin anyhow? Filthy animal, strolling over the kitchen surfaces, shitting in the flowerbeds.

But this was no cat, and he'd been unable to settle back into the game. The floor above had creaked, not just once, but a series of light footfalls.

"Chi va là?"

Inside, the computer hummed. The hackles on Pietro's neck rose a little more. He slowed his breathing, placed his left foot against the door, and slowly pushed it further open.

"Come out. Now." His English was limited; he never cared for the sloppy language, lazy vowels.

A loud roar made him catch his breath. An enormous weight crashed against the door, buckling his ankle, slamming against his arm. He screamed as the bones cracked and shards of pain ripped through him. Inside, the Sig Sauer fell, pins and needles spiking through his fingers. Desperately, he tugged his arm but a second roar, a second impact, and it felt like his entire hand had gone. Through the spots peppering his vision, Pietro leaned into the door, hearing a groan as the intruder tumbled back. Then the door swung free and pain gnawed at his forearm. Breathing it out, he padded the carpet with his good hand, desperately searching for the Sig Sauer. He heard a cough, short, mechanical, felt a thump to his thigh, and he fell sideways, yelping as the bullet tore away his flesh.

Proof of Life

His left hand touched the cold of the gun, and he grabbed it. One chance. He pulled the trigger, fireflies in the dark, seeing the intruder, a chiaroscuro freeze-frame, as the Sig Sauer barked twice, throwing lead wildly across the room. The pain in his arm and leg made him nauseous. His eyes filled with flashing red. Rolling his body, shifting it against the door, pressing it closed, he aimed the Sig Sauer into the darkness, another couple of rounds impotently smashing into the ceiling.

Then the room stilled, the computer spun down, sleeping. Pietro strained to hear in the darkness, pushing away the dizziness, feeling the blood draining from his head, trying to focus on the shuffling shape.

***

The door was ajar, a sliver of light across the office. He must have passed out. For how long? Dragging himself up, gritting his teeth as the pain bit again, he cursed his weakness. If the intruder escaped, he was a dead man; Moretti had no concept of failure. Hard but fair. How fair would he be after this?

The landing was deserted. At the far end, the door stood open, moving with the breeze through the house. Pietro dragged himself along the wall, his leg twisting under his weight. He needed to call someone. Where was his phone?

The sound made him turn. The intruder framed in another doorway, the look of amazement mirroring his own. Without thinking, Pietro swung out with his good arm, but the man parried, sending him falling to the floor. His energy was draining away. Ignoring the pain, he flung out both his arms. A boot sole struck his cheek. Catching hold of the intruder's trousers, Pietro dragged him down, hearing the clatter of a gun against the skirting. Seizing his chance, Pietro lunged for it, inches short as the man pounced onto him and dragged his head back. The weight on top of him, the pressure in the middle of his back robbed him of air, tearing at sinews, crushing his windpipe. For a fleeting moment, Pietro thought of Claudio and Renata, of Elisa, tucking them up for bed. Of the dreams they had for the future. He would not die like this.

Summoning up every ounce of his waning strength, Pietro pressed up from the floor and toppled the intruder onto the carpet. He turned and pounced, feeling the intruder's knee in his chest, sending him somersaulting into the air, weightless, flying, spindles from the banister cascading with him as he fell back towards the Italian tiles and the brightest white light he had ever seen.

Proof of Life

Chapter 8

Thirty minutes later, the police arrived at Moretti's villa, surprising given the Carabinieri headquarters were only a kilometer away. They sent only a single patrol car. Two officers in gray uniforms adjusted their belts, crammed on their hats, and buzzed on the intercom. After a few mumbled words, they buzzed it again. Then they shrugged and left. There was no sign of the assassin. Maybe he wasn't after the information Moretti was selling? Maybe killing Moretti was enough?

Still, the Carabinieri would return, and when they did, all hell would break loose.

I walked in the shadows back to the Ford. The streets were quiet. Just a peaceful fall night. Somewhere a town dog barked, the leaves rustled above me. My chest hurt from the pummeling the goon had given me and I had a lump the size of an egg on my skull. I was battered and bruised and needed to sleep. But I still had a problem to solve.

The girl.

The fluorescent hands on my Omega told me it was 9:40 pm. Four hours before my flight checked in. My things were in the car. I could high-tail it to the airport and be out of the country before she woke the next morning. She was safe for the night in an anonymous hotel room. Then the Polizia could deal with her. She was not my problem.

Was she?

So why had she prayed on my mind all evening?

Rome was alive with CCTV. Perhaps not as much as

Proof of Life

London or Beijing, but the chances of leaving the city without being seen were slim. And innocent people rarely flee with the killer. By now, she would be the prime suspect. After a few uncomfortable days in a cell, a couple of interviews, the British Consul would rescue her, surely.

Unless the assassin reached her first.

By now, he would have seen the CCTV. He would know the license from the Ford, even the route out to the motel.

Back in Moretti's apartment, I'd winged him in the right arm. Just a graze and some torn clothing but he'd be mad. Already he would be tooling up, tracking us down. No loose ends. Hell, he may already be driving away from the motel, having spread Steve's head across the cheap velour headboard. Or sitting, waiting patiently for me to return.

I had my tickets, my gear, the thumb drive. My head willed me to make the choice, turn West towards Leonardo da Vinci airport. But my heart, my conscience, wouldn't let me abandon the girl.

When I returned to the motel, the nightwatchman looked out from his office and nodded. There was no blood trail smeared into the carpet along the corridor. Inside, the TV was on. I readied the Glock under my jacket and I eased open the door. The girl was lying on the bed, remote in her hand, a kaleidoscope of shapes and colors as the TV flickered to itself. I took a breath, relieved. Even I knew dead people didn't snore. Latching the door, taking off my jacket, I folded the counterpane across her, fished a spare blanket from the wardrobe, and settled into the uncomfortable chair.

As the Glock lay across my lap and my eyelids fluttered, I wondered what I had gotten myself into.

Chapter 9

Thursday, September 5

I awoke with a start, at once alert, but the room was still and quiet. Angling my watch to the light, I checked the time. 3:08 am. My default time for insomnia, when my mind careered along at a million miles an hour while my body stood on the brakes. A faint amber stripe snaked through the curtains and across the bed, up and over the shape between the sheets. The girl was breathing, slow and regular. Twenty miles away, an airplane sat on the apron, a queue patiently waiting at the terminal, an unanswered call for Franklin Farrell to proceed to the gate. Dejected at the thought of another day away from home, I made my way into the bathroom and swilled cold water across my face, drank a glassful, rank with chlorine. With sleep now a distant hope, I dragged in the briefcase, took my MacBook from my backpack, and latched the bathroom door.

The paper in Moretti's briefcase was headed Amber Rock. My boss Pliskin had given me those two words and told me to go seek. I went, I sought. Hopefully, I'd found the right thumb drive and not a bunch of continental pornography. Pliskin had a sense of humor, but I doubted it would stretch that far.

In the *Moleskine* notebook, the writing was almost italic as it raced to the next word. Expedient. Not rushing, but with an air of self-importance, just like Moretti himself. He'd formatted it as a daybook, notes and jotting from phone calls taken whilst kicking back in the big old leather desk chair. There were times, dates, names, but without context, it was

Proof of Life

meaningless. Then several entries caught my eye. Names and some words—DeMarco, Trueman, Velasquez and Gilbués, Tom Jardine and the amounts—€500,000. €100,000 in advance. And of course, *Roccia Ambrata*—Amber Rock. There was a nasty smell about it all. Blackmail. Tom Jardine was a freelance journalist I'd seen a few times on the news channels. Was he next in line for the assassin's attention?

Only one other name resonated. I had not heard it for a long time; a name from another age. Born in Chicago, Maxwell Anderson worked in the UK as an analyst with the Office for Nuclear Regulation. He and his wife Kate had disappeared on a boating holiday back in 1990. They were never seen again, declared legally dead in 1997.

Tom Jardine è a Cagliari. Sta cercando la barca di Max Anderson.

Tom Jardine is in Cagliari. He is searching for Max Anderson's boat.

Could it be a different boat? A different Max Anderson? Somehow, I doubted it. And was Anderson mixed up in Amber Rock too? Maybe it was the reason Pliskin and my employers were so interested?

I photographed the page with my phone and turned my attention to the thumb drive. There were around a dozen folders, mostly business documents, records, accounts, photos. Some of the names I recognized, some I didn't. They were none of my concern. Only three folders interested me. Technically, they were none of my concern either, but I was intrigued.

The first, labeled *Roccia Ambrata,* contained a stack of pictures. Each showed a similar scene. Clay-colored desert, peppered with rugged die-hard bushes as far as the eye could see. Ultramarine skies dappled with scudding marshmallow clouds. There were no buildings, no sign of human habitation, apart from a dirt road disappearing toward low hills on the horizon. Except for around ten images. In these, a three-meter high chain fence, topped with concertina razor-wire, stretched as far as the eye could see. A compound or a prison? Closed-circuit cameras stared down at the photographer from motorized poles. Here and there, along the wire, there were faded signs:

> Amber Rock +1 (202) 555 0374
> Danger to Life. Do Not Enter.
> Trespassers will be prosecuted.

In one photo, a stone-built dome, like an igloo, no bigger than a shed, stood alone baking in the heat. It looked like the cairns I'd seen on Scottish hillsides.

The second folder was named *Sentinel Group*. Another list of names, which meant nothing to me, except again Max Anderson appeared. There were photos, news reports, publicity fliers, all featuring the same set of people, which I assumed to be the members of the group. They were having a fine old time, traveling the world, attending every Climate Change conference and Energy Symposium going. Perhaps the expenses were good.

The last file, headed *Max Anderson* intrigued me the most. It contained press cuttings relating to his disappearance nearly three decades ago, and of the fruitless search afterward.

Was Amber Rock a place? Did the name refer to the compound surrounded by razor wire? If so, how? What part did Max Anderson play in all this, and why had it all resurfaced now?

And what else did Tom Jardine know?

***

I'd told Stephanie Jordan I worked for the government. Which government was always debatable—and deniable. When I left the US Marines, or rather they left me, I'd gotten the call out of the blue from a private security organization. TORUS Security Inc. They said they needed people with my

Proof of Life

particular military background, shame to waste taxpayer-funded training, yadda, yadda, yadda. Turned out the call was genuine. They helped rehabilitate my shattered left shoulder, expanded my skillset, and gave me a cute codename—Beckett. Of course, TORUS didn't exist, nor did the External Covert Operations Bureau, the department that employed me. Not officially, anyway. We had clients throughout the world who would deny knowing us, projects they would deny were even going ahead and a revenue stream so convoluted even Harry Houdini couldn't untie it. So if things went to shit, we—I—could not turn to them for help.

Pliskin had been my handler for a year now and always knew everything. From his cave in London, Washington, Caracas, wherever, news seemed to reach him first. Pliskin and I had no secrets. Well, not many. Grabbing my phone, I dialed the satellite uplink. Despite the hour, he answered almost immediately. He always did.

"Beckett. You have had a busy day." The tone was superior and dry; somehow I always thought he was mocking me.

"You don't know the half of it."

"Unfortunately, I do. Still, Moretti has been terminated. Our clients will be satisfied and we have canceled your flight back, so that will have reduced the expenditure. The assassin is a Sicilian, Renzo Baresi. He honed his skills with the *Cosa Nostra* and dropped off-grid five years ago. We matched his face from CCTV. You need to find him and terminate him too because, have no doubt, he will come for you. And to answer your next question, you have been paid in full. We expect his termination to be on the house, so to speak."

"Hey, Pliskin. You're all heart."

"The girl. Stephanie Jordan."

I raised my eyebrows. "You *are* well informed, Pliskin."

"No. Sky News is well informed. I just watch Sky News. Taking the girl was a rash move. No act of kindness goes unpunished. Your chivalry is laudable, but it also saddles you with a problem. What do you intend to do with her?"

"Find Baresi, I suppose. Clear her name, take her somewhere safe until this all blows over. I am not sure yet. If Baresi has Sky News, he will know she was there too, so I figure we are safer together than apart."

"We are not a charity and you are not a social worker. Amber Rock is your concern. You need to make it your primary focus."

"C'mon, Pliskin. I owe her that much. If I hadn't turned up, she would either be dead or in the clear. As it is, because of me she's neither."

The line stilled as Pliskin considered. "Be careful, Beckett, and remember where your loyalties lie."

Proof of Life

Chapter 10

Crawling back under my duvet bivouac, I watched the girl for a moment, listening to her slow, regular breathing, the expression of terror lost in the embrace of sleep. I knew Pliskin was right. Rescuing her had been a rash move; it made her a fugitive, too. I could've left her or handed her over, but that ship had sailed. Now, Baresi would come after us both, so, until I could convince the Polizia she was innocent, I was stuck with her. Forensics may help—or at least make them think. Moretti and his goon were killed with the same gun, but because we took it, there was nothing to say who fired it.

Under my shirt, the bruises from my beatings compounded my misery.

And me? Moretti was dead, and I had the Amber Rock information. Technically, I could pass the thumb drive to Pliskin and declare the job done. I could retreat home and continue to uncover Amber Rock from my couch.

But for the girl.

Also, I couldn't get Moretti's notebook off my mind. *Tom Jardine is in Cagliari. He is searching for Max Anderson's boat.* Like it or not, something had sparked my curiosity. Who had sent Baresi to silence Luciano Moretti? Would he now be gunning for Tom Jardine?

And what the sweet Jesus was Amber Rock?

***

Proof of Life

The sun, leaking through the flimsy drapes, cajoled me reluctantly into consciousness. The egg on my head and the crick in my neck told me getting up was likely to hurt, but my stomach insisted I ate. Eventually, my stomach won, and I threw off the blanket and groaned myself to my feet. My clothes were creased and grimy and the high-end shirt was a write-off, but even they were in better shape than I was.

Turning, I caught my breath and cursed. The girl was gone. So was my jacket and pocketbook. I was mad. I liked that wallet. Hand-worked cowhide and a pocket for pennies.

So she had gone. I didn't blame her. Maybe her chances were better on her own? Maybe not, but I was pissed at her timing. If she'd have skipped the previous night while I was at Moretti's, I could have made my flight out. But at least she had the sense to leave the guns, and my backpack looked untouched. Drawing back the drapes, I checked the parking lot. The Ford was still there.

A sound outside the door made me turn. Footsteps on the carpet, not simply walking past but standing, maybe listening. I grabbed the S&W, clicked off the safety, and crept around beside the wardrobes. In the dressing table mirror, I could see the door reflected.

I was amazed it took so long for Baresi to find us. Amazed but not surprised.

A keycard swiped in the lock, then a second time, followed by the weary clack of the mechanism. The handle eased down and the silhouette of a body eased through the gap, tiptoeing around to the far side of the bed. I raised the gun and aimed for the head.

"Stephanie!"

She let out a squeal and dropped the carrier bag she was holding, backing into the wall, screwing up her eyes. Momentarily confused, I drew down the S&W and stepped out. It was definitely her, but she was different. Her hair was short and spiked and—*auburn*? She was wearing spectacles. Round, dark frames. And my goddamn jacket.

"What the hell? Where have you been?" I held up my hands in apology. "I'm sorry, sit down. Please."

Tentatively, she lowered her arms and sat on the bed, still looking at the gun. "I couldn't sleep. I needed to go out for a walk. Clear my head."

My mouth actually fell open. "Really? Half the police forces in Europe have your picture and you went out for *a walk*? And—that?" I gestured at her hair. It changed the whole shape of her face. Not even her own mother would know her. "How did you…?"

"There is a *Tabacchi* about a kilometer away. I saw my photograph on the newsstand outside, so I went into the *Farmacia* and bought scissors and hair dye. I used the bathroom down the hall."

"And the glasses?"

"From my bag. I usually wear contacts. I figured if they plastered my passport photo all over the news…"

"No one ever looks like their passport photo, Steve."

"But I look even less like it now," she huffed. "I thought you'd be pleased. Instead, you point that bloody gun at me."

"Look, I said I'm sorry, but you must know how stupid that was? The guy in the Tab…Taba…"

"…*Tabacchi*. It's a…"

"Whatever. That guy has been staring at those newspapers for hours. What if he recognized you?"

"Well," she spat sassily. "He didn't."

Her eyes flicked between me and the gun. She was still in the white blouse and A-line skirt, both covered with dust and dirt. Her unmade-up face, etched with anxiety, was red with tears. I felt another pang of guilt. Was I being too hard on her? One minute she was taking dictation, next on the run for murder. In her place, I would worry too.

"You okay?"

"What do you care?" She began gnawing on a nail.

"You need to remember we are both in this shit together." Through the drapes, it all still looked quiet. Maybe we'd gotten away with it. For now.

"I thought you'd be glad I showed some initiative."

"I am glad, honest I am." I could feel myself digging deeper. "I love what you did with your hair. And your glasses but wandering the streets in a town where you are public enemy number one? Really?"

She edged over to the bed and sat down heavily, dropping her head into her hands. She was shaking and sniffing back the tears. "This is all so—so screwed up. I have no idea what is going on."

I sighed, sat on the bed next to her. "You and me both, Steve. It's a screwed-up world. Far more screwed up than you can imagine. Who is right and who is wrong? Who deserves to live and who deserves to die? I don't know."

"So why Sr. Moretti? Why did he have to die?"

"He's a dangerous man. He dabbled in everything nasty in the world. Ultimately, he dabbled where he shouldn't have and someone couldn't allow that. So they shot him."

"Who shot him? You?"

"I do not know—yet, but not me. The guy who pulled the trigger was a hired gun. Someone else sent him. Look at this." I pulled the notebook from Moretti's briefcase. She squinted in the gloom, then moved into a shaft of light from window,. "Amber Rock? What is that? A precious stone, a place?"

I shrugged my shoulders. "Google only got references to

fossilized amber resin. Amber is valuable, but not worth murder or blackmail. Something else is going on and we got caught up in it."

"These others. Tom Jardine? Max Anderson, Trueman, Velasquez, Gilbués, DeMarco?"

"Jardine's a journalist. A documentary maker who pokes at open sores to make a buck. Anderson's a name from the past. He died in the early '90s. The others? Who knows?"

"Amber Rock and Trueman," she said, translating as she read. "An opportunity. €500,000. €100,000 in advance. Speak to DeMarco. Blackmail?"

"Yea. As I said, Moretti was a bottom dweller."

"And September 4th. Oh, my God. That was yesterday. *DeMarco. Discuss a deal on Amber Rock. Meet with Franklin Farrell. A time-waster.* He got the last bit right." She chuckled mirthlessly, flipping back and forth through the notebook. "What does it all mean?"

"Nothing, Steve. Nothing at all. Moretti got greedy with the wrong people. Whatever this information is, it's dynamite in the right hands. Moretti didn't care who bought it; one side seeks to expose it, another seeks to suppress it."

"*Jardine è un problema.* Do you think he will be next?"

"If it's worth €500,000, maybe more? Perhaps, Tom Jardine is getting greedy too?"

***

We tidied the room and packed away what little we had. It was a forensic soup, but there was nothing we could do about it. We needed to move as soon as possible. The girl sat on the bed, legs pulled up, arms wrapped tightly about them, flicking through news channels. She paused, at her passport photograph. The police had fingerprints belonging to the missing PA. They now implicated her in the murders.

Proof of Life

Max Anderson was playing on my mind. Moretti's was suggesting he was still alive. That he'd faked the sailboat disappearance to start a new life with his wife, Katherine. What was so important he would give up everything to do that? If indeed it were true. And just what did Tom Jardine know that, after thirty years, no one else did?

"So what now, Beckett?" Her voice was measured. Maybe acceptance of the situation, or of the inevitable.

"We need to get moving. Find breakfast and some fresh clothes. Try to keep ourselves alive. That guy, Jardine. We need to find him before they do. Pliskin is going to email details of his whereabouts."

"Who's Pliskin?"

"Great question. I'll let you know when I find out. He's the nearest I got to a boss."

"And who does Pliskin work for?"

I smiled. "What about you, Steve? English, right?"

"Salisbury."

"So, what brings you to Rome?"

She looked into middle-distance, a different life. "I am in my placement year from University. Bath. Honors in Modern Languages and European Studies. They found me a job with a temping agency in Rome to brush up my Italian."

I raised my eyebrows. The nearest I got to university was watching some geeks on a TV panel show. "How are you finding that?"

"It was going great until 12 noon yesterday."

"Sorry, but at least you're not in a cell." Her expression told me it was scant recompense. "So are we good?"

"We're good-*ish*."

"I'll take that."

Chapter 11

"So, Beckett. Twice in one day. People will talk." As always, Pliskin's voice was calm, assured, a well-spoken, urbane Harvard lilt. "I have emailed over a dossier on Tom Jardine." Enough chit-chat, straight down to business.

"Thanks, Pliskin. I am grateful."

"You may wish to reconsider. The authorities are pinning Moretti's murder on you, with the girl as your accomplice. They believe she took the position with Moretti to give you an opportunity to murder him."

"If only I'd had the opportunity," I whined. "Life is so unfair sometimes."

"Indeed, but we will gloss over that indiscretion. You and the girl were both caught on CCTV. The incident is still taking up column inches so the police need to be seen taking action. They will be on the lookout for you."

I checked the notebook. "On the day he died, Moretti was meeting someone called DeMarco."

"Popular name, especially in Italy. It could be a cover for Baresi, the hitman. An appointment with death, so to speak."

"Trueman. Moretti's diary also mentioned someone called Trueman. Also Velasquez and Gilbués?"

"The names have come up before. We could not ascertain their significance."

"And Max Anderson?"

"What of him?" Pliskin's voice changed. Suddenly

devoid of any interest, almost purposefully so.

"The notebook also mentions Max Anderson's boat. Perhaps I need to investigate further."

"Max Anderson disappeared twenty-seven years ago. Many have looked. No one has been successful. There is no sense turning over old stones." I could hear the irritation in Pliskin's voice. A raw nerve pricked.

"But…"

"We tasked you with removing Moretti because we believe Amber Rock is important. Moretti staked his life on it and lost. Find out who contracted Baresi, who they work for and how it links to Amber Rock. Find these people, Jardine, DeMarco, Trueman, Velasquez and Gilbués. Hopefully, they will enlighten us all."

"And the girl?"

"Turn her in, set her loose. The sooner that happens, the sooner she can return to her own life."

"You want me to hand her over?"

"Yes, I do. If they had arrested her yesterday, the lack of real forensics would have cleared her. By *rescuing* her, you have implicated her and yourself. In turn, it threatens us. I cannot allow that." There was something hard and mechanical in Pliskin's voice. Was this a company line, or was he just a cold-hearted bastard?

"The girl stays with me until we find out the truth. I am not abandoning her, Pliskin."

"Concentrate on Amber Rock, Beckett."

"And Max Anderson? What if he isn't dead but…"

"Beckett?" Again the audible irritation. "It is essential you keep your eye on the ball. You can chase ghosts and good causes once that is done. Perhaps I should remind you who pays your fee? Who funds us so we can continue to do so? Find DeMarco, Trueman and the rest. Discover the truth about Amber Rock. If you stumble across Baresi and throw him to the Italian police, then all the better."

***

I dropped some of Moretti's cash on the dresser to cover the cost of the room and we high-tailed it through the first-floor fire escape. The less attention we drew to ourselves, the better. Our Ford was where I had left it. The rest of the parking lot was empty. I started the car and eased it out into the light morning traffic. Safety in numbers.

"Where are we going?"

"Sardinia."

"Sardinia?" The girl paused, open-mouthed, as she buckled up.

"Moretti's notebook says Jardine is flying to Cagliari today. It's the capital of Sardinia. It also says he's going to find the missing boat. We need to tag along for the ride if only to warn him of the danger he's in."

"I don't know about a boat or this Max Anderson."

"Anderson was a nuclear scientist. He disappeared in a boating accident a long time ago, presumed dead. Ancient history. Now he's being talked about again and in the same breath as Amber Rock. Moretti thought that important. So does DeMarco. Maybe even Trueman or the others. If Jardine is looking for the wreck, five gets you ten he thinks the same. We need to find Jardine first before anyone else."

"Won't they be looking for us, too?"

"Probably," I smiled, "but I have a plan."

Proof of Life

Chapter 12

The town of Civitavecchia is around twenty-five kilometers northwest of Rome, an ancient maritime town built in the second century. It has a sixteenth-century fort, a museum, and the remains of a Roman thermal bath complex. More importantly, it was where our ride to Sardinia docked. Sadly, the ferry traveled overnight, which meant an entire day to kill. An entire day trying to impress a sullen, scared woman whose sense of humor had deserted her.

Women were not my thing. My folks couldn't have kids, so adopted me, effectively making me an only child. This didn't bother me when I was younger. I read a lot, so I had plenty of other worlds to play in. Then came adolescence, acne, and girls. They were an alien species. I left them to do their thing and I did mine, throwing myself into my studies, played football, soccer, judo and karate. I became self-sufficient. Since then, girls had come and gone. Now they are all gone. It's tidier that way.

After half an hour, we pulled into a huge retail park I'd seen on the map. It was as big as a football field and I figured we could use some of Moretti's cash to make us less conspicuous.

"Go in and buy yourself some new clothes." I held out a bunch of notes. She just stared at them. "Some jeans, t-shirts, underwear. Maybe shoes, a coat?"

"I can't go in there. What if someone recognizes me?"

"You've done your hair. You got glasses. Why would anyone recognize you?"

Proof of Life

She looked aghast, as if I had spit-roast a poodle or something. "Clark Kent had bloody glasses but everyone still knew he was Superman!"

"Just stay away from phone booths," I snickered, rather cruelly.

"How can you joke about it? We are on the run for murder."

"You're on the run for murder. For me it's murder and kidnapping, remember? Still, we won't be on the run much longer if you don't get your ass into gear and use your head."

"You really are a bastard." She folded her arms and sunk back into the seat, ignoring the euros in my hand.

"C'mon. Just give me a break! Whether or not you like it, you are in this up to that pretty neck of yours, and…"

"*Pretty neck? A* bastard *and* a chauvinist."

"… *And*—if you *don't* use your head, neither of us will last very long. As a blonde—ex-blonde—in an A-line skirt, you stick out a mile. The quicker we sort that out the better."

"How do I know this isn't some trick to get rid of me? What if I get back here and you've driven off?"

"Stephanie. I have two loaded firearms. If I wanted to be rid of you, you'd be cold in a dumpster by now. Anyhow, my flight left at 3:35 am this morning. So you have to forgive me if my patience is wearing a little thin. Whether I like it or not, I'm stuck with you for the long haul. Now, get in the damn store and buy some clothes."

"You go first."

"What?" The conversation had turned infantile; two kids arguing about who does the chores.

"You go first. You buy the clothes. Size twelve."

"And how's that going to look? Buying women's clothes?"

"I don't know. If anyone asks , style it out and say *per mia moglie* and hope for the best they believe you. Oh, and get some food." She flashed a humorless smile, then gazed out at the white panel van parked next to us.

"Jeez." Accepting defeat, I slammed the door rather too hard and stormed away.

The superstore was practically empty, probably more staff than customers. I had ditched the waistcoat, which was just as well as our picture had made the front page of *la Repubblica*. Still, the staff seemed to be more interested in surviving the ennui of a midweek shift than dealing with customers. Not knowing how long we would be on the move, I used the rest of Moretti's cash to buy a couple of multipacks of underwear, some jeans, sweaters, t-shirts, and a faux leather jacket, along with a couple of holdalls to keep it all in. The range of beanies and baseball caps was limited, but I chanced my arm on a couple. I had forgotten to ask Steve for her shoe size but even in my naivety, I knew buying shoes for a woman was a step too far.

***

The ferry to Sardinia crossed the Tyrrhenian Sea overnight. We would be in Cagliari in time for breakfast the next day. Nevertheless, I wanted to arrive early at the port. Change our clothes. Grab a coffee. Hopefully, on a night crossing, we could hunker down and avoid too much attention. Keep an eye open for Baresi, the Sicilian hitman. My gut told me, having missed once, he would come after us again. Late morning, the port apron was still deserted, so I took the Ford around the block and parked in a side street where we would be less conspicuous.

"Do you think he knows where we are?" Steve rested her elbow on the open window and chewed on a nail. I grabbed a pack of sandwiches and a can of coke from behind the seats and handed them over. More nutritious than keratin.

"Baresi? Probably. I expect he has resources."

"Resources? Well, so have you. Can't you call your office? Maybe they know where he is now?"

"I doubt it. He's smart. He would use a drop phone, bought for cash and disposed of afterward. Also, he will also have memorized his escape route like I did—if I'd gotten to use it. Simple tricks like avoiding CCTV, mixing with crowds, changing his appearance. Using false papers."

"My papers are in my bloody bedsit across the city." She picked at the sandwiches as if I had laced them with arsenic. "Or more likely in a cardboard box at police headquarters. Even sitting here, with different clothes, different hair, I still think the police are going to jump out at any moment."

"Welcome to my world."

"I don't want your bloody world. I want *my* world. Safe. No guns. No bodies." She would never be happy until she was free of the murder charge, and that made me part of the problem. In the space of a day, my life had also turned to shit. Pulling my faux suede baseball cap over my eyes, I reclined the seat.

Late afternoon, the port apron was a little busier. I drove around, paid the fee, and took my place in line. The harbor was the usual sprawling concrete and steel affair; a promontory spoiling the coastline of Italy. A stark eyesore against the oily sea-green of the water, patrolled by surly, uniformed officials who hid behind shades and spoke into walkie-talkies. Other passengers lolled against their cars, smoking endless cigarettes. The air smelled of salt and diesel as the enormous engines whined up, and clouds of black smoke belched out of the funnels. Nearer to the water, foot passengers jostled and shouted as all Italians do. By the time they waved us on up toward the gaping stern of the ferry, it was dark and the cold had left condensation on the windows. As one of the ferry employees shackled the car down, I hustled Steve into the melee of sweaty, fractious people, all intent on bagging the best seat.

Instead of business class over the Atlantic, I would spend the night squirming in an uncomfortable leatherette seat, listening to the throbbing of the ancient ferry's engines. Rather than operating incognito, they had plastered my face all over the world's news with a suspected murderess in tow. What's more, there was a ruthless Sicilian on our tail. Maybe a few days in Sardinia would allow things to calm down? Allow me to figure a way out of this mess? Somehow I doubted it would work out that way.

"What will you do when you find Tom Jardine?" She was leaning back on her hands. The sun had flushed her face, softening her features. Beneath the veneer of weariness, her eyes were still wide, on stalks.

"Discover what he knows about Amber Rock and Max Anderson. The information on Moretti's thumb drive was only a taster, so I need something to keep my boss happy. If he can lead us to Moretti's killer, that puts you in the clear."

"You think he's on board?"

"Baresi? Probably, he's had a day to work out where we're going. He will not risk anything on a crowded ferry. When the time comes, I'll deal with him."

She leaned back in the uncomfortable seat, her head on her hand, elbow on the arm, quiet and pensive. Her eyes had dropped to my tote bag; she was thinking about the guns inside. "By deal with him, you mean…?"

"Probably. When the time comes, it will be him or me. I want it to be him."

"Don't you get sick of all this? Running, hiding, killing. Always looking over your shoulder?"

Did she really care, or was this just chit-chat? I stared straight ahead at a snack bar set into the forward bulkhead,

Proof of Life

a plump woman balancing takeout coffee on a pizza box, a plasma screen showing our pictures above the news ticker. This was business. I had to be careful about what I told her.

"It's all I have ever done," I said. "I got good at keeping myself safe."

"Ah, so that's why you were spark out on Sr. Moretti's floor."

I smiled wryly. Sarcasm was not a good look on her.

"I should have listened to my instincts. Waited a beat. Let the killer come out. Or even bugged out and gone for a coffee." I wouldn't let my guard down again that easily. At least I hoped I wouldn't.

"Still, you were prepared to kill Moretti, and the other guy—the Sicilian. Even me if you had to. All my life, I've been taught to despise death, to despise the people who murder. How can you be so comfortable with that? Is human life so meaningless you can snuff it out with no remorse?"

"Hey, I have remorse. Plenty of it." For a moment, I let the tiredness and frustration burst through. "I am not some damn psychopath with no conscience. I served in Iraq and Afghanistan. I saw people blown to pieces, my best friend choking on his own blood." The Marines had taught me to dissociate people from death. They were targets, marks, subjects. Shit happens, then you move on.

"That's different. War is war but killing Moretti? How can you justify murder—for money?"

"Not every war is fought with tanks and bullets, Steve. Most are fought in boardrooms and hotel rooms, undercover and in private. Not every soldier wears army fatigues and carries an AK47. As for Moretti, he has personally been involved in the trafficking of arms, drugs, and humans. How many people do you think have died because of him? Hundreds? Thousands? And he looked none of them in the eye when he did it. In Iraq, we aimed down the barrel, through the scope into the eye of people who were doing the same to us. An honest transaction. Oh, and it's not about money. I already have plenty of money."

"So, why not leave it to the authorities? Why is it your responsibility to play God?"

"C'mon. You know it doesn't work like that. Life isn't just good or bad. Dark or light. One man's terrorist is another man's freedom fighter. Anyway, who do you think employs me? The authorities. They don't get their own hands dirty. A little plausible deniability. Isn't it enough to know someone is removing the bad guys?"

"But if good and bad are just different truths, who's to say you are following the right one?"

"The world is a messed-up place. You just gotta pick your side and hope you picked the right one. Society needs order. It needs rules. We all must accept the rules or seek to change them. Those who don't want to play by the rules, who threaten the stability of our society, who refuse to accept the rule of law must ultimately be removed from it. The needs of the many outweigh the needs of the few."

I'd been through the morality of my job a million times. Right or wrong, good or bad, it was my job.

"And Baresi? When he catches up with you?"

"We both know what we're doing, Steve. We understand the game. Another honest transaction."

Proof of Life

Chapter 13

Steve fell quiet, and soon the gentle vibration of the hull rocked her into an uncomfortable doze. It would be another five hours until we docked, so I pulled out my MacBook and read the information Pliskin sent me about Jardine. There were documents, photos and more scanned newspaper cuttings. A potted history of the man's career.

Tom Jardine was 60 years old, a freelance journalist and writer, originally from Glasgow, Scotland. He specialized in lurid exposés and moral crusades, with several bestsellers under his belt. Human trafficking, drug-running, illegal arms. He'd written articles on the reality of recycling in the Western world—Indian waste heaps and floating barges of trash simply pushed under someone else's carpet. On Governments agreeing to the Kyoto Protocol with no intention of honoring their pledges, passing the buck to nations in need of cash and aid more than fresh air.

He was the pain-in-the-butt do-gooder type who held people to account. The sort everybody loathed whilst secretly admiring. On the whole, he aimed his barbs at the establishment. The powers-that-be who should know better. He spooked governments, upset the status quo, revealed the wheeler-dealing behind the thin veneer of honorable politics. In fact, he seemed to have his fingers in every shit-pie in the world. Now and again, we all need someone to rake up the silt at the bottom of the pond.

What shit-pie was Tom Jardine delving into now? What did he know about Max Anderson that had eluded the rest of the world? The $64,000—or rather €500,000—question.

Proof of Life

Of course, he may know nothing. He may be engaged in a fishing trip, literally, but something told me I could not ignore him.

At the same time, did I want to know?

***

After a couple of hours, I left Steve sleeping to search for a washroom. To my dismay, Baresi sat in the forward restaurant, drinking coffee. He was prodding a wooden stirrer into his takeout cup, as if fishing for a contact lens, nodding lazily while pretending to listen to another guy I didn't recognize. Short and stubbled, with large bulbous eyes and a shining bald head, the other guy was leaning forward, gesturing aggressively. Beneath the table, Baresi's white trainers bounced incessantly, his mind elsewhere. Had he seen Steve and me napping? I found a different washroom, as far away from the Sicilian as possible, then I circled back to Steve. She was lolling across the arm of her chair, fast asleep. There was no sense alarming her but still, I primed the Glock and held it under my jacket.

PART TWO - SARDINIA, ITALY

Proof of Life

Chapter 14

Friday, September 6

As the first shards of morning sunlight threaded their way through the cabin windows, the boat passed the 19th-century lighthouse which guarded the mouth of the two-kilometer-long Gulf of Olbia. Sardinia is one hundred and seventy kilometers long and fifty wide. A teardrop in the Tyrrhenian Sea between Italy, France, and Spain. Bordered by rocky coastlines, covered in forested hills and treacherous roads, it is a great place to hide if you don't want to be found. A great place for Max Anderson to hide, maybe?

I returned to my seat as the tannoy barked out instructions. The engines had throttled off, signaling we would soon enter the harbor, when they would thunder into reverse and churn up the silt on approach to the dockside. Steve was stretching, looking around nervously.

"Are we there?"

I nodded. "You want to watch the boat dock?"

"I've seen boats dock, Beckett. What I want to do is hide. My passport photo was on the news channel all night. I feel like everyone's watching me." The other passengers were yawning, collecting their things and going up to the deck to get their first view of the lighthouse and the Gulf. They were oblivious to each other, let alone us.

"I saw the picture," I smirked. "You changed your hair and everything."

She harrumphed and thrust my bag into my chest.

Joining a line, I was relieved when we emerged out into

the fresh sea air, slightly nauseous from the odor of diesel and the reek of unwashed humanity. The sun fought through the wispy, cotton-wool clouds, casting a sprinkling of diamonds across the steel gray sea. The enormous prow of the ferry carved a crystal white path past the lighthouse and between the headlands before slowing and performing a shuddering pirouette into another broad gray slab of concrete spoiling the coastline. Not waiting for the huge flat butt of the ferry to edge into the dock, we pushed through, following directions to the car deck around thirty feet below.

"Those two men. I don't like the way they keep looking over. It's kind of creepy." She was resting her elbows on the railing, with her back to the bulkhead. Baresi and his friend were on the opposite side of the deck, trying to look nonchalant, failing dismally. The short one kept cocking his head, checking we were still there.

"You know Italian men," I winked. "Attractive girl, even with the spiky hair and specs. Goes with the territory, sweetheart."

"Call me sweetheart once more and you'll be over these railings and into the sea. *Capiche?*"

"Look, we'll be away from here soon. Just don't keep looking at them." Holding Steve's arm, I guided her through the swell of passengers. We were safe in the crowds. Baresi and his pal could wait, but I needed to know whether they had a car. If they were foot-passengers, we could skedaddle before they found their rental in the dock.

They had a car.

A white Cinquecento about twenty vehicles back from ours. That might buy us a minute or two once we were through the gates and out onto the road. Then it was a race across the island to find Tom Jardine before they did.

Chapter 15

Away from the ferry, the drab concrete apron soon gave way to a palm-lined concourse leading toward the town of Olbia. The sun was already burning off the early morning haze, and it promised to be a fine day. Olbia was in the North. Cagliari was three hours south down a featureless road that scribed a serpentine route across the island. The Sicilian's Fiat was always going to be slower than our Ford, but I was in no hurry as long as we found Jardine first. Once on the autostrada, I switched on the radio and tuned to some Europop station to keep myself awake while Steve dozed. But after an hour and a half, my eyelids were weighing heavy, so I pulled into a rest stop and parked out of sight.

"You want a coffee?"

Steve blinked a couple of times. Then her brow furrowed. "Those two men are following us, aren't they?"

"Uh-huh." I wondered if she knew Baresi was one of them? "I guess if they knew we were coming to Sardinia, they already know where we are heading, so there's no point trying to out-run them. You want a pastry too?"

Queueing for the checkout, I counted six white Cinquecentos heading South, through the plate-glass window. As common as rats in a grain store, and just as difficult to catch. Steve sat out back on a grass bank with the sun on her face. Behind her, a bed of bougainvillea teemed with butterflies and chirping sparrows. The traffic noise was no more than a low rumble.

"What happens when they catch us?" She shaded her eyes, squinted up at me, took a cup from the cardboard tray.

"I'm kind of hoping they don't, but I try not to think too far ahead. Right now, we need to find Jardine, preferably before they do."

"And if we don't?" She looked at me over the cheap supermarket sunglasses. The tiredness and the fear showed in her eyes. Living on her nerves, struggling to hold it together, at least until she could find a way out.

"As I say, I try not to think too far ahead."

"Well, that may be okay for you, but not me. Every second I am scared shitless wondering what the next second may bring."

"My boss, Pliskin, said I should cut you free. Hand you over to the Polizia. He says the evidence against you is flimsy. They would soon realize and let you go."

"Nice chap, your Pliskin."

Her eyes were glassy. I handed her a clean supermarket handkerchief. It was the extent of my ability to empathize. It pays not to dwell too deeply on others. They get under your skin and then they quit on you. Or you lose them.

She sipped her coffee, singed her lips, and frowned.

"And why *didn't* you cut me loose when you had the opportunity? God knows you must have wanted to. You could have left me asleep in the motel, driven back to the airport, and been out of Italy by now."

Was she a mind reader? "Because eventually they'd find out about me. My face would be all over CNN and my career would be over."

"So the only reason you dragged me along is to keep *you* safe? Assassin, kidnapper, chauvinist, *and* arrogant bastard. Jeez, Beckett. You've got the set."

"Are you going to question every judgment call I make?" Irked, I glanced away to a safer view of traffic through the hedging.

"Yes, I bloody well am, so get used to it."

Then something snapped. I was stinging from the failure in Rome, full of self-reproach and just a little afraid of the repercussions with Pliskin.

"Hey. You think I don't know how crap all this is? That I don't feel bad about what you're going through? That I didn't lie awake last night knowing I have to keep you safe?"

"Yes, but…"

"Yes, but fucking nothing. So you're in a mess. *I will sort it.*"

"Don't you shout at me." She turned and pointed a matronly finger.

"I know it's a pile of crap, but you have to trust me. I *will* sort it." I flashed back to Basra, a dark cellar, the thuds of mortars. The eyes of Corporal Tim Neal as I held a filthy rag to his neck and pissed myself. I had said the same then only for the sepsis to make his wife a widow three weeks later.

"I'm scared." She hid behind her shades.

"Yes, you said. Twice now." I took a deep breath, cleared my head. I wasn't angry at her, just at everything else. "I've learned to live on my instincts and it's worked out okay so far." She made to speak, but I wasn't done. "Sometimes I'm as scared as you are. You got to learn to embrace the fear and not let it consume you. To use it, feed off of it."

She crossed her arms, unconvinced.

"Just go with it, Steve. Like I have to. Okay?"

After a quarter of an hour, the stone wall had left a pattern on my butt, so we took the remains of our coffee back to the car. We still had a way to go, and Baresi was probably ahead of us by now. Steve resumed her sullen sulk, arms crossed, keeping her eyes firmly on the side window, occasionally mopping at them with a tissue.

Proof of Life

"I'm sorry, okay. I shouldn't have shouted." I felt the need to justify myself. Wrongly, as it happened.

"Just leave me alone and drive the bloody car."

Soon, the land became flatter as the green mountains opened onto a rich mosaic of farmland. The road was straight and featureless, the traffic sparse. After an hours, and as sudden as a punch in the face, we moved from nothing to the suburbs. By world standards, Cagliari was a small but sprawling city, a maze of clogged streets and rat runs as the great and the good gesticulated and hooted their way to work. I drove around the western perimeter along with the juggernauts, delivery drivers, and city-breakers toward the port—the most likely place to find someone preparing to sail out into the Mediterranean.

At least that was the plan.

"Behind us. Two cars back." Steve reached through the passenger window and angled the mirror.

"You sure?" I could see nothing but a Peugeot minibus.

"Of course I'm not sure, but they picked us up as we left the main road."

"CZ 947HT, a Rome registration?"

"I can't see."

"Okay, buckle up. I'm going to get creative." Beside me, Steve huffed and sunk lower into her seat.

Baresi had picked his battle well. In the suffocating morning traffic, three miles from the port, there was nowhere to hide and nowhere to go. Twenty yards ahead, a side road opened up. I gunned the throttle and swerved off into a maze of low-rise houses and shops, immediately regretting it. Now, we were against the flow, threading the Ford through a snaking channel between parked cars and oncoming traffic. With my foot switching from throttle to brake, ignoring the complaints from the engine, I made a couple of blocks before Baresi appeared in the rearview.

The road dog-legged right. The Ford healed over on its weak suspension, tires squealing on the warm tarmac. I hooked a left, waved a hand of apology at the startled pedestrians, taking out a wing mirror against a parked car. Shards of glass cascaded in, eliciting a shriek from Steve. Ahead, the road narrowed, lined either side with parked vehicles, but I kept my foot down, praying I knew the width of the car, waiting for the graunch of metal panels. Baresi was closing, then dropping back as another pedestrian leaped to safety. The white Cinquecento filled the rearview. Ahead, our road joined the main carriageway, a solid snake of commuter traffic and no way through.

"Beckett!" Steve pushed back in her seat and covered her eyes. Instinctively, I smashed the brake pedal to the floor, inches from the junction, slewing the Ford to a halt. I looked back, saw the gun, jumped as the rear windshield crazed into a thousand fragments and a slug thumped into the dash.

"Sorry guys. We gotta go." I revved the small engine, edged it forward, bullied my way out through the line and onto the other side, but the Cinquecento followed me through. A second round smacked into the cheap radio, killing the Eurotrash. As I jammed the stick shift into second and floored the throttle, I hooked a left, regretting the move as the road again filled with parked cars and pedestrians. Another bullet, then another, cratered the trunk with a dull clank. How many goddamn bullets did he have? Seeing another side road on my right, I hauled at the wheel and slid the Ford around the tight turn, then stamped back on the gas. As the parked cars whooshed past the mirror, a trailer appeared, as if in slow motion. A solid wall of terracotta piping towering into the air, closing down our escape. Steve was screaming beside me.

"You're not going to make it!"

The gap behind the trailer was barely wider than the Ford, but I kept my foot down.

"Beckett! You're not going to make it!" She was holding on to her belt, shielding her face with the other hand. The fat, bald guy was leaning out of the Cinquecento; another bullet gouged along the side of the Ford.

"You're *not* going to make it!"

Then, like a cork from a bottle, we were through. Beyond the angry roar of our motor, the Cinquecento squealed to a halt.

"For a minute there, I didn't think you were going to make it."

"Me neither," I puffed, "though you may have to climb out through my side."

Chapter 16

A trailer full of pipes would not hold up Baresi for long. With a gun in his hand, probably not at all. They had waited on the outskirts of the town for us to arrive, then followed us. That told me one thing.

They didn't know where Jardine was.

But then neither did we. Cagliari is a large, bustling city and a popular tourist resort. He could have checked into any of a thousand hotels after his flight. For all I knew, he could have flown into Rome and been on the same ferry as us.

After an agonizing quarter-hour, threading through the dense, claustrophobic streets and dark, tree-lined avenues, eventually we picked up signs for the port. Ten minutes later, I parked the Ford in amongst a cluster of similar cars, as anonymous as we could make the battle-scarred vehicle. Steve was shaking but took no coaxing out into the sunshine. She donned her baseball cap, grabbed her tote bag, and stormed off. Then she stopped and turned.

"Just where are we going, Stirling Moss?"

"Stirling...?" I shrugged. Must've been a Brit reference. "We need the harbormaster's office."

"And we're going to stroll in, announce ourselves and ask for this Jardine character?"

"Pretty much, yeah. Well, *you* are."

***

Down by the water, Cagliari changed its character completely. The run-down, maze of congested, narrow

Proof of Life

streets gave way to wide boulevards, grand hotels, more reminiscent of Marseilles or Cannes, all barely spoiled by the concrete apron marring the coastline. Squinting against the sunlight, we crossed a palm-lined road and the empty lanes for the ferry port, and walked along the water's edge.

The Andersons left from Cagliari before they vanished in the sea to the South of Sardinia. If Jardine thought he knew where the boat was, he would need to dive for the wreck. And he would need a berth to load up his boat.

Immediately, we saw the enormity of our task. The harbor was vast and sprawling. Home to boatyards, a port for cruise ships and ferries, a naval dock as well as two marinas for pleasure craft. It was clear we were going to have our work cut out finding someone we didn't recognize renting a boat we couldn't identify.

I bought bottled water from a roadside vendor, and a couple of burgers loaded with pancetta and blue cheese. I was still ravenous. The pastry earlier just didn't cut it. We ate on the move, following the signs around the bowl of the harbor towards the Port Authority office. The sea air was fresh, the sun was warm, the benches along harbor were very inviting, but we couldn't stop. Baresi was already closing in.

The Port Authority was on one of the concrete slabs jutting out between the two marinas. In its time, imposing and overbearing, Art Deco, maybe Bauhaus, its geometric design reminded me of a 1930s aerodrome terminal. Now its tired cream walls hung with sagging cables.

Steve stopped short. "We can't go in there. What if someone recognizes us?"

"So you wait here. I'll go in."

"But what if *he* comes back?"

"Okay, okay, come inside. Browse the leaflets or something. It'll be fine, I promise." With the Glock nestled beneath my jacket, I was ready for Baresi. If he made another appearance. Steve still stood, racked with indecision. I grabbed her hand. "We are tourists, okay? We look like tourists and need to behave like tourists, so smile, honey, and pretend you're having a great time looking at the boats. Anyway, I don't speak Italian, so you will have to."

Steve puffed, and against her better judgment, relented.

The offices were cool and clinical, silent except for our footsteps on the tiled floors. Behind the reception desk, an overly made-up woman, wearing a white blouse and neckerchief in company colors, raised her head and smiled. I smiled back as she said something I didn't understand. Before I could speak, Steve was in like Flynn with the machine-gun Italian. The woman nodded and flicked on the official company smile. She peered intently into the keyboard before returning a salvo of rapid-fire Italian back.

"Jardine. Tom Jardine." Steve smiled, fiddled with her shades.

The woman typed feverishly onto her keyboard, her brow furrowing in concentration, and sent another volley of fire from behind the plexiglass screen, which Steve returned. After a minute, I picked up a courteous *grazie*. Steve turned away and gestured urgently towards the door.

"I'm impressed." For once, I actually was.

"Impressed? I was shitting myself the whole time. Did you not see my face all over the TV screen opposite reception? Let's get out of here before she realizes."

But, buoyed by her success, just a little swagger had returned as we walked away.

***

We were in the wrong place. *Il Cantiere Navale*—the shipyard—was around a mile west. I pulled up in a small, forlorn parking lot at the bottom of a dead-end, litter-strewn with weeds manhandling their way through the asphalt. Maybe the wrecked Ford would look less out of place there?

Unlike the commercial port, which hummed with life, the shipyard was quiet, almost eerily so. A small, rectangular, self-contained marina surrounded on two sides by industrial buildings and cluttered yards haphazardly filled with light vessels in various states of repair. The air tasted of diesel oil and tar, and was filled with the sounds of heavy machinery, of shipwrights jet washing barnacles, of ropes and backstays playing percussion in the fall breeze. In these places, strangers stuck out like a wart on an elbow. Someone had probably already noticed us, as they would Baresi and his buddy, if they put in an appearance.

Following an alley between two brick workshops, down onto the boardwalk, we found the sparsely filled marina. A mile out on the water, the derricks of the commercial port sat like hopeful anglers along the breakwater, their booms cast over the harbor, watching patiently as the monolithic cruise ships and workaday ferries occupied the high-end berths. But down here, it was quieter. Around twenty boats, most of them awaiting repair, or just content to occupy a cheaper berth, cash-in-hand, no questions asked. It made sense. Tom Jardine would be down here. Fewer people to notice. Fewer people to care.

"Over there?" Steve raised her hand, shielding her eyes from the glare from the water and pointing the other towards an old Sea Hawk dive boat swaying and bumping against its fenders. The air was thick with engine fumes and bilge water spattered back into the sea. Its white hull wore a thin stubble of green algae which extended down to the waterline. Above the green, in a florid italic script, the name, the *Genevieve*.

"You looking for someone?" It was a hard Glaswegian bark, cut from sheet steel.

"Tom Jardine?" I shaded my eyes and peered up at a head silhouetted against the sky, surrounded by a pall of cigar smoke and straggled hair. A pair of feet, crossed at the ankles, lazily rested on the railings above the cabin.

"Who wants to know?"

"My name is Farrell, Franklin Farrell. I think we share a mutual interest, sir."

"Oh, yeah. And what might that be?"

"We're both looking for Max Anderson."

"Do I look stupid?" A cigar butt arced over the side into the murky olive waters, scattering the small fish just below the surface.

"Sir?"

The head leaned out over the bridge rail, eclipsing the sun. "Everyone knows Max and Kate Anderson disappeared in 1990. It was in all the papers. You would have been but a bairn."

"Uh-huh. I was around fourteen months old." Everyone knew? Seven billion people on the planet. Only a handful would care.

"So what is this? Some kind of school history project, laddie?" Despite the light behind him defusing through the untidy mop of hair, I could sense he was glancing about anxiously. His voice was low, struggling not to be overheard. He disappeared momentarily, then heaved himself onto the chrome ladder, set his feet on either side, and slid down to the deck.

"No, sir. I am in insurance." Beside me, Steve did a double-take and frowned.

"American?" Jardine scratched his chin and idly rearranged some of the gear on the deck.

"Yes, sir. Washington, DC. Max Anderson insured his

life with our company and his wife Kate was the beneficiary. When they were legally declared dead, we were paid out. If there is any doubt about their death, my company needs to know. We may need to recover the money."

"Doubt? What doubt could there be, after all this time?"

"Luciano Moretti? He had doubts and someone killed him over them."

Jardine pulled another cigar from his breast pocket and flicked a lighter, drawing the flame as he considered. Then he gestured towards a couple of PVC chairs along one side of the deck.

"Come aboard, sit down—and, for fuck's sake, stop calling me *sir*."

Chapter 17

Tom Jardine was a Scotsman. With his physique, he could have played prop for the Glasgow Hawks rugby team. Over six feet tall and almost as wide, a lush outcrop of whitening ginger hair pulled into a crude ponytail behind a face carved from granite. A rough goatee competed with a couple of days of unruly stubble over his sun-ravaged, fair skin. His steely blue eyes held a single, irrefutable message - *Don't mess with me.* Though, at the moment, they were concentrating on the monumental breakfast in front of him.

We'd adjourned to a small harbor-side café, empty, except for a bored waitress weaving her finger through a ringlet on the side of her head. Jardine chose a scuffed melamine table away from the kitchen and the mindless Italian babble from the radio. He also had his back to a wall.

"So, Mr. Insurance Man, what *really* brings you to Cagliari?" Jardine eyed me suspiciously, the x-ray eyes of a journalist seeing through the BS.

"Luciano Moretti thought you were searching for the Andersons' missing boat. I want to know if you find it."

He shoveled in a mouthful and took the chewing time to consider. "And just where did you hear that?"

"Moretti kept a notebook. He wrote a few things down. A rumor Anderson was still alive and you might know what happened to him. That you might know where his boat was."

Jardine nodded at Steve. "And her?"

"My girlfriend, Steve, er Stephanie. I thought we could kill two birds and take a vacation too." Steve's face hardened and a sharp pain shot up my shin. Jardine raised his eyebrows and smirked lecherously. Our first test passed.

"What do you know of the Andersons?" he asked.

I shrugged. "They rented a sailboat called the *Spirito del Vento,* intending to sail from Cagliari to Xlendi in Malta, and they never arrived."

"Why are *you* here, Mr. Jardine?" Steve interrupted, leaning forwards, flexing a mid-Atlantic accent.

Jardine stopped masticating and smiled wryly. "I like her, Farrell. Gets straight to the point." A piece of egg made a bid for freedom and a fat paw dragged it off his cheek. His eyes flicked between the pair of us, organizing his thoughts.

"I am a journo, love. I'm chasing a story, my next bestseller. As your man says, they never found the Andersons, so they may not be dead. I'm going to find that boat, find out what really happened to Max Anderson."

"By all accounts, they had the entire navy out looking," I countered. "What makes you think you can find the boat when no one else could?"

"You gotta know where to look." Jardine smiled enigmatically and tapped his nose with a greasy finger.

"And you do?"

No response. Another mouthful died for the cause.

"What do *you* know that no one else does?" asked Steve.

"I don't *know*, love. I'm working on a hunch."

"Which is?" I asked.

Jardine flashed another enigmatic smile. "Excellent breakfast. Needs proper sausages, not these arty-farty chipolata things."

He sat back in his chair for a long moment, taking a slow pull of the syrupy coffee. The café was still empty; echoing to the Italian radio blasting out a talk show at one hundred miles an hour. Outside, the sun was high and the overnight fishing skips were bouncing their way across the waves and into the harbor. An honor guard of white vans stood ready to take their loads across the island. Beside me, Steve was braving the coffee, too. I had yet to pluck up the courage. Instead I pushed some scrambled egg around my plate, to busy my hands, allow time for the pause to become uncomfortable. Eventually, the big man lowered his cup and wiped a calloused hand across his beard.

"Do you dive, Mr. Farrell?"

"A little."

"Meet me on the boat at 5:00 pm. I could do with a little company. Maybe we can find the boat together."

***

We left Jardine to his breakfast promising to be on time. His gaze almost burned a hole in my polo shirt. He was still sizing us up. In his position, I would be suspicious, too. As it was, we may have led Baresi straight to him.

"You know, I am still not sure I understand a damn thing about you. Insurance? Girlfriend?"

I puffed, exasperated. "I was lying, Steve."

"You're good at lying. Maybe you should be a politician."

"I make enough enemies as it is but, hey, I got us a seat on the bus, and that's all that matters. We have a chance to see how involved Jardine is. Now, let's get out of here before Baresi finds out where we've gotten to."

Proof of Life

Chapter 18

With hours to kill before Jardine's boat sailed, I needed to find out more about the Andersons' disappearance. I had the official blurb from Pliskin but you can't trust what you read in the papers. The *Biblioteca Regionale*—the regional municipal library—was two miles away, somewhere to lie low; the last place an assassin would look. We left the bullet-ridden Ford, we retrieved our stuff and took a cab into town.

Our taxi dropped us on the tree-lined Viale Trieste. Sun-dappled, on the more salubrious side of the street, the library was über-modern inside. Spacious and clean with working air-conditioning, not to mention a quiet mezzanine floor where we could keep our heads down. While Steve requested microfiches for the time of the Andersons' disappearance, I reread the notes in Moretti's diary, using the translations Steve had handwritten below each one:

21 Maggio 2019

> Un pettegolezzo. Tom Jardine sta cercando la barca di Max Anderson.
> *A rumor. Tom Jardine is looking for Max Anderson's boat.*

20 Giugno 2019

> Incontro Tom Jardine per discutere di Roccia Ambrata.
> *Arrange meeting with Tom Jardine to discuss Amber Rock.*

> Roccia Ambrata e Trueman. Un'occasione? €500.000. €100.000 in anticipo. Parla con DeMarco.
> *Amber Rock and Trueman. An opportunity? €500,000. €100,000 in advance. Speak to DeMarco.*

Proof of Life

Moretti had heard the rumor. Like me, he would check the papers, browse the Internet, so he knew of the Andersons' fate. By June, he was linking the disappearance with Tom Jardine and Amber Rock, and salivating at the potential for profit. Already, he had lined up his suitors.

1 Agosto 2019   13:00

> Jardine. Pensa di aver trovato la barca di Anderson. Vuole mettere all'asta le informazioni su Roccia Ambrata.
>
> *Jardine. He thinks he has found Anderson's boat. He wants to auction information on Amber Rock.*

So Jardine was the source. What was his motive? Why was he interested in such ancient history? He had seeded Moretti's auction with the information on the thumb drive. Maybe—probably—he had more. In his position, stirring up the silt at the bottom of a thirty-year-old pond, I would keep something back. A little insurance.

15 Agosto 2019

> Roccia Ambrata - Jardine un problema. Max Anderson deve rimanere dov'é. DeMarco vuole fermare Tom Jardine.
>
> *Amber Rock - Jardine is a problem. Max Anderson must remain lost. DeMarco wants to stop Tom Jardine.*

I reread the translation. "Steve. This line? *Must remain lost?* Is that a literal translation?"

She turned from her screen and looked over my shoulder. "Well, strictly, it reads must remain where he is. *Must* could be *needs to*, *rimanere* could be *stay*, I suppose—*Max Anderson needs to stay where he is*."

So, within a fortnight, Moretti was having doubts about Jardine. Or maybe someone else was—DeMarco, Trueman? What did they need to stop? The auction, or Jardine's attempts to find the boat? Suddenly, almost subliminally, Moretti had gotten in over his head.

4 Settembre 2019 10:00

Piazza Navona. Appartamenti Donnichi. Stanza 12. DeMarco. Discutere dell'accordo su Roccia Ambrata.

Piazza Navona. Donnichi Apartments. Room 12. DeMarco. Discuss a deal on Amber Rock.

I rooted around in my backpack and found Moretti's cellphone. He blocked out the day he died for the appointments in Rome. His last call was to a cell number at 1:30 pm and they had called back—+1 (202) 555 0374—the number against DeMarco in his contact list; the same number on the pictures from Moretti's thumb drive. The call lasted ten minutes until what was left of his head hit the carpet and the call was dropped.

Someone set him up to take the bullet.

4 Settembre 2019 14:00

Franklin Farrell. Un perditempo.
Franklin Farrell. A time-waster.

Steve smirked. It cut me to the quick, but we were still none the wiser over Amber Rock. A place? An organization? Apart from the fossilized resin references I had seen before, and a few to a particularly good scotch malt whisky, a realtor in California, and a three-year-old racehorse from Australia, we drew a blank on the Internet. And who were Trueman and DeMarco? Again, the references were all benign. Nothing tangible. After an hour, we gave up. Maybe Jardine would tell us something on the boat later?

It was after midday before a tall, dour woman brought three cardboard boxes containing microfiche reels. She led us across to a couple of readers and, in Italian, delivered terse instructions on how to load and operate them. At least, I think that's what she said. The reports into the Andersons' disappearance were on the second reel, such that they were. The *Spirito del Vento* left the old port of Cagliari on the 6th of June 1990 and simply disappeared. A wispy line of white spume, slowly breaking up on the morning swell. Friends back in London told of the Andersons' plans to travel over to Xlendi on the island of Gozo. To rekindle some of the romance of their honeymoon. After a night on the water, they were to sail on to Marsala, Sicily before another overnighter and a final leg to the small Maltese island. But they never reached Xlendi. They didn't even get to Marsala.

They simply vanished.

Before GPS and cellphones, one could sail for days without human contact. The weather was good, the swell low, and Anderson was an accomplished sailor. Although they had a two-way radio, they didn't use it. Friends alerted the authorities when the boat failed to turn up in Marsala as arranged and the Sicilian Coastguard was called. Using plans lodged with the *Capitaneria di Porto,* helicopters retraced their route, boats scoured the area for debris but they found nothing. Within a week, the stories faded from the front pages; within two, they had gone completely.

We copied a few of the more detailed pages and a few photos. I even found some information on the Sentinel Working Group to which Max Anderson was seconded, but nothing linked to Amber Rock. I was tired, hungry, and losing faith. What did Tom Jardine know that the combined resources of three countries did not? Why did he think he could find the boat when no wreckage had ever washed up?

There was only one way to find out.

***

The sun was still high behind a ceiling of feathery clouds when we left the library. We grabbed some takeout and a coffee, then hailed a cab back to harbor. The engine still coughed and spluttered, the bilge pump still urinated into the murky green harbor. Above the boardwalk, a small white Fiat van was parked next to the boat, and a man, sun-browned and sweating, was heaving oxygen tanks across to his mate in the cockpit at the rear. Seeing us arrive, Jardine called out in Italian to one of the men who scanned us up and down and laughed.

"What was all that about?" I asked Steve.

"I only caught a little. He asked if the wetsuit would fit the tall, skinny guy. I think he meant you." After two years of pumping weights to strengthen my damaged shoulder, it was a dagger to my heart.

Compared to her fellow vessels in the harbor, the *Genevieve* was small, probably around thirty feet. Purpose-built for diving, she had an open cockpit and a swim platform to the stern. Forward, a ladder led over the cabin to a flying bridge. Oxygen tanks, wetsuits, and other diving paraphernalia lay in orderly piles over the deck, while Jardine oversaw the loading from the shade of the bridge. He had a laptop on his knees. Maybe he was doing his research, too. Forewarned is forearmed. Closing the lid, he slid down the ladder and stretched out a hand to Steve as she negotiated the gangplank.

"So you came along for the ride then?" His smile revealed a row of nicotine-stained teeth.

"Night-life in Cagliari is nothing to write home about," Steve replied sardonically, "so we were at a loose end."

"Well, I hope you got your sea-legs, lassie," winked Jardine, "because we'll be out on the water all night."

"Two sweaty men and a chemical toilet," she replied. "Oh, joy!"

Jardine threw back his head and guffawed. "Nae bother, my delicate little rosebud. You can have the cabin to yersel. Me and your man will pish o'er the side." And he guffawed once more as Steve stomped off and sat sullenly on the bench seat. With her world turned on its head, I knew she was overwhelmed but, to her credit, she had begun to come round. No choice but to ride it out, to rely on me to pull her through. I just hoped her faith wasn't misplaced.

The two men finished loading the gear. Jardine slid down the ladder and handed over an envelope of cash. The smaller, older of the two, checked the notes, nodded, and shook Jardine's hand. Then, with shouts of *Ciao*, they headed back out along the harbor road. As Jardine throttled up the engines and I cast off the mooring line, I noticed the van pull up alongside a white Cinquecento by the harbor wall. Was I taking Jardine a little too much on trust? Was I reading too much into a conversation between friends through a car window? Or maybe I was just tired.

Still, I checked the Glock in the small of my back.

Chapter 19

We sailed out of Cagliari as everyone else was coming in. Jardine rounded the southern tip of the island, then took a bearing Northwest, clipping the slight swell and making good headway. Leaving Steve to her thoughts, I joined him on the flying bridge and looked out over a sea painted orange by the setting sun. Jardine had engaged an autopilot to sail to the GPS coordinates he had programmed in. If Max and Kate Anderson had enjoyed this level of technology, then maybe the Coastguard would have had something to go on.

"So, what makes you think you'll find your answers out here, Mr. Farrell?" The big Glaswegian turned to me, his tangle of ginger-white hair billowing in the slight evening breeze, his face haloed orange through the mist of a cheroot.

"I suppose I've just run out of other places to look."

Jardine took another long draw, the ember glowing fiercely. Then he picked a speck of tobacco from his tongue and smiled. "In my experience, laddie, that's the time to stop or you might find things you'd rather not know."

Across the waves, the sea was a flat plane between the darkening night sky and the mirror-calm sea. How many secrets were locked beneath, lost to an unforgiving alien place that rarely gave up its secrets?

"I could ask the same of you. They've been dead a long time. What makes you think your sources are reliable?"

"Who knows? Like you, this is the only lead I have left."

I swiveled in my chair. "Lead?"

Jardine tapped his nose theatrically with a finger. "A

good reporter never reveals his sources. Suffice it to say, I have been looking for the *Spirito del Vento* for four years and the story has never varied. They set off for Marsala, Sicily, and never arrived."

"And what makes you think you can find them now?"

"Because, Farrell, the story varied. Once. They were all looking in the wrong place."

"The wrong place? What? The Coastguard? The Navy? Everybody? Come on!"

"Look at the screens. Weather, radar, sonar, radio, GPS, even the bloody BBC. There must be a thousand people on the planet who know the exact location of this boat right now. Over the internet, maybe thousands more—if they were interested. That's an EPIRB, an Emergency Position Indicating Radio Beacon." I followed Jardine's finger to a fluorescent device on the outside of the bridge. It was about the size of a sports drinks cup with an antenna on top. "If we went down right now, a squadron of helicopters would be out looking in minutes. The *Spirito del Vento* had none of this stuff. Well, they had radar and a radio."

"So, the only way anyone could know they were in trouble was if they sent a distress call?"

"Aye, and even then, they would rely on location details from the boat. No message, no location."

On the screens, a rash of green dots edged across the radar panel. Others were lit up with an array of numbers and lights. "But you know different?"

Jardine nodded and drew on his cigar, the mildest pungent aroma of tobacco in the stiff breeze.

"A year ago, I was checking through Freedom of Information responses when I came upon the reports of the disappearance. A fishing boat out for bass and bream had snagged its nets on some debris, probably an old wreck or a

World War II aircraft. They reported seeing a boat matching the description of the *Spirito del Vento* on the horizon as they freed their lines. On its own, the report was ignored. After all, it was miles away from their last known position."

"Could have been anyone."

"True, but two sightings? In another FOI report, asking about near misses in the waters off Sardinia, I found details of a boat matching the same description, riding at night without lights, on the ferry route from Port Torres to Marseilles. Late evening, same day, the same place the fishermen saw their boat. They were hailed, switched on the lights, were cautioned, and continued on their way."

"Pretty flimsy, Jardine. Two sightings of a boat that may have been the Andersons, but could just as well have been anyone." I looked out over the sea, at a panorama of flat gray with Sardinia barely visible off to the East. "The Mediterranean is small, but it's no postage stamp."

Jardine shrugged, flicked off a piece of ash. "So we could have a wasted trip. Then again, as you said, maybe I've run out of other places to look."

The smell of beans and bacon drifted up from the cabin below. I suddenly felt hungry. Perhaps, as my adopted father Joe used to say, when we traipsed the boardwalk along the Jersey Shore, it was the sea air. Dementia had robbed me of my father, but not the memories.

"She's a great wee girl, that one of yours. I'm starving."

I liked Steve being referred to as *my wee girl,* but I wasn't sure it was a good thing. I was too used to my own company.

"I'll let you tell her," I smiled, "given the mood she's in."

Proof of Life

Chapter 20

At around 10:00 pm, a small alarm sounded on the dash above us, showing the autopilot had reached the pre-programmed destination. Jardine checked the position, powered down the engines, then spooled out the anchor.

"So, here we are, Mr. Jardine. Where exactly is *here?*" Steve had hunkered down in a corner with a blanket around her shoulders. She had yet to get her sea-legs and, unable to face supper, nibbled uncomfortably on a digestive biscuit.

"Anywhere you want it to be, lassie. No boss, no taxes." He switched off the electric lamp on the bulkhead. Immediately, we were wrapped in a blackness so thick you could taste it. The salt, the ozone, the cool of the still air, the profound silence. The absence of noise. But for gravity and the movement of the boat, we could have been on a rock in space, a million light-years even from light itself.

"Fantastic, isn't it?" continued Jardine. "Just you, me, and the gentle rise and fall of the boat over one hundred feet of nothing. Up, down, up…"

"Bastard!" Steve hauled her way up the bulwark and pumped on empty over the side. Jardine switched the light back on and guffawed loudly.

"Cruel, Jardine, cruel." I pulled my jacket closer. The night had turned cold, and I was shivering against the chill. "Answer the question. Where are we? I need to send a postcard to my folks."

The big Glaswegian huffed and sat back heavily. "We're west of Sardinia, about one hundred kilometers off Port

Proof of Life

Torres. Apart from the ferries and fishermen, no one comes out here. There are enough wrecks inshore to keep the divers happy."

"And the lights are *off*," I added pointedly.

"Well, no sense drawing attention to ourselves, is there? Maybe Anderson thought so too?" Jardine cracked his grin. "And we are *off* from the shipping routes at the moment."

"Just exactly what are you hoping to find, Jardine?"

He shrugged. "Maybe nothing, maybe something. The boat, of course. This is where those two reports placed her—here or hereabouts—not South, off the coast of Sicily where she should have been. Why would Anderson tell all his friends, tell the harbormaster at Cagliari, they were going to Sicily and Malta, then sail out here? It's hardly Piccadilly Circus."

Alone in the water, I felt a sense of separation, as if we three were all the world. It unnerved me. That the frenetic bustle of Cagliari, the chaos of Rome, were the fading remnants of a dream. I'd spent time in the deserts and hillsides of Afghanistan before a sniper's bullet shattered my shoulder. I'd known the profound silence, the sense of separation before, exposed and vulnerable. It raised the hackles on my neck. One was never totally alone.

"You think the boat's still here?" I asked.

"Maybe." Jardine cocked his head, drawing in another lungful, the glowing cigar illuminating the lines on his face. "I believe the Andersons came out here, and they scuttled her. The boat is down there, a hundred feet below us."

"Scuttled? Why would they scuttle her? Why here?"

"Why not here? Quiet, less chance of being seen. Less chance of being seen searching. There are hundreds of wrecks in the Mediterranean left over from the war. Most in the South Mediterranean; convoy ships heading in from

Gibraltar across to Libya and Egypt, hugging the coast of Morocco and Algeria. Also, the convoys relieving the siege of Malta. But there are also many wrecks in the Sea of Sardinia, failed sorties from Barcelona, Marseilles, even Genoa, and Livorno. Most are war graves. The divers only ever come a few kilometers off the coast, then mainly North-East of the island, Olbia, Tavolara, and South, around Cagliari. That leaves hundreds of wrecks undisturbed. Where better to hide a sunken boat than amongst others?"

"And you believe the Andersons are down there too?"

"That's the question, Farrell. Did they fall or were they pushed? Who else was here the night the boat went down?"

I imagined the hull tilting as it sat lower in the calm, empty sea, the inrush of freezing water as it seeped through their clothes, the terror as, finally, the deck disappeared from beneath them. Then the hours of insidious cold, treading water before it drew them under. I shuddered at the thought of their bodies many fathoms below, the bones picked clean by tiny fish, green with algae.

"And what's your interest in finding Max Anderson?" I asked. Steve had retired to the cabin, curled up on the bunk. Jardine swigged the remains of his coffee and tossed the dregs over the side. For a long moment, he eyed me thoughtfully before avoiding the question.

"Word on the street is you killed Moretti. You and the girl?" He nodded towards the cabin. "I couldn't help noticing the Glock, Mr.—Beckett?" He winked in a way that, on another day, might have made me smile. My heart quickened. A punch of adrenalin. My cover was thinner than a polecat in January, but so quickly? This guy was good.

"No, sir. Someone else took care of that. Not to say I wouldn't have. He got there first, is all."

"Did you recognize the guy who did it?" Something Jardine didn't already know.

Proof of Life

"He is Renzo Baresi. Ex-Mafia. A trained killer. A ghost."

"And you? What's your interest in Moretti? Apart from killing him, of course." Jardine pulled a half-bottle of scotch from his bag. He poured a slug into his mug, offered the bottle over. The warmth radiated through my chest.

"You know about the auction?" Jardine nodded. "My employers wanted what he was auctioning. Unfortunately, someone else did too and sent Baresi over. I got Moretti's notebook. It mentions you. I figured he would come for you next. This time I beat him to it."

"So, now you're going to kill me? To send me to *sleep with the fishes?*" He smiled and raised his eyebrows. Out on the sea, facing an armed killer, Jardine seemed remarkably calm.

"No, sir." I reached for the Glock, pressing the lever and catching the magazine. Then laid them both at my feet. "Moretti also mentions in his notebook you commissioned the auction. That you originally provided the information he was auctioning off. I'm here to find out what you know before *Baresi* sends you to sleep with the fishes."

"And why should I tell you anything, Beckett? Since I saw the news on Moretti, I've had a day or two to check you out. Nothing. No search history, no social media, no email. That makes me nervous. Just who the hell are you?"

I took a slug of whisky. "I work for the government."

"Not insurance? You surprise me. Now, which government would that be?"

I ignored the question. "I believe the people who sent Baresi want to suppress the information. Maybe they also want to suppress you."

"And what do you know about Amber Rock?"

"Amber Rock? The mineral, the racehorse, or the scotch whisky?" I played dumb. After all, I knew nothing anyway. "I've also had a day or two to do my research, and there is nothing. If Baresi, and whoever is paying him, had their way, there never would be. Someone is going to a lot of trouble to keep it under wraps."

"You know what Max Anderson did for a living?" Jardine asked through an enormous cloud of smoke.

"He worked for the World Nuclear Association."

"More than that, Beckett. He worked for the British Office for Nuclear Regulation. He investigated breaches in nuclear law, as defined by the International Atomic Energy Agency, the OECD, EURATOM, and others. My guess is he latched onto something big. Something he kept close to his chest."

"You have any idea what?" The thought of Max Anderson as a nuclear spy amused me. My father was a glorified accountant. The most excitement he saw was a misplaced decimal point.

Jardine shook his head soberly. "No, but he wasn't the only one. Todd Gruber worked for the Nuclear Regulation Committee in the US. They found his car in Chesapeake Bay with him inside. The Coroner said he drove off the road, probably asleep. Pete Fernandez, an analyst working for the Atomic Energy Commission, fell off a building. Harvey Brooks crashed into a tree on a clear, dry road. Joanne McKenna, also working for the ONR, apparently stepped in front of a train. Stacey Carter, road crash. Ramon Perez, electrocuted by a faulty TV. Carl Hayes, suicide. The list goes on. All unexpected, all connected to the US nuclear industry, all working as analysts. The verdict was always suicide, accidental death or misadventure, despite any evidence to the contrary. Atomic energy in the States, the early '90s. It was a dangerous career to be in."

"There must be thousands working in the industry. Statistically, some will die. What makes you think they are all connected?" I wasn't convinced.

"Amber Rock. I don't know for sure what it is. A group of people, an organization maybe. All I know is each one of these dead scientists got mixed up in it before they died."

"Mixed up in what?"

Again, Jardine shrugged and opened his hands. "I've met no one who knows for certain. Anyone who *does* know, either won't say or ends up dead."

"The first rule of Fight Club," I suggested.

"Eh?"

"Never talk about Fight Club."

Jardine smiled. "Something like that. Over the years, I have done a lot of digging, called in a lot of favors, and found out hardly anything, except the name keeps popping up in relation to these dead scientists. They all found out something before they died. Something monumental. All those people died between 1988 and 2006. Each one had been investigating that secret and Amber Rock found out. Each one took what they knew to the grave."

"And you think that's what happened to Anderson? He was investigating this secret and someone silenced him too."

He nodded and drew from his cigar. "Explains why he was out here on the sea. Why no-one has seen him since, but no. Out here, miles from their filed route, the Andersons were running away."

Chapter 21

Saturday, September 7

As night turned to early morning, Jardine retired to his padded helm seat and was soon snoring like a rusty hinge. I stayed on the deck, alone with my thoughts. The comforting swell of the sea did little to stop my mind from racing.

Before adolescence had set us against each other, my dad and I used to fish out at Rock Creek. Saturday, we'd clean the car together, load up the boat, the tent, and the tackle. Mom packed a cool box and a hamper and we'd head out for an adventure. He'd park the station wagon at the golf club and we'd paddle upstream awhile—downstream on the way back is always better—then we'd pitch the tent just off of a shale beach under the trees. We were a mile or two from Brightwood, a couple from Chevy Chase, yet we were the only people on Earth, lying back with the smell of a fire and a sky sequined with stars, a billion galaxies, a billion worlds. Only now do I value the aloneness. How precious time with my dad really was. Now he was in a nursing home losing those memories and I was adrift in an empty sea, trying to hold on to them.

How many other souls, on their boats, or beds, or fancy Perspex-lidded spaceships, were out there looking back, unable to put their cares to bed? How many, consumed by their responsibilities, were waiting on the next morning, dreading the day? How many just plain hoped for the best?

"Beckett?" I jumped as Steve's silhouette filled the doorway to the cabin. Wrapped in her blanket, a chrysalis emerging from a wool-blend cocoon, only her nose was

Proof of Life

visible. "Can I sit with you for a while? Out in the fresh air?"

"Depends. You stopped hurling yet?"

"Funny. Very funny. My guts are so empty, I can hear an echo when I belch."

I shifted across and she eased herself down beside me, pulling her blanket tight around her, ensuring a discrete gap, either from me, or the Glock on the deck between us.

"You okay?"

She turned, and I caught a smile in the weak moonlight. "I suppose. My ribs ache, my throat aches and I'm so hungry, I could eat this bloody blanket. A few days ago, I was on the adventure of a lifetime; a gap year in Rome, an assignment on the Piazza Navona. The most dangerous part of my day was choosing a sandwich filling. Now I'm out on the ocean with two men I hardly know and no idea what's going to happen from one minute to the next. It's a lot to get used to quickly."

I empathized. It was the life I chose when I started working for Pliskin. Perhaps that's where we differed. The danger, the not knowing, was part of the excitement. Living on the edge, wondering when I would be pulled over it. I was single, alone. No one to care for except myself. That was not everyone's bag.

"You need to hang in there. I promise we'll find Moretti's killer and put you in the clear."

"…or die trying, eh?" She gave me another smile.

"Preferably not."

"Yeah. That would be a shame."

My stomach took a lurch. Just when I needed to focus on the task at hand, I was letting her get to me.

"Do you think Jardine's right? The Andersons' boat is down there?"

"A sunken boat means nothing, Steve. Depends on who sunk it and why. Who was aboard as it went down. Even if the Andersons went down with it, there's probably very little left. Bodies don't last long in the ocean."

"Jeez, you're a cheery soul, Beckett. Wish I'd stayed in the cabin with a saucepan to puke in."

"Years of practice, lady. Years of practice." I leaned over on my elbow, facing the silhouette, sensed she was doing the same. I caught a fresh spritz of scent, to mask the smell of the vomit.

"And if the boat isn't down there?" she asked.

"The mystery goes on. Where are the Andersons? Where is their boat? Everyone loves a good mystery—Amelia Earhart, Roswell, the Loch Ness monster even. Nobody wants a crashed plane, a weather balloon, or a log floating on the water. They want alien abduction, a spaceship, or a Plesiosaur. If we find the boat, there's still going to be the question of why here, why not on their route to Malta. Where were they going?"

"Jardine reckons they were running from Amber Rock."

"You heard?"

"In a brief interlude from chucking up my lunch, yeah. The story of nuclear analysts being bumped off. Do you think it's true?"

"Who knows? Jardine sells column inches. He tells a good story. Remember Moretti's notebook? Jardine supplied the information being auctioned. All he is doing, looking for the boat, is raising the value of his own stock."

"But he said those other nuclear analysts were all killed because they knew too much."

"As I say, Steve, he tells a good story. We don't find the boat, the story's bullshit, the mystery remains. We find the boat with the Andersons inside. The mystery deepens. Was it an accident or were they murdered? We find the empty boat. Another layer. What happened to them? Did they escape? Were they taken hostage? Were they killed and dumped elsewhere? However you look at it, whatever we turn up—or don't—tomorrow will change nothing, except the column inches Jardine writes."

"And you, Beckett? What's the point in following him out here on his wild goose chase?"

"It's my job. Jardine knows about the Andersons. He knows more about Amber Rock than he has told us so far. I need to buddy up with him, make him spill his guts."

"Unfortunate turn of phrase."

"Sorry, Steve."

She sighed, long and deep. "And Jardine. What's your take on him."

I looked up to the flying bridge, listened for the sonorous rasping, assured myself he was still asleep. "I don't trust him as far as I could spit a dead rat, and that's not far at all."

"Oh, goody. I am on a boat with a psychopath who is in denial about killing people and a treacherous Scotsman. Let's hope we don't deal a murderous Sicilian and make the set."

Chapter 22

At first light, Jardine kicked me awake and ordered me to make him coffee, muttering *you snooze you lose*. Steve was a bundle of legs and arms sticking out from under a blanket on the cabin bunk. I made a pot of joe and warmed up some prefabricated food from the cupboard under the galley. By 7:00 am, we were ready to start our search.

I helped Jardine drag the Fisher SSS-100K side-scan sonar from a locker under the starboard-side bench seat. It looked like a small Exocet missile but towed behind the boat, it could scan the sea bed hundreds of meters on either side, showing images on Jardine's laptop. He planned to scour a couple of square miles, grid-iron fashion, up and down until he got bored or lucky, whichever came first. He marked off rough squares on a map on the bridge. If he found nothing in the one, he would turn around and move on to the next.

We launched the scanner from the stern, playing out the rope into the gray-green murk, dropping twenty-five meters before Jardine locked it off on a cleat. Then he opened the laptop and adjourned to the bridge. Beneath us, the twin engines growled. The bow rose, and the boat crept forward.

"Beckett. We've got company." Steve was sitting on the stern cradling a cup, a blanket around her shoulders, looking to the horizon. Out across the idle waves, a group of small boats sat bright against the horizon.

"Probably fishing boats. I'll speak to Jardine."

***

Proof of Life

The scanner traveled back and forth all morning but revealed little. A bland ochre-brown landscape occasionally pockmarked with blurred blobs which Jardine assured me were rocks. The wavy path of the scanner was mesmerizing, and soon my eyelids weighed a ton, so I dozed in the warm fall sun, lulled away by the steady hum of the motors. Then I remembered the boats, far off on the horizon. I picked up a set of binoculars and checked. They were still there, surrounded by flocks of hopeful gulls. Whilst we had patrolled several hundred square yards, they had not moved.

"Jardine. There are other boats."

"Probably fishermen." He gestured for the binoculars. "Sardine boats," he said dismissively. "You can see the cast nets. They'll be gone by mid-afternoon. Poor fishing here. The water over there is deeper. Nothing to worry about."

It was after 1:00 pm before we saw anything worthy of note. Jardine nudged my shoulder, and I started awake.

"Look at this, Beckett." He had throttled back the engines and the image on the laptop screen froze. A wavy yellow background with a jumble of earth-colored blobs was scattered about the picture. In the lee of the scanner, their shadows dragged away like brush strokes gradually running out of paint. Slowly, my eyes became attuned to the shapes.

"Is that a jeep?"

Jardine nodded and pointed to some of the other blobs. "A tank. Another jeep, some packing crates, I guess."

"A ship?"

Jardine nodded again. "Loads of them around here."

He resumed the scan and I became transfixed by the screen, learning to read the images. Eventually, we came across the mother lode. A ship almost filled the screen, its back broken at an impossible angle. All around the cargo laid like sugar spilled on a kitchen floor, an eerie field of green, yellow and brown. In response to my next question, Jardine unfurled the gridiron map and pointed at a small triangle.

"We are here. Well, the sonar is. Directly over the *Navarine*. She's a French escort vessel torpedoed by a German U-boat in 1941. Fifteen hundred souls went down with her. A designated war grave, so no one dives on her."

Over the next few hours, our scanner trawled across other wrecks like the *Navarine*. Broken aircraft, fishing boats lying on their sides, more cars, tanks, and field guns.

"What's that, do you suppose?" I craned over the screen and peered along the line of his finger. A gigantic mass scored a brown trough from one edge to the other.

"Another ship?"

"Well, yes. The *Etienne DeFarge*, a Corvette class loaned by the British to the French. Torpedoed in 1942. No. *That.*"

He enlarged a portion of the screen until the dark scar almost filled it. In the shadows, was a discernible shape; a bright yellow triangular frame pointing away from the wreck.

"A mast, rigging," I surmised. "Maybe radio antennae. The ship's on its side."

Jardine smirked at my greenness. "Nah. It's the prow of a Corvette class. You can see the four-inch cannon still on its turntable. The radio masts are further back."

He pulled a folder from his bag, searching through for a picture. He placed the photo on the screen and twisted it into the same orientation as the mysterious shape. "Single masted sailing boat."

"Just like the *Spirito del Vento*." My heart leaped.

Jardine beamed triumphantly. "There's only one way to be certain."

Proof of Life

Chapter 23

I'd told Jardine I knew how to dive. Whilst not exactly true, it also wasn't a lie. I had gained my certification years ago with the Marines, squinting through the silt of a shallow lake in Wisconsin. I was a little rusty on the details, but Jardine seemed to know what he was doing. At least, I hoped he did. Steve had spent the morning with her thoughts. Worrying about Moretti, her job, her life, about being left in charge of a $200,000 boat while the boys went diving. But also worrying about the small dots around three miles away.

"Jardine says sardine fishers. If they were interested in us, they would have come over." The boats were so distant I couldn't make out the detail without glasses. Just that they were there, holding station, occasionally catching the sun, sending a spark of white our way.

"I don't like it. We are too exposed out here."

"You'd rather be back in Rome with Polizia and CCTV? You're jumping at shadows and I don't blame you. The Glock is in the cupboard over the sink. Fetch it. Keep it with you. No safety. Just pull the trigger."

"That's your answer to everything, isn't it?" She huffed testily and returned to the cabin, slamming the door, making Jardine look up briefly.

"Women, eh?" he chuckled, heaving at the neoprene pants. "Bring her something nice back. A shell or a pretty colored rock."

It broke my heart to leave her alone. Alone is the worst feeling. No one to talk to. No one to help or tell you you're doing things right, that it's going to be okay. Just trust in a gut instinct that has let you down before. She looked vulnerable, and I was leaving her alone.

Despite the sun in the cloudless sky, the water made me shudder as I tumbled backward from the Sea Hawk. We both checked our breathing tubes, checked our gauges, and hooked our fingers into the traditional okay signal. Paddling forward, finding the anchor line disappearing into the murk below, I steadied my nerves and led the descent, literally out of my depth. I kept my eyes downward, listened to the regular push-pull of my breath through the re-breather, tasted the slight tang of aluminum and compressor oil. I felt the inevitable claustrophobia as the world turned teal green. It was my *bête noire*, my weakness since an IED left me trapped in a wrecked Hummer.

Above, the shimmering sun had all but faded. Shoals of tiny fish darted about, fleeing on mass as we descended deeper. The *Etienne DeFarge* emerged like a sleeping leviathan through the murky fog, her great underbelly frosted with plants and shellfish. She was lying in a hundred feet of water, about ninety-five feet deeper than I had ever dived before. I felt the pressure crushing my eardrums, swallowing periodically to relieve the pain. And then my feet touched the bottom, kicking up a cloud of silt, dulling the twilight world. Jardine gestured and together we swam over to the towering hulk of the ship. It took a moment to realize I was looking at her keel; as she lay on her side on the seabed. Jardine pinned a magnetic marker to the hull, fluorescent orange, to guide us back. Then I followed him along the rib of the keel until we reached the prow. Or what was left of it. The port side had collapsed. Curls of rusting metal bowed outwards like the petals of a great undersea flower. A nod to the enormous explosion that sent her and her crew to their murky graves. My first wreck dive, I half expected to see human remains, scattered like fall leaves by the undertow.

But there was nothing. Just a huge, rusted hulk, forested with barnacles and algae, and clouds of fish darting in and out of the mangled superstructure.

We swam across what would have been the foredeck. Now it was a hole, concave and black. Beyond, the four-inch gun sat atilt on its turntable, pointing helplessly to the surface. In front of it, the other boat was lodged against the warship's tilted deck, at a precarious angle, held by fragile guard rails and the twisted, damaged superstructure. The masts jutted out. No sails, just rigging. Washing lines hung with trailing fronds of seaweed, all coated a deep moss green. Exchanging a glance with Jardine, we swam over, ran our hands across the stern, wiping away the green algae. My heart was thumping as I made out the name.

The *Spirito del Vento*. Jardine was right.

While the Scotsman swam below the boat, I swam above, inspecting the cabin, the windows, running my hands along as I went. I twisted the handle on the door, but it was locked, which puzzled me. Why lock a door on a boat in the middle of the ocean? I rubbed a patch of glass clean, shone my flashlight through, but the dark and the reflection on the window hid everything inside.

Jardine appeared from the stern, opening his arms and shaking his head. *Nothing.* He tapped his gauge. The needle was approaching red. He only had a few minutes of air left. Strangely, my gauge still read over an hour, so I swept a hand around. *I'll stay down for a while.* Jardine shook his head. Diving alone is dangerous, not recommended. I willed him to reconsider. We were on the cusp of solving a thirty-year-old mystery. We couldn't leave now. Finally, he relented, laying a finger on the gauge, indicating a number, tapping the glass, and pointing up. I crooked my finger and thumb - *okay.* Jardine reciprocated, then disappeared into the darkness.

My heart was racing, I was breathing far too quickly,

using up precious minutes, so I took a beat to calm down. A moment to forestall the demons inside that wanted to tear off the cloying rubber mask.

Beckett, you got this.

The hull of the *Spirito del Vento* seemed intact, no gaping rent like the *Etienne DeFarge*. Beyond the ravages of three decades on the seabed, she looked in good condition. In fact, I could see no reason she was here at all.

I found something on the seabed, a piece of the wreck to jemmy the lock, holding my breath as the boat groaned and creaked, relieved when the door gave way and I could prize it open. I shone my diving lamp inside, disappointed there were no remains. No grinning corpses. After so long, it wasn't such a surprise. The sea claims its victims mercilessly.

Maneuvering through the narrow opening, my heart stopped for a moment as the boat shifted on its precarious perch. The hull ground against the rusted hull of the ship. Then it caught, sending a wash of silt blooming around the vessel. I breathed again, aware of the confinement, of the danger. I needed to be quick or risk being entombed like the crew of the sunken warship.

Inside, it was a confused, topsy-turvy world. Bunk squabs spilled, cupboard doors lay open, tipping crockery and cutlery. Everything was piled at the lowest point, green and furred, swarming with urchins and anemones. Small crabs and shellfish peppered the windows and all around, shoals of fish darted about. Beneath the tiny galley, through the open cupboard door, there was a dim light, the sea outside shining through. The reason for the boat's watery end. A seacock is a device used to vent liquid through pipes into the sea or let in water to cool engines. Normally, it is isolated from the rest of the boat keeping it watertight. On the *Spirito del Vento*, the seacock had been wrenched from its mountings. Water would have inundated the cabin, swamping the boat and taking her down in minutes.

Jardine was right. Someone scuppered her.

Feeling the boat teeter again, I listened to my voice of reason. With no bodies, no reason the boat was deliberately sunk, my quest for the Andersons and Amber Rock lay elsewhere. My gauges showed enough air for the slow ascent to avoid any risk of the bends. So I quit while I was ahead.

The boat had shifted; angled down toward the seabed. The door had hinged closed, banging on the jamb in the current. Reaching for the handle, I noticed something dancing, a faint glimmer struggling through the years of green algae. A small pendant, its gold chain looped over the handle. Rubbing away the green, I could see a motif but couldn't make it out, so I stuffed it into the sleeve of my wetsuit. At least I would have something to occupy my mind on the long journey back to Cagliari. But as I retraced my route back to the *Day-Glo* marker, the pendant pressed against my arm. I was puzzled. They had intentionally stripped the boat of everything personal before smashing the seacocks. Without the name on the stern, without the serial numbers on the small diesel engine, it could have been any sailboat. So why leave the pendant? Was it overlooked in the haste to leave the boat? As I slowly followed the line towards the surface, I wondered if Max Anderson was trying to tell us something.

Eventually, as the dimness gave way to aquamarine, then to sunlight, the dark shape of the *Genevieve's* hull broke the surface. Then my heart missed a beat. Sitting, maybe thirty feet away, was another hull.

Proof of Life

Chapter 24

The two boats were tethered together, a sag of rope writhing on the waves. The Sea Hawk and another longer, narrower vessel. A wooden hull painted sky-blue and white. Was it one of the bright dots three miles away? So low in the water, I couldn't see the horizon, just the chop of small waves as the two hulls creaked and splashed in the swell.

I recalled the van and the Cinquecento back at Cagliari, the uneasy feeling as they parked up together. Baresi.

Where was Steve?

She had seen the sardine fishers. I did nothing. Jardine convinced me there was nothing to worry about and still I did nothing, despite the alarm bells in my head. I'd left her alone on the surface at the mercy of Baresi, and I felt ashamed. Was she already dead as they searched the cabin? Or was she also sinking down to lie in the war grave below?

Surfacing under the swim platform of the *Genevieve*, I kept my head down. By now, Jardine would have surfaced, removed his gear, and been up on the bridge, smoking a cigar, but he was nowhere to be seen, nor was any of his gear. Inside the cabin, there was movement, shadows across the windows, but I couldn't tell how many people. Had Jardine surprised the Sicilian and paid the price? Or was he in the cabin, conspiring, even begging, for his life? Maybe he was trading his for mine and Steve's?

The cabin door opened and Baresi strode out, hand on hip, and a face like a bear with a hangover. With the other hand, he was holding my goddamn Glock.

Proof of Life

"Quanto tempo ancora, capo? The voice carried across from the second boat. *How much longer?*

"We go when I say we go, Carlo. I need to deal with Beckett first." Baresi's reply was in English, probably for my benefit. He dragged a hand across his scalp and scowled, then returned to the cabin. With Jardine gone, with Steve and I sent the same way, Baresi could collect his paycheck and tell Amber Rock he had secured all loose ends.

I couldn't let that happen.

Replacing my mouthpiece, I sank below the surface and swam over to the second boat. I hoisted myself up the iron hull and peered over. The wooden deck glistened in the sun. There were no fish, no nets, no dead Scotsmen. Up in the open cabin, the small rotund man from the ferry was slouching at the helm, reading a magazine, turning it through ninety degrees to admire the pictures. I removed my tanks, mask, and flippers and let them sink. Then I eased up the ladder, untied the two boats, and dropped back into the water. Within a moment, a curse cut through the air.

"Che cazzo!" The small man dropped his magazine and raced across the deck, hands flailing at the loose end of the dangling rope as it snaked over the gunwale.

"Merda, merda, merda."

I pulled myself back onto the deck. The small man was bent over, one leg flailing as he stretched out for the rope, grabbing at whatever he could. I thought of the knife strapped to my ankle. I left it there. The fat man had a poor choice of friends but didn't deserve to die. Instead, I grabbed a piece of his t-shirt, dragged him back onto the boat, then slammed his head forward into the bulkhead, feeling his muscles relax as he slumped into a heap.

"Stay!" I slid into the water and crossed to the *Genevieve*.

The current had eased the boats apart. If Baresi wanted to get back, he would need to swim. One down, one to go.

There were windows on three sides of the *Genevieve's* cabin and a windowed door on the fourth. It was effectively a fortress. The Sicilian was inside, waiting for my head to break the surface, waiting to take it off with my own gun as soon as it did. In a wetsuit, my options were limited; all I had was the diving knife. I could throw it but I was no circus act. It would probably miss. In the port side locker, below the bench seat, there was a flare pistol. Hauling myself out of the water, crouching low as I crossed the deck, I snapped open the catch, deadening the sound against my palm. I found the waterproof box of cartridges and loaded one. Then something pressed into the middle of my back and I froze.

"Beckett. Come stai?"

"Good to see you too, Baresi." I turned slowly. Expressionless, drawn, he was as tired as I was, yet his eyes were narrow and scornful. A slight nod of appreciation I knew his name already. Pointedly, I put down the flare pistol and raised my hands, knitting my fingers behind my head.

"I should make you swim over and bring my fucking boat back." He nodded over the starboard and I risked a glance. The sky-blue and white boat was around twenty feet away, the small man still out cold on the deck.

"Where's the girl?" Behind him, the cabin seemed empty.

Baresi half-smiled. "She's okay—for now. Perhaps you should focus more on your own predicament?"

He waved the gun towards the cabin. I walked slowly, feeling the muzzle through my wetsuit, scanning the deck for something I could reach before a hollow-tip shattered my spine. The breeze was cooling the saltwater on my face, my heart was thumping in my chest.

Why hadn't he plugged me already?

I needed time to think, so I stopped, half-turned. "You know this is a waste of time, don't you?"

Proof of Life

"Move." Baresi huffed. He pushed the muzzle deeper.

"Moretti was blowing smoke up all our asses. You killed him and he had nothing. No information on the Andersons. No lost boat. He was stringing us all along for the fee."

"But here you are diving on a wreck. Looking for the boat. It's you blowing smoke, or your friend Jardine."

"Jardine's dead," I bluffed. "The bastard double-crossed us, so I cut his breathing tube. He told us he had something new. That he knew where the Andersons' boat was. When we got down there, all we found was an old fishing trawler." I stared at Baresi for a long moment. Watching for any change in expression, but there was none, so I carried on. "And Moretti? If he had information on Amber Rock, it wasn't at his villa. So here we are. Moretti's dead, Jardine's dead, now Steve and I are going to die, and for what?"

Baresi shrugged indifferently. Could he tell I was lying? Was Jardine hunkered down in the cabin, watching the floorshow and smoking one of his foul cheroots?

"What do I care?" he scoffed. "I have no interest in missing boats or missing people. I don't even care about Amber Rock. All I care about is my money. Now move."

"And you think they will pay you? The only payment you'll get is a bullet in the head. Let's face it, Baresi. It happens to anyone who knows too much."

Baresi smiled, dug the gun deeper. "I'll take my chances."

I reached the cabin door, twisted the handle. Steve was lying on the bunk, bound and gagged. Her eyes were closed.

"She is taking a nap. It has been a stressful day so far. It can only get worse." His English was good; better than my Italian would ever be, mocking and superior.

"So, why not just shoot us back in the harbor at Cagliari. Why go to all the trouble of following us out here?"

"I am an Italian. We are all artists, poets. And what could

be more poetic than this, eh? You come looking for Anderson, to the place where his boat disappeared, only to end up disappearing like him. Even in the same place."

"Well, it's not Dante but I suppose it has its merits."

In a swift movement, I grabbed out at the metal ladder up to the bridge and swung around on it, turning on Baresi, kicking him square in the groin, hearing the wheeze. The Glock barked, and my ears rang as shards of glass fiber rained down. Baresi immediately countered. His broad fist smashed into my jaw. I remembered Moretti's apartment, my bullet winging him, so I grabbed out at his left arm, gripping for all I was worth. His face contorted, and he let out a howl. Spinning around, I threw him up against the bridge ladder, hearing it ring as his head hit metal. Above me, he held the Glock, straining to bring the barrel down to my face. I was tired after the dive. The lactic acid in my biceps stole my strength as the gun inched lower. Still, I pressed my finger into his wounded arm. Summoning every ounce of energy, I smacked Baresi's wrist against the handrail, feeling the sinews crack as it twisted over the metal. His left hand grabbed at my face, his palm driving my head back until I could feel the muscles tight in my neck.

Baresi's eyes were wild as he growled, mustering extra reserves of energy, and the Glock inched still lower.

Then he stopped. He grinned as a shadow fell over us. My eyes lit up in an explosion of colors. My knees buckled, as everything went black and I remember thinking, this is becoming tedious.

Proof of Life

Chapter 25

Water slapping against the outside of the hull. A lazy distant Latin rhythm through the glass fiber. My head was playing Icelandic thrash metal. I could taste brine. I could smell blood. Something solid nudged me in the kidneys.

"Beckett. Wake up, for God's sake." It nudged again.

Irked, I opened my eyes, confused as the world lay askew. Gradually, things came into focus. The cabin of boat, spilled cupboards and drawers. The inch of water across the floor.

The staring eyes of Baresi's partner. *No loose ends.*

Another nudge. This time harder, irritating. I tried to move my arms and felt more pain as something bit into my wrists. Cable ties. I have felt that pain before. No problem when your hands are in front. Mine were behind my back.

"Come on, Beckett. Please." Steve's voice was frantic, pleading, tearful. The toe of her trainers struck out again.

"Will you just stop kicking me, for Chrissakes."

"Oh, thank you, God. Thank you, thank you, thank you."

"What's happened? Where's Baresi?" The water was icy against my cheek and getting deeper. That couldn't be good.

"I don't know. Gone. Do something." I couldn't see her. Her voice was behind me, from one of the bunks.

I shook away the fog in my brain, suddenly alert. "We need to cut these ties. And quickly. We need something sharp. What can you see?"

Steve looked around. "There's nothing, Beckett. They took your knife and the gun."

Proof of Life

I rolled onto my back. Steve was on the bunk, her hands and legs bound with ties. Over her head, a Perspex fronted First Aid Box hung from the wall.

"Above you. Can you kick at it?"

"I don't know..."

"Yes, you do. Lie on your back and kick. Hard!"

Leaning back, legs tied together, she flung a kick up, landing ineffectually against the transparent front of the box. Then again, each time getting more and more frustrated. After five or six attempts, she had gotten nowhere, unable to put enough power behind the kick. So she changed tack, concentrating her weight underneath the box and heaving.

"You...bloody...sodding...fucking...bastard." Above her feet, the box began to bend. With a crack, the front panel split. I willed her to carry on. The water was now so deep I was choking. I needed to raise myself up against the bunks.

"One more good push, Steve. You can do this."

Again she kicked, again the plastic flexed and snapped.

With a last kick, the lid splintered and exploded, spilling the contents onto the floor, splashing into the oily blood-tainted water. The scissors were small, round-nosed. I fumbled around the floor, grabbed them, and shuffled further up the bunk.

"Shimmy around till I can get to your wrists."

I squirmed up onto the bunk, my back against Steve's wrists, my fingers searching for the tie holding them together. Slipping the blade inside the tie, I sawed.

"This is going to hurt."

"Just bloody get on with it, please."

I was catching her skin, pulling the tie tighter around her wrists, but I just kept going until it snapped. Steve yelped and spun on the bunk, grabbing at the scissors, and returned the favor. Salt stung my broken skin. On the floor, Carlo lay bleeding out into the water. A dark hole in his forehead leached blood into the lake of seawater.

"Hurry, Steve." The boat was leaning dangerously. Time was running out. When it reached its tipping point, it would go over fast. Ignoring the pain, gritting my teeth, I stretched at the ties until, with a snap, my hands were free. Groaning as the blood rushed to my numb arms, I pushed myself up and cut away the ties around our legs.

"We need to get out of here before it goes under."

"No shit, Sherlock!"

I frowned. A scintilla of gratitude was all I asked.

The door would not budge. The pressure of the rising water against the outside held it fast, trickling around the old, ineffective seal. Soon, the engine room below would be full, and we would plunge to the bottom.

"We'll have one go at this, so you need to be ready. We need to combine our weight against the door. Push against the water. Then, hold on to my arm like your life depends on it…because it does."

I put a shoulder to the door, then pulled Steve close and together we leaned our weight against it. Gradually the trickling water became a spray, then small fountains pouring over the threshold, until the door gave way and a torrent of water cascaded through. We tumbled out on the deck. The water was up to our waists; the floor falling rapidly.

"Swim. Away from the boat, out from the undertow," I shouted. "I have to do one more thing."

"Don't leave me, Beckett. Not now!"

"Just swim, or it will pull you under. Go!"

There was no time for a debate. Shaking her hand free, I dived below the surface and looped my arm around the handrail. I hung on as the boat finally reached the critical point and plunged downward. I unlatched the locker and found a handle on top of the orange package within. My ears were imploding as the pressure tried to crush my skull. My tired lungs ached once more, willing me to gulp water and yield to the inevitable. I released the rail and pulled until finally the orange package came free. Then I tugged the bright red cord on top. There was a thunderous explosion, a series of seismic thuds through the water. My arm was wrenched half out of its socket and I was airborne, legs flailing, clinging onto the raging beast as it arced upwards and crashed down onto the surface.

Then, everything stopped, and water showered down.

Chapter 26

I hauled Steve aboard the tiny life raft and we both lay under a setting sun, getting our breaths back and wondering what the hell just happened. The other boat was long gone. So was Baresi. Not even a dot on the horizon. Jardine, too, was gone. For three hours we listened, scoured the rippling blue plane, expecting him to shout and wave, but he never did. Maybe he was regaling the crew of the *Etienne DeFarge* with his stories, filling their cabins with cigar smoke? Maybe he was caught in the rigging, waiting for the crabs and fishes to scour his bones clean?

So Jardine was gone, and with him, my last hope of finding the truth about Max Anderson's disappearance. But he'd been right. Someone scuppered the *Spirito del Vento*, hundreds of miles from her last known location. But the Andersons? Had the sea consumed them? Had *they* scuppered the boat? If so, what happened next? Or had someone overpowered them, like Steve and I, then left them inside the locked cabin as she sank.

I was no further along.

We sat in silence, shaded by the small apron attached to the raft as a sunshade. What was there to say? Rather than keeping Steve safe, I was continually dragging her back from the abyss. Perhaps Pliskin was right. I should hand her over to the Polizia. How much longer would she endure this until she asked me to?

Eventually, the distant sound of rotor blades thudded across the sky. The sun was setting as the dazzling white light of a Sikorsky Sea King belonging to the *Guardia Costiera* came over the horizon. Soon, we were shielding our eyes from the spits of water kicked up from the downdraft, watching a guy in a jumpsuit spiraling down a wire. They had responded to the emergency beacon, which had activated as I wrestled with the inflatable raft. I spun them some BS about renting out the boat for some diving, about a damaged sea valve which left us sinking. They seemed to buy it. Or maybe they didn't care.

Baresi had tracked us from Rome to Sardinia. If he'd gotten hold of Roma CCTV, he'd know about the Ford and could track it, but how did he know about Jardine, about his search for the *Spirito del Vento*? About where he was searching? Had he already seen Moretti's notebook?

The Sicilian and I were the same. In another life, I could have become him. Maybe I already had. He had his mission and I had mine. We would both go to any extreme to achieve our goal. And our masters? Pliskin needed to know about Amber Rock. Amber Rock needed to cover their tracks. What lengths would either of them go to? Then there was Max Anderson. Thirty years ago, Amber Rock was killing nuclear scientists, and he believed he would be next. How far would *he* go to ensure they didn't succeed?

On the raft, in the chopper, Steve kept her counsel. If she was shaken by the death of Moretti, she was terrified by Renzo Baresi. Until then, it had all been a TV movie, where the peril is real, the jinks are high, but the good guy saves the day. Escaping a sinking boat, with nothing below her but the deep blue, had left her traumatized. But more than the terror, there was the realization she had entered a new world, parallel to her normal, middle-class English upbringing. One where guns scrambled brains and even the good guys broke necks to survive. One where she was a little afraid of me and everyone I met.

***

The helicopter took us to the Emergency Hospital in Cagliari, where they put us into separate cubicles. They gave me a pair of paper underpants and an unflattering open-backed gown. Less chance of me running with half my butt on display. A brusque young intern checked me over. Apart from dehydration and an angry pink blush to my cheeks, he gave me a clean bill of health and wittily advised me to confine my activities to dry land in the future. Through the opening in the drapes, a tall, wiry man, almost certainly a police officer, stopped him and they engaged in an animated exchange. Several times, in amongst the machine-gun flow of Italian, I caught the name of Luciano Moretti.

The pendant I'd found on Anderson's boat was tight in my clenched fist. Now, without clothes and no chance of escape, I sat on the bed and let it spiral in front of my eyes. It was around the size of a nickel, but maybe twice the thickness. The metal beneath the dried detritus shone keenly and was obviously gold; the harsh, salty water would have eroded anything else. Rubbing away some of the surface muck, I could make out a wavy line, a sawtooth pattern of colored enamel—a snake, maybe. In an arc around the top, there was a word, but I couldn't read it. On the back, there was some engraving. Thirty years in the Mediterranean had rendered that unreadable too.

"What's happening out there?"

The nurse glanced across as she checked the monitors. "The police want to speak to you and the woman. Doctor Santos says twenty-four hours. The police officer is angry because in here, the doctor is boss."

"Twenty-four hours?" I couldn't sit with my butt out for that long. The rescue would be all over the news. Baresi would certainly have seen it.

"Yes, Sr. Farrell. Dehydration is serious. Doctor Santos wants to keep you in for observation. We are finding a

Proof of Life

private room." She was a small woman with piercing brown eyes and a stern face that demanded obedience. She reminded me of my mom, Pat. Not one to be messed with.

"Look, nurse. I need to get out of here." I had never been too good at the puppy-dog eyes. Women, especially attractive ones, saw straight through them.

"When the doctor discharges you. Twenty-four hours."

"Can't I discharge myself? Sign some papers or something?"

"My shift ends in one hour. Then you are my colleague's responsibility. For now, you stay in this bed."

I flopped back, defeated. "Nurse. I need you to do something for me. Do you have paper and a pen?"

The nurse huffed admonishingly, as if I was destroying her busy schedule. She reached into her breast pocket and pulled out a pen, took a leaflet from a rack on the wall, and handed both to me. Quickly, I scribbled an international phone number on the white margin.

"Ring this number. It's collect. When they answer, tell them 'taxi for Beckett'. Tell them the address of the hospital. Then put the phone down. You got that? Taxi for Beckett."

She had the number. She had the code phrase. Now, I had to hope she would use them.

"But what about the Polizia?"

"You're only booking a taxi, nurse."

She folded the leaflet, over and over, until it was the size of a charge card. Then she stuck it in her pocket and left.

***

The curtain hooks pinging along the track woke me from my doze. In the opening, the tall police officer I'd seen earlier threw a pile of clothes onto the bed. A shoulder holster nestled under his sweating armpit.

"I am Ispettore Ernesto Bartholdi." He flashed what I took to be a warrant card. "The doctor says you are no longer at risk, so we are moving you. Get dressed. Hurry."

As he left, I glanced at the clock. So much for twenty-four hours; it had barely been three. Behind the *Ispettore*, a uniformed officer, the size of a small shed, turned to fill the doorway. Much as I hated the idea, Steve and I were probably safer in Bartholdi's custody than out on the streets. I dressed in the jeans and faded prickly black sweater, and slipped on a pair of ill-fitting trainers, wondering how many other people had worn them before me. Outside, I heard more machine-gun Italian. No doubt the doctor was shoving disclaimers and indemnities under Bartholdi's nose. No doubt Bartholdi was waving them away.

Presently, two uniformed officers entered, dragged my arms behind my back, and snapped on handcuffs. They frog marched me out, along a series of plain, gray corridors to an anonymous door.

"Steve. You alright?" Her hands were cuffed too, and she wore similar ill-fitting garments.

She turned and glared. "What do you think, *Beckett*? At least I'll be safer with the police than with you." She was far from alright.

"I'll take the fall. I'll admit everything. You were just there, right? Soon, all this will be over."

"Non parlare, per favore." An elbow stung my ribs, sending the wind from my lungs. "Do not talk, please."

Outside, night had fallen and the chill air smelled of stale food, stale sweat, and a fresh frisson of fear. Silent except for the faint roar of hospital air conditioners and a low rumble of early morning traffic. In the small yard behind the hospital, a plain blue Iveco people carrier and two marked police cruisers were waiting patiently.

"Where are you taking us?"

"Non parlare. Into the van. Avanti, avanti."

Another dig in my back and I stumbled forward. The officer behind Steve nudged her. Soon we were both on the bench seat, anxiously watching the lights of Cagliari flash by.

We were leaving by the back doors. It felt wrong. The demeanor of the officers, the decals on the cars. Deep in the slurry at the back of my mind, my spider senses were tingling. And where was *Ispettore* Bartholdi?

Chapter 27

"Where are you taking us?" The van was no police vehicle. It smelled of sweat and the pungent Turkish tobacco that stains teeth and fingers. A coconut air freshener swung from the rearview. Just like us, it was fighting a losing battle.

"Non parlo Inglese." Around twenty, swarthy, dark-haired, and stone-faced, the officer in front kept his eyes forward. On the other side of Steve, the second officer was older, paunchier—say forty. They were each holstering a Beretta 9mm. The driver eyed us in the rearview mirror, a hairy arm resting on the stick shift. We moved at a steady speed through the sparse early morning traffic as the sirens blared and blue lights flashed off the shopfronts. Briefly, I considered escape, but the odds were too steep. I could probably take the two guards with a swift elbow, but the driver? As it was, the doors had locked automatically, and we were helpless, shackled to the headrests in front.

"I need to speak to my lawyer. I'm American." Well, it worked in the movies.

"Non parlare." The two officers continued to face forward, except one moved a hand to his gun. I took the hint and sat silently, watching the blue strobe lights of the car in front, hearing the beat of my heart. Steve's breathing was short, quivering, and it tore me apart there was nothing I could do for her. Nothing I could do for myself.

Then the blue strobe lights stopped.

I blinked away the spots as the cruiser in front peeled off down a side road. The one behind had gone too. A knot formed in my gut.

Proof of Life

"Beckett?" Steve looked nervously over.

"Something's been bugging me since we left hospital."

"What do you mean?"

"The cruisers, out front and back? They had blues and twos, decals, the works. This van is unmarked."

"And?"

"*Non parlare*," the cop in front barked impatiently.

"I don't know," I lied, "but we are not going to the police station."

Leaning around, the front guard's eyes fixed on us menacingly. "*Non parlare*. Okay?" The nose of his Beretta edged around the front headrest. He pulled back the trigger.

After around half an hour, we turned off the main road and climbed a darker, dustier track into the hills. The lights of Cagliari were distant, through the trees, an orange strand on the horizon. Around us, blackness clung to the outside of the van, stones rattled against the floor pan. Five minutes later—could have been ten or twenty—with a jolt and a creak of springs, the driver pulled over and killed the engine. As the younger officer alighted, the older one unhooked our cuffs. Apart from the chirp of cicadas and the crunch of their boots on the gravel, it was deadly silent.

"Out, please. No funny business."

"Hey, I thought you didn't speak English?"

"*I* do. *He* doesn't." He gestured with the gun at his counterpart. "Young people, huh? They know nothing." Though his face was in shadow, I could imagine the mocking smile as we slid along the seat squab and stepped out onto the road. Now, even the cicadas stopped their grating.

The younger officer manhandled Steve out of the van. She kicked out, catching him full on the shin. He returned a backhand across her cheek, eliciting a yelp.

"Hey, asshole. There's no need…"

"I said *non parlare*." The old man thrust his Beretta against my chest and I stopped short, helpless to intervene.

The younger one twisted Steve's arm until she cried out again. Like a cat with a bird, callous, unfeeling. Then they pushed us both against the van, backs to a grubby window, our hands cuffed in front of us. I thought back to the nurse in the hospital cubicle. Should I have worked harder to convince her? Now it was too late.

"Turn around. On your knees. Both of you." The older officer waved his pistol at me. Behind him, the face of the driver flashed orange as he lit a cigarette.

"Beckett? What's happening?" Her face was in shadow. The tremble in her voice betrayed her fear.

"Let the girl go. This has nothing to do with her." I made to turn, to plead with the men, but a sharp kick buckled my knees and sent me to the ground, wincing at the impact of stones through my borrowed jeans. Beside me, Steve was mumbling something incoherent over and over, pressing herself closer to the van.

"And you, lady. Come on!" The older officer swiped the gun across her face again. She squealed and raised her cuffed arms, collapsing to her knees. I wanted to leap up, throw my arms around the man's scrawny neck, and twist the cuffs until his bloodshot eyes exploded from his skull. But I knew I would just seal my fate more quickly. Steve would be even more alone. Anyway, I had seen enough roadside executions to guess what was coming next. Newsreels of Kosovo, Afghanistan, and Iraq. The crack, the bodies falling limp. The lines of dusty, blood-spattered corpses along the road to Basra. I wondered what went through their minds. Images of their loved ones, memories of a life about to end, regrets? I felt the gravel bite my knees. I felt the wind on my face, but nothing else. Awkwardly, I bowed my head forward.

Maximum target, minimum risk of fucking it up, leaving me a vegetable, choking on my own blood.

The older guard spoke. "Sr. Baresi wishes you to know, this is nothing personal, but you are causing him a problem. The people we work for want no loose ends."

Behind me, the hammer of the Beretta clicked back.

"I'm sorry, Steve."

Chapter 28

I closed my eyes and waited for the shot. In a split second, my life would be over. They would erase me from the Earth and no one would mourn my passing. Not my mother; I had mourned her myself two years ago. Not my father; dementia had peppered his mind, taking with it memories of me. Not even Steve. Not for more than half a second anyhow.

Between 1975 and 1979, an estimated two million Cambodians were slaughtered by the Khmer Rouge. Each one had a history—lives, loves, families. Each one ended up a sun-bleached skull with a round hole. Was that to be my fate? Discovered in a shallow grave. A nameless corpse. A forgotten history?

Thirty years on, people still remembered Max Anderson. What had he done that deserved to be remembered? What was so important I needed to find him alive? Maybe some things are bigger than just one man. Maybe each of the two million Cambodians played an infinitesimally small part in the overthrow of Pol Pot. Maybe I was the only one who could discover what Max Anderson knew.

A wave of anger surged through me. Anger at my weakness, my inability to keep Steve safe. My stupidity which had led her to her death. The hubris of a trained soldier who thought himself invincible and now, brutally, finally has to face the truth. Most of all, I felt anger at Amber Rock, at Pliskin, at all the others who hid in the shadows while other people did their dirty work. Other people died, and they wiped the blood from their hands.

Proof of Life

This could not happen. I would not die, tethered and kneeling head down in the dirt, with tears tracking through the dust on my cheeks. The rage tightened in my chest; the blood pumped through my forehead, into my arms, my legs. With a growl, I threw myself backward. The old man wheezed and tumbled over. A bullet crazed the van window. Steve screamed. A second bullet whistled past my head. With the old guard reeling, I folded over, kicked up onto my feet, and landed a crushing heel across his windpipe. His eyes rolled and he spluttered for breath. The younger man wheeled round, drawing up his Beretta. Steve kicked out at his shin and he shrieked with pain, sending a bullet into the dust. Then I was on him, my knee in his back, my manacled hands around his neck, yanking it back. My wrists were wet with blood as the cuffs carved at my flesh. I used the pain; wanted it. I needed to feel the burn in my flesh as he died. His hands flailed by his side. His breath rasped through his throat. Between my hands, his hyoid bone snapped. His larynx fell into his windpipe. Bone ground against bone. He let out a slow gurgling moan, and the breathing stopped.

One more.

Another bullet clanked against the van. I dived across to the fallen Beretta and spun around. The driver stood open-mouthed, his gun out in front, swinging back and forth as he sought a target. Along the short barrel of the Beretta, I saw his wide-eyed stare and squeezed the trigger. Lie down with dogs, you get up with fleas.

Or you never get up.

Back at the van, the old man was struggling for breath, coughing blood, his hands around his throat. I aimed the Beretta at his face.

"Who are you? Who sent you?"

He wouldn't answer, couldn't answer. His throat was split, the froth of blood on his lips mixing with air, flooding his lungs. In his eyes, my contempt for him was reflected. The breathing stopped, and the eyes glazed over, looking straight through me, seeing nothing.

The show was over. The cicadas resumed their concert. Above the ticking of the cooling engine, someone was sobbing, and I wondered if it was me. In the ethereal calmness, after the inevitability of death, my heart pounded like a jackhammer, my lungs gasped for air and I was shaking.

Steve had fallen down beside the van, hands over her face, quivering uncontrollably. She was mumbling, plaintive, low, an animal noise. What could I do? I sat beside her, put my arm around her, and watched the glow of the driver's cigarette fade to black.

Proof of Life

Chapter 29

After a while, my hands stopped shaking, and the red fog left my mind. Now I had to think. We couldn't stay there forever. The dusty track may be remote, but Berettas were noisy and it was getting light.

I frisked each of the corpses and found keys to the cuffs. There were no personal effects, no identification, certainly nothing to prove they were actually Polizia. They had even stripped their uniforms of badges. The older guy carried a cell, a drop phone with a single number in the memory. His Beretta had fallen from his hand, a bullet still in the breach. I ejected it, held it up against the dull light of early dawn, imagined it cracking through my skull, turning my brain to mush. But it didn't. The guard was slow. *You snooze, you lose.*

I cleared up as best I could, heaving the bodies into the van, emptying the rounds from the Berettas into my jeans pocket, and tossing the guns on top of the corpses. I kept the old man's gun. I took the handbrake off the van, then pushing against the back, feeling the weight shift, I rocked it until the wheels began to turn. Then momentum took over, and it quietly trundled off the dirt track into the deep ravine, bumping and scraping through the bushes, crashing noisily into a rocky stream at the bottom.

Soon, Renzo Baresi would know his men had failed. He would come for us again.

Steve was sitting across the dusty road, staring into middle distance, replaying the shit I'd put her through in the last few days. Probably terrified at what I might put her through next. She shivered against the cold, barely noticing as I removed her cuffs and flung them over the edge. Without my Omega, I could only guess the time, but a thin strip of gold was edging its way over the horizon. Soon the day would warm up. Soon there would be people about.

"We need to get out of here, Steve."

She looked up, nodding absently. Her eyes were empty. A private hell of mutilated corpses and sinking boats. Of lead ripping skin and bone. Of eternal oblivion. I lifted her to her feet. It was not the time for talking, but I needed her help. Opening the old guard's phone, I started a text to the only number it held. Handing it to Steve, I told her what to type.

'Lavoro fatto, capo.' *Job done, boss.*

I pressed send and waited a beat. Almost immediately, the screen lit up with a response—'sei sicuro?' - *are you sure?*

'Sono sicuro.' *I am sure.*

Then I switched off the phone, ripped out the battery, and hurled them both as far as I could out into the ravine.

We walked back along the dirt track in silence. What was there to say? Sorry for getting you into this mess? Sorry for the bullets and the bodies and the damn near-fatal drowning? Steve looked forward, expressionless. Right now, she was busy just placing one foot in front of the other, incapable of anything else. In the weak light of dawn, I could see the tear tracks on her face. I waited for the tirade of anger, of undirected hysteria, but it never came. She just kept on walking.

The fact was, I wasn't sorry. Baresi had tried to silence us twice. Twice he had failed. If Steve had stayed in the Piazza Navona, she would be dead. On the boat, without me, again she would be dead. The Sicilian was proving ruthless and unstoppable. I needed to change that.

By the time we reached the main road, the sun was edging over the horizon, turning the gray to amber and pulling a wispy haze from the hills. I guessed around 5:00 am. The road was deserted, but wouldn't stay that way for long. This was farming territory, and those guys hardly slept at all. Cagliari was South, to our right, so we turned left, our long shadows leading the way down the empty tarmac.

"Where are we going, Beckett?"

Her voice startled me in the silence.

"Somewhere safe."

Proof of Life

Chapter 30

Sunday, September 8

I didn't know where we were going. It was just *away*. Somewhere no one would know to look. A haystack in need of a couple of needles for a while.

The main road was featureless, a ribbon of brown and dusty sage green, devoid of traffic. Lines of hedges and stone walls, gates with chains, stop taps feeding irrigation pipes, barking dogs prowling barren stony yards. After an hour, we passed a dirty *Vendesi* sign, leaning against an old rusting gate. Beyond, a rutted track, florid with yellowing weeds, led up into a copse of trees. No one had been here in a while. There were places like this all over rural Italy. Farming was not a young person's game, especially in a recession.

"Let's see if anyone's home."

Steve just stood. On autopilot. Opening the gate with a teeth-jarring creak, I pulled her through, closing it behind us. The less anyone knew of our whereabouts, the better. The driveway wound through gnarled walnut trees, the ground littered with unharvested fruit and crisp leaves. At the other end, a small farmhouse, shuttered and dilapidated, stood in a clearing hidden from the road.

"Stay here while I check it out."

Steve slid into the soft carpet of leaves. She drew up her knees and linked her arms over them, pulling her world in around her, unmoved as I took out the Beretta. Maybe she was already annealed to guns, hardened to the violence?

Proof of Life

The farmhouse was boarded up long ago. An unkempt yard strewn with die-hard weeds. Some crumbling outbuildings. Nature was already reclaiming it. I prized open a shuttered window and dropped into the room, sending dust dancing in the sunlight. A wave of oppressive heat hit me, pulling the sweat from my skin. There was the odor of mildew and dry rot. As my eyes acclimatized, I took in a large family room converted to a hospital ward. They'd pushed everything back to accommodate a large iron bedstead, a small chest of drawers, and a well-read pile of magazines and books. In the corner, a couple of chairs gathered around a bamboo and glass occasional table. An ancient TV stood on another table facing the bed. A patina of dust coated everything. A lamp, dry glass, and a photo of two elderly people. It reminded me of my home in.

My mom, Pat, spent her last days at home. We moved the furniture aside and loaned a bed from the hospital. Each day, the conversation became less and more disconnected, her eyes more distant. There is no peace, no calm in death. Just staring eyes and a slack, yawning jaw. Joe was away in Philadelphia and never forgave himself for not being there. Then one day, he walked through the front door and couldn't find his way back. I found him a place where he could watch reruns of game shows and take his meds. I hoped the people who lived in this farmhouse were as lucky as Joe had been.

Back at the walnut grove, Steve was sitting under a tree, still staring, still somewhere else. I helped her up and led her around to the rear window.

"We should be safe in here."

***

"Looks like they lived here. In this room."

Steve made no response.

"You okay?" I could make her outline, sitting on a chair on the other side of the room.

"I'm fine." Clipped, hostile. "I just want to be left alone."

The silence soaked into the room once more. I found a candlestick and fresh candles over on the sideboard, lit one, and set it down on the chest of drawers. The light flickered in Steve's eyes. She was wiping away a tear. I felt helpless and empty, so I lay back on the bed, my hands laced behind my head, trying to rationalize what had just happened.

The moment was on loop. The rear tire of the van, a small patch of gravel road, the dark as I closed my eyes. The endless wait for oblivion. I'd never feared death. In my tours of the Middle East, it was a constant companion, just a sniper's aim away, but somehow it would never happen to me. They would always aim for someone else. But the dusty farm track in the hills of Sardinia changed that. I believed I was going to die.

After a while, Steve walked over and picked up the candle. Without a word, she left the room. As darkness draped its veil across me, a door shut, and the latch bit. If she was going to run, she would anyhow, somehow. If she did, maybe it was one less problem for me.

And for her.

Proof of Life

Chapter 31

I woke with a start, briefly disoriented, hearing a shout fade into the half-light, realizing it was my own. The room was still. A gray dusk with white shards of light cutting the mote-filled air. My mouth was as dry as a Temperance Society tea dance, so I left Steve for a while to scout out the property. Looking up at the sun, I figured a little after 9:00 am. The ground was cracked and sun-scorched, tufted with hardy weeds and sinuous straw-colored climbers weaving around the tumbledown brickwork. In the lean-to buildings, there were pieces of ancient farm machinery from another century. Beneath a tarpaulin, I found an old Citroen GS, sat on its haunches, peppered with rust and dirt. Under another, a Honda scooter waited expectantly. It too was dusty, rusty, and past its best, but there was air in the tires. After a little coaxing, the engine eventually played ball. Filling it with gas from cans in the back of the barn, I pulled it around to the side of the farmhouse.

When Steve finally surfaced, she returned to the uncomfortable wicker chair and sat cross-legged. She was still in no mood for conversation. I replaced her candle with the last new one we had and lit it.

"I need to go back into Cagliari for a while. Will you be okay here?"

She just looked through me and shrugged. I placed the Beretta and spare rounds on the chest of drawers, knowing she wouldn't use them. Hoping she wouldn't need to.

I reached the shipyard at the harbor. The afternoon sun was sticking my shirt to my back. The scooter was not built

Proof of Life

for distance and the can of angry bees, which passed for a motor, smelled of burned aluminum. Although it groaned and mumbled the entire way there, it still made it. Rounding the corner, the Ford Focus was in the parking lot, although someone had searched it, perhaps Baresi or one of his men. It could have been kids, seeing the back window out, assuming it was abandoned. Anyhow, there was nothing to find. Our bags were in a coin-operated locker at the railroad station. Maybe I had a premonition of what was to come. I needed to recover them before Baresi cottoned on we'd escaped his execution squad. Removing the license plates, I set a fire under the car and rode back to the railroad station.

Sturdy as the small Honda was, we needed better wheels. The station parking lot was awash with CCTV, so I headed a few streets away, found another white Ford rental, and swapped the plates. I was kind of sad to silence the can of angry bees and leave it to its fate. Like a trusty steed tied up outside the abattoir.

Once I'd recovered the bags, I boosted the new Ford and headed through the town. It was a quiet Sunday afternoon. A smattering of tourists and hopeful store-holders. Church bells pealed, summoning the faithful for an afternoon of religious self-flagellation. Even so, the sparse traffic found a reason to rev and hoot. Pigeons scavenged. So did I. My head was still aching, so stopped at a supermarket, bought food, water and fruit.

So much had happened since the Piazza Navona. I used the drive back to filter out the noise. Clearly, Luciano Moretti was part of that; his part now over now. Then there was Baresi. They hired the Sicilian to silence Moretti and anyone else who became involved. I recalled the words of the old man: *Sr. Baresi wishes you to know this is nothing personal. The people we work for want no loose ends.* Baresi was also a hired monkey, just like me. Someone else was the organ grinder.

But who?

Everything centered on Amber Rock. It had to. *DeMarco. Amber Rock and Trueman. An opportunity? €500,000.* Moretti thought it worth big bucks, DeMarco didn't want to pay, silencing him before he could sell the secret. And what now of Max Anderson? Scuppering the *Spirito del Vento* way off course was a ruse. But who carried it out? Amber Rock? Or the Andersons. Max Anderson was and always had been the key to understanding Amber Rock. If I found him, I could warn him to keep his head down.

If he was still alive.

I parked around the back of the farmhouse, fetching the cover off the Citroen, laying it over the Ford. It left a few tire marks on the sunbaked driveway, but one would need to look closely to see them. Steve was still in the same chair, but she had fallen asleep. I tethered the MacBook to my phone, finding a news report on RAI. Bartholdi, the Inspector, appeared on-screen, a furrowed brow and creased shirt, like he hadn't slept, and gabbled something in Italian.

"Do you think he was behind what happened earlier?"

I turned. "I thought you were asleep." Her eyes were two pinpoint reflections of the screen. I passed over the bottle of supermarket water, watched as she took a draft. Felt guilty again for putting her through all this.

She shrugged. "Not much of that about, right now."

"Baresi worked for the Cosa Nostra in Palermo. They have a very long reach. Perhaps he called in some favors?"

Steve moved over and leaned into the computer. "He says the two people recovered from the sea had escaped from custody. They are believed to be armed and dangerous, blah, blah, blah. Something about an audacious gang raid on the hospital, looking for getaway vehicles."

"So, if he was involved, he is trying to distance himself. Better to look like a poor policeman than a crooked one."

"Beckett. When is all this going to end? When does the killing stop?"

I had no answer, so I gave her the best I could manage. "Baresi lost face when we caught him at the apartment. He needs to restore his reputation and the only way he can do so is to silence us—for good. So this stops when either we or Renzo Baresi are dead, Steve."

She returned to the chair in the half-darkness beyond the flickering screen. "So you get Baresi before he gets you?"

"Maybe, but eventually, he will find me. I just have to be ready when he does."

"And me?"

On the way to Cagliari, I had time to think. If I turned her in now, I would condemn her to death. The fact was, Steve also knew too much. If not about Amber Rock, then certainly about Baresi. The people he worked for needed to tie up loose ends. So did he.

Chapter 32

Monday, September 9

That night, Steve didn't want to be alone. I gave her the bed, took a blanket to the uncomfortable chair, and dozed with the Beretta across my knee. I understood the demons stalking her mind because I had my own. Swimming below the surface of my consciousness, hiding around the corners of my memories. Benign, biding their time. Waiting for an opportunity to feast off my naked soul, strip away the flesh of my sanity. And when they are gone, the world returns to normal. What they leave is hardened, annealed to the horror.

I needed to call Pliskin. For now, I let him wait. What could I tell him, except we were alive? He would have seen the news. He would already know. Anyhow, there was nothing to report. No more on Amber Rock. Though I knew Max Anderson had not drowned all those years ago, that was all I knew.

Eventually, Steve's breathing slowed to a regular rhythm as she succumbed to the darkness. The next thing I knew, the room was bathed in the soft glow of morning through the cracks in the shutters. I massaged the cramp out of my back and butt, and opened the last bottle of supermarket water. When Steve roused, her eyes were still distant, like she was somewhere else and had left her body behind to take the flak. I hoped it was somewhere more pleasant, less threatening. Trouble was, I needed her here with me.

"How're you feeling?" I asked.

She turned and stared through me. "Like warmed-up shit." With no make-up, her skin was drawn and ashen except for the dark rings under her eyes. She nodded over to the wicker chair. "You sat there all night?"

"Uh-huh." I stretched my spine, overemphasizing the ache just a little.

"Dickhead. Why didn't you lie on the bed—over the sheets, of course? Maybe you wouldn't have snored so much."

She forced a sardonic smile. The first time since Jardine's boat. I offered her the water bottle. She took a draft, then rubbed her hands over the outside, collecting the condensation and massaging it across her face. I waited for the onslaught, convinced I deserved it, but it didn't come. When she spoke, she was calm and rational.

"I had time to think things over last night—while you snored. I—*understand*—what you did yesterday. It was us or them. I know that, and I understand a Sicilian hitman is gunning for us, and you have to get him before he gets you. And me? I know I could return to Rome, hand myself in, but Baresi would still come after me. Like it or not, this isn't just going to go away."

All I could do was nod.

"So, until we find out what really happened, until the Polizia know Baresi is the actual killer, we must keep going. We must find Max Anderson, or at least find out what became of him."

"Baresi is a dangerous man. What happened on the boat, out there on the hillside. We were lucky. We might not be so lucky next time, and I couldn't have that on my conscience."

"As you said, you just have to be ready when he comes."

***

I needed to clear my head. I left Steve with the Beretta and walked up the clay-brown hillside behind the farm. We had slept in late and the sun was already high, coaxing a million sparrows into song. There must've been a rain shower during the night and the leaves on the unkempt olive and walnut trees glistened a vibrant gray-green. About two-thirds up the hill, a dry-stone wall that had seen better days ran for a hundred yards in each direction. Over it, the land was better kept, the ranks of olive trees heavy with fruit. There was the hiss of irrigation pipes.

A question was buzzing around my mind, like a fly round fresh dung. How could I find someone who had been missing as long as Max Anderson? Assuming he had escaped the *Spirito del Vento* and spent almost three decades undercover, by now he would have *become* his cover. He may even be dead. Around sixty years old, many folks don't make it that far, especially with someone chasing them. Just how had Anderson staged such a perfect disappearance?

I leaned against the wall and looked back down over the derelict farm, then back across to the working farm. Two sides of the economic coin. Times were hard for farmers. Some went under, some had the funds to survive the downturn. It all came down to one thing.

Money.

I'd been on operations for less than a week. My free cash was running short, but I had a charge card and a bank account to top up my funds. Anderson left a well-paid job. When he disappeared, his bank would have frozen his accounts. With no money, almost three decades on the run, how could he and Kate have survived?

There was only one answer. They had planned their escape in advance.

Proof of Life

Chapter 33

"Who are they?" Steve leaned in over my shoulder and peered down at the MacBook. I'd opened up some more of the shuttered windows, lightening up the room, and I could see she'd put on makeup, enlivening her features, disguising the weariness. Her scent prickled my nostrils.

I'd spent some time sending the contents of Moretti's thumb drive to Pliskin, across the slow uplink on my phone. One photo showed a man and a woman seated at a table outside a café. The man wore khaki shorts and a maroon polo shirt. He was squinting against the sunlight, pointing at something out of shot. The woman had long hair, brushed back behind an Alice band. She was leaning her chin on her palm, gazing intently at the man. There were coffee cups on the chintz table cloth.

"Max and Kate Anderson. He'd be older now—if he is still alive. This picture must have been taken before he disappeared in 1990."

The folder, labeled *The Andersons*, contained around forty pictures, mostly featuring Max, Kate, or both. The image files were dated earlier in the year, but I had learned to distrust the metadata on files. If the file has been copied or changed, this date changes, so they could have been taken any time. There was a strange quality to most of them, voyeuristic, as if the Andersons were unaware. A hired photographer, maybe, or a private detective. Which made some sense; if the Andersons were investigating Amber Rock, then maybe someone was investigating them too.

"Do you think they died on the boat?"

Proof of Life

"I don't know, Steve, but my guess is no." Their boat was in the wrong place. Somewhere no one thought of looking. But for Jardine, no one would have found it.

Six years ago, after graduating from Parris Island, the Marines sent me on detachment to the Defense Intelligence Agency in Quantico. With a blizzard blowing in from the sea, a troop carrier had crashed on landing at Andrews. No one had been seriously injured, but even without corpses, it was obvious the plane was carrying passengers. Baggage and other personal effects were strewn about amongst the tangled wreckage. Yet with the *Spirito del Vento*, there was nothing. No clothes, shoes, or books. No mementos, ornaments, or navigational charts. Nothing *personal*. If their killers had scuppered the sailboat, they would have done so with everything inside. As it was, the boat was empty.

Maybe Jardine was right? They had run away, but from whom and to where?

"They seem happy together" I had skipped to another shot of Max and Kate. An easy, candid shot on the deck of a boat, raising a glass of something. Their faces were close, lit brightly by the sun. A moment frozen in time.

"A holiday? They spent a lot of time sailing."

Steve smiled wryly. "Ironic when you think how they are supposed to have died. And it's always the same boat."

All sailboats looked the same to me. After the other day, I tried not to think too hard about them.

"The *Diktynna A*." Steve scrolled to a harbor-side shot, the name across the stern. "Not the *Spirito del Vento*?"

"No," I replied casually. "That was a rental."

"So every picture shows them in the same harbor on the *Diktynna A*, yet they rented a boat for their last ever trip?"

"What are you getting at?"

"I don't know. It's just they seemed to spend all their

time on the *Diktynna A*, so why did they rent one? Surely they could have used their own?"

"Maybe their boat was being repaired, or it's not their boat?"

I opened the folder entitled *Amber Rock - Sentinel Group* and brought up the press clippings. They were from industry magazines, casual photos in lobbies, formal line-outs captioned with names. Always the same group around a restaurant table or seated at a conference. Or standing in a bar, raising a glass. I read the caption below one photo and held my breath.

Sentinel delegates taking a break.

L to R, Harvey Brooks, Carl Hayes - NNSA, Fabrizio Rossi - INFN-LNL, Joanne McKenna, Max Anderson - ONR.

...Harvey Brooks, crashed into a tree on a clear, dry road. Carl Hayes, suicide. Joanne McKenna, fell under a train... I was staring into the eyes of corpses, with Tom Jardine's coarse voice rasping in my head.

"Steve. These are some of the people Jardine spoke about the other night on the sea."

"When you *thought* I was asleep in the cabin."

I frowned. "...Jardine told me of others who had disappeared or been killed. He thought there was a pattern, which is why he was looking for Anderson."

"Todd Gruber. Stacey Carter. Ramon Perez, Carl Hayes, someone called Joanne."

"McKenna. Yes. That's her, and there is Carl Hayes." I pointed at the screen. The five in the photographs having a whale of a time jet-setting across the globe. Did their friendship persist after Max Anderson disappeared? Jardine's stories sounded like wishful thinking; disparate facts knitted into a story. Now I wasn't so sure. The clippings originated before Max and Kate disappeared. The same four

Proof of Life

faces, repeatedly. And a new name—Fabrizio Rossi.

Older now, less hair, Rossi was a Professor Emeritus—*Dipartimento di arricchimento e sicurezza del carburante*—which Google told me meant the Department of Fuel Enrichment and Safety. He worked out of a group of laboratories run by the Italian National Institute of Nuclear Physics, based in Legnaro near Padua, Italy. We could drive to Padua and ask Rossi outright about Max Anderson, but charging into a government institution unannounced with a price on our heads might not be the coolest of moves. Anyway, he would probably clam up. Instead, I found an email address online and, as Franklin Farrell, asked for a meeting. Some bullshit about research. I crossed my fingers and pressed send. If that didn't work, then we would go charging in.

The Andersons both worked for the Nuclear Regulatory Committee, out of London. Max seemed to spend his time attending symposia, becoming pally with like-minded people. In their free time, they enjoyed sailing or at least partying on a boat called *The Diktynna A*. Then something serious happened. Something that led to the deaths of several of Max's colleagues around the world. Max got spooked, and he and Kate staged their disappearance.

What was it Harvey Brooks, Carl Hayes, Joanne McKenna, and the rest found out that got them killed? How did the Andersons stage their own disappearance? I was on the verge of a breakthrough in my search for Max Anderson, like a small child standing on tip-toes to see through a candy store window but only reaching the sill.

***

I left Steve with the MacBook and shut myself in the other room. I dialed Pliskin's number. He answered after one ring.

"Hi, Pliskin."

"Beckett. Good to hear your voice."

"Yeah. Damn near drowned, damn near shot but okay."

"I am relieved. I saw the news broadcasts of your audacious escape from the hospital."

"Less escape, more kidnap and execution." A shudder ran down my spine. I recalled the click of the hammers, Steve whimpering, the bullets missing their mark.

"Anyhow, Beckett, whilst I enjoy chewing the fat, I trust this isn't a social call."

"It's a long shot but I need to know about the Andersons' finances."

"The Andersons? I thought you had come to the end of that particular blind alley?"

"So did I, but it turns out they may have escaped the *Spirito del Vento,* after all. I need you to locate their financial records from the time the Sentinel Group photograph was taken until their banks finally closed the accounts down?"

"I thought I asked you to focus on Amber Rock?" Flat, expressionless, somewhat peeved.

"Believe me, Pliskin, I am, but right now the only road that leads there passes through Max Anderson. If I find him, I will be much closer to Amber Rock. Staging a disappearance takes planning and preparation. Somehow they funded it long enough to make a new life for themselves. If I could follow the money, maybe I could find them, and in turn, learn about Amber Rock."

The line stilled to static. In the background, the coded chirrup of voices. Other handlers, other dilemmas.

"Alright. I will see what I can find. Digital records are sketchy so far back, but there will be information from when they were declared legally dead. There might also be something from the investigation into their deaths."

Proof of Life

"Also, a sailboat called the *Diktynna A*." I spelled the name. "Any chance you can see what you can dig up on it?"

"Unusual name. I'll see what we can do."

"There is one more thing. Steve—Stephanie Jordan, the girl. She needs a new passport with a different identity."

"Beckett?"

"We need to go back to Italy, but we need to keep a couple of steps ahead of Baresi. I have a lead but it's in Italy."

"Honestly? You have a lead? The taxpayers of the world who fund your expensive vacations will be stunned, or are you just yanking my chain again?"

"Okay, more a hunch than a lead. Look, Pliskin, we are as hot as chilies in a sauna right now. If we set one foot outside, Baresi is sure to find out. You need to trust me."

The line stilled as Pliskin considered. "Send me headshots. I have your GPS location. You will have the passport in the morning. And Beckett. I am warning you. You are stretching our patience very thin. You need to give us something, show some progress. One more slip-up and we will recall you—forcibly if necessary—and pass the woman over to the police."

Chapter 34

After less than forty-eight hours, the half-light of the shuttered farmhouse and the claustrophobic smell of must, had become too much. We were both getting antsy.

I read the news pages on my MacBook. Our glorious president was making an ass of himself, and his team was trying to make it sound good. The vice president had become so adept at dodging, he could play interference for the Redskins. But when stupid is in the news, it is usually hiding something important. The president may be an ass, but he is a shrewd one. The ticker read of some furor about power stations and uranium mining contracts, a dock strike in New York, murder in Rome, fugitives on the run in Sardinia. Somehow none of it seemed real.

Uranium Contracts? Dead Nuclear Analysts? Maybe I was thinking about this too deeply?

All we could do now was wait. Wait for Rossi to respond and wait for Pliskin to send a new ID for Steve. I couldn't persuade Rossi to respond. Maybe he never would. So, we looked around. We found tinned food in the larder and bottles of wine under the stairs. Steve suggested a picnic *alfresco* away from the gloom. I rummaged in the kitchen for a corkscrew and a can opener, then we took a blanket and adjourned to the backyard for some fresh air and to find a side of ripe olives and walnuts. Soon the heat of the sun, the chirrup of the cicadas, pulled down my eyelids.

"How long do we wait for the professor?"

I turned to Steve's silhouette against the sun. "I don't know. We can't stay here forever. We need to get off of this goddamn island. Right now, he's our only lead."

She held out the bottle. The wine tasted like battery acid.

"Jeez. Who needs Sicilian hitmen when you got this?" There was a back-taste, the sort you get from cheap mouthwash, or expensive gasoline. It reminded me of the sterilizing solution I used when brewing hooch as a teenager in my dad's shed.

"Tell me, Beckett. Just what is so important about this *Amber Rock*, anyway?"

I hoisted myself onto an elbow, shading my eyes from the sunshine. She was wearing a t-shirt and shorts I'd bought in Civitavecchia. The sun was blushing up her face and, for once, she seemed to have relaxed. To have accepted the situation. To live in the moment. In the end, it is all we have.

"I wish I knew, Steve, but they are prepared to kill to keep it secret, even after almost thirty years."

Out front, the sound of a motorcycle, deep, throaty, rattled off the stone walls. I flipped the safety off the Beretta, and nodded to Steve, who disappeared into the barn. Around the corner of the farmhouse, the rider, a shapely woman dressed from head to foot in black, took an automatic from inside her leathers and cautiously approached the front door.

"You looking for someone?" I eased out from behind the wall, leveled my own gun, and stared down the barrel.

"I'm from Arkham & Brown, sir." The visor muffled her voice. Italian. Clipped vowels. With her free hand, she held up a small white plastic business card.

Hearing no shooting, Steve had garnered the courage to stand behind me. "What the hell is her game?"

"Relax, Steve. Standard operating procedures." I pulled out a similar card and held it aloft. A small LED on the back of the card flashed red, then green. In my pocket, my phone uttered a shrill two-tone beep. The business cards each contained electronics and a small transceiver. Each card read the holder's thumbprint. Then, via our respective satellite phones and the TORUS mainframe, confirmed both cards and holders were genuine. I breathed again.

Still, we both kept our pistols raised.

The biker reached into her top box, pulled out a slim manila package, and placed it on the ground. Then she climbed on her bike, pressed the starter, and disappeared in a rooster-tail of dust. Conversation was not a prerequisite with Pliskin's people.

"What's that?" Steve nodded at the package.

"Pliskin got you a new identity while the Polizia are trashing your old one. It means we can travel over to Padua and see Fabrizio Rossi."

Her brow furrowed. "Ruth Davis? What sort of name is that?"

"Dependable. It's a good name."

"Do I look dependable?"

"Well…" Right now, she looked like a child denied a cookie, brewing a tantrum.

"I've never been to the States, let alone Edgewater, Cleveland." She scratched her short red hair. "And I've got no idea what a computer analyst does!"

"Aw, just put on the fake Yankee accent you Brits love to do and bluff the rest. You'll be fine."

***

At around 8:00 pm, out of the blue, an email arrived from Professor Fabrizio Rossi. It took me by surprise, as I never expected a response. He had replied using a personal email, not the university one I had found. Seems he bought the bullshit story about a research and development project, flattered I thought his advice would be useful. He agreed to meet my alter-ego, Franklin Farrell, and suggested a coffee bar near the IFNF laboratories in Legnaro. I replied with effusive thanks and a suitable time in a couple of days.

I set the alarm on my phone, but I was awake most of the night. The creaks and cracks in the woodwork of the old house left my nerves on edge. Though I knew we were safe, the primeval inside me still saw ghosts in the dark. In the end, I rested my head back, listening to the creaks of the stairs, imagining the people who had walked those treads before. Wondering if anyone would ever walk them again.

PART THREE - VENICE, ITALY

Proof of Life

Chapter 35

Tuesday, September 10

"Where are all the bullet holes?" Steve stood with the tarpaulin raised, staring at the car underneath.

"It's a different car, Steve. One nobody's looking for."

"Except for the poor chap you stole it off."

"It's a rental. The rental company will replace it and claim on their insurance. As far as they know, it's in a chop shop being stripped. Besides, I swapped the plates too."

"Bloody hell! Assassin, burglar, chauvinist, car thief. Is there no end to your talents?"

I winked. "Stick with me, kid. You'll go far."

We were in for a long trip, and I was eager to get off Sardinia. If we made good time, we could be on the return ferry later in the day and travel across Italy at night. Legnaro was in the north, near Padua. Once we landed, nearly ten hours and 800 kilometers away by road.

The ferry was already docked at Olbia, towering above the concrete apron, being turned around for a 12:30 pm sailing back to Civitavecchia. There were some cars in the parking lot, including several white Cinquecentos. Baresi's wasn't amongst them—unless he swapped plates too. I purchased tickets, then parked up off the lot, to grab brunch from a harbor-side cafeteria.

***

Proof of Life

"A penny for them?" I stopped stirring the first proper coffee I'd had in days and looked across at Steve. She was distractedly pushing a fork through a bowl of spaghetti, which was fighting back. Through the salt-dashed plate window, the ferry's funnel was belching soot-black smoke. Port workers in hi-vis vests, pumped diesel, loaded supplies, and whatever else a ferry needed. The boarding lines were a third full; they would only ever get two-thirds full if our trip over was anything to go by. We still had an hour to wait.

"I was thinking about my parents and my sister. What they must be going through."

"Tell me about them." I put down the spoon. Did I really want to know, or was I just being polite? As far as her family knew, she had murdered her boss and been missing for over a week. All they had was the media and hope.

"Not much to tell. Dad is a solicitor, and Mum is a GP. We have a pleasant house in a posh part of Salisbury. The Rotary Club, Women's Institute, golf on a Sunday, then home for a roast. It's all comfortable. Very *British,* really."

"And just a tad boring?"

Steve smiled. "Well, yes, maybe. Mom and Dad are home-birds. Dad deals with family law—probate, divorce. Mom walks two hundred yards to work and back. Charlie's in sixth form, her A-levels."

"Steve and Charlie? Your folks wanted boys?"

She smiled wistfully. "Stephanie and Charlotte. Made us sound like nuns."

"So that's what brought you to Italy? Wanting more?"

"I wanted to see the real world. To experience things beyond the cathedral, beyond the genteel, middle-class *Britishness*. The smells, the sounds, the people."

"Careful what you wish for…"

"Indeed. Not quite what I had in mind."

"And then some. They approve of your wanderlust?"

"Oh, they are okay with it. They still have Charlie."

"But?"

"But when she goes off to university, I am not sure how they will cope with an empty nest."

"Your folks will be fine. Sure they will worry, but they will worry less each time your face appears on the BBC. They may not know how much trouble you are in, but they know you are alive. Trouble has a habit of working itself out."

I could tell from her eyes she wasn't convinced.

"And you Beckett? Where's home for you?"

A small alarm began to ring in my head.

"Bethesda, Maryland. Not that I see it much."

The house in which Joe and Pat Wexler raised me as their adopted son resounded with their memories and echoed their absence. No one was missing me. No one tuned in to the BBC to see my face. No one cared I was alive—except Baresi. And then it was for all the wrong reasons.

"And what do your parents think of your *profession*?"

When I joined the Marines, Mom was still alive, and Dad had all his marbles. To be honest, they were glad to see me go. I was a rebellious teen. Somehow, they adjusted. Or did they just sit in the wingbacks watching Oprah all day until I returned on furlough?

"Mom died and Dad is in a care home. He doesn't think much about anything anymore—except jigsaws."

"I'm sorry, Beckett." She laid a hand gently over mine. My body shuddered, the touch of another person. Unfamiliar. I smiled at her and drew my hand away. The alarm sounded louder.

Name, rank, and serial number, soldier.

Proof of Life

"Ah, it's okay. I was adopted before I was two. I have no memory of my actual parents, so nothing to miss."

Steve turned back to her spaghetti, slightly abashed. "Do you ever think of them? Your actual parents?"

"Rarely," I replied. The truth was, I thought of them all the time. Especially now. "My Dad used to say, the past is a closed book, the future is an undiscovered country, and all we can change is the present."

"Wise man."

"He was."

"You think you'll ever look for them?"

"I've always thought no, but just lately, I get the feeling they're looking for me."

***

The vehicle boarding lot was busier when we returned to the port. I joined the line, now less conspicuous amongst the horde of other vehicles. It's harder to hit a moving target, so I was eager to start the road trip across Italy and find another bolt hole until we met with Rossi.

No one appeared to be looking out for us. The Carabinieri sat in their cars, idly watching the queue of foot passengers, ferry attendants in their two-tone blue uniforms and official peak caps, seemed unconcerned as they smoked themselves sick and enjoyed the sunshine. When it was time to load up, they swung their arms like pendulums, beckoning the cars aboard, as if their lives depended upon it. Maybe they all secretly hoped the two fugitives *would* board and become someone else's problem?

With another eight-hour crossing to fill, we bought beer and candy, and hunkered down in the quietest spot we could find, next to a view of the sea. In the main lounge, the TV screens were still showing the news on loop. There were no pictures of us now, just a byline in the ticker and a paragraph in the quarter-hour update. But then, who in their right mind would try to enter a country where they were already wanted for multiple homicide?

Who indeed?

Proof of Life

Chapter 36

The crossing to Civitavecchia passed without incident. Onboard, I purchased new shades and baseball caps, complete with the ferry line's logo, to replace the ones we lost on the *Genevieve*. Then I spent the trip dozing, half-heartedly scrutinizing the other passengers. The daytime crossing was more animated than the nighttime one, the undercurrent of chatter louder, the people more restive. Steve lolled against her arm, watching the waves go by. In Renzo Baresi's place, I would have eyes on the ferry. Cameras. Someone at the docks, maybe even boarding as a passenger, watching for a tall American and a petite auburn-haired English girl. But I spotted no one; not even so much as a furtive glance as we took comfort breaks. Maybe he still believed we were face down on a hillside being picked at by crows? Maybe he knew we weren't? That we had boarded a ferry and were sitting ducks when the ferry docked?

Baresi had my Glock, but I still had his S&W and all my spare ammunition, which I'd left in the railroad station locker. I also had the old man's Beretta. With the rounds I'd taken from the other faux officers, it amounted to twenty. Enough for protection, not enough for a gunfight. If anyone came hunting, I would need to be frugal, creative, or both.

By late evening, the orange bowl of Civitavecchia loomed large on the dark coast. I nudged Steve and together we beat the rush down to the vehicle decks. Before long, a guy in a hi-vis vest unbuckled our Ford and started swinging his pendulum arms.

The INFN-LNL, where Fabrizio Rossi worked, was

around five hours away with no traffic. The route drove inland to the romantically named *Autostrada del Sol*, or Motorway of the Sun, one of Europe's oldest highways running from Naples all the way North to Milan, apparently cutting travel time along the spine of Italy from days to a matter of hours. We would take a diagonal path from the Tyrrhenian Sea in the west to the Adriatic coast in the east, arriving in the early hours of the next morning. I'd traveled the road before, with my parents, stopping along the way in Orvieto, Siena, Florence, Bologna, even taking a detour to Pisa. There was so much to see, yet tonight we would pass it all, unseen beyond our snaking tunnel of headlights.

***

"What are you thinking about, Beckett?"

We'd been traveling North for around an hour. The traffic was sparse. Lumbering articulated trucks getting a head-start on the day. Coaches thundering along while oblivious tourists snorted and snored. A smattering of workers, leaving their loved ones for trips away.

"Ah, nothing."

"You've been quiet since we docked," she said. The lights from the dash caught a curious smile on her lips, a sparkle in her eye as if she could read my mind. I hoped she couldn't. No one should go there. The top of my hand still bore the memory of her touch, and it concerned me.

I had been thinking about us—Steve and me. Or more accurately, not us.

For some men, the opposite sex are just other people. They can laugh and joke, work, play, and flirt. They can separate love from lust, sex from passion, romance from a roll in the hay. They can breeze through relationships like a .38 caliber through jello, devoid of the emotional attachment that reduces other mere mortals to simpering fools. And then there are those like me. Relationships are a rollercoaster, either high on the passion of the moment, or deep in the misery of its absence. Full-on or full-off. Every relationship immediate and forever until the inevitable moment there no longer was one. Or I realized there never was one; it was just my mind playing dirty tricks. So I avoided getting close wherever I could. I suppressed that side of my nature, or at least tried to ignore it. But right now, with Steve, I was on the tipping point and I was in no hurry to pull back. That's the problem with women. They play on the irrational side of your brain.

Bottom line? When all this was over, when the job was done, she would fly back to England and me to the States. I would never see her again. Because, while I worked for TORUS, there could never be an *us*. Not with anyone.

"I was thinking about you and me."

There, you fool, you said it.

Steve shifted in her seat, her face now lost in shadow, unreadable. "Me and you? In what respect?"

I had faced ruthless drugs gangs in Colombia and Guatemala, cleared a street of insurgents in Basra, but this felt like stumbling over hot coals trying to ignore the pain. I kept my eyes on the road, on the ribbon of yellow-orange opening up in the beam of the headlights, on the rhythmic *thud-thud* of expansion seams in the road, tied up in my embarrassment. I hoped she was teasing. I hoped a team of dissidents would ambush the car and give me something else to focus on. She reached a hand across, laid it on my arm. Another shudder of excitement, of terror, I wasn't sure.

"Let's take each day as it comes, eh? Like you said yesterday, it's best not to think too far ahead."

Each day as it comes. I could live with that.

Proof of Life

Chapter 37

Wednesday, September 11

Legnaro is a nondescript dormitory town about four klicks south-east of the city of Padua. The INFN—the Istituto Nazionale di Fisica Nucleare—occupied a modern business park, cheek to jowl with other complementary scientific institutions. Share coffee, share staff, share secrets, that sort of thing. Professor Fabrizio Rossi, however, had decided against meeting there, preferring instead a small café just off the town center at 10:00 am. Maybe he had some secrets he wanted to keep to himself.

We arrived in the early hours, with Steve asleep beside me. I turned off at a sprawling service area, so we could get gas, have breakfast, and not be noticed. Even though I'd swapped our rental's license plates with an identical white Ford, they still bore a Cagliari provincial code which stuck out like a baboon's butt in the snow. So out in the boondocks, I took my screwdriver and swapped plates again with a late model Fiat. Hopefully, it should keep the Carabinieri guessing for a while. Then Steve and I crossed between the parked-up trucks and found the restrooms.

According to Wikipedia, Fabrizio Rossi was seventy-six years old, a *professor emeritus*. They obviously thought he'd earned his corn or were keeping him on out of kindness. Or because he had nowhere else to go. The page cited a string of awards and commendations for things I didn't understand. He'd worked extensively in nuclear cold fusion and had more than a passing interest in the Large Hadron Collider. The rest went over my head. There was a single line about his involvement in the Sentinel Group. Around the time of Max Anderson's disappearance, Rossi had been a vocal proponent of nuclear energy when its popularity was at rock bottom. The price of uranium ore on the open market had plummeted. His projects revolved around quick, easier, cheaper methods of extraction and refinement. Another guy swimming against the tide. I couldn't help thinking it must be significant. The research he undertook was not cheap, so somebody must have been footing the bill. Unfortunately, Wikipedia was short on detail there.

We took our time over coffee and pastries. No sense arriving early to meet an academic whose idea of time-keeping probably relied on a sundial. So, by the time of the rendezvous, or *appuntamento*, as Steve corrected, the traffic had congealed into a sinuous living creature around the streets of the small town. The café itself was more a trattoria, set back between a couple of small shopping complexes, with tables screened off from the traffic by rows of potted conifers. I parked up in the pay-and-display lot across the road. A few more absurd European coins for the privacy of walls on three sides.

The café was more or less deserted, echoing to the metallic clanks and thuds of coffee machines and the hiss of steam. Waitresses gossiped as they sprayed cleaner and ran a cloth over the tables. A few patrons on high stools at the ornately curved polished wood bar gesticulated and shouted—like every other middle-aged Italian I had ever seen. We found an empty table at the back, next to a designer-distressed fireplace. Beside it, a sad spindly pot plant pleaded for *acqua e luce*. What is it with Europeans and potted plants they can't keep them watered?

After a few minutes, a rather effete waiter sauntered over with our drinks and an overweight woman peered around the mock Doric pillars, muttered *Ciao,* then left. I checked my watch. Rossi was late. He had suggested I carry a *New*

Scientist magazine and, ever the one for cold-war melodrama, I had purchased a copy. As it was in Italian, so I was reduced to looking at the pictures. Still, for the drama to be complete, he had actually to turn up.

I glanced at Steve. "I hope he's not going to stand us up."

She smiled. "Give him a chance. He's only a couple of minutes late. Read your comic and relax." She sipped her latte and burned her tongue. She was far from relaxed. Even the relative solitude of the booth was far too public, given her star status in Italy. I flicked impatiently through the magazine, catching snippets of text I understood and loads of science I didn't. There was a story on uranium mining, pictures of Kazakhstan, Canada, the mid-west United States, Australia, but I didn't have enough Italian. I recalled the news the other day. It had mentioned uranium. Was this the news the president was trying to bury with his idiotic antics? But then, there had been a high-school shooting, monsoon deaths in India, and a mountain of other bad news too.

Still, uranium featured a lot in the news right now. Rossi's specialty. Was uranium the reason for Amber Rock's resurgence after thirty years below the surface?

Steve nudged my elbow. "He's here, I think."

I checked my watch. "Only forty-five minutes late, then."

Rossi was easily recognizable from the photos on Moretti's computer; time had been kind to him. He was short, slim, and severe, with an unruly mop of receding gray-white hair, and spectacles on a chain around his neck. With brown corduroys, a bottle-green check shirt, and a creased blue blazer, it looked like he had got dressed in the dark. But his brown eyes were sharp and probing.

"Signor Farrell?" Round vowels coping with the English, subdued and conspiratorial. Too quiet even for the waitress who followed him for his order. I nodded and maneuvered the *New Scientist* pointedly. He flicked an eye briefly at Steve.

"This is a colleague, Ruth Davis. You wanna coffee?"

Rossi turned his head and peered at the waitress. "Un espresso, per favore." She scurried away. He screeched out a chair and sighed his way into it.

"So, Sr. Farrell…"

"Franklin, please." I drawled affectedly, offering a hand.

"Thank you. Of course, Franklin. What is it I can do for you? You mentioned land reclamation?"

"Yes, sir. My company is in land reclamation, brownfield and polluted sites. We are looking to acquire some of the old mining sites in the States and redevelop them for commercial use but first, we have to clean them up."

"And how can I help?"

"Well, sir, these are uranium mining sites, so there is spoil contamination and radiation, settlement pools, not to mention the other chemicals used in the leaching process. This is your area of expertise?"

The old man straightened up and raised his eyebrows, impressed with the knowledge I had gleaned from the TV news over the last few days. "I am flattered, Sr. Farrell. Yes indeed, this used to be my field of expertise in the Department of Fuel Enrichment and Safety but you must know I am retired now."

"Yes, sir, but you are still renowned in your field. A *professor emeritus*, no less."

The old man's brow furrowed. His first attempt to dodge had failed. He tried again. "I'd heard the US was considering reopening some of these mines? Would it not be better to purchase the land and sell it back to them for a profit?"

"True, signor, but many of the old sites are depleted. Those are the ones we will be targeting first." I was rapidly reaching the extent of my knowledge.

I sat back, pleased with my counter-play, but Rossi again raised an eyebrow as the waitress returned with his espresso.

"The older the facility, the worse the problems of decontamination. They buried radioactive sludge in the early facilities, even the residues of uranium in the tunnels and the old processing plant. With a half-life of anywhere between 25,000 and 4.5 billion years, it would all need to be removed. And the radon risk as the radioactive uranium decays. The increased risk of kidney dysfunction and cancers through the emission of beta and lambda radiation. All this would eat away any profit you might make later."

"Radon. Yes." I was out of my depth. Staring down at the *New Scientist*, I wished I could read Italian.

Rossi sipped his espresso and laid it down on the table, precisely and theatrically. Then he leaned forward and scrutinized us both, taking his time.

"Just who are you, Sr. Farrell. Who are you, really?"

Proof of Life

Chapter 38

"Alpha radiation," spat Rossi. "Uranium emits *alpha* radiation. Anyone who knew their subject would have corrected me. So I ask again. Who are you, and what do you really want?"

I pushed the *New Scientist* aside, regarded the old scientist. Behind the small, round spectacles, Rossi's eyes had sharpened. The old man became more guarded. He pulled his flimsy jacket about him, scratched a stubbled cheek.

"We are trying to find Max Anderson."

Rossi chuckled. "Max Anderson? I have not heard that name for many years." He waved a hand dismissively. "I am afraid you are wasting your time. You must know Max Anderson and his wife died a long time ago."

I passed across my cellphone, the group photo from the symposium. "This was taken in the early '90s. The Sentinel Group. You recall it?"

"Vaguely. What of it?"

I pointed at each person in turn. "Harvey Brooks, Carl Hayes, Joanne McKenna? They're all dead too."

Rossi ran a hand through his hair. He labored over another sip of espresso. When he spoke, his voice raised half an octave, mock astonishment. "The photograph was taken a long time ago. People die. Such is life. They had stressful jobs. Accidents happen, even suicide."

"I accept that, sir, but falling from buildings, car accidents with no apparent cause, suicide, boating accident? Falling under a train? And this wasn't over many years. They all died between 1987 and 1990, and there were more before, maybe even more afterward. But not you? Out of the people in this photograph, three are dead, one is missing, and only you have survived. Maybe it's the Mediterranean diet, Professore? All that olive oil?"

"What are you implying?" Rossi took off his spectacles, letting them swing on their lanyard, and stood sharply. "I don't have to sit here and be bullied by—*you*." He sunk the rest of the espresso and pushed away his chair noisily. I played a high card.

"I believe Max Anderson survived the boating accident."

Rossi stopped and turned. His eyes studied us, looking for the bluff. Then he clicked back on message. "Anderson is dead. He died in 1990. You are wasting your time."

"No, Professore. I dove on the boat, on the seabed. It was scuttled, and the Andersons were not on board."

"Ridiculous!" Again the sneer, but this time his eyes betrayed him. "Max and Kate Anderson were lost on their way to Malta nearly thirty years ago. No one found the boat!"

"That was the story, sir, but the sailboat went down nearly 800kms off-course. Someone cleaned her out, locked the cabin doors, then scuttled her. There was no sign of the Andersons. No luggage, no personal effects, nothing."

"Anderson is dead. The matter is closed. If you go hunting his ghost, all you will find is trouble."

I smiled. "Yes. Everyone keeps telling me that."

"And you should take their advice," he said wide-eyed, earnest. Again, he turned to leave.

"What about Amber Rock?" It was Steve, from left field.

He puffed, obviously tired of the conversation, the merest hint of panic crossing his face.

"What do you know?" He sat back down, leaned his

elbows on the table, eyes narrow and challenging. "A boat whose whereabouts are vague. A series of explainable deaths over a period of time. You know nothing—because there is *nothing to know*." He slammed the table slightly too heavily, rattling the condiments. "As you Americans say, shit happens. All these deaths, the Andersons' disappearance; they were all investigated. There is no evidence to support anything but unfortunate accidents."

Of course, he was right, and he'd called our bluff. We knew nothing of any note. Just fragments of information floating around a sea of supposition. So why was he so rattled? I reached into my jacket, took out my pocketbook, and removed the pendant. I had cleaned some of the staining off of it. Though the enamel was old and discolored, the image was clearer. A snake writhing across the surface, balancing a ball on its tail. The word *Akurra* enameled above.

"I found this in the boat, Sr. Rossi."

The professor settled back into his chair and stared at it for a long moment, flipped it over, glanced at the back, and raised his eyebrows. Then he abruptly handed it back, rubbed a hand across his tired face, and sighed.

"I am sorry I cannot help you. It was a long time ago. It will serve no purpose to dig up the past, I assure you."

I was pushing the right buttons. I just needed to push a little harder. "Harvey Brooks, Carl Hayes, Joanne McKenna, Max Anderson. All involved in Amber Rock. All died under suspicious circumstances. Now I have positive evidence one of them may still be alive. Don't you have any interest at all in knowing what became of the Andersons?"

Rossi glanced nervously over his shoulder; there were no bugs, no cameras, no one listening in. Even so, he looked. I figured he had probably looked over that shoulder most of his life. Pulling a pen from his pocket and a napkin from the holder, he scribbled down a few words.

"We can't talk about this now. Meet me here, 9:00 pm tonight. Tell no one and make sure no one follows you." As he slid the pen back into his pocket, he pursed his lips and sighed.

"You should let the sleeping dogs lie, Sr. Farrell. They have the habit of coming back to bite you."

Chapter 39

We watched Rossi bluster through the door, rattling window blinds, stilling the hubbub for a second. Steve picked up the pendant, licked a finger, and rubbed at the image of the snake, bringing a luster to the maroon enamel.

"Where did you say you got this, Beckett?" I sensed she was a little peeved. Another confidence she wasn't party to.

"From the *Spirito del Vento*. It was hanging on the locked cabin door handle—on the inside. It was the only tangible evidence that anyone was on board before she sank."

Steve peered closer. "Do you know what it represents?"

"Back in Sardinia, when I couldn't sleep, I looked it up on the internet. I think it's the rainbow serpent, an Australian symbol, but other than that…"

"*Akurra*. What is that? A place?" She ran her finger across the word etched on the surface.

I shrugged. "I think it's the name of the snake. The pendant is probably a keepsake, left behind in their hurry to leave the sinking boat."

But that wasn't what I believed. I was sure they had left it there for me—just me—to find.

"Do you trust Professor Rossi?"

I was asking myself the same thing. "What do you think?"

"About as far as I could throw him," she snorted.

I raised my eyebrows. "They have laws against geriatric abuse in the US." But I understood. He was obviously being evasive, but at the same time, fishing, trying to find out what we knew. Understandably, he was nervous. Over the years, he too had witnessed the deaths of a long string of industry colleagues, of close friends even. Perhaps he assumed, in old age, he'd shaken off Amber Rock. That until we turned up, they had forgotten him.

"I guess we have to trust him. We have nothing else."

Steve puffed deeply and laid out the pendant. "It could be a trap."

"We don't have a choice. You saw his reaction. He knew something. We have to keep close, watch each other's back."

She reached over and picked up the napkin.

"Venice?" Her voice raised an octave, and her eyes widened, somewhat bemused. "Really?"

"Uh-huh. We are only thirty miles away." The handwriting was scrappy, the ink slightly leached on the napkin, but there was no mistaking the location Rossi had chosen for our assignation later.

"I've never been to Venice," Steve remarked.

"We'd better make a move then."

Chapter 40

We reached the causeway across to Venice, around 1:30 pm, following the signs over the shimmering lagoon, to the port at the north-west corner of the city. On our right, the colossal cruise liners towered above the harbor-side buildings, adding thousands of bodies to the oppressive jam in the city, all of which would mysteriously vanish at tea-time when the all-inclusive buffets came out. Beyond the port, Venice had no roads, so we left the car at the bus terminus and progressed into the rabbit warren on foot. The Beretta nestled in the crook of my back. I hoped it would stay there. In the narrow alleys of Venice, it would wake the dead.

Our assignation with Rossi was several hours away; several hours pounding the unforgiving sidewalks of the city. I didn't know how long the meeting would last, maybe an hour, seconds if he got cold feet, so I phoned ahead and booked a hotel in Mestre to give us time to plan our next move. I used Franklin Farrell's charge card. At least Pliskin knew where we were heading when he picked up the tab—if the cost didn't give him a coronary first.

Venice was an enigma. I'd been there many times with my parents, alone and on furlough with a group of buddies. I never grew tired of it. A city perched above the water on millions of ancient log piles driven into the mud beneath, bisected by the busy, serpentine Grand Canal. The only thing holding it together was the discarded chewing gum on the sidewalks. One day, the water would rise, or the city would sink, but for now, it remained a unique renaissance theme park, more often these days, a paddling pool. A few years ago, jostling amongst the tourists in front of the Doge's palace, I watched the moored gondolas bumping and splashing as a mammoth cruise ship inched through the lagoon. How long could the twenty-first and fifteenth centuries endure each other before one conceded defeat, or the other saw sense?

"You been here before?" I was a kid anticipating a visit to the candy store.

"No, not yet. Not sure I want to be here now." Steve had been quiet the whole way from Legnaro. She simply didn't trust Rossi. Beside me, she was craning up at the architecture or down into the murk of the canals, probably wondering what the heck I was leading her into now.

"It's okay. It's truly magical but also a little scary at night. Lots of alleyways. Easy to get lost."

"You're not reassuring me, Beckett."

With time to kill, we wound a path across to the Grand Canal, to the colorful, aromatic *Campo de la Pescaria*, the fish market, whiled away a few minutes behind the stalls that topped the Rialto Bridge, gazing out at the array of watercraft churning up the aquamarine water. Then, we followed the yellow signs high on the wall—*Per San Marco* towards Saint Mark's Basilica. After a quarter of an hour, we reached the unrivaled splendor of the Piazza San Marco and the imposing Byzantine Basilica.

"Hey Steve, See those horses up there?" I pointed up at the arches of the Basilica, the horses rampaging over the balcony. "The Venetians stole them during the sacking of Constantinople in 1204. In 1797, Napoleon Bonaparte used them as models for the ones on top of the Arc de Triomphe. Those collars around their necks? They were added because the Venetians cut off their heads to get them on their boats."

Steve folded her arms and looked at me. "And you know those aren't the actual horses? They're copies. The real ones are on the inside of the Basilica?"

"Well, yes. I was getting on to that."

"And they rebuilt the Campanile in the early twentieth century after it collapsed?"

I sighed.

"And the face of the Torre dell'Orologio was not destroyed by a James Bond villain crashing through to his death, contrary to popular belief?"

"Ah, c'mon, Steve. I love this place."

"So bring me back when there isn't a price on my head. Look, we've done the sights, now can we get out of this bloody great big open space? I keep thinking, any minute now, I'm going to hear a bang and it'll all be over."

"Take it from me, lady, you wouldn't hear the bang."

***

Refusing the eye-wateringly expensive coffee at the Caffè Florian, I headed across town to the Campo Santi Giovanni e Paolo, a gothic cathedral off the beaten track. Adjacent, the Scuola Grande di San Marco boasted magnificent 3D trompe l'oeil relief panels. Refusing even those, Steve dragged me to a restaurant where we could hide under the canopy of parasols, with our backs to a wall.

Okay, I was pissed. Venice is *Disneyland* for history nuts, and when your dad is a history nut, it kinda rubs off a little. Looking at Steve moping, sucking coke through a straw, I saw my mom. Putting on a brave face, hoping it would soon be over. And I got it. We may be walking into a trap. This was not my first rodeo. In Helmand, the roads were littered with improvised explosive devices—IEDs. The next mile, the next yard, the next step, could be our last. So we kept the banter up and our eyes down. Even then, we missed a few.

Now, we were in Venice, amongst a million tourists. Surely we could take a beat to enjoy the linguine?

Proof of Life

Still, Rossi's choice of meeting place didn't help. A long life in a highly paid professorship afforded him a residence in the upmarket district of Santa Croce, but he hadn't invited us there. Instead, he'd suggested neutral ground—the Scala Contarini del Bovolo, or as Steve informed me, *The Contarini's Snail Staircase*, a weird folly languishing in a rarely visited corner of the floating city.

***

At night, Venice took on a different personality, quickening the heart and making the blood run cold. The sun had fallen behind the tall buildings, and the tourists had deserted the dark alleys for the lights of the Piazza San Marco. The nearer we got to the Palazzo Contarini del Bovolo, the louder my military training was screaming at me to turn back. But we would not get a second chance with Rossi. Maybe we were already too late? Maybe he was scuppering his own sailboat and disappearing?

Using a tiny, creased map purloined from a street vendor, we followed the canyon of claustrophobic alleyways. Away from the tourist traps, it was narrow and dark, ranks of doors and windows caked with a centuries-old fur of dust and dirt. Ill-lit tunnels of orange light, ending in an abrupt drop into a murky canal or a frustrating rendered wall daubed with graffiti. The place had an air of purposeful dilapidation, an odor of mold and drains. Then, as my hopes of ever finding the place were fading, we came across an archway above which, lit by a puny incandescent bulb, a sign proclaimed *Scala Contario del Bovolo*.

"Not sure I like this." Steve was keeping close, peering apprehensively down the passage. Over her shoulder, twenty yards away, a slit of amber cut the absolute black of the passageway. The hair on my neck stood on end.

"Just keep your wits about you. Keep your back to the wall and be careful of windows and doorways."

"You sure know how to show a girl a good time."

Several missed heartbeats later, we emerged in the relative brightness of the *Corte del Bovolo,* about the size of a tennis court, overlooked by shuttered apartment windows. Fallen render, creeping black mold up dirty walls, gave it the same air of neglect as the rest of the city's backstreets. The sorry lawn, sun-bleached green and brown, dotted with wellheads and small empty plinths, looked like a graveyard. Surrounded by high black railings, it threatened hidden assassins, sudden ambush, death.

The palazzo itself, and its ornate staircase, deserved the epithet. A sweeping snail-shell forming a turret of high arches spiraling to the rooftops. But under a single street lamp, there was an unsettling Gothic feel. Long shadows and dark windows, swathes of fathomless black. Steve linked an arm through mine. It felt good, but my heart was beating fit to burst, my mouth was dry. All I wanted to do was run.

The gate was unlocked, squealing like a stuck pig as we inched through. Rossi was already here. Letting the Beretta lead the way, we climbed the steps.

"Sr. Farrell."

Steve let out a small squeak, and my heart almost ripped from my chest. I swung the gun toward the voice.

"Please put that away. I am unarmed. All I have is my intellect. Some say I have lost that lately." From the darkness, Professor Rossi chuckled nervously. Slowly, my eyes adjusted. He was on the landing above, an ethereal, floating face in the dim green of the emergency lights.

"Are you alone?" I asked.

"Can anyone truly be alone in a city as densely populated as this?" Rossi came out from the shadows. His long overcoat buttoned to the lapels. A voluminous yellow check scarf billowed from the top, cradling his round head.

Not a straight yes or no.

"What is this place?" Steve was rubbing her arms. The night was drawing in, and the air had turned damp and cold.

"Come with me. I'll show you." Rossi crooked a finger. "Let us take the stairs up to the highest arcade. You will thank me for the view."

Yeah, and the long drop.

Against my better judgment, I followed him up three flights of marble steps, with Steve close behind. The curved walls were sandpaper under my fingers, recent patching to age-old weathering, the steps worn concave under my feet. Outside, the rooftops descended lower, and the darkness of the sky closed in around us. Finally, in front of us, a single straight narrow staircase led up to the highest arcade.

I recalled Moretti's apartment, the narrow stairs, the door. A profound feeling of *déjà vu* hit me.

Chapter 41

The uppermost landing opened onto a circular arcade. Timber domed and surrounded by arched windows, it looked out over an undulating mountain range of pan-tiled rooftops, tinted by a weak moonlight, and punctuated with TV antennae and dim-lit dormer windows. A handful of campaniles, sodium orange against the darkening sky, and the grandest of them all, the *Campanile di San Marco*.

Rossi was admiring the Venetian skyline, a silhouette against the balustrade. I had to give him his due. The view was spectacular.

"The Contarini family acquired the palazzo in the 1480s when it was actually two separate buildings—an older part, late Gothic, and a more recent rectangular building. Pietro Contarini considered it inadequate to express the prestige and grandeur of such a powerful family, so he commissioned the architect, Giorgio Candi, to join the two parts with a tower. Unfortunately, that was forbidden by order of the Doge, who wanted the *Campanile di San Marco* to command the skyline, so Candi got creative. He added something that *was* permitted—a staircase. Only, he attached it to the outside of the buildings, extending beyond the roofline. So from this arcade, the Contarinis could thumb their noses at the Doge and his rules."

I listened, somewhat distractedly. Maybe if I took an interest in this crumbling pile, he would be more forthcoming on other matters. Steve looked over the balustrade, puffed her cheeks, and retreated inside the room to read the visitor's information board.

Proof of Life

Rossi turned his back on the view, one side shrouded in darkness, the other lit by the moon, a man divided. "So, tell me, Sr. Farrell. Just what do you want with me?"

You have to give to receive. So I told him of Moretti, of Steve's plight, of my search for Amber Rock. The discovery of Max Anderson's boat. That he may still be alive. Rossi stood motionless, letting the silence soak into the air before turning dismissively back to the view. "You are wasting your time. Max and Kate Anderson died when their boat sank. Metaphorically, if not literally."

"So you said? Then why this charade, the whole cloak and dagger thing?"

He turned back to the skyline. "I love this city, its antiquated architecture, the narrow streets, the chaos. I love the whole theater of life here. Take this building. A folly, a joke, its story lost in a back street. Like Max Anderson. He has hidden for thirty years. His story too is lost."

"Present tense? So, you believe he is alive too?"

Even in the gloom, I could see Rossi's shoulders rise and fall. Another chuckle. "Who knows?"

"But he didn't drown in the Mediterranean Sea?" Steve spoke from the darkness at the top of the stairs.

"I think that is obvious to us all, don't you, my dear?" Rossi's tone was condescending. I bet his students loved that. Steve let it go.

"So, Professore," I asked again. "Why all this cloak and dagger?"

"You remind me of Anderson. Inquisitive, intelligent. Like you, he asked many questions, made some powerful enemies. Secrets. Some have a half-life longer than uranium and are twice as deadly."

Across the rooftops, a bell rang mournfully. The wind gusted around the stone pillars. Rossi pushed off the balustrade and stepped into the moonlit arcade. He sighed as if an immense tiredness descended upon him.

"The '80s and '90s were turbulent times for the Nuclear industry, Sr. Farrell. I was a professor at the IFNF; one of the foremost experts in my field. They asked me to head up the Sentinel Group, an international working party, set up by the World Health Organization, overseeing the nuclear industry. That's where I met Anderson. He worked for the Office for Nuclear Regulation in London. Brooks, Hayes, McKenna, Anderson, and myself. We were all advisers to Sentinel. We met regularly, four, maybe five times a year, somewhere in the world."

"To cut a long story short, in 1982 something went wrong—badly wrong. Something that reflected poorly on me and would eventually come to the attention of the Sentinel Group. For a year or so, I kept it hidden, but I was working with the best minds in their field. Brooks, Hayes, McKenna, and Anderson. Soon they started piecing things together. Snippets here, memos there. I had to act to protect everyone—to protect myself."

"So you killed them?"

"I didn't kill them," he snorted, offended by the accusation. "I am just a pawn in this game. There are much more powerful people at work than a mere professore."

I played a hunch. "Who? Trueman? DeMarco?, Velasquez? Gilbués." Moretti thought these names important. Rossi ignored the interruption.

"Harvey, Carl, Joanne, Max. They stuck their noses in where they didn't belong. They were all warned off and didn't listen. Only Max saw sense. He learned the wisdom of silence. Now and again, a rumor surfaces. When it does, it is squashed."

"And the pendant? What's it's significance?"

"Just a keepsake." Rossi reached out. He dropped

something into my palm. A disc on a chain, glinting gold. Whether he could see the puzzlement on my face or just knew it was there, he continued. "We each had one. A souvenir from a conference in Melbourne. Our last conference together."

I turned it into the light, ran my thumb over the enamel, clearer than the one I had found. A zigzag pattern of green, blue, and red across the back of a writhing serpent, on a bed of engine-turned gold. Over the head, the word *Akurra* in black enamel. I turned it over. The same engine-turning but no engraving.

"So, what is the image? The rainbow serpent?"

"Serpent?" Rossi retorted, scornfully. "You know nothing, Farrell."

"So, enlighten me," I snapped. I was sick of playing games.

"Enlighten you? Why should I *enlighten* you? These people will stop at nothing to keep their secrets hidden. Moretti thought he was untouchable. Thought he could profit from Amber Rock. Now he knows better."

"Amber Rock?"

"See?" Rossi smirked patronizingly, a guardian with faint praise for a ward who had gotten his math right. "You already know too much. If you find Max Anderson, he will join all your dots together. Then everything they have worked for will be under threat. Almost forty years ensuring the secret remains hidden. They will not allow that. *I* cannot allow that."

The dark tower, the silver-gray light of the moon, the half-silhouette of a crazed professor. Had we drifted into a 1940s B-Movie? All this melodrama was raising the hackles on the back of my neck. The feeling we had indeed walked into a trap. Wondering how long until it was sprung.

"You expect me to cease and desist? To return to the States, tell my boss Amber Rock is a myth, and get amnesia? To ignore the possibility Anderson may still be alive?"

Rossi's eyes fell to his feet, then locked onto mine, catching the light, cold and steely. Behind him, a door opened, lighting the gallery, and a familiar tall, balding figure stepped out.

"To paraphrase Ian Fleming—no, Sr. *Beckett*. I expect you to die."

Proof of Life

Chapter 42

As Baresi raised his gun, I threw myself into the shadows. A bullet gouged plaster from the wall behind me. The Sicilian advanced from the shadows. In his hand was my Glock fitted with the silencer, recovered from the *Genevieve* when he half-caved in my skull. I envied him. The Beretta was a popgun in comparison, but it ain't what you're packing, it's how you use it. I sent a couple toward him, pock-marking the walls.

"Baresi. This is becoming a bit of a habit. Don't you have a life?"

"Tell me about it," he sighed, his voice full of ennui. "I am seriously out of pocket with this job and I really want to go home, but a deal is a deal. My hands are tied."

"Makes a change from *my* hands." My joke fell flatter than an undercooked souffle. A cough and a round ricocheted off the floor.

"Where's the girl?" Baresi too was keeping to the shadows.

"Probably getting a pizza. She's frightened of the dark." The barrel of the Glock flashed orange, and another round bit the floor at my feet. I stood firm. "You need her too, Baresi. We both know that."

"She is here somewhere. You both arrived together. How long do you think she can hide from me, eh? She's *una segretaria*. Without you, I give her five minutes."

"Per l'amor di Dio." Rossi threw his arms up in despair. "We don't have time for these silly games. Kill him!"

Proof of Life

"Don't lecture me, old man," barked Baresi. "If you are in such a hurry, shoot him yourself. I am always clearing up after your messes."

"What? Like Sardinia? You have one job—but you delegate it to imbeciles. That is why we are here. Someone had to take the initiative and bring the them to you."

Rossi had balls, arguing semantics with a Mafia hitman, but he was also riling Baresi. Distracting him. I would not have a better opportunity. Springing up, I dived for Rossi, turning him, drawing him close. A human shield. As his back hit my chest, he let out a surprised gasp.

Stalemate.

"Kill him, you fool!" Rossi's voice had risen an octave. "What do you need—an invitation?"

Baresi sighed. "I don't take orders from you." Again the Glock spat orange. Rossi thumped backward against my chest and fell limp, gasping breathlessly. Letting him fall to the ground, I leaped back into the shadows as another shot ricocheted off a column, spitting shards of stone across the arcade. Twisting around, Baresi launched another fusillade, slamming harmlessly into the brickwork behind me.

"You have nowhere to go, Beckett, except down. Either you jump and die on the stones below, or they take you out in a bag. You choose."

Across the circular gallery, slumped against the wall, Rossi's breathing was shallow, short staccato bubbling wheezes. Baresi's long shadow fell across the floor. He was still in the doorway. I risked a look. He rewarded me with another stinging shower of brick dust. Under my jacket, my shirt felt clammy, sticking to my skin. Then the pain came, insidious and gnawing, like a skewer through my ribs. The round that hit Rossi was a through-and-through, finishing in me. My mind fizzed. I felt light-headed.

"It's over, Beckett. You have led me a merry dance, but

now it is you and me. You have nowhere to go. Throw out the gun. Make it easy on yourself."

"Come and get it, asshole." It was my turn for foolhardy bravado. The shadow was less than a yard long now, an arm outstretched along the wall, canted down, the sharp eyes focusing along it, into the dark. He was coming closer.

"Again up the stairs. Again the dead body. Again you take the rap for a murder I committed. Poetic, no?"

"Well, it's not Tennyson, but I get your point. Poetry's not really your bag, Baresi. Better not give up the day job."

Across the gallery, Rossi was soaked in blood, his chest heaving as he struggled for breath. He raised a hand weakly and gave the tiniest of nods. I reciprocated, then I launched myself around the corner, flooring Baresi with a groan. The Glock clattered to the concrete. Before he could regroup, I reigned blows across his face, bouncing his skull off the floor. Suddenly my vision filled with stars as his foot struck my groin, and I collapsed helplessly onto my back. Baresi immediately leaped to his feet and towered over me. He smiled as he saw the blood on my shirt and aimed a boot at the wound. My ribs buckled, pain ripping through my torso. Reflexively, I rolled away, tasting the brick dust as my face hit the floor, feeling the air driven from my lungs as he kicked and kicked again. A few feet away, the Glock begged me to reach out and hole the bastard, but the blows kept coming. I just couldn't reach it. When he stopped, I gasped helplessly for air. Through a field of stars, I saw him lunge for the gun. I kicked out a leg, caught his foot, sending him sprawling. But he rallied and rolled, grabbing the Glock, swinging it around, another round digging a groove across the floor. Gritting my teeth, I barrel-rolled back into the shadows, feeling my ribs grind. I reached for the Beretta, felt my empty waistband. It must have fallen out as I dived for the floor. My eyes on stalks, I searched, but I couldn't see it. Slowly, agonizingly, I dragged myself up against the parapet wall, suddenly utterly drained. I was all out of options, and Baresi knew it. Across the gallery, Rossi's head was lolling to one side. Barely alive, he still stood a better chance than me.

"So, this is it, Beckett." He grinned, raising the Glock. "No hard feelings, eh?"

Chapter 43

I propped myself up against the parapet wall, staring up at the round black hole in the muzzle of the Glock—my Glock. I couldn't help smiling at the irony. Outside, apartment lights were coming on, voices on balconies. Baresi's eyes flicked about nervously.

"Time's up, Baresi. Either piss or get off the pot." My voice sounded strange—hoarse, strained.

From the corner of my eye, I caught a movement, heard an animal roar. I saw a flash of red, then a metallic clunk. The tall man's eyes rolled, and his knees folded like an origami deck chair before he landed in a heap with a grunt. Behind him, Steve, tears filling her eyes, smiled weakly and dropped the fire extinguisher.

"We have to get out of here."

Steve reached out a hand and pulled me to my feet. She gasped. "Jesus, he shot you!"

"It's just a flesh wound," I groaned, leaning heavily against the wall. "Shit happens, then you die." Two years ago, when the sniper's bullet had exploded in my shoulder, it felt like I had lost an arm. In contrast, my side hurt like hell, but the pain was bearable, at least until I ran out of adrenaline. With one hand clasped against the wound, I picked up the Glock and felt shards of pain through my ribs. Maybe more than a flesh wound. Baresi was barely conscious, rubbing the back of his rock-hard skull.

"Now, it's your turn, you bastard."

The Sicilian turned his head in amazement, shuffling

Proof of Life

away, keeping his hands in the open. "What?"

I aimed the Glock at his forehead.

Baresi just snorted contemptuously. "So now you shoot me Go on then. Pull the trigger. Spread my brains over the wall, just like I did to Moretti. Eye for an eye."

I pressed the Glock to his brow and felt the movement of his breathing, smelled his cologne tinged with the animal sweat of fear. My finger cradled the twin *safe-action* triggers. Felt the minute give in the mechanism.

"Do it, Beckett. Once and for all." Steve was watching, contempt in her eyes, hate in her voice, low and primal. She had knelt where he knelt, waiting for the bullet. Now she understood my world.

"Yes, Beckett," he sneered. "Pull the trigger. Or are you some kind of *pussy?*" Baresi spat the insult.

My mind replayed the previous week, the traps, the terror, the fear. Escaping Moretti's apartment, the shoot-out at the villa, the execution squad. I could feel the gravel in my knees, the hilltop breeze through the silence. How I had waited for the shot, for oblivion, as he did now. I wanted to make him pay for Jardine, for the sinking of the *Genevieve*. I could feel my finger squeezing the trigger, taking up the play, tensioning the springs.

"Do it, Beckett."

Then out of the blue, one of those throwaway social media memes came into my mind—*a moment of patience in a moment of anger saves you a hundred moments of regret*. I took a breath. The Glock rose and fell as Baresi did the same.

Baresi was an assassin. Killing was in his blood, in the DNA that made him what he was. He exchanged lives for money and showed no mercy or remorse. A robot. The only reason he'd followed us from the Piazza Navona, out to Sardinia, then back up to Venice, was money. If not me and

Steve, then someone else would be lying in their own blood so he could get paid.

I was nothing like him. The Marines trained me to kill. Quickly, effectively but not without cause. Everyone I killed either threatened me, my comrades, or the freedoms I'd signed up to defend. When I am forced to take a life, I have already justified it in my own head.

Now Baresi was unarmed, helpless, taunting me to take the shot. And I could not do it.

Easing my finger from the trigger, raising it above my head, I brought it down with a bone-crunching crash on the side of Baresi's face and watched him crumple to the ground once more.

***

Rossi was against the wall, leaning up on an elbow. There was too much blood. His time was short.

"Tell me where Max Anderson is?"

"You want him to die too?" Little more than a whisper, Rossi forced out the words. Blood laced his lips. "You have seen what they will do. Max Anderson is better off lost."

"I can protect him, Professore. Help me find him."

"No. You don't know who you are dealing with. This is bigger than all of us. They will not stop until they have wiped out every memory of what happened, every last person who knows."

"Who will? DeMarco, Trueman, Velasquez, Gilbués? Please Professore. Give me something."

"I have told you. Leave those dogs to sleep. No good will come of it. Trueman is gone. The others are gone. It is over." Rossi's breathing was shallow and short, bubbling in his throat. He reached up a hand and grabbed the lapel of my jacket, pulling me close. "*Trova la signora delle reti*, Beckett. The

Lady of the Nets. It is the one thing they know nothing of. She will tell you of the serpent. Akurra. Trova la signora and you will find Anderson."

Then the rasping stopped, and the world fell silent. Rossi's eyes were fixed on mine, but they saw nothing as his jaw yawed open. I let him slip to the gallery floor, saying a quick prayer for his soul, a plea to an Almighty I didn't believe in to forgive him his indiscretions. Pascal's wager; it is wiser to believe than to not.

The commotion outside was now palpable. Footsteps echoed off the walls, flashlights played across the arched windows.

"We have to go." I frisked Rossi's body, taking his pocketbook and a small notepad. To make it look like a robbery gone wrong. Baresi was clean; a few Euros which I let him keep. I left the Beretta, to implicate him in Rossi's murder—at least for a while until they checked ballistics. Taking a deep breath, I hauled myself up, grabbed Steve's arm, and made for the stairs.

Chapter 44

Despite the hullabaloo, the courtyard was still quiet, except for a few excitable Italians shouting down from balconies. I checked my Omega. 10:00 pm. The crowds in the town should be thinning, but if we could mingle, we could make it back to the car.

"Do up your jacket." Steve spun me around, away from the smattering of tourists.

"Uh?"

"Your shirt is covered with blood. Do up your jacket, put your arm around my waist and stay close. Pretend we're a couple. Perhaps, we can hide it."

"A couple? Oh." For a moment, I toyed with some quip about time and place, but Steve's eyes told me to let it go.

As we quickened our pace away from the Palazzo Contarini, I was dismayed to find the streets as busy as ever, so hugging Steve close, we joined the throng as a group of three *Carabinieri* sprinted past toward the alleyway. Soon the air behind us echoed to the sound of shouting and gunfire.

The nearer we got to the Grand Canal, the busier it became. Venice is never quiet. Restaurants and bars packed to capacity, and the air a heady mix of Mediterranean aromas and cacophonous chatter, but all we could focus on was escape. The Carabinieri were out in force, on every corner, chattering into radios. Fortunately, Venice is the playground of the pickpocket. They were too preoccupied with the crowds to take much notice of us—at least for now.

Joining the snake of tourists, we weaved through the

impossibly tight walkways. The buildings seemed to lean in over us, turning the streets into tunnels of noise. I was sweating, and my vision was blurring. The pain in my ribs was getting worse, but I bit my lip and carried on. In my head, my Marine drill sergeant was bawling as I crawled through the rain and the mud. His wild, contorted face and his spit on the back of my neck as he bawled and cussed. I kept going, doggedly placing one foot in front of the other.

"What happened back there, Beckett? He will chase us forever. Eventually, you have to kill him. You know that?"

"In time, Steve. But not now. I am too angry. Angry people make mistakes. Angry people miss shots. They miss opportunities. They burn bridges."

Had I missed an opportunity tonight?

Eventually, we reached the Ponte dell'Accademia, with its never-ending corridor of white steps, a graceful arc cresting over the dark ribbon of the canal. The tourist train which had pushed us along had gradually thinned as its passengers peeled off into shops and photo opportunities, or just stood. A hundred yards behind, a scream rang out. Then a bee buzzed past my ear. A moment later, the crack.

"Shit! Baresi. How the f...? What the hell is his skull made of?" I wheeled around and caught sight of the outstretched arm between a crowd of confused heads, behind Baresi's eyes blazed.

"I told you to finish it, Beckett. No good deed goes unpunished."

I recalled Steve's pathetic mewling back at Moretti's apartment. "Too right. Maybe I should have never brought you along."

"Maybe you shouldn't have."

The bridge opened onto a small *campo*, lined with billboards and graffiti. The crowds had headed for cover, and we were totally exposed. I risked a glance back. Baresi was on the crest of the bridge. He was holding the side of his head with one hand as he again leveled the Beretta. Instinctively, I gritted my teeth and pulled Steve sideways as the bark of a lone tree exploded beside me. Then we ran as best we could. With one eye on the route on my phone screen and another eye down the treacherous side alleys, we lost ourselves in the maze of claustrophobic streets as we raced towards the bus station. Baresi's pounding footsteps echoed off the ancient walls—behind us, parallel, in front, confusing, disorienting. My head was spinning. I was nauseous, but Steve urged me on. And then we teetered over the murky black of the canal.

A dead end.

From along the towpath, silhouetted against a single street lamp, Baresi stepped out and raised his gun once more. There was an eerie silence, just the faintest murmur of the distant crowds and the slap of the water against the bank ten yards away.

"Did I mention when I was a boy, my father worked on the docks?" There was a hint of amusement in his voice. "I know these streets like the back of my hand."

I leaned against the wall, now thoroughly exhausted. "Rome, Cagliari, even the middle of the damn Mediterranean. Now here. What is it you want, Baresi?"

"I want to get paid. That is all. This is nothing personal. Moretti had to be silenced. So did Rossi. They knew about Amber Rock and were going to reveal what they knew to the world. My employers couldn't let that happen. Then you turned up."

"But Tom Jardine? Steve Jordan? Must they die?"

"Casualties of war. Like Mario at Moretti's villa. I don't recall you shedding too many tears over him. Deep down, you and I are the same, Beckett. People pay us to do the jobs

Proof of Life

they don't want to do themselves. We are the hired help. Some you win, some you lose. This time you lose."

He drew back the hammer of the Beretta.

"So Beckett. Do you want to watch the girl die first, or do you want her to feel a few seconds of pure hopelessness before I kill her too?"

The Sicilian's callousness emphasized the difference between us. I don't just kill; it would make me nothing more than an animal. There is a reason behind every death, and every execution is quick. Assassination. An honest transaction. Baresi was enjoying this job too much.

"Just get the fuck on with it, asshole." Once again, I closed my eyes against the inevitable. Then I heard the click on an empty chamber.

"Merda!"

Steve's hand reached into the waistband of my jeans. She leveled the Glock towards Baresi.

"Drop your gun. Now!" Her voice was high-pitched and taut.

Baresi mumbled more expletives as he rifled through his pockets for another magazine of bullets, further cursing as he realized they wouldn't fit. Steve pulled the trigger, sighed, and pulled the trigger again.

"The slide lock. Take off the slide lock."

Ten feet away, Baresi ejected the spent magazine with a clatter across the pavement. Then Steve pulled the trigger again. The Glock coughed, sending brick dust spilling from a wall, and she stumbled backward at the recoil. She fired again, the second disappearing into the night. I doubted she could hit a cow's butt with a Chevrolet, let alone kill Baresi. However, everyone gets lucky now and again. She fired a third shot. There was a spray of red, and Baresi yelped, the empty Beretta flying from his hand.

"You bitch! My fucking arm!"

Turning on his heels, clutching his injured arm, Baresi jumped over the towpath. But instead of a splash, there was a thump and the sound of an outboard motor disappearing into the distance.

The pain in my side was making it difficult to breathe, sending needles through my ribs. How much blood could a man lose and still function? Like spilled milk on a kitchen floor, it spreads.

"Let's get out of here." Grabbing the warm barrel of the Glock, I wrenched it from her hands. She was almost catatonic, eyes round and terrified.

"I shot a man."

"He'll get over it." Kicking at the Beretta, I sent it skittering across the cobbles and over the edge with a reassuring plop. Squinting away the stars in my eyes, I pulled at Steve's hand. "C'mon. Let's go."

***

It was gone midnight when we reached the bus station. The parking lot was empty, and the Ford stood out like a turd at a pool party.

"Can you drive?" I was becoming breathless. My right side was numb.

"About as well as I can shoot—and I've never driven outside England. Sorry."

"Never too late to learn." I threw the keys and turned to the passenger door before she changed her mind. As she fumbled with the seat adjuster, I programmed the hotel details into the sat nav, then fell back exhausted.

If Steve had been a poor driver, then I was in no state to complain. The sound of the engine, the road, my own roaring breath filled my head. I suddenly felt totally spent.

Proof of Life

Through the window, the lights of the port bounced rhythmically past. Beyond them, there was only the inky black of the lagoon. In the distance, I heard a voice—I think it was Steve—but the words were drifting like wind through the corn, and the lights were gone. The road was gone.

Then everything was gone.

Chapter 45

Thursday, September 12

The cellar drummed. Brick-dust and concrete rained down. My heart was pumping fit to burst through my ribs. In the darkness, a woman was sobbing. A man was pleading. I crouched down low and covered my ears.

Don't leave us here.

Then I was reaching out in the clinging black void, but my fingers gripped nothing but the slime of seaweed.

I'll find you. Stay where you are. I'm coming. I promise.

My legs were running on a treadmill, going nowhere.

Don't leave us here.

Confused, I turned. The voice was behind me, echoing off invisible walls. Or was it above? The woman's sobs were close, and I turned again. The seaweed wrapped and writhed, tight tendrils around my legs.

Find us, Aidan. We are here waiting.

Disembodied, nebulous, directionless. I was crying, wailing frantic yet soundless. The tendrils gripped tighter as I struggled towards the sound, pulling me back, dragging me through the floor.

Please, Aidan. You are our only chance.

And I fell through into the moss green of the water.

Find us, you've come so far. Keep going. Don't give up now.

My lungs were aching as I sucked the oxygen into my

bloodstream, and it plumed crimson through the hole in my side. Far away, through the darting shoals of fish, a boat canted over, a man clinging to the deck.

Trova la signora delle reti, Beckett. Just a few more feet. Trova la signora. You can do it.

I reached out, feeling the fingers brush mine, wrapping around my hands and writhing up my arms, dragging me towards the abyss, the mangled, rusting wrecks, and the torn bodies. The head was sliding over my torso now. Rearing up, its eyes met mine, hissing and growling as its tongue flicked at my face and its mouth gaped wide.

***

I awoke as the last echoes faded into the wall. I kept my eyes shut, the face of the serpent imprinted on my retinas. A machine played a regular beep, and the steady stream of oxygen cooled my sinuses. The hairs on my arm stung as a Band-Aid tugged, and I could feel the cannula thick in my vein. There was a smell of ether and disinfectant. But no pain, so I kept my eyes closed for a while longer and tried fruitlessly to hang on to the dying wisps of the dream.

Were Max and Kate Anderson out there somewhere? The whole rainbow serpent thing. Had Max left a clue behind, nearly thirty years ago, for me to find? And what did Rossi mean? *Trova la signora delle reti and you will find your father.*

"Doctor! He's awake." It was an unfamiliar voice, deep, rich as Colombian coffee.

There were footsteps on the plastic tiles.

"Good morning, Captain Beckett." In contrast, cold, detached, with a forced lilt. New England, educated—Massachusetts, Maine, maybe. In my mind's eye, I pictured someone tall, chiseled, cropped blond, with a broad, disingenuous, professional smile. I was wrong. Doctor Mahoney was around fifty, short with several chins, sharp, severe eyes, and the squashed nose of a Pekinese. The stubble on his chin and crotchety demeanor told me I had occupied a good proportion of his early morning. He was still wearing creased, green scrubs. In one of those ironic twists of fate, his arms were a forest of black hair, while there was only a short shaved ridge around his bald pate. He grabbed my arm, digging in a thumb, as he watched the second hand of his watch.

"You'll live. I'll be back shortly." He dropped my arm and disappeared into the hallway.

"Wow. He's a laugh a minute." I smiled at the guard. A towering monolith in a navy blue crew neck and pants, a sky blue beret canted at a technically accurate angle. He was standing, somewhat pointlessly, next to an easy chair.

"Well, sir, you did wake him at three this morning."

"Remind me to buy some flowers." I pulled myself up in the bed. The pain in my side pulled me back down. I had almost forgotten my ribs. "How's Miss Jordan?"

"We needed a jimmy to prize her hands from the steering wheel, sir. They found her a room, and she took a pill."

"Where am I?"

The guard kept looking straight ahead. "Doc Mahoney will be back soon, sir. The Major asked me to stay with you."

"Asked or ordered?"

"That is a matter of opinion, Captain." The guard's mouth flicked up at the corner. He grabbed a remote and aimed it at the TV. "You made the morning news, sir."

NBC News showed Venice, the Snail Staircase, a body bag, the bus station filled with flashing lights, and urgent shouting Italians. "Bet that's impressed your major."

The guard risked a smile. "One way of putting it, sir."

***

Proof of Life

The doctor arrived at 9:00 am. I'd been counting the seconds.

"Captain Beckett. You are a lucky man." The professional, superficial grin hid his irritation.

"Excuse me, doc, but I don't feel so lucky." The dressings were pulling against my skin. The whole of my side felt like a rhinoceros had charged me down.

"On the contrary. The bullet had already passed through another person. The risks of infection are huge. And, by then, it was the shape of a bent dime. Luckily, it passed between two of your ribs, damaging intercostal tissue and grazing the bones. Another inch and it would have broken a rib, maybe even fragmented on impact and spread shrapnel through your lungs."

I smiled wryly. "An inch the other way and it would have missed completely." Behind the doc, the guard allowed himself an oh-so-brief titter.

"But it didn't. That must tell you something about your life choices." Another professional, superficial grin. "Anyway, all I have to do is patch you up and ship you out."

He spent a few seconds reading the clipboard. Then he looked up over his spectacles.

"I will prescribe some painkillers and antibiotics, and you should get the dressing changed every two or three days. Oh, and give yourself a chance to heal. Resist the urge to indulge in a gunfight, at least for a week or two."

Once I was dressed, the guard escorted me across the compound to the building where the head honcho had his office. I felt like a schoolboy being taken to the Principal for smoking weed behind the bleachers. The Major was in his chair, head down in his paperwork. He didn't lift it as I entered. He was puffing on a briar pipe. The aromatic smell of *Golden Harvest* reminded me of my dad, Joe, Sundays watching the game and meatloaf for tea.

"Sit down, Captain." Emphasizing the difference in our ranks—my former rank. He wore the blue uniform of a US NATO air officer and had the appearance of Clark Gable, right down to the pencil mustache, gravelly smoker's growl, and poorly disguised bad temper.

"Sir." I couldn't see a cane. Nevertheless, I wished I had a magazine to put down my pants. He set down his pen, labored the action, how much I was screwing with his day.

"My name is Major Lou Dennis. I'm responsible for this unit and everyone in it. And I want you gone."

"Unit, sir?"

Dennis lifted his head, tutted, and tamped the tobacco in his pipe. "You're at Aviano, Captain, specifically the US Army Tactical Logistic unit. We got a call last night. Brought you here. Doc Mahoney fixed you up."

Aviano?

Aviano airbase was a NATO facility, about an hour north of Venice. I'd never been there—until now.

"You and the woman will remain in the hospital wing for forty-eight hours. Then, I want you gone, pronto. Before the Base Commander realizes you are here."

"But Major…"

"No buts, Captain Beckett." Again the rank emphasized. "I am as happy as the next man to help our fellow Americans, but with the commotion you caused last night… I called in so many favors, I have a drawerful of IOUs. Not to mention the clothing bill." He gestured at the new clean regulation shirt I was wearing.

"And we are both very grateful, sir."

"Really? Do you realize the repercussions if the authorities track you back here?"

"Sir, what happened in Venice…"

Proof of Life

"Goddammit!" Dennis rose to his feet and slammed his hands down on the desk. His eyes were blazing. "I don't give a flying fuck what happened in Venice. I don't even care about Rome, Sardinia, or any other part of this godforsaken country that you have shot to pieces. I just want you off of this base before someone gets a warrant and drags us both to the glasshouse." A vein in Dennis's forehead was drumming in four-four. He dropped himself heavily back in his chair and wiped a hand across his face. Then he picked up his pen and distractedly scanned the top paper of a set, but it was clear his concentration was shot. I sat quietly until all his ammunition was spent.

"You have to realize the spot you have gotten me into here, Beckett. This base plays a pivotal role in the region. Humanitarian missions, peacekeeping. We are still stinging from the repercussions of 2009 and I am damned if I am going the same way as my predecessor."

I recalled 2009. The extraordinary rendition of an Islamic cleric from the streets of Milan had ended in an international incident, not to mention the conviction for the kidnap of nearly two dozen CIA agents and a USAF colonel. I could almost feel the Joint Chiefs of Staff breathing heavily on the nape of Dennis's neck. Pliskin's hot breath was on mine and I still had no sign of Amber Rock or Anderson.

"Maybe, I could call my boss? Talk it over? I just need a few more days to follow up some leads and then we'll be gone."

"I don't care if you call the goddam pope." He slammed his hand down again. "Just get the hell off of my base."

Chapter 46

The guard escorted me back to the hospital wing in silence. I noticed he took me the back way, past the dumpsters, probably resisting the urge to hurl me into one. I also noticed his hand on the gun holstered on his belt. A second monolithic guard relieved him and took up station outside my room. He was thick-necked and broad-shouldered, around two hundred and fifty pounds and taller than me by about a foot. Standing at ease, flipping to attention as I arrived, the corridor shook under the movement. His eyes locked on to me like homing beams on a cruise missile.

"Sir, I am Airman Desaux. I have been ordered to ensure you stay in your room, and you leave the base in due course." He grinned, a businesslike, somewhat supercilious grin.

"Your major made that perfectly clear, Desaux."

"You didn't hear it from me, Captain, but the doc has signed you off until Saturday, and in here, he outranks the major. He wants to monitor your injury. You need to keep your head down for a while, at least until you leave the base."

"Do you know where Miss Jordan is?"

"She's under house arrest in the female quarters, sir. Just keeping her safe."

I pulled my satellite phone from my jacket and used a *Pluswipe* to remove the dried blood. There were three missed calls from Pliskin. I guessed I owed him a call-back, but I wasn't in the mood. My ribs ached and my pride ached even more.

Proof of Life

Apropos of nothing, I recalled Rossi's last words. Trova la signora delle reti, Beckett. The Lady of the Nets.

"Airman Desaux? Can I get Wi-Fi in here?"

Desaux shook his head somberly. "No, sir. Major's orders. No external computer equipment can be connected to the network."

"Well, can I get an internal one, then? Desktop, tablet, anything?"

"I'll see what I can do."

***

Like it or not, I needed to return Pliskin's calls.

"Beckett. What's the occasion? It's not my birthday, is it?" Again, he picked up on the first ring.

"Not as far as I know, Pliskin. Anyway, many happy returns just in case."

"How are you feeling? Major Dennis said a gunshot wound to the abdomen."

"The thorax, Pliskin. You know Major Dennis? Pleasant fellow. Very protective of his airbase—and speaking of airbases, how did I get here?"

"Miss Jordan used your TORUS phone. She drove the car out of Venice and across the causeway but could not locate the hotel, so she pulled over onto the shoulder. She called me, and I called Dennis."

It explained the blood on the phone, on the fingerprint reader that unlocked it. "Anyway, I'll live."

Pliskin grunted. "For me, it's is a mixed blessing. I have been getting a good deal of flak on your behalf today. This lead you followed. I hope it was worth it."

Was it worth it? What had I learned from Rossi? "Major Dennis wants me off the base."

"I can't say I blame him. It's rumored the Scala del Bovolo cost around one million euros to renovate, and already you have left bullet holes and bloodstains in the fresh plaster. Not to mention the cost of a door in the *Calle dei Puti*. And don't deny it. You were caught on camera as you passed a restaurant."

"Someone lured us there under false pretenses. What could I do?"

"For a start, you're a fully trained US marine. It's is why we employed you. Should you not expect the unexpected?"

I let the question hang. Of course, Pliskin was right. He was always right. "And did they catch Renzo Baresi on camera too?"

Pliskin grunted again. "Baresi remembered his training—and where the cameras were."

"But he didn't remember to reload his pistol. My Glock damn near took his arm off."

"Waking half of Venice in the process—and you didn't fire it." The line paused as Pliskin collected his thoughts. "So, what did you discover in between target practice?"

"The person we met. Professore Fabrizio Rossi."

"Professor Rossi? He was in one of the press cuttings on Moretti's thumb drive. Now he is in the obituary columns of *la Repubblica*." Pliskin's amazing recall no longer surprised me. Still, he'd had two days to digest the contents of both.

"He knew Anderson before he disappeared," I continued. "They worked together on an international working party dealing with nuclear safety."

"The Sentinel group, yes."

"Man, if you already know this stuff…" My irritation must have been obvious. "It's my life we are risking here. Don't you think you should tell me?"

Proof of Life

"My apologies, Beckett. The press cuttings mentioned the Sentinel Group. I did some research. Anyhow…"

"Anyhow Rossi was also undertaking commercial work on new uranium extraction techniques. Apparently, there was an accident or an incident. He didn't elaborate, but it was something serious in the early '80s."

"Nuclear accidents are far more frequent than one would imagine, Beckett. Between Three Mile Island in 1979 and Chernobyl in 1986, there were several high-profile incidents across the US. Still more across the world. Many of them barely made the inside pages."

"Yes, but Rossi implied this was different. Significant enough to cause a lot of embarrassment or damage if it became public. He claims someone coerced him into keeping it under wraps, and to squash any rumors that surfaced—which he did. In return, he kept his reputation. Over the years, it became harder to keep the lid on the story, though. Even the members of his own team suspected something. So they were dealt with. Now, every member of the Sentinel Group, pictured in that article, is dead. Brooks, Hayes, McKenna. Now, even Rossi is dead."

"And Anderson is missing presumed dead."

"Precisely. I believe Max Anderson put two and two together and realized he was in danger. That eventually, they would find out he also knew."

"So he ran?"

"So he ran."

"What do you propose, Beckett?"

"Nothing has changed here. I need to find Max Anderson. Assuming Baresi doesn't find him first."

Chapter 47

At 3:00 pm, Airman Desaux's fist on the frosted door pane woke me.

"Miss Jordan to see you, Captain. Oh, and your computer."

Steve pushed her way through and hurried over to the bed. She made to speak, but I laid a hand on her arm, flicked my eyes towards a smaller, leaner man, peach-fuzz and shirtsleeves, who wheeled in a computer on a trolley. He attached it to wall sockets and handed me a *Post-it* note.

"Guest password, sir. Please don't store data on the hard drive as I will wipe it. Oh, and the firewall is aggressive, so don't do any illegal searches."

I nodded my thanks as the door closed, and Airman Desaux eased himself into the chair outside.

"How're you feeling?" She nodded at my ribs, which immediately twinged in sympathy.

"Doc Mahoney says I'll live. You?"

I knew it was a rhetorical question. She'd changed clothes, freshened her makeup, but she couldn't disguise the weariness. The gradual erosion of everything normal in her life, a sliding scale until she settled at my level.

"I didn't know what to do. I thought you were dying."

"You did just great, Steve. Probably gave Pliskin a coronary, using my phone but hey." I took her hand, squeezed it reassuringly. "Shit happens, and you just have to deal with it. You dealt with it."

Proof of Life

She crossed to the window, to a view of the barracks and the rear of an airplane hangar. A Spartan transport plane rattled the panes as it came into land.

"When is all this going to end, Beckett?"

I had no answers, so I gave her the best I could manage. "Soon, Steve. It will end soon. It has too."

"But what if Baresi is smarter than us? So far, he seems to be one step ahead at every turn. He found Jardine out on the Mediterranean, then he tracked us down to Venice."

"He got lucky, is all." But it wasn't what I was thinking. If Baresi was working for Amber Rock when Rossi reported someone was turning over stones, it made sense they would send him to Venice; he knew the territory. But Sardinia, Cagliari, even a random point in the middle of the sea?

How could he possibly have known?

Back in Sardinia, I'd run this round my head until my brain ached. Without Moretti's notebook, there was no way Baresi could know about Jardine, least of all what he had planned. My best guess was he tracked the Ford from the backstreets of Rome to the harbor, maybe even stuck a device under a wheel arch, then followed us on his cellphone.

That would get him to Jardine, but how had he known where Jardine was heading?

Maybe there was a device on the *Genevieve* too?

***

Steve sat heavily next to me on the bed, and we both crossed our ankles like a pair of bookends. I lolled my head to one side, looked at the curve of her mouth. These days, it seemed set in a permanent pout.

I found a TV News broadcast. The Carabinieri blamed the shootings on rival drugs gangs taking a pop at each other.

At least they did publicly. There were no photos, except a youthful Fabrizio Rossi, probably in his thirties, carrying the caption *Professore nucleare assassinato*.

"What happens to me, now?" she asked.

"The way I see it, Steve, there are two options. You could ask Major Dennis for safe passage back to the UK. Let the authorities there look after you. They would release you on police bail until they prove your innocence. If you stick to the story—you saw an unknown gunman shoot Moretti, and he has been chasing you ever since…"

"And somehow, I traveled to Sardinia, nearly got drowned, and then made my way here?" She gestured around the safe room in a NATO compound miles from Rome.

"I'm sure Pliskin can pull some strings…"

She grabbed the remote and turned off the TV, then folded her arms and puffed out her frustration. "And the other option? You said there were two?"

Or I could keep her with me until they had apprehended Baresi and cleared her name.

"There is only one sensible option. At least in the UK, you'll be safe."

She turned to me, dumbfounded. "Baresi will travel across Europe to blow my head off, but not to England? No, Beckett, he's after me too. You have to get him before he gets us."

"It has a naïve simplicity about it, but yes." My tone was far too humorous.

"And—I need to know why Sr. Moretti was killed."

I lolled my head over. She did the same. Her eyes bored into mine, and I knew I was just about to be hoodwinked. The shrewd poker player, bidding high but holding crap.

"And," she continued, "we still don't know the truth about Max Anderson and all those others. We are the only ones who know he is still alive, apart from Baresi."

"*Could* still be alive, Steve. Until we find him, we don't *know* jack."

I understood Pliskin's pragmatism. Steve was a complication I didn't need. Logically, I should cut her loose. I couldn't protect her from Baresi forever.

"Those are my problems, Steve. If anything happened to you… I couldn't have that on my conscience."

The thing was, deep down, I didn't want her to go. I was in unfamiliar territory. A street full of emotional IEDs tying me in knots. I flicked the TV back on, changed channels to an episode of Frasier, overdubbed with a clipped Italian voice that owed more to the bark of a terrier than Kelsey Grammer.

"There's another option." The glint in her eye could only mean trouble. "We stay together and find Max Anderson. Strength in numbers."

I snickered. "Strength in *numbers*? There's two of us."

"And I managed to scare off Baresi in Venice."

"True—but more luck than judgment."

"Still, without me… Look Beckett." She grabbed the remote, despatched Kelsey Grammer, and hurled it away.

"I believe we are *that close*—," she measured a tiny gap with her thumb and forefinger, "—to finding Anderson. We need to see this through. Bring Baresi to justice for the murders of Luciano Moretti, Tom Jardine, and Fabrizio Rossi. This is not just about your *Amber Rock* anymore. This is about Max and Kate Anderson. If what they know is as explosive as Rossi and Moretti suggest, then the world needs to know."

Of course she was right. The history of Amber Rock

went back at least a generation, long before Renzo Baresi. Nevertheless, someone felt they needed to keep it hidden. And just what drove two successful people to abandon their lives, their careers? To simply disappear?

"I want to see this thing through, Beckett. To clear my name once and for all. I am going to stick to you like gum on the pavement until you sort it out, or they all stop wanting to kill me."

Proof of Life

Chapter 48

That evening, Desaux arranged for Steve's supper to be sent to my room. We lay on the bed watching TV until Steve fell asleep. The room was dim, lit only by the orange base lamps through the window. The bedside clock said 11:30 pm. I checked my Omega, disappointed somehow the clock hadn't lied. My side was throbbing again, and the rest of my body had stiffened up in sympathy, so I popped a couple of pills and washed them down with lukewarm water. Then I laid my head back, in no rush to aggravate the pain further, enjoying the restful gloom, safe in the knowledge that at least, in this room, there were no Sicilian assassins.

But I couldn't settle. Too many loose threads were fluttering around my head. How could the Andersons stage such a perfect disappearance when Steve and I couldn't even travel across Italy without Baresi on our tails? Pliskin had yet to come back to me about the Andersons' finances. Maybe they would tell me something. Also, they'd need a new identity. Maxwell Anderson is not a common name but easy enough to track down, given thirty years to look.

I opened my MacBook, stole some electricity, and took another look at the photos. I sorted the ones featuring the boat—the *Diktynna A*, checked the ones without a boat. Something confused me, but my tired mind would not bring it forward. Most could have been vacation photos. Cloudless skies, deep azure seas, rocky shorelines, rising to low hazy hills. A rash of cypresses punctuated by groves of olives and vines. It was typically Mediterranean, but it didn't help. There were nearly 30,000 miles of coastline like this and hundreds, if not thousands, of islands. Any of a dozen

Proof of Life

countries. The buildings were all low-rise, pan-tiled, and stuccoed, with an air of age and neglect. Dusty roads edged between ragged stone walls and sparse hedges winding upwards to a barren skyline.

Some photos showed a town. Shops, mini-markets and cafés along a main road. Hordes of tourists meandering and chatting. Waiters outside restaurants smiling solicitously. And a gleaming white church with a prominent domed roof. Beside it, a bell tower, equally majestic, equally brilliant white, dominated the corner of the square. Everywhere, dusty scooters and automobiles were scattered haphazardly. I zoomed in on a few. They were mostly small European hatchbacks, but the license plates were indistinct.

Other pictures showed a harbor filled with ranks of pleasure boats and hopeful pilots hawking their boat trips from behind colorful placards. The Andersons, carefree, dangling their feet over the harbor-side, deep in conversation, as Max gestured toward the sea, a boat, some remarkable architecture, or even just the weather.

Then it hit me like a lump hammer. The Andersons never faced the camera. They were unaware the pictures were being taken? These weren't holiday snaps. They were surveillance photos. No wonder Moretti valued them at half a million euros.

Someone already found the Andersons.

"What are you doing?" Steve stretched and looked over. I ran through my theories, stopping on a picture of Max and Kate in a restaurant. Though grainy and without flash, the details were distinct. "Notice anything?"

Steve craned in, her eyes flicking across the screen, lips pursed. She shook her head. So I zoomed in closer

"See there." The camera had caught a glint of light below Kate's neck. "She's wearing the rainbow serpent pendant."

"Could be any pendant. I have about eight."

I wouldn't be deviated so easily. Scrolling across to Max's neck. "Look. No pendant—because he left it in the boat."

Steve frowned as my Tada moment fell flat. "Flimsy. He could have forgotten to put it on."

"What about his hair? Longer, wavier, a little grayer?"

"Because his hair grew, it's a sign he survived a boating accident? My hair grows in four weeks. The gap between the Sentinel photos and their disappearance was years."

"But Moretti's notebook. You said *Max Anderson must remain lost* could read *Max Anderson needs to stay where he is*. Where he is! Not lost but wherever these pictures were taken. Moretti knew where Anderson was hiding."

Steve wrested the MacBook from me and swiped through again. "Do you know where they were taken? Some of them look familiar. Something about the harbor, the buildings in the background. I'm sure I know this place. I've been there on holiday with my folks. I recognize the white church with the red roof, the bell tower."

"So, where it's it?"

"It's Crete. I know that. I was only eight and more interested in the beach. My dad was going through a phase. He wanted to see the wonders of the ancient world. We visited the Palace of Knossos. I remember the bull fresco and the stories of the Minotaur."

"So this is Knossos, Crete?"

"No, it was one of the other excursions we took, but I can't remember where to. We drove in a coach for hours, then a boat. There were eagles and a castle on an island."

"A castle?"

"Something like that."

***

Proof of Life

Outside the door, Desaux had called it a day, replaced by an equally monolithic guard who preferred earbuds and a steady foot-tapping rhythm to silent intimidation. Steve drifted back to sleep, annexing the whole of the bed, leaving me in the uncomfortable guest chair. I stared out at the rear of the aircraft hangar, the apron busy with night duties, but all I saw was the wheel of the van, the Snail Staircase. All I heard was the subdued puff of my Glock pistol. All I felt was the thump as Rossi slumped back and a bullet careened through my rib cage. My wounds would heal, the bruises would fade in time, but my mind was a different matter.

The first time I shook hands with death, I was fresh out of training on my first tour of Afghanistan. My section was attached to a multi-national ISAF offensive, clearing insurgents from Helmand Province. We spent most of our time sweating our balls off in a baking Humvee M1151. Within a week, one of our squad caught a bullet to the throat and bled out. He had arrived in Virginia in a check shirt and brown corduroy trousers. He returned in a metal box draped in a flag. We all wised up quickly after that. Even so, it felt like a play. Where other people got killed.

Then the Humvee hit a mine.

That day—ironically Friday 13th August—started in darkness, strangely silent, coughing in the fume-filled cabin. There was a stench of burned rubber and ordnance, and it was hard to breathe. Something was crushing my chest, no pain, just the claustrophobia. A panic rising from deep within and overwhelming me—the need to escape. I lost control, thrashing about, fighting demons who stayed just out of reach. Only I couldn't free my legs. I was helpless and screaming for my parents. Then I must have passed out.

When I came to, I realized I was upside down. There was the drip of liquid, a hiss like steam from a pressure cooker. I stretched out my hands, but all I found was Brad Katzner or the top half of him. I must have passed out again, coming round to the grating whine of the pneumatic cutters—the *jaws of life*. A frenetic free-for-all, voices shouting for medics, stretchers, *find a vein, get a line in, where's that goddamn morphine*. Still, there was no pain, just a warm, comfortable peace.

As I flitted in and out of consciousness, everything made sense to me. The angst of my teens, the loneliness I had always felt being different. The truth was, none of it needed to make sense. Life is not good or bad, successful or a failure, happy, sad, or any of a million shades of gray in between. It just is—and one day, it won't be anymore. For three of my comrades, it ended that day.

I wasn't afraid of dying. I was afraid of *not living*.

***

Being a reluctant guest of NATO, Major Dennis had blocked Wi-Fi access and loaned me a clunky desktop machine older than the adolescent who installed it. I had to assume it monitored every keystroke I made and every search through the digital masonry of the base's security firewalls. So instead, I tethered my MacBook to my phone and used the TORUS uplink. Slow but private.

Trova la signora delle reti, Beckett. The Lady of the Nets. What did Rossi mean?

I brought up a browser and typed in the phrase, surprised at the number of references returned. Seems *the Lady of the Nets* is an epithet. Apart from travelog entries, restaurants and bars, all references led to the same basic myth. The huntress goddess of Mount Dikte, Zeus's birthplace, supposedly Zeus's daughter. She caught the eye of King Minos who, not content with Queen Pasiphae, pursued her for nine months to steal her virtue. When at last he caught her, rather than submit, she threw herself into the sea where she was saved in the fishermen's nets, hence the epithet *The Lady of the Nets*.

Proof of Life

Almost drowned but saved. That sounded familiar.

Her name was Diktynna or Dictynna, take your pick, but she was a big deal, especially in Crete—where Steve had seen her castle.

Frustratingly, there turned out to be many castles in Crete, believed to be the cradle of civilization in Europe, with King Minos, Pasiphae, and the unsavory stories of the Minotaur. Since then, the Romans, the Byzantines, the Arabs, Venetians, and the Ottoman Empire had all ruled there. Even Barbarossa the pirate had rocked up to plunder. The Venetians had recognized the island's strategic importance in the Mediterranean, midway between Africa, Europe, and Asia, and had colonized it for centuries, developing its culture, influencing the architecture, and building a fortress pretty well every few miles along the coast. After independence in 1898 and becoming part of the Greek State in 1913, all the island had to fear these days were the battalions of inquisitive tourists. Steve's curious father had plenty to get his teeth into but little to guide us to the location of the photos.

Still, a goddess called Diktynna, the name of the sailboat in the photos, and castles in Crete? It was a long shot.

But even a long shot was still a shot.

Chapter 49

Friday, September 13

In the morning, I was on the bed on top of the sheets. Steve was tight against my back, under them. The warmth, the closeness, felt good. Like she'd been there all my life and I'd just not noticed. As I moved, she stirred but settled back, her soft, regular breathing barely moving the bedclothes. For the first time since we met in Moretti's apartment, her face was still, the lines of anxiety smoothed, pale eyelids over the wide, frightened eyes. She looked—normal.

In any other life, she would not give me a second glance. Now fate had thrown us together. How would she feel about me when all this was over?

***

Desaux brought breakfast at around 8:00 am, snickering as he realized we'd stayed in the same room all night. Eggs over easy, toast, some Italian hams and cheeses, a pot of java. We sat together, staring out the window at the utilitarian buildings as we ate. It was like a last hearty meal before a short walk to a long drop. In the airbase, we were safe, but we were impotent. Out there, the price on our heads flashed like a neon sign yet, that's where the answers lay.

"Have you still got Baresi's gun?" Now she'd awoken, the lines had returned. Her eyes somewhere else.

Bemused, I fetched my backpack and found the Smith & Wesson, the silencer and clip, the remaining bullets. She took it, hesitant at first, but once I had convinced her the safety was on, she gripped it tighter.

"Can I keep this?"

"You said you'd never fired a gun before."

"Well, I did the other day, and I cocked it up completely. For over a week now, I have had two professional killers dueling it out, with me in the middle. When it came to the crunch, I held your gun and didn't know what to do with it. If Baresi had not run out of bullets, we would both be dead."

"So you think the answer is to pack heat? Against a Sicilian assassin?"

She looked at me, slightly taken aback, as if I'd criticized her ass in a new dress. "Why not?"

"Because you don't know the first thing about guns. It would be like giving a child a hand grenade. Eventually, they're going to yank out the pin."

She huffed. Taking a deep breath, she flicked the magazine release, and set aside the clip, pulled the slide back three times, ejecting a round, locked it, and inspected the empty chamber. She released the slide lock, flicked on the thumb safety, and gave me an accomplished grin.

"Yeah, any kid in kindergarten knows that much these days." I sneered petulantly and returned to my coffee. "You only need to watch a cop show…"

She huffed again She sized up the weapon, feeling the balance in her hand, thumbed off the safety, and aimed at the opposite wall. Relaxing her breath, she fired on an empty chamber, the barrel slide shooting back. Then, flicking the safety back on, she slammed in the magazine and set it down.

"A week ago, I'd never seen a real gun. Then I was holding this thing in your face without the first clue what I was doing. Since then, I've had one pointed at the back of my neck and shot a man in the arm. And I still didn't know what the heck I was doing. Rossi was dying. For all I knew, you were dying too, and I was completely helpless."

I felt ashamed as she relived all the shit I'd put her through. I set down my coffee, allowed her to speak.

"The other night, I sat in the car at the side of the road, watching you slumped in the passenger seat. There was *so much blood*. You were mumbling incoherently, barely conscious. I had never driven on the wrong side of the road. I haven't even got a license, for heaven's sake. I was just completely helpless watching you bleed out."

"But, Steve, you weren't. You called Pliskin before the police got to you. You did good, Steve."

"But not good enough." She nodded down at my side. My stitches again pulled. "So yesterday morning, I asked Major Dennis for help. After he'd stopped throwing an *eppy*, he sent me down to the range, where a nice boy called Sean, showed me how guns work. I know it might not save me, but at least I have a chance now."

Knowing I was beaten, I handed her the silencer and watched as she mated the thread and screwed it down.

"Better the devil you know, Beckett."

***

When Doc Mahoney and Major Dennis finally allowed me to leave, we would need to get to Crete. But how? Public air travel was out. Too many security guards and metal detectors, considering we would be carrying weapons. And I didn't relish 30 hours and two thousand kilometers by road, given my injury. That left one option. Driving down to Brindisi, the ferry to Greece, and then another ferry from Pireas across to Heraklion in Crete. Another drive of thirty hours with a hole in my side. Also, outside the base, the world and his spinster aunt were on the lookout for us. We needed something less public.

Proof of Life

So I called Major Dennis; he wanted me gone as much as I wanted to be away. I practically sold a kidney to persuade him he should help us reach Crete. The major called the doc, who examined me and frowned—that was just his natural expression. He concluded I needed another day, at least.

As luck would have it, the C-27J Spartan transport plane we had seen landing came from Chania, Crete, to pick up some spares for the NAMFI missile base. It was due to fly on to Pisa to drop and collect from Camp Darby Army base before returning to Aviano, then home to Crete. Realizing his opportunity, Major Dennis damn near sold a kidney of his own to ensure Steve and I were on it the next morning. He had even burned some more of the clothing budget to kit us out as orderlies, so we would look less conspicuous. Still more of the budget went on spare rounds for our handguns and the armed guard who would see us off NATO property at the other end.

The rest of the day in Aviano was wet and gray. Leaving Steve to pack what meager belongings we had, I tackled one last job—one with the full blessing of Major Dennis, if unofficially. At around 11:00 am, Desaux and another monolithic barrel-neck airman took me to a nondescript garage where they had parked the Ford away from casual observers. The florid bloodstain across the upholstery brought a lump to my throat. Together, we took it out to a secluded spot just into the foothills of the Alps, with Desaux following along in an unmarked Citroen. Then we torched it and they drove me back.

At least Major Dennis would sleep easier now.

PART FOUR - CRETE

Proof of Life

Chapter 50

Saturday, September 14

At 6:22 am, the base was a hive of activity. Desaux drove us around to the apron in time to see our ride from Pisa land, kicking up vortices of spray from the broad tires.

The C-27J Spartan is a huge, khaki-green, lumbering beast, like a Hercules transport plane that shrunk in the wash. Spartan was an apt name. Inside, it was a tube, large enough to load several high-mobility armored vehicles and offload them quickly and whilst under fire. Treacherous rollers, mounted in the floor, could send a man in combat gear reeling over onto his back to the ridicule of his squad. Fully loaded with paratroopers, it would become sticky and odorous. Maybe that's what persuaded them to jump out?

While fork-lift drivers loaded up, Desaux led Steve and me to seats up front, forward of the payload. Desaux sat across from us, his gun substituted for a taser. Even though the plane was not pressurized during flight, the last thing he needed was to annoy Major Dennis by putting holes in the fuselage. Through the open door to the flight deck, the two pilots were flicking switches and chattering on the radio. Aft, the loadmaster who would accompany the payload, pressed a button and the tailgate consumed the morning sun.

"I don't like this, Beckett." Her expression was blank, like the hundreds of soldiers in the back of troop carriers. Scared, going through the motions and taking it as it comes.

Guess it also described me.

Proof of Life

"It'll be fine. We need to go to Crete, and this plane is going to Crete. Relax. Enjoy the ride." But there were still butterflies in my gut. We had no plans, no backup, and no idea where we were going.

Chania International Airport was a busy commercial airport, splitting the load with Heraklion around one hundred kilometers away. The Greek Aviation authorities had struck a deal and allowed the NAMFI to occupy a smattering of buildings in the boondocks South of the airport, so, while the sleek white tourist jets hit the tarmac and turned left towards the terminal, our Spartan turned discreetly right.

Desaux led us from the plane toward a compact Ford and gestured for us to get in. Beside me, Steve tensed up and grabbed my arm. The last time we were ordered into the back of a vehicle, it didn't end well.

"Where are we going?" Steve stood her ground.

"My orders are to take you to the center of Chania, then leave you there."

Steve folded her arms rebelliously.

Desaux frowned. "Just get in the goddamn car—*sir, ma'am*."

As Desaux climbed into the driver's seat and started up the engine, my phone buzzed in my jacket pocket. It was Pliskin. The message—*call me*. So I did.

"Pliskin?"

"Ah, Beckett. Crete. Chania. A slight breeze, twenty-eight degrees. I hope you enjoy your mini-break."

"Yeah. Thinking of doing some sightseeing. Bugging out for a while. Maybe get a tattoo of Zeus." I was not in the least surprised he knew where we were, but it puzzled me he didn't ask why. Maybe he already knew.

"And the girl—Miss Jordan?"

"After Venice, she needs some time on the beach too."

There was a brief telling silence. I imagined Pliskin mouthing obscenities in silent rage.

"As per your request concerning the *Diktynna A*. There is an entry in the UK Small Ships Register. She was built in Southampton, England, and first registered in 1985 as the *Melusina*. The owner was Paul Massey, an English industrialist who unfortunately died of lung cancer in 1989. A Jacqueline Robbins bought the boat from his estate and re-registered her as the *Diktynna A* in January 1990. After that, the details are sketchy. The registration lapsed after five years. Unfortunately, we could not trace Ms. Robbins or anyone else of a similar name at the registration address, a post office box in London. Payments stopped in 1990."

"So, could she be a colleague of the Andersons? Someone they knew?"

"Not that I can find, Beckett. We found records for the boat purchase. She used a banker's draft from an account that subsequently closed. After all this time, the bank has erased the details."

"So we have no address for her?"

"Not then. Not now."

"How can someone just disappear from the planet and leave no trace?"

"Maybe you should direct that question to the three faux police officers in the van in Sardinia." Pliskin paused for a moment, perhaps amused at his sadistic wit. Somewhere, families had lost sons or fathers, newspapers were printing missing persons stories. Pliskin continued. "So, the *Diktynna A*. Diktynna is the name of a Cretan Goddess."

"Uh-huh." I didn't want to tell him I'd googled it.

"Well, I assume you are not intending to schlep around Crete in the hopes of divine inspiration, so you may wish to visit the Museum of Archeology in Chania. There is also an extensive harbor dating back to Venetian times—if the boat is relevant."

"So that's why we are being driven to Chania?"

"Major Dennis was only too glad to oblige."

I closed the call, feeling more confused than ever. Was Jacqueline Robbins just a casual acquaintance? Would there be time for the surveillance photos *before* they disappeared? In the photos, their hair was longer. More likely, Robbins had helped them leave, and later, someone snapped them, enjoying life on the deck of the boat.

The pictures were taken *after* their disappearance.

***

"What was all that about?" Steve gestured at the phone.

"Seems Pliskin knows of our holiday plans."

"Holiday plans? What…?"

I gestured at Desaux's iron neck, seeing his eyes flick away from the rearview.

Outside, blue skies and scorched grass passed by at a leisurely pace, the occasional dust-covered car whooshing past, but, in the middle of the day, the sun was high and most people kept out of it. The road was an endless stream of scrub grass and tumble-down stone walls, interspersed with scatterings of buildings seemingly cast down like corn feed for chickens. Every now and again there was the promise of a village—a gas station, superstore or taverna, a collection of houses and shops, which soon petered out to sun-bleached scrubland. Even here, everything had an air of neglect, of not being well kept or only half-finished. I suppose the Spanish call it *mañana*. Along the way, we passed the main NAMFI facility, hiding behind its low walls, forbidding high fences and vicious razor wire.

After a while, the nothingness gave way to real civilization. The houses became smarter, peppered with apartment blocks and lush bougainvillea tumbling over balconies, shops, and supermarkets. We were descending the winding road leading down toward the town of Chania, a gleaming white mosaic, tumbling into the azure waters of the bay beyond. Eventually, Desaux pulled over on an anonymous town street.

"This is where I leave you."

"And *this* is where?" I peered despondently through the windows. Dusty cars lined the street on both sides. Beyond the sidewalks were shops and apartment blocks, balconies almost touching across the road, telephone wires hanging like liana in swathes. We were not in the tourist quarter; the shops were travel agents, realtors, clothes shops, pharmacies, and the occasional bar and restaurant. The sort of place where the locals would live and the tourists rarely ventured—which suited me.

"Chania Old Town. I was ordered to leave you outside the old market but this time of day, it will be crowded with tourists. This is more discreet. Fewer people to notice you arriving—if you get my drift, sir. A friend of mine works at the rent-a-car on the corner. Mention my name and he will fix you up with a car, no questions asked."

"You're a good man, Desaux."

"Can we stop the old pals' act and get out of this bloody car?" Steve loosened her seat belt and heaved open the door. Desaux offloaded the bags from the trunk and reached out a hand, somewhat self-consciously.

"Good luck with your search, sir."

Proof of Life

Chapter 51

As Airman Desaux disappeared down the street, my stomach was telling me I was hungry. The sun was at its height, like opening an oven door, scorching on my skin. We crossed to the shady side of the street but still stuck out like clowns at a wake in our khaki NATO issue fatigues. Along the street, several of the doorways had signs saying they rented rooms.

"These all look a little seedy to me." Steve wrinkled her nose; there was a distinct smell of drains. "Why don't we speak to your new best friend's friend? The rent-a-car guy? Maybe he can suggest somewhere where we won't catch fleas and dysentery."

"You can take the girl out of Salisbury…"

"So I have standards? Who knows what they do in these places? They probably rent by the hour."

"Right now, we have little choice. Anyhow, we won't spend a lot of time here."

"Thank God for small mercies."

Desaux was as good as his word. His friend, the rent-a-car guy, hired us a small Citroen for one hundred euros cash. One week, and the only stipulation—bring it back full of gas and undamaged. I showed Franklin Farrell's US driver's license, but he waved it away without a glance. I got the impression my hundred euros were off the books. For the entire transaction, the swarthy muscle-bound man didn't stop texting. Steve asked about rooms. He looked us up and down, smiled lasciviously, and pointed us to a doorway across the street where a small, squat woman sat on a wicker chair in the shade. She was one of those archetypal grandmothers they manufacture in a Greek factory somewhere. Gray hair tied up into a bun, a wraparound floral apron straight from the Nineteen Forties, and a pair of sharp eyes scrutinizing us through a leathery roadmap of tanned age lines. She showed us to a couple of passable rooms and, by mid-afternoon, we had changed and headed to the harbor for something to eat.

Down by the water, tourists crammed the streets. After the midday surge, the waiters were lolling about, regaining their stamina for the evening, ogling the women and waving laminated menu cards solicitously. Steve pointed, and we sat under the shade of the restaurant's palm-thatched veranda. With her spiked auburn hair and shades, sipping cola through a straw, Steve blended in perfectly, unrecognizable as the terrified blonde girl on the news reports, although even those had dwindled now. Behind her, the waves sparkled and lapped laconically against the ancient harbor walls, rigging rung against aluminum masts, and traffic buzzed moodily along the road. As we waited for seafood, my mind drifted back. A mental itch I had failed to scratch.

"Back on the boat? What happened?"

Steve looked up from her glass. "Well, I forgot about the other boats on the horizon. I was more concerned with you and Jardine. The sun was burning my neck, so I went into the cabin, found a cold drink, and must have fallen asleep. The next thing I knew, I was staring up at that bloody Sicilian hitman. He was searching the cabin. I screamed. He jumped a mile, then he grabbed me and started asking me about *Roccia Ambrata*—Amber Rock. If I knew where Moretti's information was. I just said I knew nothing, I was just a secretary. Eventually, he got bored and gave up."

"And then?"

"He left me in the cabin. He'd put those bloody ties on my wrists and ankles. I was shit-scared. I thought he was going to kill me like Moretti. Instead, he went out onto the deck and waited. Next thing I know, the door opened, and you tumbled into the cabin, out for the count. Then he tied you up, and I heard him hammering somewhere behind me. He stood up, stared straight at me, and smiled. I will never forget those eyes. Callous and cold. Like he didn't give a damn. After he left, I started kicking you. I thought you'd never wake up."

"What about Jardine? He came up before me."

Steve shrugged and sucked through her straw noisily. "As I say, I was shit-scared, all I could see was Baresi. Why? What's on your mind."

"When I resurfaced, I dealt with the pilot of Baresi's boat then moved back to the *Genevieve*. I couldn't see Jardine; not even his wetsuit or tanks. I assumed Baresi had dealt with him. Anyhow, Baresi saw me and we fought. I had Baresi pinned against the ladder up to the bridge, holding his gun arm with one hand and his free arm with the other. Still, he laid me out."

"And?"

"So if I had both his arms, who the hell hit me?"

***

After supper, we took a stroll along the harbor wall, taking our time. A balmy afternoon gradually drifted into a balmy evening, lazy with holiday-makers, music, and the smells of food and the sea. For the first time in over a week, I allowed myself to relax. Hopefully, Baresi would not find us for a day or two. A day or two for us to run further away.

We did normal stuff, ducking in and out of tourist shops, eating yogurt ice cream, and frowning disapprovingly at catch-penny knick-knacks, probably manufactured in the

Proof of Life

Far East. Then we found a noisy bar on the seafront, listened to music, and drank beer. Across the road, through the milling crowds, a few lights studded the inky blackness of the sea. Lonely, isolated. For once, that was not me.

"So what will you do after your degree?" I wasn't great at small talk. I needed an *in*.

Steve shrugged, her mind pulled back from somewhere far away. "I hadn't thought that far. Something which involves travel, seeing the world."

"Who needs a degree?" I gestured around her. "Rome, Sardinia, Venice, and now Crete."

She raised her eyebrows, scrunched her face in mock horror. "Er, secret identities, life-guard training, ordnance, ballistics, field medicine, not to mention the psychology of murderers. Should get a bloody Masters when I get back."

"The University of Life, lady. And no student debt."

She smiled and looked down at the table.

"You thinking about home?"

"Yeah. Mom and Dad. Right now? Probably climbing the flock wallpaper and contacting Amnesty International, if my dad's got anything to do with it. He's—excitable. Sees everything as a world-class problem requiring a monumental solution. Probably because his job is so boring."

"And your mom?"

"Oh, she'll approach this with the same level-headed stoicism she does everything. What doesn't kill you makes you stronger, and all that. She'll sit patiently, waiting for news while all the time, the anxiety will burn her up from the inside. The British disease. Stiff upper lip. Then one day, it'll all be over and she'll flick her bedside manner back on, vindicated. *See? Nothing to worry about after all.*"

Steve stopped and looked away at the TV. A soccer game, a low hubbub of excitable commentary, that no one was watching. She brushed a tear from her cheek. I felt like shit for asking.

"I'm sorry, Steve. I'll get us another beer." When I joined the Marines, I'd heard a saying: *It is also a victory to know when to retreat.*

When I returned, she'd repaired the makeup and sat cross-legged on the tall stool, a foot bouncing to the rhythm of the cheap music, turning her mind to happier things. A stiff upper lip of her own? I set down the beers and looked at her for a moment. Really looked at her, like I'd not done before. The smooth line of her jaw down to a chin with the faintest of clefts. Her mouth, asymmetric, one corner always turned up in a half-smile. Her eyes were wide, pale blue in the glow of the flickering candle.

There was an inevitability about the evening, and it left me afraid. Steve was out of my league. Educated, beautiful, funny, and I was some bum abandoned by the Marines, trying not to get killed. Trying not to get her killed.

"And who's there for you, Beckett? Whose warming their toes by your fire, waiting on the moment you return?" I looked away, embarrassed she'd caught me.

"I live alone. Relationships don't really work in this line of business."

"There must have been someone, sometime. Unless you're… You're not…?"

I raised my eyebrows and made a face between shock and disapproval. I probably looked deformed.

"Not that I know of. There have been a few. There was one, but it was over a long while ago."

I recalled a rainy night outside Dusseldorf, Marta Neumann, silhouetted against the lamplight, rain dripping from her hair, an *auf wiedersehen* that became goodbye. An immense, gnawing sense of loss. A pain far greater than a

Proof of Life

sniper's bullet smashing into my shoulder. "Nothing more recent, though. Well, nothing serious."

"Love 'em and leave 'em, eh Beckett?"

I shuddered. There was something in her tone. Intimate. No longer detached. Now she'd set her emotional IEDs. I felt myself dancing toward the minefield, about to be blown to pieces.

"More leaving than loving, Steve. Now they've all left."

"Not all of them, Beckett." She leaned over, the warmth of her breath on my cheek as she kissed me.

I shuddered again, only now I was enjoying the sensation. Lost in the promise it offered. A question had been making its way to the surface of my beer. It lingered in the ant trail of fizzing bubbles appearing from halfway down the bottle. Now it emerged with the froth and begged to be answered, but not with words. I cupped a hand behind her neck. Held her close, moving her mouth to mine and kissing her, long and deep. The Europop, the soccer game, everyone in the bar, drifted away. For a moment, she became my world.

Our lips parted, but we stayed close. Suddenly awkward, I sat upright, my hand lingering as it left her shoulder.

"I don't know if this is a good thing, Steve."

"Gunfights, boats sinking, bodies everywhere, and you don't know if *this* is a good thing?" She sipped her beer, wetted her lips, ran a tongue over them.

"You know what I mean."

"Maybe you're right, Beckett, but as you said, best not to think too far ahead." She leaned in once more.

"What happens in Crete…"

Chapter 52

Sunday, September 15

I watched her reflection in the mirror, silhouetted against the morning sun through the thin drapes. The outline of her face as she freshened up her hair, the sinuous curve of her neck, the contours of her breasts and hips. Her skin was pale and smooth as marble, a dark horizon between the stark morning and the lingering memory of the night.

"What are you thinking about?" Steve half-turned. I felt cheap, like some voyeur, getting my kicks when no one could see me.

"What happened last night? Me and you." I was embarrassed, unable to find adequate words for what I felt.

"It takes two to tango, Beckett."

"Yeah, but someone still has to lead."

"And you think that was you? Nothing happened last night I didn't want to happen. Now, Rome, Sardinia, Venice. They were a different matter. Don't think a night of passion gets you off the hook. You still owe me big-time."

So why did I feel like a shit?

Thrust so close together, there was an inevitability about what had happened. Love, lust, passion, there are a thousand names for it, and a thousand reasons I should have resisted. Kept her at arm's length until I could safely hand her over to the authorities. This was business and I'd made it pleasure, blurring the line, forgetting which side of it we both stood.

Proof of Life

When this was over, would I be able to just walk away?

"Why the tattoo?" I asked, for want of something to say. On her right hip, she had a red rose in full bloom—vibrant, beautiful, fragile. I wasn't great on tattoos, even less so when on women, but around the size of a silver dollar, it was as erotic as hell. She turned and smiled. Her eyes were warm, the bed was cooling, and I already felt bereft.

"*Carpe diem*, Beckett. Seize the day. Like a rose, life is short, and we spend too much time concerned about the past, worrying about the future, we forget how precious the present is. Living the moment, smelling the roses."

"Whoa, deep!" I lay back on my hands and thought about it. How long could this rose bloom before Baresi made it wither and die?

"Actually," she winked. "I was with a group of girls on a night out in Bristol. Hurt like hell for a week."

She took my hand and perched on the edge of the bed, still naked except for some supermarket panties in a shade of mauve. My eyes lingered too long on her breasts as she stretched her arms through the sleeves of a t-shirt.

"Love 'em and leave 'em. Remember, Beckett?"

Once more, she was reading my mind. The truth was, I wasn't the *love 'em and leave 'em* type. I was hard-wired to fall in love with every woman I met, to squirm in the straitjacket of pointless infatuation until they breezed on out or I came to my senses. One day, this would be over. She would return to Salisbury, England, and I would be left broken. So deeply in love with a memory. I pulled her close, letting my lips run over her neck, smelling the fresh perfume.

Then I whispered, "Carpe diem, Steve."

And we made love once more.

***

We breakfasted down at the harbor. The sun was already hot on our necks, so we stopped to buy sun cream and water, welcoming the air-con in the tourist shops. My mind was still on the previous night, Steve's body against mine, the feel of her skin, the gnawing quandary it left me in.

We were close to the secret of Max Anderson's disappearance. I could feel it. Something about Crete, about Chania. Something comforting and peaceful. It was a place I would happily disappear to. The architecture, the harbor, the bars, and the shops. We had seen them all in the photos from Moretti's computer. I was certain Max and Kate had made it to Crete. All we had to do was find them.

But what then? Where would that leave Steve? Where would it leave me?

"Do you think I will ever be able to return to a normal life?" Strolling in the heat, with the salty breeze off the ocean, Rome, Cagliari, Venice, even Renzo Baresi, all seemed a lifetime away. She was wearing shorts and a t-shirt. Her legs had already started to redden.

"Depends what you see as normal." I stared out at the line separating the white crests of the Mediterranean and the smooth harbor. Between the rolling breakers of the previous week and the dead calm of today. "Will life ever be the same? No. We are shaped by our experiences. For me, this is normal."

"Yes, but me as a secretary or PA," she mused. "Even back at University—it seems like a lifetime ago."

"That's what places like this do to you."

"True, but a few days out. A few days of sunshine, good food, and a chance to relax. That's okay?"

"Yeah. Right now, that's okay."

Proof of Life

Chapter 53

Of course, the *Diktynna A* was not berthed in Chania—neither in the Old Venetian Harbor nor the newer, more modern, Nea Hora Marina, a twenty-minute walk away. After thirty years, it was always a long shot, so we bought ice cream and chilled for a while, watching the tourists go by.

The Archaeological Museum of Chania was three hundred yards from the Old Harbor. Housed in an airy converted church that used to belong to Venetian monks, it comprised a vast gallery of vaulted ceilings and columned archways. Along the central nave, there were statues I didn't recognize and glass cases containing relics I didn't care about. People who focus on the past often forget the present. All I could learn from a museum was that the people who carved this stuff, who worshiped these icons, are all dead now. But at least it was cool. Steve got an enormous kick from it. Like a kid in a candy store, the benefit of higher education, and a geeky father. I respectfully peered into several of the glass cabinets, craned over to read the blurb off of the little white cards pinned to the wall and I checked out the gift shop, dropping five euros on a leather *good luck* bracelet which I hoped Steve would like. Then I sat out in the small courtyard garden, dozing, thinking about the previous night, and waiting for her to get bored. I'd just gotten cozy when she peered around the doorway, wide-eyed, squinting in the sunlight and beckoning frantically.

"Beckett, over here."

Heaving myself wearily from the comfortable bench, I followed her back into the nave, around halfway down,

Proof of Life

where she gestured at a yellowing statue that had seen better days. Gazing wistfully into the distance, the woman was missing both her arms and one leg, the metal support acting as a crutch. All I could think of was *Long John* Silver from *Treasure Island*. Beside her, probably peeing up the tree stump which formed the only piece of scenery, a rather scary headless dog waited patiently. The little white card read:

Statue of goddess Artemis.

It was found at the Diktynnaion sanctuary (Menzies Kissamou), 1913.

"Diktynnaion sanctuary, Beckett. That must be Diktynna." Steve was excited, like a kid who'd found a cake in the pantry and wanted a slice.

"Says Artemis." Distractedly, I flipped a finger at the card. Educational as the museum might be, my interest had waned as soon as I crossed the threshold.

"Can I help you?" We turned in unison to find a smiling docent—a tall, olive-skinned woman wearing a light blouse and skirt and a name badge called *Evangeline*. Steve stepped forward. Probably so I wouldn't embarrass myself. "We are looking for information on Diktynna. A friend suggested we try here." Steve gestured at the sculpture. "Is this Diktynna?"

The docent smiled again, somewhat condescendingly, her mind shuffling her Rolodex of amazing Cretan facts.

"The mythologies of Diktynna and Artemis *are* rather intertwined, but no. This statue dates from the Roman occupation, between the first century BC and the fourth century AD. The deity Diktynna predates the Romans."

I rested my chin on my thumb and forefinger, attempting to look erudite. "So, tell us about Diktynna."

"Follow me." The docent twirled and set off, her heels sending resounding cracks across the tiled floor. She spoke as she walked.

"Diktynna was worshipped as a goddess throughout all of Crete, but mainly in the west, where most temples were built in her honor. The Diktynnaion sanctuary, where the statue was found, is north of here, on the Rodopos peninsula. It is still an important site in Cretan mythology."

The docent stopped by another small figurine. A fulsome bare-breasted woman, in a floor-length bell-shaped skirt, a writhing snake in each hand. Another dog sat on top of her head, intact and a lot less scary.

"This is a replica of a statue found in the excavations of Knossos; the original is in the Archaeological Museum of Heraklion. We believe it to be Diktynna, in her role as goddess of the earth's blossoms."

"Isn't she also called *The Lady of the Nets*?" I was bored with parrying random facts like a bombardment of frisbees.

The docent smiled and nodded, a little too patronizingly. "You see her skirts are fashioned from fishing nets? Do you know the legend that surrounds her?"

I shook my head, obligingly. I wanted to get back to our room, to cool off, make love and try to find some shred that would bring us nearer to the Andersons.

"She was the daughter of Zeus and of Carme. A favorite of Artemis, she loved hunting and nature. She was a beautiful woman, born in Western Crete, remaining a virgin by choice. The legend says King Minos II fell deeply in love with her, and chased her around the island for nine months, until finally she leapt from the cliff where the Diktynnaion sanctuary stood. She was caught in the nets of the fishermen, earning herself the name of Diktynna—Goddess of Nets. The fisherman who saved her took her to Greece, where he too fell in love with her. Once more, to protect her virtue, Diktynna fled to the sanctuary of Artemis, where the goddess rewarded her for keeping her vow of chastity and made her immortal."

Proof of Life

The docent spoke with passion and, bored as I was, it occurred to me there were too many coincidences to ignore. A sailboat called the *Diktynna A*, a Cretan goddess of the same name, and photos of the Andersons that were almost certainly taken after they disappeared. Steve's intuition had been right on the mark. The Andersons had cast themselves in the water and fled to sanctuary in Crete.

"So, what is your interest in Diktynna?" asked the docent.

"Just curiosity. My family owned a sailboat called the *Diktynna A*. I wondered where the name came from. I thought it would be an ideal opportunity to find out and grab some culture along the way."

"Interesting. I wonder if the *A* stands for Aegina, the island where the fisherman took her? Where she ended up?"

"Aegina? Where is that?"

"It is in the Saronic group, around one hundred and fifty kilometers north of Crete. Of course, *A* could stand for Anatolikós—meaning Diktynna of the rising sun, or Diktynna of the East. In the east of Crete, the myth goes many centuries further back. Over the years, the goddess has had many names—Diktynna, Britomartis, Achaea, Kore, even Artemis, Vritomartis in the Cretan tongue."

"Britomartis, Vritomartis?" My heart sank. I had hoped coming to Crete would narrow our search. Now it had widened again. Another place, even another island. More hiding places for Max Anderson. Maybe Crete was just another wild goose chase?

"Yes, the cults of Britomartis were mainly in North-East Crete. The Festival of Britomarpeia was held in the ancient city of Olous, where they built a temple to her. They also had images of her on their coinage."

She reached across to a bookshelf and leafed through one of the glossy tourist catch-penny books, padded out with photos and the same text in several languages. "These coins were found in the excavations of Olous." She stopped at a page and held out the book. Just some corroded pieces of metal, but I took her word for it.

"Where is Olous?" asked Steve.

"Near the town of Elounda. Unfortunately, it is now underwater following the volcanic eruption on Santorini in 1540 BC, and the natural movement of tectonic plates, but there are still artifacts below the surface, and it makes for excellent diving."

I shuddered. I'd done enough diving to last a lifetime. Then something occurred to me. I pulled out Fabrizio Rossi's Akurra pendant and handed it to the docent.

"Does this mean anything to you? It's the Rainbow Serpent, we think. With Diktynna and snakes, I was wondering…"

The docent turned over the pendant in her hands. Her brow furrowed as she tilted the locket towards the light of the window. "It's not the Rainbow Serpent. She is quite different. A multi-colored snake. This one is rather drab. It looks like an Australian deity, but I deal only in Greek ones, I'm afraid."

"Ah, okay. Still, it was worth a try. I was told it was a tourist souvenir from Melbourne."

The docent raised her eyebrows and handed it back. "Maybe, but an expensive one. This is solid gold. Where did you get it?"

"The bottom of the Mediterranean."

Proof of Life

Chapter 54

Afternoon once again brought the Cretan equivalent of siesta for the locals, leaving the streets to vendors relieving tourists of their euros from the trestle table stalls, bowing under the weight of tack. The air hung heavy with sage and thyme, and spices and gaudy seashells that would never make it through the green channel at Customs. Counterfeit watches they would not waste their time stopping. Even the traffic had died off. Down at the harbor, we found a seat with a view across the ocean. Somewhere to think.

"What do you make of that? Diktynna, fishermen, all that baloney?" Separating facts from mumbo-jumbo wasn't my strong suit.

Steve pushed her shades onto the top of her head and smiled. "You're a Philistine. I love legends and mythology, wondering where the stories came from, how they grew into myths as they were passed down the generations."

"Benefits of a higher education," I suggested.

Steve gave an affronted huff, scrunched up her face. "No, Beckett. An inquiring mind. There's a difference."

"Whatever. I meant about the *Diktynna A* and the Andersons? I'm not sure we are any further along. Either it's a leap of faith or a fool's errand, and we won't know which until we find them. Or we don't."

"And which do you think it is?"

"Jardine was convinced he knew where their sunken boat was, and he was right. Maybe he's right about them being alive too."

"Okay, he had a tenuous lead, and it worked out. They could still have been killed and thrown overboard, or taken by pirates. If Jardine's right about Amber Rock, maybe they got to the Andersons too?"

"Yeah, but the cabin was empty, the door was locked from the outside, and the boat scuppered. Would Amber Rock, or even pirates, waste time clearing her out before they sunk her? And what about the *Diktynna A*? Jacqueline Robbins bought her at around the right time. Someone photographed the Andersons on board."

"Someone bought a boat and changed its name, then sailed off into the sunset. On the way, she and the Andersons crossed paths and had a drink or two."

"…after they went missing?"

"That's an assumption, Beckett. There are no reliable dates on the photos."

"But Rossi. He told me to find the *Lady of the Nets*—Diktynna."

"Or Britomartis, Artemis, Kore or a hundred and one names. The man's life was ebbing away. He could have been hallucinating for all we know."

"Aw, come on! Is there not a single thing you think is a clue to what happened to the Andersons?"

Steve smiled at the waiter as he placed drinks on the table. She leaned over, a glint in her eye. And a warmth I had rarely experienced before.

"When you get frustrated, the edge of your mouth turns up like a spoiled brat denied sweets?"

Reflexively, I raised my hand and puffed. Steve laughed.

"You're so cute when you're annoyed."

"I am not annoyed," I retorted, somewhat annoyed.

She leaned over, kissing me full on the mouth, lingering

for a long moment. I tasted the bitterness of the wine on her lips. I suddenly felt tremendously horny.

"No, Beckett. Everything around here is Diktynna. It's too obvious. The coins were recovered from Olous—in the East. *Diktynna A* could mean *Diktynna of the East*, like the woman at the museum suggested. Okay, so it could be the island of Aegina. Maybe Max's little joke? The *Diktynna A* ending up where the *goddess Diktynna* ended up. I think we are closer than ever. I just think we are looking on the wrong end of the island, so let's exhaust all avenues here first."

Her reasoning was faultless. "You want we go over to this Olous place?"

"Why not?" Her eyes were alive. The museum had fired her imagination, and now she was on a mission, no longer running away but moving toward something.

"Oh, by the way, while you were looking at pottery and shit, I got you this from the gift shop." I handed over the small paper bag and she peered curiously inside.

"The *Evil Eye*? Really?" Open-mouthed, she held the bracelet up; the small blue bead spun, glinting in the sunlight.

"Evil? No, that's the *All-Seeing Eye*. The lady in the gift shop said you got to make a wish and tie it on. When the leather string breaks, your wish will come true."

"And you believe that nonsense?"

"Pascal's wager, Steve. If you believe, and it's not true, you've lost nothing. If you don't believe and it's true, well…"

"Seriously?"

"No, I'm shitting with you." I reached over and took the bracelet, tying it on her wrist. "Now make a wish."

Steve screwed her eyes up as if the effort of wishing was physical. Then she opened them, smiled, and we shared another long, deep kiss.

Proof of Life

Chapter 55

Monday, September 16

When I awoke, the sun had yet to rise. Unable to sleep, I left Steve under the sheets and went looking for breakfast. It annoyed me I had paid for two rooms. The streets were empty, except for gray-haired grandmothers holding armfuls of bread and cheese, chattering on corners. A few people were reluctantly off to work, their faces buried in smartphones. There was an apocalyptic silence; peaceful yet unnerving, broken only by the subdued roar of unseen street-cleaning trucks. Steve was still asleep when I returned, the soft rise and fall of the bedclothes, the sigh of her breath. For a long moment, I dwelt in the memory of her back against my skin, the way we made love, and of the remains of the night, wrapped in each other's arms, unaware of the world and hoping the night would never end.

But end it did. At 5:00 pm. A missed call from Pliskin.

Of course, I should've phoned back immediately. Procrastination is the thief of time. Instead, I laid out breakfast and procrastinated some more, looking through the small window out over the yard behind the hotel. Flagstoned with diamond-shaped beds, at its center, a gnarled tree, probably older than the building, writhed its way to a canopy of green. Even in the shade, the plants blossomed out over the path. Aubretia, Bougainvillea, and Hibiscus, a small patch of herbs, all doing their thing in this oasis away from the world. I envied them. For as long as I could remember, I had been chasing or running, searching or hiding, fighting and killing. Maybe it was time to stop. To hang up the Glock and drive a taxi in this island paradise for a while. And when I got bored with that…?

The bedclothes rustled. Steve propped herself up on an elbow. "What time is it?"

"7:30. Early yet. I got breakfast."

She threw back the sheet, naked except for underwear, red tan lines around her neck, arms, and thighs, and sat on the edge of the bed. She got up, kissed me, and disappeared into the en-suite.

I couldn't put off the call to Pliskin any longer.

"Beckett. Bright and early. You saw my email then?"

"Uh-huh," I lied. I had not checked my emails since leaving Aviano. "Bright and early? What time is it there?"

"I don't know. The perpetual darkness of the comms. room. No windows, no clocks. Perhaps it's for the best. To stop us dreaming of things—or people—we can never have." My heart jumped. There was something in his tone. Something reproving. Did he know about Steve and me?

"Anyhow," he continued. "What have you discovered during your Mediterranean sojourn?"

Pliskin probably already knew the stories of goddesses and fishermen. He knew everything else. "We haven't found the boat yet, but we made some inquiries and we have some leads. We are still not sure the Andersons came to Crete, but nothing confirms they didn't."

"Well, maybe I can help you. Do you have the email?"

I pulled my MacBook from the wall charger and flipped it open. The email contained a series of spreadsheets. Bank statements. Financial stuff.

"Jeez, Pliskin. You've been busy. It's early here, so do you have a summary?"

"You suggested Max Anderson would need to prepare

for his disappearance. It seems you were right."

"Was that a compliment?"

"Please don't get carried away. We all get lucky sometime. Okay, a précis. In 1982, whilst at University, Max and Kate opened separate personal bank accounts with the Midland Bank in Oxford, England. Later, they also opened a joint account at the same bank. By 1988, they each had a healthy balance in their personal accounts, with the joint account ticking over, paying bills. By 1990, all three accounts were empty. Each time they paid in money, it was withdrawn in cash soon after, leaving only enough for living expenses."

"They were preparing to split?"

"Indeed, Beckett. By 1990, until their disappearance, they lived on practically nothing. Each had bequests from their parents that subsequently vanished. They also sold the house in Camden Town and moved into a rental. The equity from the house sale has also vanished. We estimate that over the four years, they spirited away three-quarters of a million pounds sterling."

"So what happened to the money?"

"We can only guess. In 1999, they were declared legally deceased. The liquidated estate and the meager life insurance payouts were shared out amongst immediate relatives. But that amounted to less than ten thousand pounds sterling."

"So, a blind alley then?" Behind me, the shower had stopped. Steve emerged, a towel draped around her. I raised a finger to my lips and put the phone onto speaker.

"Not quite," continued Pliskin. "Knowing the money must have been transferred somewhere, and with Jacqueline Robbins our only other lead, our attention turned to her."

"I thought you said you found nothing on her."

"That was then. This is now. This time, we checked residency records and bank accounts outside the UK. We tried France, Spain, Italy, and Greece. After discarding the noise, we had three hits; one in Greece and two in Italy. So we checked bank records and struck pay dirt. In 1988, Jacqueline Robbins opened an account with the Hellenic Bank in Athens. By 1990, the account contained roughly the amount the Andersons had spirited away."

A shiver ran down my spine, a frisson of excitement. "So, what are we saying? Kate Anderson and Jacqueline Robbins are the same people?"

"There is no *we* in team, Beckett, but yes, that is what *I* am saying. The Andersons acquired the identity of Jacqueline Robbins to disguise their escape. I have found the transactions that paid for the *Melusina* in 1989, and re-registered her as the *Diktynna A* in the Spring of 1990. Robbins also paid for a berth in Mahon, Menorca."

Menorca. Not a million miles away from the wreck of the *Spirito del Vento*.

"Then," continued Pliskin, "in 1991, she paid fourteen and a half million Greek Drachma to a realtor in Athens. Around one-hundred-and twenty-six thousand dollars."

"They bought property. Any idea where?"

"I'm afraid not. The realtor succumbed to the poor Greek economy. We only have the transaction in a bank account."

"So Kate Anderson aka Jacqueline Robbins is somewhere in Greece?"

"Yes. At least she was then."

Steve's eyes were flicking back and forth, trying to assemble the fragments. Her wet hair was dripping onto the counterpane as she listened intently.

"So what about the boat—the *Diktynna A*?" I asked.

"You recall, I told you, Robbins berthed it in Mahon?"

"Uh-huh."

"Two days before the Andersons' disappearance, Robbins flew from Cagliari to Malpensa, in Italy. Two hours later, she flew on to Menorca Airport, Mahon."

I took a slug of coffee, hoping it would clear away the fog. Jacqueline Robbins, Kate Anderson. Accounts in England and Greece, money moving backward and forward. I was losing track.

"So what you're saying is the Andersons traveled to Cagliari, rented the *Spirito del Vento,* but only Max Anderson sailed to the rendezvous point?" I jumped as Steve spoke out loud.

"Good morning, Miss Jordan, or should I say *Ruth Davis*." Steve grimaced, forgetting the phone was on speaker. At the other end, Pliskin sighed. "Beckett, this is supposed to be a secure line. Anyhow, yes. Five days earlier, Kate Anderson, as Ms. Robbins, flew to Mahon and sailed the *Diktynna A* to the rendezvous point. Then they transferred to the *Diktynna A*, scuppered the rental boat, and sailed off into the sunset. If your guess is right, they sailed to Crete."

Steve leaned over. "It's *my* guess, really, Mr. Pliskin. I recognized some buildings in the photos of the Andersons, only I had forgotten where on Crete, as I was only eight when we came here."

I rapped my finger against my mouth furiously, trying to persuade Steve to keep quiet. She returned an infuriating broad grin, mimicked a zipper across her face, and sauntered around to the wardrobe.

"Beckett, take the goddamn phone off speaker."

Sheepishly, I pressed a button and raised the phone to my ear. "Right, you're off speaker."

"Good." Pliskin's voice had turned monotone, annoyance seeping into every consonant. "Remember,

Proof of Life

Beckett, this is not a vacation. You have been employed—as in we are paying you—to find out about Amber Rock. We are indulging your search for Max Anderson, but I have to tell you, our patience is wearing gossamer thin. Have I made myself clear?"

"Crystal, Pliskin. Crystal."

"So, what are your plans?"

"I guess we try to find the town Steve's family visited."

Pliskin was unimpressed. "As plans go, that's pretty broad. Crete is a big island."

"Yes, but the museum? Diktynna? We have a few leads."

"Keep me informed. I don't want to keep ringing you to find out if you are still alive."

"I will, I promise." I crossed my fingers behind my back.

There was a pause as Pliskin collected his thoughts. Above the static, I could hear the faint noise on the encrypted line. Tens, maybe hundreds of calls like mine, chopped up, encoded, and sent around the world in the blink of an eye. It sounded like an old-fashioned spool tape recorder playing backward at high speed.

"Renzo Baresi was seen in Rome boarding a plane to Heraklion, so you should expect company. You and the girl are still his primary targets, but now he has a new one. He knows you are close to finding Max Anderson, and he wants to be there when you do. Three birds, one stone, so to speak."

"What do you want me to do?"

"Find Anderson before Baresi does. Protect him. Eliminate Baresi. Then, and only then, bring in Max and Kate Anderson."

***

By the time I hung up on Pliskin, my coffee was cold, and I had lost my appetite. Steve was sitting on the bed, dressed in a pastel blue vest top and khaki shorts.

"We have to make a move."

She looked up, doing that pouting thing women do to spread their lipstick evenly. "Are you—mad with me?"

"Pliskin's my boss. That little trick with the phone just now…"

"Oh, come on! Your expression was priceless."

"Look, Steve, my job is on the line unless we pull our thumbs out of our butts and find Anderson. Now let's go."

Proof of Life

Chapter 56

The Citroen rental had no sat-nav or air-con. It was like driving a tin can for three hours across a hot plate. The wind through the open window barely ruffled Steve's short-cropped hair as she sulked behind her shades. So I was mad at her for interrupting the phone call, for getting me into trouble with Pliskin. I knew I couldn't stay mad at her for long. Lines had to be drawn, even if she trod them into the sand later.

Crete is actually a collection of small islands around one long one, around two hundred miles from east to west; about twice the length of Long Island. Of course, it was a world away from New York. Whilst Montauk to Manhattan is an easy drive—until Farmingdale when the traffic snarls—the roads in Crete are smaller and wilder. The drive takes in flat fertile plains, plunging gorges, and narrow mountain passes. Fortunately, our route was along the northern coast. The South was less populated and much wilder, the desolate spine formed by the White Mountains, the Idi Range, and the Dikti mountains in the East. It was easy to see why the island was so alive with myth and legend. Cut off from Greece, it has its own economy, its own ecosystem, and its own history.

As we neared Heraklion, the capital of Crete, the expressway took a sweeping curve across the outskirts of the city before dipping close to the airport, where even now, Baresi may be fastening his belt for landing, or smiling at border control. The Sicilian definitely had an excellent source of intelligence. We had flown incognito in a cargo plane, yet still, he knew. Somewhere, there was a leak.

Proof of Life

Our new destination, Agios Nikolaos, was on the edge of the Mirabello Bay, a nick cut out of the North East of the island. Then we needed to follow the signs for Elounda, where the ancient city of Olous lay beneath the sea. Needing a break, I pulled the Citroen into a gas station and parked off the pumps. Outside the car, the blazing sun instantly dried the patchwork of sweat stains on my shirt before starting to roast me. Still, I like the dry heat. It's good for my shoulder, good for my mood. Rain always gets me down.

Steve propped her shades on top of her head and smiled. She reached out a hand, and I took it.

"Don't think you have gotten away with it. I am still mad at you." But the smile on my face was transparent. The line had already been trampled.

Together we browsed the small supermarket, stocked up on bottled water and snacks. Another of the ubiquitous elderly ladies in a wraparound apron sat on a plastic chair behind the cash desk, glued to a TV whispering the news. Some riot on the streets of Paris. Another fatuous statement on energy from our illustrious president and a lorry blockade somewhere on the mainland. Out front, a rough-haired dog with xylophone ribs yanked at his rope and barked as we returned to the car. It all seemed a thousand miles from where we had been over the last week.

The E75 took another sweeping loop, this time out towards the coast. Above holiday lets and beachside villas, the sea was a stark azure blue, faintly dappled with small white breakers, dotted with ships making their way into the harbor, and tourist boats sailing out for hedonistic pleasure. Agios Nikolaos was still around an hour away, so I settled back into the rhythm of the road, fretting over the conversation with Pliskin. Of the lengths the Andersons had gone to in order to engineer their disappearance, even their deaths. If I failed to measure up if Pliskin turned nasty, would I be able to disappear? Maybe I would meet Baresi first? Eventually, there would be a showdown. One of us would win. Frankly, it didn't matter who. Dead men don't fret over anything.

We left the coast behind and plunged into the hinterland of scree-covered cliffs and fathomless gorges, where spindly trees and dogged bushes clung on precariously. The road became a monotonous ribbon of beige, and the easy hum of the engine weighed on my eyelids. I turned on the radio and pressed buttons—bouzoukis, accordions, and the all-pervasive Europop. I turned it off. I had enough problems.

"Eagles!" Steve was pointing out of the window.

Ducking my head, I looked up at the sky above, but couldn't see a thing. "Eagles?"

"Yes. Golden eagles. I remember being in a coach, me and Charlie looking out of the windows for golden eagles after the guide said they were in the hills. We passed a monastery on the edge of the road."

"So, we're going the right way?"

She shrugged. "I was eight, but maybe."

Sure enough, another mile or two around a bend was a monastery, shoe-horned into a tiny space beside the road. I didn't see any eagles. By the beaming grin on Steve's face, I knew they would be hovering somewhere overhead.

After a while, the steep sides fell away to plains, to flat, barren land broken only by outlets, car lots, and gas stations. There was still an air of sullen existence, of *survive* rather than *thrive*. Agios Nikolaos was a tourist town and a busy port. At its center, there is a pool that is supposed to be bottomless. Maybe I could throw Baresi's cold dead corpse in one day, but for now, we skirted around the town and headed North.

"You recognize anything else?"

"Not yet. Sort've familiar, but it all looks the same, really."

Proof of Life

The road back out of town was typically Mediterranean, hugging a serpentine coastline, dotted with tavernas and hotels, holiday lets, and premium villas, climbing the hillside and enjoying the view. But even here, vacant or abandoned lots interspersed them. Dusty cars and scooters packed into any space left unfenced. Back in Bethesda, people cut their front lawns with a scalpel. They painted their shingles to death. Weekends spent cleaning cars, cleaning windows, cleaning every damn thing. I am sure the Cretans are house-proud. I just don't think they give two shits about anything outside their front doors. After all, there is a local authority for that sort of thing, right? I had read the Greeks were creative with their tax accounting and the authorities, even more so with the little they could excise. Still, everyone seemed happy in the sun, and the system worked just fine.

Soon we were back out into the tan-colored hillside, covered with an acne rash of green trees and bushes, here and there a small villa or two, shimmering in the baking heat.

"Can we pull over a moment?" Steve pointed to a lay-by.

"This familiar?" I drew the Citroen over and peeled my back from the seat. The car had become a furnace.

"Vaguely. I keep seeing the white church with the red roof, and the castle on an island. I am sure we're close."

Mirabello Bay stretched away to the mountains in the South, swathed in a blanket of haze. Only the white tails of speed boats and dark scars of islands broke the ink-blue plane of the sea. Below us, swanky hotels and holiday lets skirted the coast back into the town.

After a while, we summoned up the courage to get back into our car and drive on. It was a wrench. I could have looked at the view all day. A few minutes later, we descended toward the town of Elounda, traveling through a strip mall of tourists lets, gift shops, and tavernas. Once, Elounda had probably been a quiet fishing village, but now, like Coney

Island or Atlantic City, locals took second place to tourist dollars and a snake of rental cars. I parked up a side street, one hundred yards from the busy main road. Off the tourist drag, there was the same air of neglect and faded elegance we had seen elsewhere. An old guy sat in his front yard under a shade of begonias, hemmed in by a small stucco wall and the line of parked cars and scooters. All he could do was look over his wall at them and hope they would get lost sometime soon. He lifted his stick in greeting, and Steve waved and shouted *kalimera,* like a native. She smiled and took my hand as we negotiated the mobile chicane of tourists and vehicles. Out on the front, it was quieter. The breeze playing off the sea felt good on my face. The marina was a rectangle of deep clear aquamarine, surrounded by bobbing pleasure craft and idle drumming tour boats. We strolled along the harbor side, only casually looking at the boats. If not for Max Anderson and Renzo Baresi, we could have been holiday-makers, John and Joan taking a week from the factory, and forgetting their workaday cares. I imagined Max and Kate Anderson sitting on the wall, legs in the water. They had made their escape, put their troubles behind them. In that instant, I yearned to follow them.

"The church with a red roof!" Steve was pointing excitedly again, like a small child seeing a puppy in a pet store. The heart of the town thronged with tourists, a melee of cars, vans, and scooters. In front, a tall bell tower shone bright white, peering out over a vast marina. Its pitched terracotta roof blazed in the sunshine. Behind it, in a neat garden of tall palms and wiry olive trees, surrounded by a box bay hedge, sat a squat Greek Orthodox Church.

"You sure?"

"Absolutely. This is definitely the place, Beckett. There's a pontoon with a restaurant on it, over in the marina. The tour we were on booked it out. Me and Charlie had to sit opposite a German couple who only spoke a little English.

Proof of Life

In the end, we went to the edge and watched the fishes swim. Charlie was only three, so Mom shouted a lot. And there's the castle on an island." She was pointing excitedly again at one of the pop-up kiosks selling boat trips.

"What is that? Spinalonga?" I took my time with the syllables, picked up a leaflet, and stuck it in my shorts pocket. "What about it?"

Steve shrugged. "I don't know. We went across the bay on a boat. Mom was seasick all the way. When we got there, it was boring. Just a castle with a village inside. There was a graveyard which was quite cool." She smiled, a warm smile at the reminiscences of a childhood I knew nothing of. Of a childhood I never had.

Chapter 57

Unsurprisingly, the *Diktynna A* was not in the marina at Elounda either. Thirty years is a long time. Deep down, I knew we had the right place. I just had to hope Anderson was still here, that he was still alive, even.

With time to kill, I suggested we travel across to Steve's castle on an island. Look around. See if it jogged any more memories. It was mid-afternoon before we embarked on the thirty-minute trip. The sea was a millpond, so we watched the world go by as the boat lumbered across. Steve grabbed my arm, and together we hung over the railings, feeling the spray on our faces, looking out at a lost paradise. Overlooked by the rest of the world, it minded its own business and kept its own time. Most visitors probably stumbled on it, as we had. Gradually, the island appeared from behind the headland, a teardrop-shaped jelly mold of tan and olive green, waisted by a line of high walls and fortress ramparts. While Steve rattled off nostalgic reminiscences, I read the leaflet and tried to make myself look erudite.

"The island used to be attached to the Spinalonga peninsula." I gestured casually over my shoulder. "There has always been a fortress and a garrison on it to protect Olous. Arab pirates were rife in the Mediterranean. Over the years, the Romans, Venetians, and the Ottomans had all maintained a presence."

"I was eight, Beckett. It was a castle, okay?" Steve gave me a withering look. I had forgotten women are usually right, even when they're not.

Proof of Life

"Well, not since the 19th century. Apparently, the Greeks finally ousted the Turks and turned it into a leper colony to deter anyone else from invading. It stayed like that until 1957 when modern medicine rendered it obsolete. Now it's just a tourist attraction."

"It's a little macabre." Steve pouted, slightly disgusted. "All those germs. I'm not sure I want to go there now."

"I'll tell the guy up front to turn around, shall I?"

We let the tour parties disembark first; this was part of their vacation, and I needed to be sure no one had followed us. Baresi had already traced us to Crete, and it was playing on my mind. Beyond the small barren foreshore, the walls of the fortress clung to the cliff face, and above them, a circular stronghold, pierced with half a dozen arch top windows kept watch on the invaders, as they chattered and jostled towards the entrance. Steve and I mingled into an American party, eavesdropped on their guide.

"Macabre is right. So much for Cinderella's castle." On either side of the main street, stone-built dwellings lay in ruins, weeds carpeted the paved floors, and gnarled trees and bushes forced themselves through the crumbling brickwork. Medicine may be a wonderful thing, but I wondered what the residents would have felt, to see their town, their home, in such a state.

"Can we get out of here? It's creepy."

We left the group and climbed a perilous stepped side-street, past more ruined buildings and out onto the rugged hillside above town, relieved when the claustrophobia gave way to the ferocity of the sun and the tempering cool of the breeze. On the crest of the island, the Venetians had cleared an area, giving them a view of the whole bay and the shoreline beyond. It also gave them somewhere to place their cannons, according to my leaflet. The west side, facing the bay's mouth, was a patchwork of demolished dwellings, slowly being reclaimed by the undergrowth leading into the town below. Seaward, a barren, forbidding rock face sloped down to the perimeter walls of the fort.

Steve sat on the remains of a stone wall and wiped the sweat from her face. "All these people. Marooned out here and forgotten."

"According to this," I waved my leaflet, "the community thrived. They had regular supplies, medical care, sanitation, everything they needed. Even starting their own businesses and opening shops. They lived well by all accounts."

The rugged hillside was hard going but soon we made it down to the dusty perimeter path, over slatted duckboards, heading northward. At the point of the teardrop, a second stronghold, the Mezzaluna Michiel, guarded the narrow straits out to the sea. A vast arc of battlements threatened a fusillade to any ships entering the bay. Above us, the dividing wall between east and west snaked through the jagged rocks and gnarly trees up toward the clearing. Despite its grotesque history, the island imbued a sense of safety, of security. Surrounded by water, well-protected. I envied the people of Spinalonga. I also felt different, disparate. As an adopted child, I guess it goes with the territory. I could picture myself out here, watching the world go by.

Down in the semi-circular yard behind the battlements, a team of workers was renovating part of the stronghold wall. Others were excavating the ruined dwellings above us. There was a sign in Greek; some kind of preservation project funded by the European Union. I'd seen other gangs across the island, but something captured my attention.

Or rather, someone.

He was standing, stretching his back. His brown scalp glistening through thinning white hair as he removed a tattered cap and wiped his brow. Briefly, our eyes met. Then he turned away to the men, chiseling stone, repointing walls, fetching and carrying. He glanced up at me again, now distracted, deep in thought. Then he clapped a colleague on the shoulder and walked toward the buildings below the walkway, risking another look. This time the expression was unmistakable—fear.

A shock of electricity coursed through me. The world shifted sideways. I grabbed for a rail, my heart racing, slightly dizzy, a strange mixture of exhilaration and foreboding. I had visualized this moment many times. Sometimes happily, often angrily. I gulped water from my bottle, but it was warm. The hilltop was empty. The man had gone.

"We need to return to the boat—now."

"What? Already?" Steve grimaced, twisted my wrist, and scrutinized my Omega. "Nah! We've got ages yet. The boat doesn't leave until 4:30 pm. It's only just after three now."

"All the same," I insisted. "We need to get back. We can come again, I promise."

I took her arm, steering her along the path, in the natural direction of the people. I tried not to look too rushed, tried not to let the panic show.

Steve yanked her wrist free and stood, arms folded. "What's gotten into you, Beckett?" We were by a small church, isolated, facing east out to sea. Tourists were milling around, taking snaps, and ringing the verdigris-stained bell for posterity, or luck, or both. "We haven't seen everything. I want to go back to the town, see the shop, the buildings and I…"

"We have to get back to the mainland as quickly as possible—and without causing a fuss. We'll come back, but now we have to go. Please, Steve. This is important."

Boats were arriving every half an hour. If the man knew a quick way back to port, he could vanish.

"I just don't get you, Beckett. One moment, you're as

nice as pie, chilling in the sun, next you're flying off into some fit of anxiety."

"This is not some fit of anxiety, Steve. Back there. Those men, working on the fort. Well, he was there. He looked right at me. Then he spooked and ran."

"What are you talking about?"

"The man at the dig. Older, smaller, grayer but definitely Max Anderson."

Proof of Life

Chapter 58

We made the exit gate in double-quick time, wet with perspiration in the unremitting heat. I queued for a couple of popsicles, wincing at the price, scanning the meandering crowd for Anderson. Down on the foreshore, there was the usual melee of tourists. The ones who, afraid of missing their ride, waited by the boats and missed half the tour instead. The man, Max Anderson, was not amongst them.

"Excuse me, ma'am, but do you or any of the staff live on the island?" The middle-aged woman in the kiosk eyed me curiously. She had avoided the wrap-around apron in favor of a pink tabard.

"No. Elefthérios comes over on the last boat each night to keep watch, and we all leave on it." Her jet-black ponytail flicked as she cast her head back to a bronze-skinned, middle-aged man in a beige short-sleeved shirt. He was drinking coffee and listening to the radio. One hand held a mobile phone to his ear, the other gestured theatrically as he tried to get some point across to the caller.

"What time is that, ma'am?"

"Around 7:15 pm. The island closes at 7:00 pm."

"And the workers, the archaeologists?"

"They have their own boat." The woman pointed to a small shallow red craft moored off the main jetty, its canopy flapping in the breeze as it bobbed at the end of its rope.

"And what time do they leave—usually?" I checked my watch—3:45 pm.

Irked, the woman looked over her shoulder and

Proof of Life

exchanged a few words with the watchman. He pointed at me and laughed.

"5:00 pm. Sometimes earlier, sometimes later. Please?" She gestured at the short queue behind me. I thanked her and found Steve in a shady corner.

"Why didn't you say something? Introduce yourself."

"Because he saw me, Steve. He knew I had recognized him."

"Well, that's good, isn't it?"

"You've been hiding out for thirty years, in the middle of nowhere, and suddenly, out of the blue, someone turns up and recognizes you?"

"I suppose. What's your plan."

"Except for the security guy, no one stays on the island overnight, so we need to get back to the mainland before him, follow him, see where he goes."

Of course, this particular night, Anderson could stay on the island, tough it out, and hope we'd give up. He could swim to the spit of land opposite and walk home when it got dark. After all, he knew the area, knew the hiding places.

As Steve finished her popsicle in the shade of a couple of knotted walnut trees, I sauntered over to the tour boats. Aside from ours, another four were moored up along with several tiny private craft. I made up an emergency, offered some euros, and we hitched a ride on a boat that would get us back sooner than our own. We hid on the top deck, in the shade, with all the other sweaty, odorous sad sacks who had gotten onto the boat early so as not to miss it. As the crew cast off, it annoyed me Anderson was not among them.

"Do you reckon he's been living here all these years?" Steve was resting an elbow on the gunwale, enjoying the breeze over the water.

"Why not? Look at the place." The sea had turned

turquoise, and away in the distance, the town of Elounda shimmered beneath the butterscotch hillsides. "He's practically invisible. Who'd think of looking here?"

"We did."

"Fair point."

Whatever Anderson knew was yesterday's news. So why was he still running? Maybe he was no longer running? Maybe he and Kate were simply enjoying their new lives, the seclusion, the sun. Until now. A brief meeting of eyes, a millisecond of recognition, had changed all that. Now Anderson knew his past was catching up with him. Even after three decades in his secure hideaway, he would have a plan. More fake passports, money salted away. I knew I had to find him before he ran again.

Our boat nosed into the harbor, vibrating as the engines throttled into reverse. Muscling through, we made the front of the line as the gangplank was lowered. A hundred yards away, the town was as busy as ever, now the afternoon sun was cooling. The restaurants were still enticing customers, touts were still selling tours, and a few fishermen sorted their nets on the quayside. I bought takeout coffee and chicken gyros, and we found a convenient perch to check the returning boats. Steve dangled her feet over the side, as Kate and Max had, many years before. In the distance, punctuating the horizon, the stubby towers of Greek windmills lined the narrow causeway between the mainland and the headland. Where the ancient city of Olous lay submerged, now nothing but crumbling foundations and an interesting place to dive. In the old photo, was that the view Max and Kate saw?

Suddenly, it all made sense. The ancient city, the island of Spinalonga, even the Minoan palace of Knossos further round the coast. Crete was rich in myth and history. Max Anderson had a degree in Classical Archaeology and Ancient

Proof of Life

History from the University of Chicago. If he had to run, why not run to somewhere that would interest him, where he could easily blend in?

"Maybe he won't come back tonight?" After an hour, we had finished our food, and I was becoming impatient.

Steve stopped swinging her legs for a while. "Beckett. It's a beautiful day. Just relax, soak up the rays." She looped her arm through mine and kissed me on the cheek. "Eventually, he'll come back for his car."

But I'd had my fill of UV for the day. I was hot, grubby, and annoyed. If only I hadn't checked out the workers at that precise moment, but lain in wait for them to leave the island. If only, if only…

"I'm going to fetch the car. Bring it down to the harbor. Just in case."

I had tracked down Max Anderson. What now? I could follow him home, ask him straight about Amber Rock, but would he tell me anything? Finding Anderson, delivering Amber Rock to Pliskin, none of it would exonerate Steve of Moretti's killing.

And Baresi was still out there somewhere, and he was still coming for us all.

***

I drove the car down to the harbor and parked near the water, using more absurd small European coins to buy a ticket. At least my pocket felt lighter, even if my heart didn't. Steve had moved to the shade next to the coach park. She was flapping her hands frantically and pointing. A fresh boatload of tourists was spilling ashore over on the cruise dock, like rats escaping a wreck.

"That's him. Khaki hat and coat."

Steve followed my finger to the man. Same blue shirt,

now covered by a khaki utility vest. The hair was under the battered cap. He was cupping his hands as he lit a cigarette. We both turned away so as not to spook him.

"You sure, Beckett? Doesn't look much like the photos."

"He's over sixty, Steve. Comes to us all. Back on the island, I knew it was him, and he knew I knew." Stooped and thin, deeply tanned and with a retreating head of salt and pepper hair, it was hard to reconcile with the happy-go-lucky smile of the guy sitting on this dock thirty years before.

Puffing on the cigarette, engulfed in a cloud of smoke, he crossed the harbor and skipped through the traffic to the other side of the main road, where he waved at a café owner, took a takeout cup, and shot the breeze for a few minutes. His sharp eyes were scanning around him, the streets, the car parks, the kiosks. Reaching over, shaking the vendor's hand, he returned to the harbor, to a battered red Toyota pickup. He opened the door and stood for a moment, finishing the cigarette, letting the PVC seats cool, still eyeing everything cautiously. Then he reversed out of the space and turned left up the main road, snarled by the throng of pedestrians enjoying a walk before an all-inclusive supper.

Proof of Life

Chapter 59

By the time we made it out, Anderson was four cars ahead, crawling through the tight shadowed canyon of buildings that overhung the main road. Leaving the town, we picked up speed and traveled a mile before he turned down a small side-road out towards the coast, through fields of sparsely planted olives in the rocky, clay-colored soil. I hung back, hidden by the rooster-tail of dust draping the air. After around five hundred yards, he turned again, onto a large gravel parking lot. I carried on a while and pulled up behind a dry-stone wall. Anderson alighted and walked urgently, pirouetting, looking around him before disappearing behind the buildings.

According to its sign, the *Taverna Aegina* had been around since the mid-Sixties. Beyond the chalkboard menus, the effusive plants tumbling from Grecian urns, the two-story building was rectangular and workaday, with painted signs and pantiles. Out front, a few early diners were sun-striped, chattering under the trellised pergola. A young girl in a white blouse and black pants stood by a lectern, awaiting further guests.

"I can see why he would want to hide away here." Again, I had a peculiar feeling in my stomach, a mixture of exhilaration, anticipation, and foreboding. Like reaching the end of a long journey and not knowing what the destination holds.

The Taverna looked over the salt lakes and the small flat island that held the remains of the ancient city of Olous, a patchwork of ragged stone walls which slid off into the sea.

Proof of Life

There was no temple to Vritomartis, no wooden statue carved by Daedalus. No sound beyond the gentle lapping of the waves, the song of a million cicadas, and the laconic creaking of an ornamental Greek windmill catching the breeze in the Taverna's garden.

"Over there." Steve nodded to the far side of the parking lot; a half-acre grove of olive trees, gray-green in the falling sun. Sprinklers had kicked off, turning the soil chestnut brown. At first, I couldn't see what had caught her interest, so I followed her until she stopped at a sun-bleached tarpaulin up against the mottled plaster wall. My heart leaped. Beneath, between two cinder block trestles, hung the keel of a boat. Old and weather-worn, it had not seen the water for a long time. My guess was around thirty years.

The Diktynna A. *I wonder if the A stands for Aegina, the island where the fisherman took her? Where she ended up?* The Taverna Aegina.

"You were on the island. Why are you following me?"

We spun in unison. The man stood, hands on hips. Again I saw the look. Fear and recognition. The accent was definitely American. East Coast, tainted through years in Europe. The tan shorts, blue shirt, and khaki hat had given way to formal black pants and a crisp white shirt.

"Mr. Robbins?" We had the boat. I played a hunch.

"Who wants to know?"

"My name is Beckett, and this is Steve Jordan. We are looking for Max Anderson."

"Anderson? I don't know any Anderson." But the flick of the eyes told me he did. He turned to the more palatable view of the salt lakes. "The name's Robbins. Will Robbins. This is my place. That's my boat."

In the smallholding next door, a rooster crowed. I thought of Sundays, of bible class. Of Peter denying Jesus.

"Is *this* the *Diktynna A*, Mr. Robbins?" I asked.

"Uh-huh. Belonged to my wife." *Belonged*—past tense.

"Sir." I took a pace forward, held out the pendant at arm's length towards him. Eying it, and me, suspiciously, he turned it over, running a thumb over the pockmarked enamel. As he angled the reverse to the light and peered through the encrusted algae, he stifled a gasp.

"We found the *Spirito del Vento* at the bottom of the Mediterranean, off Sardinia. This was in the cabin."

"And? So you dove on a boat and found some treasure." He regrouped, handing it back dismissively. Then his face hardened, his eyes widened, and he stepped back. "Hey, aren't you the two from Italy? The two on the news who killed that guy?"

"We *were* in Italy. I had a meeting with Luciano Moretti. He had information on Max Anderson, about Amber Rock, but someone got to him first and set us up. We just got caught up in it all."

"Caught up in what exactly?" Robbins ran a hand across his brow and through his thinning hair. The beads of sweat had sprung up again, gray patches in the pits of the clean white shirt. He looked about the parking lot, over the crumbling stone walls, across at the Taverna—anywhere but at us. "Look, I have things to do…"

I needed to throw in my ace.

"We know about the boats. The switcheroo in the Mediterranean. The *Diktynna A*, once the *Melusina*. How you swapped boats then scuppered the *Spirito del Vento*."

"I have no idea what you're talking about. I know nothing about any other boat." But the fear in his voice was palpable as he thrust a finger towards the rotting hulk. "*This* is my boat. The *Diktynna A*. I don't know any Anderson. You have the wrong man."

Proof of Life

"Please, Mr. Robbins?"

He turned back, fixed his eyes on me for a long moment. "Not here."

***

Out in front of the Taverna, the parking lot was filling up. Automatic lights had started, festooning the foliage with bright fireflies of color. Beyond the boundary, the causeway and the salt lakes were but a smudge in the darkness. Robbins found a hurricane lamp, sat in the undergrowth next to the gate, and lit it. Then he whistled—a peculiar two-tone sound—and a small mongrel dog came bounding over. Steve flinched and drew back.

"Don't worry, Miss Jordan. He only bites people he doesn't like. When he wags his tail, it means he is still deciding. When the tail stops..." Then he turned, looked us straight in the eyes. "Are either of you two armed?"

In Robbins' shoes, I would ask the same, so we gave him the guns. He dropped the Smith & Wesson into a mailbox on the perimeter wall. He checked the Glock, looked me over for a long moment, then rammed it in his belt.

We walked down towards the water, where the breeze was heady with brine. Unlit, remote, the darkness clung thick and cool, broken only by the light from Elounda, a string of pearls shimmering on the distant shoreline. Robbins sat down on a wall, the ruined foundations of some small dwelling or shop, or just a wall. He placed down the lamp and whistled for the dog, who came trotting back, wagging its tail, stopping only briefly to pee up a rock.

"So, you got your audience, Mr. Beckett."

Away from the lights and the people, the pretense was futile. He had called our bluff, and now we had to show our hands in the hopes he would show his.

"I work for an organization that was hired by the US government. They sent me to Rome to meet with Luciano Moretti. I was early and stumbled in on Moretti and his minder. They had both been shot."

"Minder? What sort of guy was this Moretti?"

"The worst kind, sir—guns, drugs, information, people. Anything he could sell for a margin, and I was there to buy."

"Says a lot about you. That you were there to buy." He chuckled mirthlessly. "Buy *what* exactly?"

"Information my employers wanted before anyone else could get it."

"And her?" Robbins' tone was pejorative as he nodded towards Steve.

"Miss Jordan was Moretti's PA, hired for the day. She was in the same room as two dead bodies and the gun that killed them. We knew the Polizia would assume one of us had fired the gun, so we ran."

"Okay. I'll buy it. Wrong place, wrong time and you ran." His eyes briefly flicked upwards, perhaps recalling a different man and woman, a different time when *they* both ran. "And what was so valuable about this information?"

"Amber Rock, Mr. Robbins. A journalist called Tom Jardine acquired a file of evidence he believed proved Max Anderson was still alive. He claimed he had tracked down the *Spirito del Vento*. Moretti thought it was worth a cool half-million euros, more to the right bidder. There were oblique references to Amber Rock and some less oblique ones to Max Anderson. So, push comes to shove, I found Tom Jardine, found a sunken boat. We tracked down Fabrizio Rossi and now the *Diktynna A*. That all led us here. To you."

Despite the ingrained tan and the flickering glow of the lamp, the color drained from his face. He pulled the Glock from his belt, chambered a round, and laid it on his lap.

Proof of Life

"Say I am *Max Anderson*. What business is it of yours?"

"My employers are interested in Amber Rock. And what Anderson can tell them about it. That's all."

Robbins chuckled again, dry and humorless. "You know, this entire area—the salt lakes, the ground in front—all this was once a vibrant city, the most important in the area, dating back to the Minoans, maybe four thousand years. Then came the earthquake at Santorini, or the Arabs, or one of many other catastrophes. Now look at it, just a pile of stones, sliding inexorably into the sea. Everything passes eventually. Even Amber Rock. It was a generation, a lifetime ago. How can it still be important?"

"Above my pay grade, sir, yet here we are. But we are not the only ones looking for you, Max. They know you are still alive and are coming to get you. Ever since Moretti's office in Rome, they have been trying to stop us from reaching you. Trying to find you before we did."

"And if you find out what this Max Anderson knows, what happens then? What happens to *him* then?"

"We are working to expose Amber Rock. We would work to protect you. If you told us everything you know, then maybe Anderson could remain lost."

"I keep telling you, it's Robbins, not Anderson." Then he added. "It's not been Anderson for a long, *long* time."

Chapter 60

Sitting amongst the ghosts of Olous, the walls of the ruined city sinking off into the darkness, an uncomfortable silence fell, broken only by the faint roar of the lamp and the quick breaths of the sleeping dog. He was lying between Steve's knees. His tail had stopped, but he showed no desire to rip out her throat. In contrast, I was buzzing. My heart was thumping fit to burst. I had found Max Anderson. A name in a notebook. A phantom, a memory submerged below the sea for a generation. I thought of Gruber, Fernandez, Hayes, Brooks, McKenna—all the other analysts Jardine mentioned, who died trying to unravel the secret of Amber Rock and the many analysts who had died since. I thought of Tom Jardine. Yet, for all that time—all my lifetime—Anderson had been here. Living a charmed existence beyond the eyes of the world. Beyond the reach of Amber Rock. A modern-day *lotus-eater* who prized his own life, his own survival, above those who deserved his loyalty.

Now, though, he was an old man, gazing up at the clear, diamond-studded sky, a lifer seeing it for the last time before the cell door slammed. The turmoil inside him was almost palpable. Thirty years hidden, anonymous and safe. Now all that was in jeopardy. He took out a battered hip flask and offered it around. It reminded me of the night on the *Genevieve*, Jardine and his tales. A lifetime ago. Another soul lost to Amber Rock.

Max took a second slug from the flask, Dutch courage, and screwed the top back on firmly. He drew his eyes down from the safety of the sky, gave a reluctant sigh, his face half shadow, half light, bisected, conflicted.

Proof of Life

"Todd Gruber, Pete Fernandez, Harvey Brooks, Carl Hayes. Even Jo—Joanne McKenna. All dead. All murdered. That's what Amber Rock means. Kapoor, Carter, Gudrensen, Lewinski, the list goes on. It's a curse on anyone who gets too close. Now I hear Fabrizio Rossi's dead. To them, time is irrelevant. They won't stop until they have killed us all. They are everywhere. They could be out there now, in the darkness, listening in with some damn parabolic microphone, biding their time."

Through the melodrama, Anderson's voice held a genuine edge of fear. I peered around at the falling blanket of night, and a shiver ran down my spine. Was Baresi out there? Was he listening in, biding his time?

"I was working in London," he continued. "Through the grapevine, I heard Todd Gruber, a colleague in the States, had died. Spring of '85, they pulled him and his white Cimarron from Chesapeake Bay. The coroner recorded misadventure. Said Gruber probably fell asleep at the wheel. Tragic but I thought no more about it until just after Christmas '85. Pete Fernandez, who worked for the Atomic Energy Commission in Germantown, threw himself off of a building in Rosslyn, Maryland."

"So two suicides," I reasoned. "The biggest killer of men in their thirties."

"And that's what we put it down to. The industry was in flux; we were all under a great deal of pressure."

"So, what changed?"

"We read the coroner's reports—to put our minds at rest. They did anything but. There was so much caffeine in Gruber's system, he was unlikely to fall asleep for a week. Also, he was wearing his seatbelt; even the expert witness stated a broken neck was possible, but unlikely. And why did he drive down to Cape Charles in the first place? And Fernandez? He wasn't happy, arguing Gruber was already dead, that they ran the car into the bay to hide the body. He was the excitable type. Like *Don Quixote*, always tilting at windmills. He saw a conspiracy behind Gruber's death."

"And was there evidence to substantiate his claims?" I had felt necks break. It took an enormous amount of pressure in the right spot or an immense amount of trauma. Gripped by a seatbelt, would bouncing over rough ground be sufficient? Perhaps Fernandez had a point.

"By December '85 he was dead too and, conveniently, it no longer mattered." Anderson took another slug, offered the hip flask. I declined.

"Conveniently? Two people in two years. Tragic but hardly significant."

"I agree. Barely a blip on the chart. If it were only two." Max shifted on his stone seat and leaned in conspiratorially. "But we found other nuclear analysts, like Gruber and Fernandez, working for the NRC, the AEC, the NNSA, all who had died suddenly. On the face of it, all the deaths were random, all unconnected, all suspicious."

"You think someone was killing them off?" It was Steve. I'd assumed she had fallen asleep.

"The whole thing smelled higher than a dead skunk in July, Ms. Jordan. Still, we had nothing concrete to go on. Again, we got on with our lives. Then, in early '87, Sentinel—you know about the Sentinel Working Group?" I nodded. "Sentinel attended a symposium in Strasbourg. It was the first time Rossi, Hayes, Brooks, Jo McKenna, and I had met in person since Fernandez died. Of course, the subject came up. Jo and I proposed we investigate formally, as a group. Hayes seconded, but we couldn't convince Rossi, nor Brooks, so we let it lie. Over the next few months, we examined the whole thing again. We found other deaths— car accidents, drug overdoses, house fires. All related to the nuclear industry and all involving analysts who had taken their own lives or died suddenly. We convinced Brooks, but Rossi stood firm. No investigation."

"What was his reasoning?"

Anderson shrugged. "Funding, staff shortages, political focus, you name it. He had a boxful of reasons to do nothing. He was an academic. Goes with the job. Effectively, it left us at a dead end."

"In June of '87, Jo McKenna and I flew to Washington to meet up with Hayes and Brooks. We revisited everything we had, correlating dates and places with official records—checking the facts. We found inconsistencies between what Gruber, Fernandez, and the others had put in their reports, and what Rossi had recorded in the official versions. Signs of a cover-up."

"That fits," I added. "When we saw Rossi in Venice, he alluded to a disaster back in '82, but he didn't elaborate. Something big. Something they would kill for. Even now, thirty years later, they are trying to keep it under wraps. You know what that is, don't you, Max?"

Anderson held my gaze for a long moment, but evaded the question. "When we got back to England, Carl—Carl Hayes—called me. He thought he was being watched. Nothing he could nail down but the same cars following him to work, the same people on street corners, behind him in the mall. I told him he was being paranoid, to get a grip. Two weeks later, he snuck off from a Fourth of July party. His boyfriend found him in the den at the bottom of the garden. He had eaten a revolver."

"Another suicide?"

"On the face of it, yes, and the coroner agreed, but they found no signs of gunshot residue on his hands. He was a staunch member of the anti-gun lobby. He abhorred guns. Anyhow, after the inquest, I thought long and hard about all this. Too many people were dying. I phoned Harvey and Jo.

I told them to take extra care and to destroy any documents they had. To forget about Amber Rock and the investigations. It was the fall of '87, and for months, we went about our business. Kate was pregnant, and I tried to focus on other, more pleasant things. Maybe Amber Rock noticed that too. Gradually, the goons stopped following us. Guess they assumed we were no longer a threat; maybe they thought bugging our phones was enough. Kate gave birth in Jul '88. Amber Rock faded away."

There was a lump in my throat. Here was Anderson, casually discussing the birth of his child—a child he abandoned thirty years before.

"But I was still scared," continued Anderson. "Scared for myself, but also scared for Kate. Becoming a father, becoming parents, kinda puts life into perspective. Some things just aren't worth dying for. We'd started to make plans a couple of years before. We salted money away, found people who could sell us new identities."

"Jacqueline and William Robbins?"

"Uh-huh. Then one night, October '89, the facsimile machine in the den fired up. It was Harvey Brooks, sending me copies of everything he had before destroying them. The files dated right back to 1982, heavily redacted, but all the names were there. Gruber, Fernandez, Kapoor, Gudrensen, Lewinski, Hayes, and all the others. Every inspection visit they had made, all signed off by Rossi. Except, at the bottom of some of them, Rossi had hand-written *Refer to Amber Rock*. I called Brooks on his landline, but I got no reply. They found him the next day. He had run his car into a tree and died in the fire."

"What did Rossi mean? *Refer to Amber Rock*?"

Anderson raised his hands and slapped them down on his knees. "We didn't know. A person maybe, a committee, an organization. Brooks faxed me one hundred and fifty pages. I was feeding paper in for twenty minutes. That damn machine was hungrier than Nico." He gestured at the dog, who raised his head and wagged his tail three times. "Even with the redactions, I could identify the inspectors, the dates, the sites. I had the originals, from when we visited Washington. So now I had three copies; one submitted by the inspector, a copy annotated *Refer to Amber Rock,* and the sanitized version Rossi sent to his peers. At last, I had proof he was hiding something."

"I called Rossi. Eventually, early '90, he agreed to meet. We met in Geneva, some boxy little room at CERN. He stood with his back to the window. I remember the rain hammering on the glass, the condensation stains on the ceiling tiles, the smell of stale tobacco—prosaic and unspectacular. I told Rossi what we had. He denied everything at first. What right had I got to question his authority? When he realized I would not back down, he told me what he told you. Some *accident* in the early '80s. Something that would be catastrophic to the whole industry if it ever came out. As with you, he wouldn't elaborate, however hard I pushed him, however much I reminded him of Sentinel's responsibilities to the industry."

"So I played the only other card I had. I showed him the redacted documents and their non-redacted counterparts, confronted him with the evidence. He got mad. Madder than I ever saw him, hollering and banging on the desk. All sorts of rhetoric about undermining his authority, meddling in things which were none of my concern, digging up ancient history. He even blamed me for the deaths of Hayes and Brooks. It all developed into some unseemly spat that made neither of us look good. At one point, a guy from outside banged the door, asked us to keep the noise down. Then Rossi let something slip. One of those throwaway things that, once said, cannot be unsaid."

"Which was?" We had gone around the block to get here.

"Amber Rock." Anderson said it with a somber finality, as if waiting for the fatal bullet. "He said *you don't know what Amber Rock is capable of. They will do anything to keep it a secret. Anything!* And he was right. They killed Jo, for God's sake. She fell under a train at Moorgate. She was claustrophobic and hated the Underground. Why would she be catching a subway train in the rush hour?"

Anderson puffed and dropped his head into his hands. "Look, Beckett. I get it. They sent you to do a job, but you don't know who you are dealing with. We had to run. That meeting in Geneva. We showed our hand, and Amber Rock bit it off. They killed Jo. Jesus Christ, they nearly killed Kate and me—and our new baby!"

I found the Amber Rock images on my phone—the deserts, the fences, the cameras looking down.

"Is this what they are keeping a secret, Max? Is this the scene of this *disaster?*"

Anderson's face widened to a look of horror, stark in the glare from the phone. "Where did you get these?" He swiped left and right, becoming more and more agitated.

"This is what Moretti was selling." I brought up the pictures of the Sentinel Group, of Kate and Max in Elounda post-disappearance. "While you were living the high-life, Max, things have moved on apiece. You've become the stuff of legend. The one that got away. Only now, Amber Rock is looking for you again, and if we can trace you, so can they."

Max rose from the stone wall, stretched out the cramp, and waved a dismissive hand. "I'm telling you, Beckett. You and Ms. Jordan. Forget all about this. Get on with your lives and leave me to get on with mine."

"Just like that?" I retorted. "We walk away? Forget any of this happened—just like you and Kate, thirty years ago?" I was losing my patience. Like with Rossi, Jardine even, I was being stonewalled. All the data but none of the information.

Proof of Life

Stories of a boogeyman to keep me away from the hearth, and I'd had enough.

"Come on, tell me. What exactly is Amber Rock? What are they protecting? Why is everyone so afraid?"

"No, Beckett. Just let sleeping dogs lie. Please."

Let sleeping dogs lie. The phrase Fabrizio Rossi had used back in Legnaro before he died. I fired a finger right in Anderson's face.

"Just what gives you the right to play with other people's lives? To poke the hornet's nest, then just take off when they all come out to sting?"

Anderson reached for his belt, grabbed the Glock, and leveled it at my face. "I'm warning you, Beckett. I'm begging you for Chrissakes. Quit while you're ahead."

Steve leaped to her feet and backed away. The dog yelped and began yapping.

"So, go on. Pull the trigger. Kill me, kill Steve, kill the fucking dog. Then you can run again. After all, thirty years ago, you left without a second thought. You abandoned your colleagues, people who trusted you, who relied on you. Left them to die while you skulked off here to your goddamn island. You abandoned your child and never looked back. Not in all those years. Not once did you check to see how he was doing—not once! You're a fucking disgrace, Max."

Anderson's hands were shaking, knuckles taut. There were tears in his eyes, flickering gold in the lamplight. "What gives you the right to lecture me? You do not know what we went through. It damn near broke Kate. but we couldn't go back. How could we?"

Anderson kicked out. There was a flash of light, a crash-tinkle of glass, and a slow, angry ribbon of blue-red flame chased across the grass. Then he collapsed down onto his haunches and wept.

Chapter 61

Anderson took a few minutes. To compose himself, maybe to realize things had changed. That Utopia was still only a town in a world of crap, and crap had a habit of creeping insidiously into everyone's lives. Then he wiped his eyes, handed back the gun, and walked back to the taverna.

He pointed us to a gingham table, set apart from the noise of the Greek folk duo ruining the country's heritage. It looked like the one in the photo from Moretti's drive, but I could have been wrong. He ordered food, gave us a room for the night, and told us to be gone by sunrise. The Adonis brought over wine—*a bottle of red and a bottle of white.* I remembered the Billy Joel song. Just friends, catching up after a while. We ate food; we talked about the Andersons' sailboat trip across the Mediterranean to the harbor in Agios Nikolaos and the Taverna Aegina. Max talked of the pendant, the breadcrumb trail he had left. How he hoped one day someone would follow it, pleased at last someone had. Heartbroken, Kate had not been there to see it.

"Pancreatic cancer. Five years back. When we left our life, our family, we also left a hole, and the cancer filled it. It was like a demon inside her, a parasite eating her up."

Anderson looked out into the darkness a long moment before continuing. "We'd always talked about making a new life somewhere. It was our dream. Then when Amber Rock started, it became a necessity. I had watched colleague after colleague die, and I was damned if that was going to happen to us. So we made our plans. Even then, I knew, eventually, they would catch up with me. I just had to hope I could deal with them when they did. So we put money away, made the arrangements. Found this place."

"And Kate? How much of a say did she have in all this?" She had left her newborn; I suspected very little.

"Every step of the way, Beckett. You have to believe me. It tore her apart she had to leave her family, but eventually, she knew it was the only way to keep us all safe."

After a while, the Greek folk duo finished their caterwauling, and the taverna lapsed into a relaxed, happy hubbub. Except around our table. The silence felt sullen and uncomfortable. Max poured out the last of the wine, stopping over my glass, fixing me with his eyes.

"So, now you know, what's going to happen to me?"

I had my orders. Anderson must remain lost, eliminate Renzo Baresi, and only then, bring in the Andersons.

"For now, sir, nothing. Only Ms. Jordan and I know you're here. If we can keep it that way, once we know it's safe, we will bring you in, give you protection. Then afterward, as Will Robbins, restauranteur, you could live out your old age in peaceful obscurity." I was over-promising.

He poured the wine and sighed. "Forgive me if I don't sound convinced. Rossi agreed to speak to you and they got to him." He stood, and drained his glass. "I have chores to do. We will speak more in the morning. Enjoy your stay." He turned and spoke briefly to the ponytail girl. Presently, in the apartments above the taverna, a light came on.

"Tell me something, Beckett, how much of this is about helping me and how much is about finding Max Anderson?" She was irked and I was embarrassed. Right now, it was all about Anderson. Anderson and me.

"Look, Steve, I promised to look after you, to work things out. I know it's been a bumpy road, but I will sort it. I just have to get some things done first."

"So you said, but you've spent the best part of the week searching for Anderson when you could've been finding Baresi and proving my innocence. How is all this helping me? How are you going to convince the Polizia I didn't kill Sr. Moretti, or Professor Rossi in Venice? How are you going to convince them I am just a passenger on this rollercoaster?"

"Okay, I admit it. Since I found the Andersons had not died at sea, I have been desperate to find them. Now I have, I still feel cheated. I came searching for Amber Rock, and all I got was some thirty-year-old spy story."

"So what are you—we—going to do about it?"

"What can we do? I need to persuade him to tell us what he knows about Amber Rock. Then I need to make sure I deal with Baresi before he finds out where we are."

"And me?"

Taking Steve away from the apartment in Rome, not flying back to the States immediately. Everything snowballed from that one rash moment of hubris. Thinking I could save the day. Now we were both in over our heads, fighting on all fronts.

"I'm going to keep you safe until I have done both."

Again, I hoped I wasn't over-promising.

Proof of Life

Chapter 62

Tuesday, September 17

Steve slept upstairs. I took the veranda; I wouldn't sleep much anyhow. The sun woke me at stupid o'clock. The dog had inveigled his way onto my lap as I slept. But now he was awake, seeking food, a quiet place to crap, or whatever, and I was cold. I checked my watch. 5:00 am, and the shutters were still closed on the taverna, so I stretched and went to the car to doze in the back until I could persuade someone to stand me a coffee. Already, the air was alive with the sounds of the waves and a million sparrows, and I felt guilty about intruding on Max Anderson's idyll. However, that didn't last long.

The Citroen sat low and squat; all four tires cut, gouged apart by a large blade. Anderson's Toyota pickup was gone, along with the inflatable dinghy on the trailer beside it. The S.O.B. must have walked right past me as I stretched out, catching flies on the bench.

Racing back to the taverna, I hammered on the door until an upstairs window opened. Eventually, the Adonis stood in the doorway, in a crumpled white vest, mumbling abuse, a mean look behind the stubble.

"Take me to Will Robbins."

The jerk just stood, scratching his nuts.

"No man. We're not open." He folded his arms, rippling the muscles. He was five inches taller and thirty pounds heavier, but he shrunk to a pea when I thrust the Glock into his six-pack.

Proof of Life

"Not today, bud. I don't have the time."

Feebly, the Adonis pointed up the stairs. Steve was on the landing, looking bewildered.

"Anderson's gone. Get our things." I ran along the landing, popping each door, sending it crashing against the wall, apologizing to the ponytail girl who stared drowsily from under the bedclothes. Anderson's room had been turned over. The wardrobe doors flung open, clothes gone, hangers on the bed. Under the window, a laptop was missing. All the drawers were pulled.

"His papers are still here." Steve waved a passport and driving license.

"He'll have others. We need to stop him before he leaves Crete, else we're back to square one."

Even after thirty years, Anderson would have a backup plan. Maybe there was another tarp with a fast motorbike underneath it? Maybe even now, he was securing tickets off the island under another name. A cleaner in Buenos Aires or Guatemala was preparing another safe house for him to escape to.

Down in the restaurant, Ponytail and the Adonis were having a domestic.

"You going to say what this is all about?" The Adonis stood tall, adopting his best surly look. Ponytail pulled her short white dressing-gown about her. I couldn't help noticing she had great legs.

"Where is Robbins?" I barked. "Where has he gone?"

The Adonis flexed his pecs. He obviously worked out, and I am sure he wanted value for money for all those hours on the bench press, but his guns were no match for the Glock and he knew it. I pulled the slide back. He stood off, raising his hands, then backed away behind Ponytail, who tutted in irritation.

"He has gone to work," she huffed dismissively. "He always goes early. He meets the other men at the dock in Elounda. Every day, they have breakfast. Always the same."

"Then why'd he take the boat? Surely he goes across with the others?"

The girl shrugged and turned to the coffee machine.

"Maybe he has gone to Plaka?" suggested the Adonis, still staring at the gun. "It's a town further along. It's easier to cross there."

"Car keys. Give me your car keys." I waved the Glock about until the Adonis handed over the keys to a beat-up Land Rover. We transferred our stuff, and I threw my keys back, pointing at the Citroen.

"Four new tires. And charge it to Robbins' account."

Of course, Anderson was smart. He could have dumped the boat in a lay-by and skedaddled to the airport, but there was something about the island that told me he'd be there. A fortress, a leper colony. For years these people learned about self-sufficiency, about survival. Remote, cut off from the rest of humanity, it resonated with Anderson.

"Maybe he has a hiding place? A refuge?" I suggested, pulling out onto the main road.

"Maybe. But how the hell are we going to find it?" Steve's eyes were flicking between the mirrors, searching side-roads, examining traffic.

"It's a small island, Steve."

"It's also a maze of bloody rat-runs."

"So we have to make sure he doesn't leave without us."

Proof of Life

Chapter 63

We reached Elounda quickly, but Anderson's pickup was not in the harbor, so I turned northwards towards Plaka. We had the road to ourselves, apart from a few scooters. And the Audi. Low, sleek and black, and, above all, clean. It had caught my eye in Elounda, parked along the quiet harbor road. Now, it was following along at a discreet distance. Discreet, if there were other traffic.

"I think we have company."

"Can you see who it is?" Steve was peering into the side mirror, but the car was hanging off a long way.

"No. Just one person."

"Baresi? How could he have found us so quickly? Nobody knew we were coming to Elounda." She ducked down, just a pair of eyes peering out of the side window.

"Who knows? Maybe he's into Greek myth, too? Maybe he spoke to the museum curator?"

We needed to lose him before we reached Plaka, but that would be easier said than done. Ordinarily, I would have taken a turning, driven into a gateway to lose a tail. But the road was sinuous, with few turnings off, the Audi disappearing briefly behind a bend only to re-appear moments later. We were passing through a stretch of bayside villas and luxury hotel complexes. I thought of turning into an estate, trying to lose them in the maze of roads, but gave it up. One wrong turn, and we would be fish in a barrel. Instead, I focused on the road, relieved when the Audi turned off into a beach resort.

Proof of Life

Maybe I was being over-cautious?

Less than fifteen minutes after we started out, we arrived on the outskirts of the coastal town of Plaka. Smaller, less commercial, the same air of casual neglect as Elounda, it was still sleeping in at 5:30 am. Across the bay, Spinalonga was so close I could almost pick it from the water. Against the aquamarine, a small red dot bobbed on the slight swell.

"Looks like we made the right call, Steve. He's around halfway across. We need to find a boat—and quick."

"At half-five in the morning? Some hope." Then she bounced in her seat and jabbed a finger out through the window. "Look. Water sports. Surely they have boats."

"At half-five in the morning?"

Steve gave me the sort of withering look I was now used to. "They'll have boats. If necessary, we'll steal one."

"You sure have changed, lady."

The drive passed a couple of poolside bars and restaurants before ending abruptly at the water's edge. A small jetty poked out into the water a little way, slapping and thudding as the swell lifted a line of small powerboats. Over the beach, a slim, blond man in a black polo shirt and shorts was manhandling a hose, trying to persuade the water to rinse the sand off of some plastic sunbeds. As we strode across, he looked up. The bags under his eyes suggested we may have woken him.

"Hi, can I help you?" The accent was Californian.

"I wonder if you can, son," I drawled. "My name's Farrell, Franklin Farrell. And you are?"

"Gene, sir, er, Eugene." He gingerly lowered the hose, allowing it to urinate over the sandy grass.

"Is that a Californian accent, Gene? Los Angeles? San Diego?"

The boy smiled suspiciously, as if he was divulging a state secret. "Bakersfield, sir."

I put a huge, matey southern arm around him. "Hey, I got friends in Bakersfield. The Weintraubs? Maybe you know them?"

"I-I…"

"Well, here's the thing. You see that itty-bitty red boat way out there? That's my good friend, Elroy. We were supposed to meet him in town at 5 O'clock but, you know how it is…" I nodded towards Steve, who was wondering what the heck was happening. "On vacation, pretty girl. I guess we, er, overslept?"

The boy's cheeks turned flame-red.

"We need a boat. A fast one. So we can catch Elroy up?"

"The boat hire doesn't open until 10:00 am, sir."

"Yes, but an enterprising guy like you?" I held up 400 euros. It was all the cash I had left. My face ached with a jaw-breaking smile.

"I can't just…"

"C'mon, son. What the eye don't see, the heart won't grieve over." I waved the notes. "They don't have to know. We'll easily be back by ten."

"What about that one?" Steve trotted out a game-show Yankee accent and pointed towards a boat pulled onto the shore. The boy began to buckle under the weight of euros, so I steered him along the sand to the boat. Made him buckle some more.

"Nice one, Ruth. That will do fine! It warms my heart to find some good ole American hospitality so far from home. Now can you help us push it out?"

The boy stood for a moment, wondering whether he should just turn tail and run. In the end, he relented and

Proof of Life

heaved the boat towards the water. I pulled the starter cord on the small Evinrude outboard motor, and we left him standing on the shore, clutching the wad of notes and pondering his last day at work.

"Keep an eye on the boat, Steve. Let's see where he docks." The bay was calm, but I kept losing Anderson in the swell. It would take ten minutes to cross, even with our more powerful boat. By then, he would have moored up and disappeared into the town.

"He's heading for the old gate, I think." She sat in the bow of the small craft, holding on to her baseball cap as the spray leaped over the prow.

Spinalonga fortress has two gateways. Midway along the western wall was the Old Gate, a large colonnaded portal with stout wooden doors. For centuries, it was the main entrance. Since the island welcomed lepers, though, it had become the tradesman's entrance, where the boats bringing supplies docked to drop off their goods. Benefactors brought alms and medicines and left them. After the last resident left, the gates were closed forever. A symbol of humanity's endeavor to eradicate the heinous disease. South, where the tourists gathered, the boats only dropped off lepers to enter through a foreboding twenty-meter tunnel called *Dante's Gate*. The first view a newcomer had of the town and the last of the outside world. Their own private circle of Hell. They only ever left in boxes, if they left at all.

Heading for the Old Gate, I pulled our boat up under the faded, peeling gray of the mountainous wooden doors. Anderson's inflatable was nowhere to be seen.

"So where'd he go?" The fortress walls were twenty-five feet high and impenetrable. Here and there, huge openings had been cut, set with bars, solid and unforgiving. There was no way he could squeeze through. Steve walked to the end of the slipway and scanned the water.

"He must have landed somewhere else."

Bemused, I cast off the boat, and we motored around the headland toward the south entrance. Concealed behind a sprawling thicket of tamarisk trees clinging to the edge of the island, I saw a flash of red.

"Over there."

We debarked and pulled the boat up onto the shale, where the beach tapered to frothing white over rocks. Against the wall, a dilapidated stone hut or store leaned incongruously, unprotected against the outside wall of the fortress. The padlock on the wooden door was open. I held Steve back and removed the Glock. We were on Anderson's territory now.

Proof of Life

Chapter 64

Inside the hut, there was a reek of dust and mold. Weak sunlight spun motes across haphazard piles of neglected tools, coiled ropes, and cans of paint. Wood planks and cement bags were piled in stacks around the edges. In the back wall—the fortress wall—there was another opening, similar to the ones outside. In it, a wooden shutter stood ajar. Gingerly, I shone my phone through like a flashlight. The beam faded to nothing along an endless corridor.

"This is his way in when they lock the gates."

"Or he doesn't want anyone to know he's here."

Climbing in, a clinging cold raised goosebumps on my arms. Letting the Glock lead, we followed the tunnel, the blackness parting then closing behind us.

"We must be under the old town by now." My voice was a whisper but sounded like a tannoy. I played the flashlight beam around. There were tool marks where the tunnel had been hewn from the bedrock, and graffiti—names and dates and brief messages I couldn't decipher. We were entering a hell that only the former residents could understand. After forty yards, the shaft split three ways. Left and right, steps led upward toward a faint glimmer of sunlight.

"He won't have taken either of these; they go up into the town, probably into the houses," reasoned Steve. "He will have picked somewhere high up, with a view of the bay and the harbor."

We continued on; the passage climbing relentlessly in the darkness.

Proof of Life

"What's that?" Steve froze. Beyond the flashlight, in the eerie gloom, there were noises. A shuffling, scratching, like the faint tick of a clock but random, disorganized. All around us, the air seemed to vibrate and move. It spooked my primeval brain. I shone the beam upwards and saw it reflected in thousands of pinpoints of light.

Bats.

I nudged Steve. "Bet you're glad you cut your hair now."

"Arsehole."

A hundred yards further on, we tripped on steps carved into the rock floor and climbed past niches opened into the walls; small offertories or shrines, rooms with old rusted bedsteads, crumbling furniture, long forgotten.

"There must be a lot of these tunnels across the island. Out of the sun, away from the gaze of the curious."

I thought of Anderson walking these corridors. "Perhaps they valued their privacy, Steve?"

Eventually, the steps reached a landing, around twelve by nine. There were rooms on either side and a large riveted steel door at the far end. Electric cables hung from the ceiling. Here and there, bats perched, ticking and squirming in the light beam. A faint crack of light edged under the door. The air felt warmer.

"I guess we've reached the top. Damn! We must've taken the wrong turn at the fork." There was disappointment in Steve's voice. And no sign of Anderson.

"I don't think so." I shone the flashlight into one of the side rooms, no more than a hollow in the island's fabric. Fumbling for a light switch, I screwed up my eyes as the weak bulb burned my retinas. The room was sparse, but not derelict. A bed, a chair, a desk, and a tall cupboard. All of which had seen better days. There was an electric heater and a shortwave radio. Empty soda cans littered the floor by a small butane stove. On the bed, a suitcase and a backpack lay open. Around them, clothes, books, papers waiting to be packed in. The laptop Anderson had taken from the taverna. "Looks like he's almost ready to go."

There was a photo in a frame on top of the suitcase. A slim, tall woman, long gray hair tumbling about her face. Her kind eyes betrayed a lifetime of pain. I showed it to Steve, who sighed wistfully.

"She's beautiful. I would have liked to have met her."

Like the *Diktynna A*, that boat had already sailed. For both of us.

"Just what is it you want with me, Beckett?" Alarmed, we turned. Anderson was framed in the doorway, pointing a twelve-bore our way. "You think you can show up out of the blue and turn my life upside down?"

"I've told you Max—Amber Rock. I am here to find out what you know. And don't give me any cockamamie bullshit about secret organizations and spooks…"

"… Says the spook, working for a secret organization."

I huffed. "I just need you to tell me what this is all about. The disaster that Professor Rossi spoke about? What happened back then, and who is behind it?"

"And why should I tell you? I have spent half my life keeping my head down, staying out of the line of fire, and now you want to drag me straight back into it?"

"Listen here, Max. I have had it with you and your goddamn paranoia. Don't you give a shit about all the others? What gives you the right to hunker down in this paradise, to turn a blind eye, while people are getting killed? Who was it who said *for evil to prosper, it is enough that good men do nothing?* Well, guess what? For thirty years, you've done nothing and evil *is* prospering. Don't you think you owe it to all the others? That the world has a right to know?"

Proof of Life

"And what would have happened if I had acted? If I had told what I know? I would be on a slab next to Joanne McKenna and so would my family. Amber Rock would still be hidden, still protected. Sometimes, Beckett, evil prospers *despite* the good men. That's the way the world works. Whatever that evil is, whoever these people are, they will continue to prosper regardless of anything you or I do."

I puffed out the exasperation and nodded at the bags on the bed. "So, where are you going to run to this time?"

He shrugged. "I don't know. Maybe, I thought I could just come here and ride out the storm? This is my life now. My island. I don't want to go back and you can't make me." Behind the fear, the guilt hung heavily on Anderson. Was Spinalonga his penance?

"So tell us what you know. Return to your life and we'll return to ours. No-one need ever know we found you."

Anderson glanced down at the twelve-bore and chuckled ironically. "No-one need ever know, anyway."

"What? You kill us and it's over? There will be others—there already *are* others. If we found you, they can too."

Steve stepped forward, perhaps to relieve the charged atmosphere. "What is this place, the tunnels?"

He sighed deeply as his mind changed tack, grateful for the diversion. "We think they are pre-Roman—most of them. There's a natural cave system under the island. In antiquity, troglodytes—cave dwellers—would have occupied them. When the Romans, Venetians, and the rest arrived, they built the fortress and stayed on the surface. The Romans expanded the tunnels and added catacombs in the North. Since the lepers left in the Fifties, the tunnels have been largely forgotten."

Anderson regarded us for a long moment, then lowered the shotgun and stepped into the room. I perched on the edge of the bed. My hands were away from the Glock.

"Until you rediscovered them." Steve was still holding the picture of Kate Anderson.

"No, Miss Jordan. I just found a use for them. In here, I sit with the ghosts of the past. I feel their struggles, their pain. It puts my own problems into perspective." He sighed, resting the shotgun against the wall. "And you, Beckett? Where are you going to run to? When they catch up with you. When they learn you, too, know too much?"

"I can take care of myself, Max."

"Yeah, sure you can. So far this week, you have been overpowered by an assassin in Rome, nearly drowned off the coast of Sardinia, and shot in Venice. They might have missed so far, but one day…"

Steve and I exchanged a glance. Anderson was well informed. He pointed at the shortwave set.

"I have the BBC World Service, and satellite back at the taverna. But I know much more than that, Mr. Beckett. One day, I knew you would turn up, though I envisaged nothing like this." He reached down, opened the bag, and pulled out an old, battered photo album. "Take a look."

The lump in my throat told me what I'd see. Without opening the cover, I passed it on to Steve. "How long have you known, Max?"

"Since you appeared on the North Mezzaluna. Then, beside the *Diktynna A*, when you handed me the pendant, I was certain. You are exactly like I was then. Standing tall, wearing your bravado on your sleeve. Acting first and dealing with the consequences later."

"What's going on, Beckett?" Steve's voice was edgy, taut. She was leafing through the album, monochrome turning to color as the years passed, as the child grew.

Max cackled, short, sardonic. "So he hasn't let you into his confidence, then?"

Proof of Life

"What confidence?" she snapped. "No, Mr. Anderson. He hasn't told me a bloody thing."

From that moment in Rome, when I read Moretti's notebook, and as we chased the specter of Max Anderson across the Mediterranean, I had struggled to keep my own ghosts at bay. To focus on the job-in-hand. Steve had accused me of caring more about finding Max than exonerating her. She was right. I held up the pendant and allowed it to spin in the dim light.

"You left this on the *Spirito del Vento* for me to find, didn't you, Max? Not just for anyone but for *me*." I swung it in front of Steve. "The engraving on the back, underneath the crap? The word we couldn't make out. It says *Aidan*."

She looked up at me, bewildered.

"Beckett is my operating name. My real name is Aidan Wexler. Thirty years ago, Joe and Pat Wexler adopted me when my real parents disappeared on a sailboat trip."

My voice was breaking up. I could not stem the tears as I jabbed a finger out at Anderson.

"You and Kate ran to this *paradise* and abandoned me with strangers. I am your son, Max. I am Aidan Anderson."

Chapter 65

Steve gasped, like the circus crowd when the highwire guy misses a step. I could feel her eyes on me and felt ashamed of lying to her. Or at least not telling her the whole truth. To her credit, she kept quiet. Max stood a moment, his jaw oscillating up and down, but there were no words. His eyes looking at another country, another decade. This was the man who abandoned his son and never came back.

I was looking at a stranger.

They disappeared when I was fourteen months old. Too young to remember. Only later did I learn how they sailed out of Cagliari and were never heard of again. As a child, I invented my own truth, more palatable than a fathomless ocean holding them captive. Seafarers lost to an exciting adventure saving the world. I wanted there to be a truly important reason they abandoned me, why they had missed my birthdays, my graduation. The Wexlers adopted me when the Andersons were declared legally deceased, and became my real parents and the only people I ever truly loved.

But all the while, Max and Kate were enjoying a parallel existence of which I knew nothing.

When I turned eighteen, Joe Wexler gave me three archive boxes. Until then, all I possessed were some color snapshots, cracked and dog-eared. I also acquired the trust fund that made me wealthier than my parents overnight.

I looked closer at the photo of Kate, trying to find the family resemblance. When my mother, Pat, lost her battle with cancer, I felt a great sense of injustice, betrayal even. The loss gouged a hole in my soul so big, I can never really

Proof of Life

fill it. All my life, I knew a piece of me was missing. The realization the Andersons were still alive gave me a chance to find it. My birth mother, my flesh-and-blood, was dead, and I'd lost some of it forever. Yet, I felt nothing.

Max sighed. "Believe me, we had no alternative. There was always the possibility they would get to us through you, so we had to cut off all ties. We had to leave you. Wexler managed our accounts back in the States before we left. He and Pat couldn't have kids, so they agreed to take care of you. They were down-to-earth, trustworthy. It wasn't perfect, but we knew you'd be safe."

"They knew?" This was a scenario I hadn't considered—ever. That Mom and Dad could adopt me, raise me, knowing my biological parents were still alive. The rage was building inside of me, a rage I'd felt as a teen, not knowing why, not understanding—until now. I trusted Mom and Dad. How could they keep something that huge a secret?

"For a long time, the Wexlers sent photos and letters but eventually they dwindled to one or two a year, then stopped when you were eighteen."

Anderson beckoned for the pendant, pulled a small penknife from his pocket, and found the seam on the gold disk. Inside was a tiny image, bleached and stained. In the light from the hurricane lamp, I instantly recognized it. A face cut from a larger photo. The face of an infant. My face.

Max pointed. "The scar on your upper lip. Did you ever wonder how you got that?"

"My dad told me I fell and cut it when I was two. I can't remember…" I raised my hand reflexively. The scar was hidden beneath days of stubble, invisible, almost forgotten.

"You were a year old." He looked away to a memory. "We were having a mild Spring, so Kate and I drove down to the shore at Brighton, England. On the way back, Amber Rock ran us off the road. I got one too." Max lowered his spectacles. A small white mark crossed the bridge of his nose. "That's when we knew we were in danger."

I turned away, letting the tears flow. When I saw the name in Moretti's notebook, I knew this moment was inevitable, hoping for it but dreading it as well. Outside, the world was waking. Life continued, humdrum, just another day. Except on this day, I met my birth father.

"We knew it had to be a clean break. No one must know where we went. *No one*. But, as I stood in the cabin of the *Spirito del Vento*, watching the water pouring in through the hull, I had such an ache in my heart, such a feeling of shame. I knew I—we—would probably never see you again. So I hung the pendant on the door before I locked it forever. I hoped that hanging there, as the boat sank, you would know the cabin was empty, that we had not perished. You've must believe me, if there was any other way…"

Steve laid a hand on my arm, and I shrugged it off.

"You met her once." Max's voice was faltering. "One time, we flew to the States, did the whole Niagara, Big Apple trip. Ended up in Central Park Zoo, at the penguin pool. The keepers had a couple of the little guys on the pavement. The kids were going ape."

He found a photo in the album; the woman in Max's photo crouching with a young boy. The boy was pointing off-camera. Unnerved, I dredged my memory, faint still frames from a movie I hadn't played in a long time.

"I remember that. I was eight or nine. The sun was scorching, and Dad and Mom went to get snow cones. The penguins were splashing water over us. This woman put her arm across my shoulders, asked how I was doing at school, all those workaday things. I was more interested in the penguins. The woman's eyes were red. I thought she must've been sick, you know, a cold."

"She was crying, Aidan. For you."

Proof of Life

Chapter 66

Anderson unlocked the steel door and led us out of the stifling tunnel. We were on a curved dusty concourse, pierced by rays of bright sunlight which striped the stone floor. The fresh air, salt on the breeze. Now I knew what the troglodyte dwellers, all those centuries ago, must have felt—alone in the dark, craving the light.

It relieved me the secret was out, but I was still struggling to contain my anger. Now it boiled over. I swung a fist that caught Anderson on the side of his jaw, sending him to the floor. Then I crossed to a window and showed my tears to the Bay of Elounda.

"I guess I deserved that." Max reached out for Steve's hand and heaved himself up, flexing his jaw. "Let's go up top, where it's more public. Where I am less likely to get another one."

Across the curved concourse, a set of steps led onto the walkway above the southern stronghold.

"You know, Beckett. You are a bugger of a man to track down."

We all swung around towards the gravelly Glaswegian growl. My mind, still reeling from the past few minutes, struggled to understand what I was seeing. Steve let out a shrill squeak. Anderson gasped and leveled the shotgun.

"Jardine? How the…" Anderson's voice had raised an octave, incredulous.

"Max *Bloody* Anderson, as I live and breathe." The Scotsman laboriously raised his hands level with the side of

Proof of Life

his head, drawing deep on a cigar mid-way. "You can put that thing down. If I wanted to do away with you, I've lost the element of surprise now, haven't I? Apart from that, seems I'm dead. So, how's it been going since Sardinia?"

My mouth flapped, but words failed me at the double irony. Two men, taken by the sea thirty years apart, now facing each other in a place of the dead.

Anderson kept the shotgun raised, wondering whether he should just take out Jardine's ribcage and put an end to it. Jardine's eyes flicked between us. His enormous face was angry with sunburn beneath the unruly mop of ginger gray hair. His check lumberjack shirt was wet with sweat, and dust caked his jeans, but he was definitely not dead.

"You tell us, Mr. Jardine." Steve leaned back out of the sun, arms folded, and glared at the Glaswegian.

"To be fair, lassie, I am a wee bit embarrassed about all that." Jardine grinned sheepishly. "You warned me about the fishing boat, and I took no notice. My bad, eh?"

"And?" The apology did not impress Steve. "Did it ever occur to you to help us?"

"Help you how? By getting myself killed? No fear, love."

"You could have stayed on the *Genevieve*," I suggested, bemused by Jardine's flippancy. "Kept your head down until I surfaced. Two against one. The odds would be better."

"I am a journalist, Beckett, a hack. I chase stories, not killers. He was a big bastard, that man. And he had a gun and an accomplice." Jardine puffed his cheeks. "What can I say? Spur of the moment. Maybe I got scared too? I figured I'd have a better chance of finding Max Anderson if I made it back to land." He gestured towards the old man with the shotgun, flicked a supercilious smile. "Seems I was right."

Steve still glowered at Jardine. She would not let him off the hook so easily.

"Okay, I saw Baresi in the cabin and I didn't want to get involved. I climbed up onto the prow, rescued my stuff from the bridge, and hid in the front hold of their boat until they reached Cagliari." The big man pursed his lips and folded his arms, satisfied he had explained enough.

"So, where have you been for the last week? Since you left us to die?" I didn't believe him. With Baresi's pilot spark out on the deck of the other boat, with me holding Baresi's arms, I was sure it must have been Jardine who KOed me. Now he had tracked us to Spinalonga, and I had handed him Max Anderson on a plate.

"I don't answer to you, Beckett, or your vigilante organization. I'm here to see Max Anderson."

Again, my dander rose. I saw the water rising in the boat, felt the resistance as we tried to escape, recalled the hillside, the Iveco van, the gravel in my knees. I lunged at Jardine, desperate to punch the bastard's lights out. Behind me, there was a metallic click as Anderson raised the shotgun.

"Hey, guys, I hate to break up this reunion, but we have a more pressing problem." Steve leaned through one of the arched windows and pointed. Down the rocky slope, a small boat had docked. Renzo Baresi had swapped the black overcoat for beige chinos and a royal blue polo shirt. There was a line of white bandage around his arm, just peeking out from under his sleeve. Beside the crumpled corpse of the nightwatchman, he was scanning the water's edge, probably looking for the boat we sailed over on.

"How did he track us here?" asked Steve.

I glared at Jardine. "The Black Audi. That yours?"

Jardine shrugged sheepishly. Whether it was didn't matter. Somehow, either with his help or without, Baresi followed him straight to Max Anderson.

Straight to me.

Proof of Life

I turned to the old man. "Max? Is there anywhere safe we can go?"

"Who's Renzo Baresi?" Anderson lowered the shotgun and peered down quizzically.

"The guy who killed Moretti. Who sunk the boat off Sardinia and nearly drowned us. The one who killed Fabrizio Rossi for opening his mouth. Now, he's here to finish the job—and that means you too, Max. Is there somewhere you can go? Somewhere he can't get to?"

Anderson was trembling. He led us back through the stronghold into the tunnels, locking the steel door firmly behind us. "We should be okay down here."

"No, Max. It needs to be away from these tunnels." If Steve and I could find a way in, then so could Baresi. Even in this maze, eventually, he would get lucky. Perhaps it was a mistake to leave our boats out on the beach.

Anderson scratched at his thinning hair. "Where you saw me yesterday, the North Mezzaluna? There is a small disused arsenal under the tourist walkway. It's not part of the tourist trail, so unless he's an Archaeology major…"

"Can you get there without being seen?"

"I guess. We can follow the tunnel across to the old dormitory block, then take the tourist path across to the Mezzaluna. We would only be out on the surface for a minute or two at the most."

"Get your things and go there. Lock yourselves in and make sure he can't see you if he gets lucky."

"And what about you, Beckett?" asked Steve.

"Jardine and I are going to deal with Baresi. Once and for all."

We followed the tunnel back toward the intersection and turned what I assumed was north. Presently, Anderson pulled us up at a black void in the wall.

"That way leads into the garrison building by the Old Gate. You can wait for your man there. We still have a way to go to reach the North Mezzaluna."

I pulled out the Glock, jabbed it into Jardine's ribs. "After you, Tom."

"Now, wait a minute, Beckett. If you think…"

"You owe me, Jardine. You left us to die on that boat. Now you led Baresi straight to us. And if you think I am going to leave you alone with Max Anderson, think again."

"Aw, come on, Beckett!"

I jabbed harder. Jardine sighed and turned into the darkness. Anderson laid a hand on my shoulder.

"Take care, son."

The light from the lamp warped his features. It was the first time my birth father had shown an ounce of compassion for me. And probably the last.

Proof of Life

Chapter 67

About a hundred yards down the tunnel, I saw the impression of steps, gray against the black, and a faint square of light oozing around a trapdoor. I took a beat. After Moretti's apartment, the Snail Staircase, doors at the top of steps concerned me. Behind us, the shuffling footsteps had faded away. Anderson and Steve were on their way to safety.

"Open it."

Jardine turned, just a vague silhouette. "The hell I will!"

Pushing past him, I braced my hand against the wooden hatch, breaking the insistent grip of weeds, tipping it back in a shower of brick dust and gypsum. Then I heaved myself up, squinting in the blinding sunlight.

"Get a move on! If you think I'm dying down here... Pull me up!" He thrust a hand through the hole, probably relieved my head hadn't exploded as soon as I stuck it up. He was beckoning with his fingers. Insistent.

For a long moment, I stared at Jardine. The man who fled from a sinking boat and left us to Baresi. Who abandoned us to find Anderson on his own. So full of self-interest, he was prepared to sacrifice everything for his Pulitzer Prize. I reached out a hand, raised him into the hole.

"No, Jardine. I will not die for you. Not today, not ever."

I kicked out a boot square across his chin. The big man gave a grunt and folded back down into the darkness. Then I closed the trapdoor and tried to forget he even existed.

I was in a small overgrown yard, shaded by a tumble-down lean-to. Around me, skeletal roofs and ragged walls cast grotesque shadows across the floors. I made for a crumbling arched gateway that opened onto the street and headed north. On my left, a street sloped down to the Old Gate, the paving worn slick by the thousands of souls that had passed through. Beside it, the garrison building, with the old, rusting boiler, waited patiently to disinfect people and goods entering the colony. Further along, Anderson and Steve appeared from the huge, square dormitory block. I hoped they made it to their bolthole, safely.

A bee-buzz caught my attention and, on instinct, I dropped to the ground as chips of stone bit my face. Not waiting for a second, I rolled up and ran across to a maze of ruined buildings, trying to gauge the trajectory of the shot. Baresi was using a silencer. That's all I needed. I had one for the Glock, but it was in the Citroen's glove compartment. A single shot from me would wake the dead of the island. Hopefully, I would only need one.

Ducking in the rubble behind a wall, I listened for the slightest movement. Birds sang, timbers flexed in the heat, waves broke on the rocks outside the walls. My blood thudded through my ears. But no footsteps on gravel, no scree tumbling down the slope. Baresi was too clever for that. He would be high up, a vantage point chosen before he even set foot on the island. The joy of Google Maps.

"Can we talk, Baresi?" Of course, it was the last thing I wanted to do, but I needed to find him.

"Where is the girl?" More a demand than a question. I swiveled towards the sound. High in the walls of a large Ottoman house forty yards away. Roofless, tumbledown, yet multiple levels, multiple windows, panoramic view.

"She's not here," I bluffed. "She stayed at the taverna."

"Don't talk shit. I saw her on the boat you stole."

"So come out and look for her." Another bee buzzed, more rock showered down. His heels were scuffing the stone floor, seeking a better vantage point. I needed to do the same. I darted through a doorway, alarmed to find three-quarters of the space filled with clinging thorn bushes. A third shot hissed past my ear in a billowing cloud of dust. Risking my neck, I pushed aside the bushes and gasped as the walls fell away to nothing but stone steps leading to another ruined house. I took them quickly, diving out of sight. High in the other house, I caught a movement past a window; a flash of blue. I swung the Glock a second too late.

"What is all this about, Baresi? Really about?"

"Who cares? Like me, you are the hired help."

"Humor me." *Hired help*. A phrase I used myself a day or two ago. Across at the ottoman house, I pinpointed the window; saw Baresi's shadow, but the angle was too sharp. The shot was long and would have to be perfect, too perfect given my ribs still pulled like heck.

"They hired me to silence Luciano Moretti and take what he had. Now *you* have what I want."

"And Rossi?"

"Another message," he replied. "As I say, hired help."

"Yes, but who is hiring you?"

"Who cares as long as they pay?"

"Amber Rock?"

A pause. Brief but telling. I needed to finish this.

"Why are you here, Beckett? On this island?" Baresi's voice echoed off the stonework.

"I needed a vacation. Like my dad, I have a thing about archeology. Rome, Venice, now here." I shimmied along to within ten feet of Baresi's window. I could almost smell the garlic on his breath, but I still couldn't see him.

"He's on the island somewhere, isn't he?"

"Who? My dad? No, he's in a nursing home. He plays

Proof of Life

checkers all day, leers at the nurses." He rewarded my humor with a shower of dust. I saw a muzzle flash in the downstairs window. One well-aimed shot, and Baresi was mine.

"Funny man. Cut the crap. Tell me where Anderson is."

"Where's the fun in that?" Around me, the ruins were low. Above Baresi, the hillside sloped upwards in unbroken tiers of tumble-down walls. Somehow I had to get behind him, above him, or I had to lure him out.

"So you know where he is?"

"Believe it or not, Baresi, no I don't. Not at this precise moment. This island is riddled with caves and tunnels. Kill me, and you'll be searching forever."

Baresi cackled. "The people I work for have patience. Eventually, Anderson will come out or he will starve."

He had a point. Spinalonga was a fortress, but it was also a prison. Right now, it promised to be my tomb. Climbing the hill to find Baresi had been a mistake. I was pinned down, and he was safe behind his window, ready to pick me off if I moved. I needed to change the dynamics.

Twenty yards across the hillside, the utilitarian concrete shells of the dormitory blocks loomed above the ruins. If I could make it there, I would have more options. Baresi would need to find a new vantage point.

In Iraq, we called it a turkey shoot. A line of buildings, empty space between here and there, tripwires, booby traps, and snipers on every rooftop. At least on Spinalonga, there were no tripwires, no IEDs. In Iraq, though, we had body armor and buddies who had our backs.

I crouched, gathered my shit together, and focused on the doorway of the dormitory building. Taking a deep breath, feeling my ribs grind, I thought of Steve, I thought of Max Anderson—my father.

And I ran.

Chapter 68

I leaped up and sped off down the hill, jinking right as a bullet ripped the rough grass beside me, throwing myself into a small hollow as another thudded into the masonry. I had counted five shots, not that it mattered. He was carrying an automatic. Six, ten, fifteen, who knew how many shells in the clip. Still, five shots had missed their target. Maybe Baresi was feeling his arm as much as I was feeling my ribs?

I was ten yards short of the doorway. Rough ground, strewn with treacherous boulders. Taking a deep breath, I sprinted again. Another bullet landed behind me, then one thumped into my thigh and my right leg turned to lead. I hit the ground hard, and the breath left my lungs. Grasping at weeds and , I hauled myself into cover. Above me, I heard the click of a clip release. Baresi was reloading. I would have a second. Gritting my teeth, I launched myself through the archway, and my leg folded, sending me rolling through a fog of plaster dust as Baresi's shots again missed their mark.

Sweat drenched my face, dancing spots crazed my vision, and my chest felt like I was breathing razor blades. My black chinos glistened in the sun, a three-inch tear matted with blood. At least it wasn't pumping out. It could wait.

"What's up, Baresi? You're way off your game. Arm hurting you?" Had he seen the bullet smash into my thigh?

"Not as much as your leg, Beckett. Tell me where Anderson is and you might walk away." He let out a sarcastic chuckle. "Well, maybe not walk away…"

"Should be on *The Late Show*, Renzo." With the slope blindsiding Baresi, I crawled to the window of the dormitory

Proof of Life

block and tumbled below the ledge. The place reeked of cat piss and must. Amongst the rubble, bed frames rusted, broken conduit pipes hung from the ceiling. The room echoed with the voices of the dead, and I was in no mood to join in the conversation.

"Right now, I hold the cards, Beckett. Die, don't die. It's your choice."

"Can I phone a friend on that one, Meredith?" My allusion to the gameshow fell flat. Maybe it lost something in translation? My leg stung, like a red hot bar searing through the skin and I felt nauseous.

I hauled myself upright. My leg would still bear my weight—just. I zoned out the pain, knowing it wasn't terminal. Halfway along the dormitory, I found a better vantage point. Baresi was hunkered down, but there was still not enough of a target. I held the Glock steady, focusing along the barrel, hoping he would move.

When he did, I wished to God he hadn't.

There was a movement, a flash of green up the hillside, and I caught my breath. Across from Baresi, Steve crept slowly along holding the Smith and Wesson out in front of her. I willed her to stop, to turn back. This was my fight, not hers. I raised an arm and waved it frantically—*go back*. Briefly. She paused and put her finger to her lips, defiant.

I needed something to keep his focus on me.

"So, Baresi. How did you know we were in Venice?" I waved at Steve again, but she was set on her course.

"Rossi phoned Amber Rock. They phoned me."

I moved along, sought a better angle. Above, Steve had disappeared behind a small group of trees. She was within thirty yards. Too far to be sure of a clean kill, especially for a novice with a handgun and more ambition than sense.

This had to end now.

Briefly, Baresi's torso filled the window frame. I held the blue Polo shirt in my sights, then winced at the sound of tumbling scree. Baresi swiveled as I squeezed my trigger, feeling the air around me shudder and seeing the spent cartridge leap from the barrel. Steve fired, the puff of the Smith and Wesson, a crack against the masonry. Baresi fired, and I squeezed the trigger of the Glock again.

Everything stopped.

My ears rang like a badly tuned AM radio, and I coughed in the dust disturbed by the percussion. I couldn't see Baresi; just a haze of plaster and brick, and red blossom spread across the window frame. Shaking away the ringing, looking up the hillside, I was confused when I couldn't see Steve. Maybe she had seen sense and dropped down into cover?

She was behind a rash of bushes, holding her leg.

Ignoring my own pain, the wrenching in my ribs, I hauled myself out into the baking sun and up the rugged hillside. There were no thoughts for myself, no fear of Baresi, just desperation to be with her, to hold her, to smell her perfume. To look into her eyes and beg her forgiveness. I kept the nose of my gun trained on the window. At any moment, I waited for the bullet that would open my skull like an eggshell. When it came, it hit the ground behind me, the aim way off. How badly was Baresi injured?

"Steve, stay down!"

"Beckett. Look out!"

I swung the Glock, saw Baresi in the doorway of the house. His left shoulder was matted with blood, misshapen, a grotesque notch gouged out. His arm swung, lifeless. With his right, he aimed his gun again. I fired on instinct, clipping his chest, watching as he fell to the ground.

For a long moment, I kept the Glock raised as the small dust cloud settled, but Baresi didn't get up. I remembered Steve and, gritting my teeth, heaved myself up and onto the path where she sat. She was propped up against a tree. There were tears in her eyes.

"He shot me, Beckett," she sniffed. "My bloody ankle. I thought I could distract him until you could, you know…"

A streak of blood crossed her shin. I couldn't see a hole.

"Looks like you both missed each other. It's a ricochet or a stone chip. It'll be fine. An interesting scar to show the grandkids. Here." I gave her a handkerchief, still crisply creased from the supermarket in Civitavecchia. "Hold this against it."

"I guess I'm not cut out for this contract killer business."

"Leave it to the professionals, lady. Your talents lie elsewhere."

I threw my arms around her and we shared a deep embrace. The tiredness I felt, the pain in my thigh, the trials of the last week, all disappeared as I held her tight, and she held me. I leaned in and we shared a kiss, passionate but brief. I tasted clay on her lips, smelled the coconut sun cream. Then her eyes widened and she pushed away.

Chapter 69

I wheeled around as behind me, a boot snapped on the brushwood. Baresi was staggering over the rough grass, his polo shirt black with blood. He stopped, swaying wildly, barely conscious as he looked down on us, his gun by his side, his eyes unable to focus. I reached around for the Glock. It was a yard away, dropped in my haste to reach Steve. A yard too far. Baresi mouthed something incoherent as he raised his gun to my forehead, a clean shot. Then, with a cynical half-smile cutting his mouth, he turned awkwardly, a few degrees to his left, and pulled the trigger. There was a roar, a sound like a hammer hitting a melon. Baresi's torso exploded in a shower of blood and flesh, which hurled him back, crumpling onto the ground.

For a moment, I stared at the lifeless form. At last it was over. What could be so important that a man could risk so much?

I turned back to Steve and caught my breath, feeling the whole world crumbling around me. Her skin was china-pale and Demerara freckled, glistening with sun cream. A splattering of blood darkened her auburn hair; still more drenched the front of her t-shirt, where Baresi's last bullet had found its target.

Not this way. Don't let it end like this.

I knelt down, lifted her into my arms. Her eyes opened, a faint smile crossing her face. Fragile, pained, full of hopelessness.

"Well, I guess this is one way it ends, eh, Beckett?"

Proof of Life

"Don't speak. They must have heard the shots. They'll get someone over here." But I knew, just as I knew with Rossi, time was short.

"Would you tell my mom for me? Tell her it's okay?"

"Sure, I'll speak to them." The tears were beginning to choke me. Pliskin would let me nowhere near her parents. Still, there was something I needed to say. Something pointless and trite. "All this. TORUS, Amber Rock, everything. I would have given it up, you know. Stayed here, managed the taverna, bugged out from this whole life. I should have left you in Moretti's apartment, then none of this... I've been nothing but a jerk."

"Jerk? In England, it's a dickhead." She smiled, coughed. A fleck of blood on her lips.

"Fair enough, I'm a dickhead."

"A couple of weeks ago, the most excitement I'd had was finding a pound coin left in a shopping trolley."

"In the US, we call them dollars." Smiling, I sniffed back the tears as they dropped into her hair.

"Since then, I've met an assassin, a government agent. I traveled Europe, albeit running, and I fell in love. But now, none of that matters, Beckett. Just promise me you'll carry on. Promise me you'll find out about Amber Rock. Why all those people were killed. You have to promise me you won't give up now."

"I promise." If I could, I'd have crossed my fingers behind my back. Promises are made to be broken.

She was silent for a long moment. Her eyes drifted away and a shock went through my body. I knew I was losing her. Then she clicked back.

"Who's Kim?" she asked.

"Kim?" I was confused. A name from left field—and now? At this moment? "I don't know any Kim."

"She was in Max's photo album. Kim Anderson."

I had to laugh. Short and full of anguish. She was dying. I was about to lose her, and all she could think about was some damn photograph? Beside her, the bracelet I'd bought in Chania lay broken, the all-seeing eye face down in the sand. I picked it up. "You broke the bracelet. Did you get your wish?"

"I think so, yes." She coughed, shallow, wincing at the pain. "I wished I could be with you for the rest of my life."

I bent over and held her head to my chest, felt the tears running from my eyes, damp in her short fringe, and just let them come.

"And you will. I'm sure of it. We can talk to Anderson, run the taverna. All this will be a memory. We can be together forever."

But I knew she had already gone.

Proof of Life

Chapter 70

A shadow fell over me and I looked up into Anderson's eyes. He too was crying. Wisps of smoke swirled from the shotgun barrels.

The Marines gave me an auto-pilot. A sealed box in my mind where everything happened autonomically. Visceral, without thought, without feelings. Now I engaged it. I laid her down, gently closed her eyes, and brushed away the tears. She looked peaceful, as she had that morning in Chania, cocooned in the bedclothes, except the warmth had drained from her cheeks.

A thousand memories flooded my brain, the petulant girl in the streets of Rome. The frightened woman, cowering against the walnut trees on Sardinia. In the sunshine of Chania with her shades on top of her spiked auburn hair. The nights we spent, barely able to sleep as fear held us captive. The nights we didn't want to end, lost in each other's arms. A week and a half, the entirety of our memories, were now alone in my head. Alone with the despair of losing her and the shame of bringing her to her death. A shame would stalk me until it finally consumed me whole.

What had I done?

I have seen dozens of bodies yet now it was someone close. Not a brigade buddy but a friend and a lover.

Death isn't the problem. It's the loss it brings with it.

Max crouched down, laid a hand on my shoulder.

"Come on, son. It's over now."

Proof of Life

Chapter 71

It cut me up to walk away. To abandon her on the hillside. But what did it matter now? I had played a trained assassin at his own game and lost. I had failed Pliskin, failed Anderson, and most of all, I had failed Steve.

So I walked. I concentrated on placing one foot in front of the next. It was all I had left. My leg was growing numb, but I gritted my teeth, reprogrammed the auto-pilot. Anderson led me into the hillside and down an endless flight of stone steps. Soon, we were beneath the North Mezzaluna. There was fresh brickwork on the walls, the mortar yet to fade in the heat. The spot I had first seen the living ghost of my father. And I prayed it had all been a dream, that I would wake in Steve's arms back in Chania.

Everywhere was quiet and empty. Even the birds had ceased their song. In the distance, the first boats were plowing their glistening white furrows across the bay. The throbbing beat of a helicopter broke the still air.

"There isn't much time, son. We need to get off of this rock before they send people over." Anderson dragged out a first aid kit, covered my wound with iodine, wrapped a bandage around my leg. It hurt like hell, but I let it hurt, drew the pain in, and seared it into my heart. He squeezed a cigarette from a pack of Marlboro Gold and offered them across. I shook my head. My leg was on fire, my ribs ached, and my mouth was as dry as the arid clay-colored hills across the bay. I was smarting from the humiliation. I just wanted all this to be over. To go back to Steve.

"What the hell did you think you were doing, letting her

Proof of Life

go out on her own? She's lying dead because of you."

Anderson jetted out a thin stream of cigarette smoke. "How was I supposed to stop her? She had the damn gun."

"I don't know—tie her up, block the exit, anything. I told you to find somewhere safe. Somewhere where she could hide for a while. Jeez, Anderson."

The old man turned his back to hide his tears. In my haste to blame someone for Steve's death, I had forgotten Anderson and the shotgun, Baresi's corpse, scattered across the path. Had Anderson seen a dead body before? Had he ever killed anyone? This spat was pointless. The damage was done. There were more pressing problems and time enough for recriminations later—if there was a later.

Anderson turned back, regarded me for a while. "Right now, we need to get the hell out of Dodge. You fit to walk?"

I nodded, and Anderson helped me to my feet. It was 7:40 am. The gates opened at 9:00 am. The island would soon be crawling with tour parties. Overhead, the pounding of the helicopter echoed through the walls. I wondered where on this godforsaken rock they could put her down. I remembered the foreshore where the boats docked. The only flat patch of dirt.

Leaving the outer gate locked, Anderson turned back into the tunnels, negotiating them with practiced ease, hanging a battery lantern before him. I switched on the auto-pilot again and followed, flipping my brain into neutral, trying to mask the memory of Steve's face, speckled with blood. I tried to supplant it with happier times, the touch of her skin, the dimple on her right cheek that appeared with her crooked smile. The touch of her lips as we kissed. After half an hour, beyond the lantern, there was the faint sound of distant waves.

"Almost there, Aidan." Max turned. "How are you holding up?"

I had no energy to speak, squinting as the bright sunlight flooded a small cavern looking out onto the vast azure blue of the Sea of Crete.

"Where are we, Max?"

"It's a cave off the northwest side of the island, under the Molin gate. The ancients used to fish from the rocks, but now, no one uses it apart from a few divers. We have a dinghy here."

"What about Jardine? I left him by the garrison. In a tunnel."

"Jardine can take care of himself, don't fret on that. Think of yourself for a while."

As soon as I sat down, the shock of my leg wound made me pass out. When I came round, I was on my own. Just the Glock, me, a bottle of Zaros spring water, and a packet of sweet biscuits. The boat was still on the rocks, under its tarpaulin. If the boat was still here, so was Anderson. My leg was throbbing like an Iron Maiden encore, so I lay back and dozed, trying to take my mind back to happier times.

"They're taking her away in an air ambulance. I thought you'd like to know." I blinked. Outside, a helicopter thudded across the sky. Anderson had been back to the refuge under the South Mezzaluna. He was sorting through his bag of belongings, loading them into the boat, pulling it into the water. He took the oars and rode straight out, away from the islands, about half a mile rising and falling over the swell. A fortunate current eased the tiny boat southwards behind the Spinalonga Peninsula and, when we were out of sight of the leper island, Anderson cranked up the outboard.

If he could escape from an island swarming with police, no wonder he could remain invisible for so long.

Proof of Life

Chapter 72

Wednesday, September 18

I awoke between clean white sheets, momentarily confused, listening to sparrows sounding reveille. The sun was low behind the shutters, sending stripes across the room. Like the hospital at Aviano, I felt comfortable, unwilling to move even a hand from the pressed linen. Then, like receding tide exposing the stones of Olous, a switch was thrown and the memories returned.

Steve was gone.

The previous day, as Anderson powered the boat along the east of the spit, I'd drifted in and out of consciousness. I recalled a doctor, or at least someone who knew his stuff, and of the injection that sent me into the arms of Morpheus.

Steve was gone, and I had failed her.

I flipped back the sheet and gingerly lowered my legs over the side. The ache in my thigh had abated, less angry but throbbing to make sure I hadn't forgotten. Under the dressing, the wound was clean. So was the furrow across my ribs. I threw a couple of paracetamol into my mouth, swilled them down, and hoped they would see me through.

On the bedside table, the hands on my Omega told me it was 8:30 am. The date window told me I'd slept a whole day. The half-empty clip from the Glock, lying next to it, told me I was a fool. I saw Baresi's eyes, the cynical half-smile, as he turned the gun away from me. Steve's eyes as she faded away.

Do you want to watch the girl die first, or do you want her to feel a few seconds of pure hopelessness before I kill her too?

Proof of Life

I'd watched her die. Now I knew the hopelessness of life without her. Not for a few seconds, but forever.

The next room was empty, the bed stripped, the shutters open, billowing nets into the room. Someone had tidied away Steve's things, sparing me that pain. All I had was the broken bracelet, the all-seeing eye that granted her wish. We were together for the rest of her life.

Downstairs, the Taverna had returned to normal, as if nothing had happened. Kitschy bouzouki music played softly through a tinny speaker. Across the causeway, the gray-green bay glistened as the sun edged over the hillside. Goats in the neighboring smallholding bleated, their bells clanking as they waited impatiently to be milked. Crete, Elounda, the Taverna Aegina, were the perfect place to hide from the world. In the parking lot, the Citroen had a new set of rubber. Everything was as it had been the previous day.

But Steve was gone, and nothing was the same.

Predictably, Anderson was gone too. He'd called a doctor, sat around until he knew I was okay. Then, using his own words, *gotten the hell out of Dodge*. According to the ponytail girl, Alina, he'd told them of an urgent business trip. Then he'd dragged some cases from the outhouse down the yard, loaded them into the Toyota pickup, and left. With a day's lead, he could be over the Atlantic, drinking duty free and imagining a new life somewhere else hot and secluded.

Ponytail, the Adonis, and I sat awhile on the verandah, waving to the Greek grandmothers in their wraparound aprons, as they arrived to run a mop over the floors. The Adonis, whose name turned out to be Dimitri, fetched coffee and croissants. I explained how I knew Will Robbins, glossing over the bad parts, shining up the good parts, finding out what they already knew—which turned out to be jack. I didn't tell them his real name was Anderson. That information could get them killed. Alina told me Will and

Jackie Robbins had owned the Taverna for as long as anyone could remember. There was a story about a lottery win and a retreat away from the rat race. Somewhere Robbins could indulge his passion for archeology. It did not surprise her to find they had a child. Jackie Robbins' eyes were always a little distant, always somewhere else.

"Do you think he will come back, Mr. Beckett?"

"Who knows, Dimitri, but until then, I guess you've gotten yourself a taverna."

He frowned. "Why would I want this place? There is a job at a water sports center in Plaka. All those boats, women, and bikinis."

"What about Alina? I thought you and her…"

"Well, you know…" Dimitri smiled boyishly. "Anyway, the rich women tip better." He raised his eyebrows. I am sure he didn't mean money. "Oh, Max left this for you." He reached around behind the bar and handed me a small sealed brown envelope bearing a single word—Aidan.

***

Aidan,

I know I've not been any kind of father, and I am sorry. Disappearing, leaving you behind, was in all our best interests. So many friends and colleagues had died needlessly. When Jo McKenna died, Kate and I knew we would be next. And unless you disappeared too, they would find you, perhaps use you to get to us, perhaps worse. For months, we agonized before leaving. Only Joe and Pat Wexler knew. They were excellent parents. When I stood in the background at your graduation and passing-out parade, I was the happiest dad in the world—and also the saddest.

Your mom and I had a better life than we deserved. We didn't spend every minute mourning your loss. We acknowledged the void and moved on. Then, when Kate passed on, they let me bury her here at

Proof of Life

home, in the garden of the Ascension Church. There is also a shrine inside. The key is in the envelope. Promise me you will light a candle before you head off? Then, you will understand why we had to leave you with Joe and Pat. Why we had to cut all ties.

About Amber Rock. Yes, I know more than I have told you, but that is for a reason. A catastrophe. Something big happened in 1982 and has remained hidden since. But too many people have already lost their lives. I acknowledge the world needs to know, but at what cost? If this is exposed, others will die, millions more will suffer. You have to take my word. I know you won't, so I offer you this. Find Trueman and you will find the rest. I beg you to be careful. You have already attracted more attention than you know. It would be a tragedy if I found you now, only to lose you again.

Be safe. Be strong.

Max

Ryan Stark

Chapter 73

The call to Pliskin was always going to be a car crash. I'd fucked up major league, and we both knew it. I'd insisted Anderson was the key, to the exclusion of everything else. It had probably cost us the chance to find out more about Amber Rock. Perhaps even to understand it. He reminded me, several times during the fifteen-minute call, I had found Anderson and lost him, all in the space of forty-eight hours. As for Baresi, he muttered *good job* through gritted teeth. I took the credit and the blame. He said little about Steve, perhaps understanding how much I was already beating myself up.

"The Greek police found her lying next to Baresi, along with the gun that killed Moretti. The same gun that killed Rossi and damaged a tree and a door in Venice. I spent a good hour convincing the Inspector General of Police that all along, Baresi had been the person who kidnapped Ms. Jordan, that she had died trying to escape."

"On a leper island, Pliskin? In the middle of the Mediterranean?"

"Indeed, Baresi was chasing Franklin Farrell, who obviously escaped and should be their primary focus for a week or two until he mysteriously turns up dead. Some feud over money, I suggested, and he agreed."

"And you're comfortable with all this?" The story didn't convince me. Nor, I suspect, would it her family, back in Salisbury, England. The line went silent for a long moment. Not for the first time, I prepared myself for a beating.

"No, Beckett, I am not. We sent you to find out what

Moretti knew about Amber Rock. Instead, you used Europe as your private hunting ground while you searched for Max Anderson. As a result, Miss Jordan lost her life, you lost Anderson, and we, TORUS, have lost a good deal of faith in the eyes of our clients. As for Amber Rock, what more do we know we didn't already?"

"A catastrophe that happened in 1982. Something big that has remained hidden since."

"And exactly what does that mean? Catastrophe covers a broad church from asteroid impact right down to a celebrity breaking a fingernail. Unless we find something more specific, we are no further along."

Unfortunately, Pliskin was right—as always. He ended the call with instructions for me to fly out of Chania the next day. He also reminded me that, for Franklin Farrell to be found dead, the Cretan police would need a body. That could just as easily be mine as anyone else's. As for my mission. That would remain the same; find Max Anderson, find Amber Rock and, for God's sake, don't let either slip through my fingers again.

Chapter 74

After lunch, I walked down to the water, where Olous had sat beneath the waves for an eternity. With so much happening in the last twenty-four hours, I wondered how the ruins could remain so constant amongst all this change. The problem was mine, not theirs. While I had to return to Washington, they would remain. No other life to lead, no need to explain away their failure. A conscience clear of guns and death, life and love. All they had was this *paradise*.

I threw a stick for Nico, who looked at me as if I was a moron and continued to sniff the ground. Together, we strolled across the causeway, feeling the breeze from the bay. Just a tourist and his dog with time to kill and a sackful of memories weighing him down. The sun was warm on my face; the birds were in full song. Everything begged me to tear up my plane ticket and stay here serving moussaka to ignorant trippers until I too became part of the landscape.

Right now, it sounded appealing.

"Pretty isn't it."

Nico turned and began barking, bouncing up and down like he was on a spring. The woman was slim, late fifties, early sixties. Two men flanked her; a short, stout one with the features of a pig, and a taller, meaner one who looked bored with life. The tall misery-guts melodramatically clicked back the trigger on his automatic pistol.

The woman was eying me curiously over a pair of fashionable spectacles, a perfunctory smile on an angular face, lined from too much sun. Her short hair—gray dyed blonde—had that coiffured untidiness women pay a bundle

Proof of Life

for. The stylish blouse and tailored black pants suit told me she was good for it. Her fingers were wrapped around two takeout coffees—one called *DeMarco*, the other *Beckett*, flicking on and off the hot surface, like the legs of those lizards in the desert.

"Pretty now, but imagine when the earthquake hit," I replied, almost sensing the tremors.

"Everything beautiful has a dark side, Beckett. Even Amber Rock."

I reached for the Glock. The tall man stood upright, but the woman waved a calming hand.

"You won't need the gun, I promise. Please, let Andreas take care of it." She beckoned across the piggy guy. Andreas was paunchy, a good two inches shorter, sun-browned skin, covered by a down of gray hair. I handed over the Glock, stock first. He ejected the magazine and sent it spinning into the saltwater lagoon. He cleared the breach, threw me a crooked grin, and handed back the gun.

"Flat white, no sugar. I hope that's okay?" She handed me the coffee. I nodded, and she gestured a slim liver-spotted hand towards a tumbledown wall. "No one's going to die today. I know you may find it disappointing after recent weeks, but I just want to talk."

"You going to tell me what this is about? Miss…Mrs.…?" I feigned annoyance, but I was just puzzled. This all had a touch of theatrics about it.

"Irina DeMarco—Irina, please. We're all friends here, and anyway, it's not my real name." Another disingenuous chuckle at her in-joke.

DeMarco?

"Luciano Moretti mentioned you. In his notebook. It was you who sent in Renzo Baresi to kill Moretti and stop Jardine. And to kill Steve Jordan."

"No, Beckett. She was hiding in the closet." Her tone was dismissive. "Baresi did not know she was there. He would have left without harming a hair on her head. Anyway, what could she tell the Polizia? She was just a day-rate secretary. Until you showed up. Until you played the hero and rescued her. Once the Polizia saw her fleeing the scene with you, it implicated her. And when Baresi saw the images, when he knew she was there, her fate was sealed. You just prolonged her agony."

"So, why chase and kill her?

DeMarco huffed. "We didn't kill her, Beckett. Baresi killed her. He needed to protect himself. Every witness had to be eliminated. Anyone who had seen his face. How else could he continue to work? It's the same with you. Once you had blundered into Moretti's apartment, you knew you had to kill Baresi. Each needs to eliminate the other, then the bell rings, and the game starts again. An *honest transaction*. Isn't that what you called it?"

I could feel the anger welling up inside, but I kept a lid on it. This was a time for clear thinking. Anyhow, she was right. DeMarco hadn't killed Steve, nor had Amber Rock. That one was down to me. I had placed her in front of Baresi's gun. I'd as good as pulled the trigger.

"So, tell me. What do you want, *Irina?*"

"Your recent trip to Europe set off alarm bells. You caused quite a stir, and I'm here to make you see sense." Her voice was cultured, sort of mid-Atlantic, maybe Boston or Ivy League. This was territory she was comfortable with. A lawyer, maybe. Like she was chairing a board meeting.

"So you got your opportunity. Shoot."

She raised her eyebrows, chuckled again. "There has been enough shooting already, Beckett, don't you think?"

With an air of distaste, she eased herself down onto a dusty wall across from me and placed her hands in her lap.

Proof of Life

The two goons remained motionless a yard or two back. It reminded me of the other night. Max and me, Nico the dog. But now there was no Steve, and it was tough to keep that from my mind. DeMarco shook a stick from a pack of Marlboro and lit it, savoring the first lungful, smoking quietly until the silence became uncomfortable.

"Look, I have a flight to catch, so why don't you just get to the point?"

DeMarco glanced about. "Just checking for *damn parabolic microphones*." She raised a coquettish finger to her smiling lips,. I felt a shock of adrenaline. So she already knew what Max had told me. Nico, sick of pissing up plants, came and sat between my feet. Choosing sides. He was a runt of a mutt, but I was grateful.

She drew another lungful, expelled a thin stream of smoke sideways. "Filthy habit, I know, but difficult to kick. Now, the point. Amber Rock."

Like I hadn't guessed.

"What about it?" I responded petulantly. "I know the name, that's all. Nothing else." It was the truth. I knew very little, maybe less than DeMarco expected, but still more than was good for me.

"In particular, Max Anderson." She shuffled slightly, adjusted her jacket. "He also knows nothing yet claims he knows everything." She searched for an analogy, looked toward Nico. "He sees a puddle on the floor and blames the dog. Maybe it was the dog, maybe the child who could not make the lavatory in time? Or it may be simply condensation from the back of the refrigerator. So he goes for the dog with the biggest stick he can find. When the dog bites back, he runs away."

"I'm still struggling to see the point here, Irina." She was making me work for two bucks' worth of coffee.

"Max Anderson saw a string of deaths, people he knew,

others engaged in his industry. Coincidences that linked their deaths. Statistical anomalies, and he manufactured a connection. He put two and two together and blamed the dog. Even now, he still does not know where the puddle came from. Whether there was a puddle at all."

"Like weather balloons at Roswell? A grassy knoll in Dallas?" It was my turn for a mirthless chuckle. "Even conspiracy theorists are right now and again."

DeMarco sighed out the irritation. "Not on this occasion."

"And Fabrizio Rossi in Venice? He was convinced something happened in 1982. A disaster, and since then a conspiracy of silence to protect it."

"A minor scientist, overlooked and, in all honesty, ridiculed by the wider community for thirty years. Even Rossi had told Anderson he was tilting at windmills, but still Anderson persisted. Still looking for a conspiracy where there was none. And now? Thirty years later, when it suited Rossi, he changed his tune. And it got him killed."

"So, if Anderson's allegations were groundless, and those of Rossi, Gruber, Fernandez and all the others, why Amber Rock? Why the mop if nobody took a leak on the floor?"

DeMarco stared briefly, annoyed I was spoiling her rhetoric, then sipped her coffee, her lips barely touching the plastic lid, reptilian. Unhurried and unruffled. "As Rossi himself told you, the '80s were turbulent times for the nuclear industry…"

"Another *damn parabolic microphone?*"

"One of many, I'm afraid." She flicked a mischievous smile. "They were turbulent times. Back then, the public concerned itself more with nuclear Armageddon than with the energy benefits it could bring them. Atomic energy meant bombs and death. Politicians, governments, even industry experts like Rossi and Anderson, were all looking for reasons to kill off the nuclear threat and, with it, nuclear energy. Sides of entirely different coins, completely unconnected. Of course, there were setbacks. Every industry has them. Aircraft and metal fatigue. Thalidomide. As Bobbie Kennedy once said, *only those who dare to fail greatly can ever achieve greatly*. The world is changing, and we must all change with it. Sometimes change is tough, sometimes there are consequences, sacrifices even."

"What? Bulldozing houses to make way for a freeway?"

"Something like that." DeMarco frowned, notched down her intellectual level to keep me on board.

"And Amber Rock?"

"Progress doesn't come without a cost. The nuclear industry suffered its fair share of setbacks. Things happened. Things our clients are not proud of. They set up Amber Rock to ensure their efforts are not defined by the potholes of failure but by the road to success."

"Poetic. And one of these failures? That's what Rossi spoke of? What Anderson discovered?"

DeMarco laughed dismissively. "Whatever happened all those years ago is long forgotten. They may have bulldozed the houses, but even the freeway has been abandoned now. People have moved on."

"So, why the sudden interest in Max Anderson? Why kill Moretti and Rossi? Why chase us across Europe? If Moretti's auction is just so much horse-shit, why not let it run its course, expose it and discredit Anderson?"

"Because horse-shit may only be horse-shit, but it still leaves a smell. Anderson still has a story to tell, even if it is complete horse-shit. Even after all these years, that would taint our client's reputation. Something we couldn't allow."

"And me? What about me?"

She leaned over until I could smell the tobacco over her

perfume. "You, Beckett, are nothing. Our clients want Max Anderson. Amber Rock wants you to find him again."

"Me?" I was incredulous. "Twice in the last few days, I found Anderson. Twice he escaped."

"Still, you succeeded when the entire world failed. You can do it again. Find him. Hand him over to Amber Rock."

"And if I don't?"

"Of course, that's your choice. The world *is* changing, Beckett. Progress *will* happen. Your trip to Europe, everything that went on here is just a byline in a report. A footnote. Things are happening that will have a profound impact on our lives for generations to come. And those future generations will see you as nothing more than a disruptor, a rebel. Someone who chose the wrong side, who failed fighting a lost cause. If they see you at all."

She finished her coffee, picked up the Marlboros, then held my gaze for a long moment. Reaching into her inside pocket, she handed me a few polaroid pictures. An old man in a cardigan, his tongued wedged in the corner of his mouth as he tried to find a piece to his jigsaw.

My dad, Joe?"

I leaped to my feet, freezing as the pig-faced goon's gun leveled at my chest.

"He's safe in his comfortable home for now. If you want him to remain safe, then it's down to you. Bring me Max Anderson. Hand him over to Amber Rock. Then you can return to run your quaint little restaurant. Persist in your crusade against Amber Rock, continue to dig up ancient history no one cares about, and we will be forced to act. We will delete you from history, along with everything and everyone you hold dear. I hope that's clear."

***

Proof of Life

I watched DeMarco all the way back to her car while Andreas stood, legs akimbo, keeping an eye on me. The barrel of his gun never wavered. His knuckles were white as he gripped the trigger. Then he eased off, threw me a mocking smile, and strode nonchalantly off toward the car. For a long moment, I considered sprinting after him, wrestling him to the rough ground and planting a fist on that fat piggy snout. With my gun empty and his full, discretion was the better part of valor. I could follow the car back to the airport. Alert security, maybe? Catch her unawares and put a slug through her gnarly, wrinkled forehead? As the lady herself said, there had been enough shooting already.

But today, I was tired. Tired of the chase, tired of the killing. Tired of the pain. I needed some peace. Maybe some of the peace Anderson had enjoyed all these years. After all, I was his son.

EPILOGUE

The Ascension Church was a lonely cream and pan-tiled building. It faced southeast along the coast, down towards Agios Nikolaos, on a barren outcrop of land that bulged into the sea. The churchyard, hemmed in by pristine dry-stone walls around a trim, sun-bleached lawn, led down to the water's edge. Sparse trees gave a breeze-blown respite to the infrequent visitor. Above the church, a single bell rocked in the breeze. The rope hung lazily across the tall cedar wood doors. The old cast iron key lay under a loose stone in the wall by the entrance—an open secret amongst the locals, according to Dimitri, at the Taverna.

Inside, the building was simple and humble. Tiled floors and unrendered walls hung with images of saints of indeterminate age and triptychs of bible stories I had slept through at Sunday school. At the far end, an ornate *templon* showed Christ ascending to heaven as supplicants looked on in awe. The entire room was smaller than my parents' sitting room, packed with offertories, ornate lanterns, memorials, and other relics. Fading photos and embossed brass plaques showing religious themes in enamel cartouches. As much as Elounda, the sun, and the sea outside brought me peace, churches disturbed me. Adulation of a supreme being that had never revealed himself, blind faith despite the evidence, and remembrance of the dead at the expense of the living. Pascal's wager.

Still, I folded a ten euro note into the simple wooden box and took a candle.

Kate's shrine was on a tiered stand covered in gold-

Proof of Life

trimmed blue felt. The brass had dulled and a few dead leaves folded over the edge of a small vase, yet the smile in the grainy color photo was as bright as the sun. I replaced the candle and lit it. The flickering flame caught something, a spark of gold, hanging in the back of the lantern. Instantly, I knew what it was. A pendant, exactly matching the others.

I found the stone too. A simple, polished marble tablet, dusty from the wind, black-filled letters, scuffed and faded from the sun.

Katherine Jennifer Anderson
Beloved wife of Maxwell Anderson
1960 - 2014 aged 54

I held the pendant tight, recalling the blurry shape around Kate's neck in Moretti's photos. I struggled to feel a connection, but there was none. A mother I had never known. Crouching further, I read the rest of the inscription, expecting some maudlin homily.

Kim and Aidan. My twin angels.
Lost but never forgotten.

Twin?

A lightning bolt pierced my heart, and I felt light-headed. Turning over the pendant, I ran my thumb over the engraving on the back—*Kim*, the name Steve had seen in the photo album. Inside, roughly cut from a larger picture, a small face beamed a smile I already knew.

I had a twin sister?

A thousand questions rained in on me. Was she still called Kim? Did Anderson know where she was? If so, why did he keep it from me? Was she also struggling to come to terms with being abandoned? Did she even know?

Did Amber Rock know about her, too?

DeMarco was right. Now I knew Amber Rock was real, I needed to find Anderson again. Make him tell me about a catastrophe hidden away for three decades. That Amber Rock felt they needed to kill in order to protect. And I needed him to tell me what was so goddamn important he could abandon his baby children to separate fates. That he could sentence their mother to a life without them.

Then I needed to smoke them out. Every last one of them and hold them to account.

But I also needed to find Anderson—again. To find out about my twin sister. To find out about me.

Piece of cake.

This wasn't over. It had only just begun.

Proof of Life

Ryan Stark

COMING SOON

The Beckett Chronicles

Proof of Death

Amber Rock Book 2

Beckett played Amber Rock and lost.

Now he knows how far they go to guard their secrets.

When he returns to Washington DC, he tries to piece together the clues. Who are Trueman, Velasquez and Gilbués? What happened thirty years ago? Why is it still important now?

Then another nuclear analyst dies.

Under the constant gaze of Amber Rock, Beckett continues his search for Max Anderson, digging deeper, uncovering new clues to the mystery.

Soon, he is at the epicenter of Amber Rock.

Meanwhile, after learning everything he understood is a lie, Beckett questions his own loyalties, even his own identity.

Can he expose Amber Rock's dark secret before it is finally buried forever?

Before they finally get to him?

Proof of Life

Author's Note

Dear Reader.

Thanks for taking the time to read *Proof of Life*. I hope you enjoyed it. If you did, and would like to help, then maybe you could leave a review on my Amazon page?

www.Amazon.com/review/create-review?&asin=B09BK3MCS2

If you would like to find out more about my other books then please read on, or visit my website for full details.

www.ryanstarkauthor.co.uk

The most important part of how well a book sells is how many positive reviews it has. Some of the best books never see the light of day; some of the worst are bought in their millions. So, if you leave a review then you are directly helping me to continue on this journey as a full-time writer.

Thanks. It means a lot.

Ryan Stark

Proof of Life

KILLING BY THE BOOK

The Daley and Whetstone Crime Stories Book 1

Dawn Silverton.

Young, beautiful, successful. Now she is dead.

Her death sends shockwaves through the Monday Club, a group of university friends still together 15 years later. Soon fingers are pointed, accusations fly as each member of the group battles their own private demons.

What long-forgotten nightmare binds them? What is now tearing them apart?

Inspector Scott Daley and Sergeant Deborah Whetstone investigate her brutal death. They see parallels to a case four years ago. The murderer escaped justice then. Has the killing started again?

The Murder Book is open. First there were eight. Then seven. Now there are six.

Hard-edged and disturbing, slowly building, reeling you in until you can't put it down. A master class in noir crime fiction, this British Detective story will keep you guessing right up to the end.

AVAILABLE IN PAPERBACK AND EBOOK.

Proof of Life

THE FARM

The Daley and Whetstone Crime Stories Book 2

A young nurse tries her hand at blackmail. Now she has vanished.

Inspector Scott Daley and Sergeant Deborah Whetstone are, drawn to a private medical clinic where they meet a web of lies and half-truths protecting a secretive research project.

Coincidence or something more sinister?

Half a world away, a young refugee starts a perilous journey out of war-torn Syria and across Europe. In a murky world of human trafficking, can she make it to the UK?

Meanwhile, back from long-term injury, Daley finds a new order in the team room. Whetstone is in his seat, heading up his team. On light duties, he tackles the growing missing persons file—the mysterious Zone 6 Snatcher.

What they discover puts them on a collision course, stretching them both to breaking point.

As Satya draws closer to freedom, as Daley and Whetstone home in on a killer, no-one is prepared for the horrors that await them as they reveal the macabre secrets of The Farm.

Like a dark, detective mystery with lots of twists? You'll love this second Daley & Whetstone Crime Story.

AVAILABLE IN PAPERBACK AND EBOOK.

Proof of Life

UNNATURAL SELECTION

The Daley and Whetstone Crime Stories Book 3

DC Dean Hewell was looking for secrets. He got more than he bargained for.

When Inspector Scott Daley and Sergeant Deborah Whetstone investigate his brutal murder, they find he is not the first. Two undercover officers assassinated. Two murders unsolved.

As a devastating turf war breaks out, West London becomes a battleground. An elusive European overlord is muscling in, orchestrating the violence and fuelling the bitter feud.

Meanwhile, with the team being disbanded, their jobs under threat, the clock is ticking. They end up chasing ghosts, drawn into a world where truth takes second place to survival.

Then they become his next target.

Can Daley and Whetstone fight to separate truth from myth before time runs out for them all?

'Unputdownable. A master class in crime fiction, it will keep you guessing right up to the end.'

AVAILABLE IN PAPERBACK AND EBOOK.

Made in the USA
Columbia, SC
13 January 2022